ABOUT THIS BOOK

Welcome to Havenwood Falls, a small town in the majestic mountains of Colorado, where nobody is what you think, where truths pose as lies, and where myths blend with reality. A place where everyone has a story, including the high schoolers. These are only but three...

Avenoir by Daniele Lanzarotta

Heidi Bennett's perfect life came to a screeching halt one night last December. Now, Heidi walks among the residents of Havenwood Falls once again, but most can't see her. The last thing Heidi remembers was dancing with her boyfriend at the Cold Moon Ball, and the events surrounding her disappearance remain a complete mystery. One she's determined to solve.

Avenge the Heart by Michele G. Miller

Sequel to *Awaken the Soul* - When Vivienne Freeman's supernatural abilities manifest, Breckin Roberts questions whether the changes are due to their soul bond or something more. They soon discover an entire history connecting their families they knew nothing about. As the fallen descend on Havenwood Falls, Vivienne and Breckin must unravel the secrets and avenge the heart before any chance of redemption is lost forever.

Curse the Night by R.K. Ryals

A shapeshifting hellhound with a look that kills—literally—Jack Peters hides behind his sunglasses and skulks in the cemeteries, biding his time until he's out of Havenwood Falls and on the road to bigger adventures. A seventeen-year-old mountain nymph, Cressida Manos has a great family and a quiet life. She's sunny, cheerful, dependable, and . . . a vandal? No one can believe Cressida capable of malicious destruction of property, and Cressida doesn't remember her crimes. The only one who believes she's innocent is Jack—the guy who caught her in the act.

HAVENWOOD FALLS HIGH BOOKS

Predestined by Valia Lind

Rediscovered by Morgan Wylie

Ashes of Fate by Apryl Baker

Stay up to date at www.HavenwoodFalls.com

HAVENWOOD FALLS HIGH
VOLUME FOUR

A HAVENWOOD FALLS HIGH COLLECTION

DANIELE LANZAROTTA   MICHELE G. MILLER   R.K. RYALS

AVENOIR

DANIELE LANZAROTTA

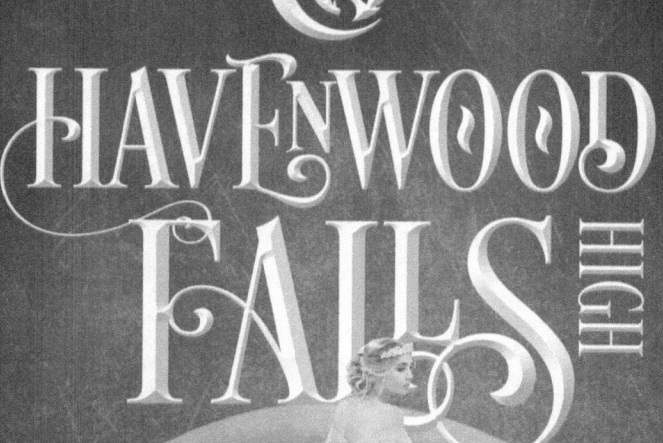

HAVENWOOD FALLS HIGH

Avenoir

DANIELE LANZAROTTA

~ A Havenwood Falls Young Adult Novella ~

ALSO BY DANIELE LANZAROTTA

To Bri for being my cheerleader.

PROLOGUE

DECEMBER 2017

I look at my reflection in the mirror, and I think about backing out of the Cold Moon Ball for the hundredth time. Tonight should feel perfect. This is one of my favorite events in Havenwood Falls. My long light-blue dress is absolutely stunning, and Mom insisted that I borrow this beautiful silver crown she won at a pageant, but none of it takes my mind away from this gut feeling that something bad is going to happen.

"You look beautiful," Mom says. I turn around, and she's leaning against the doorframe, keeping her distance, as she has been sick over the past few days.

I bite my bottom lip, feeling uncertain about this whole night.

"What's going on?" she asks.

I take a deep breath and glance down toward the infinity symbol on the promise ring Jace gave me last year for my sixteenth birthday. Without taking my eyes off the ring, I say what has been on my mind since last night, when I talked to him. "Jace said he needs to talk to me about something important."

Mom tilts her head to the side and gives me a reassuring smile. "I hope you don't think he's breaking up with you. You two have been together since middle school, and you get along better than most adult couples I know." She laughs.

I feel myself relax. She's right. I've just never heard him sound so serious before.

The doorbell rings, and Mom smiles again. "I'll get it. I'll let him know you will be down in a bit."

I look at the mirror one more time, take a deep breath, and tell myself to get it together.

As I walk out of my room, I see Jace at the bottom of the stairs, with his back to me. He's wearing black pants and a black peacoat. I can almost guarantee that instead of a dress shirt, he's wearing an old band T-shirt under his coat. The thought of that makes me laugh for a split second, before that gut feeling consumes my every thought yet again. As I make my way down the stairs, I even manage to fake a smile. The moment Jace turns around and looks up at me, his mouth hangs open, and I know by the way that he stares at me that Mom is right. Just like that, the fake smile quickly turns into a huge grin.

We say goodbye to my mom and head outside. Jace puts his hand on the small of my back as we walk away, and I freeze in place when I see his dad's black Camaro convertible parked on the street.

"Do you want to drive?" he asks, and my eyes widen.

I laugh and look at him. "You're kidding, right? I'm surprised your dad let you drive his favorite child."

Jace chuckles, showing off his dimples. He always jokes about his dad loving that car more than anything or anyone else.

"There is no way I'm driving it," I say.

He grins at me. "We should get going. We already missed the first part of the evening."

As we drive up toward Havenwood Heights, Jace turns the music up loud, and I find myself distracted by the Christmas decorations along the way. When I was little, Dad used to bring me to this area every Christmas and just drive around. And no matter how many times we did that over the years, the sight of the large houses with

Christmas lights glowing, and Mt. Alexa in the background, is always breathtaking.

When we get to the Mills mansion, one of the biggest houses on the street, Jace parks his dad's car as far away as possible from other cars around.

"Wait." He stops me when I reach for the door. He gives me a crooked smile before he gets out and rushes to my side. He opens my door and extends his hand to me. Once out of the car, I see just how far we have to walk. I laugh. "You did have his permission to take the car, right?" I ask jokingly.

Jace chuckles as he slips his hand into mine. "Yep, although he did have a few glasses of wine earlier. Maybe I should've gotten that in writing."

I just shake my head.

"So, what shirt are you wearing tonight?" I ask as we make our way to the door. "Pink Floyd or—"

He cuts me off. "What makes you think I'm not wearing a dress shirt?"

I glare at him, and he grins. "Okay. You got me. And you got it right on the first guess. Not bad." He winks.

Stepping into the ballroom is like being transported into a different world. I stop for a minute to take in the place. The crystal candelabras everywhere and the fresh cut flowers on each of the tables around the room make the ballroom look stunning, just like it does every year. But my favorite part has really always been the large skylight on the ceiling, allowing for the most breathtaking view of the moon. I've always wondered what it would be like to be in this ballroom when it is empty, just laying down on the floor at night, in silence, staring at the moon. Jace nudges my shoulder with his, leans against me, and whispers, "Ready to go, Cinderella?"

I giggle. "Yes."

Jace and I walk toward the tables filled with drinks and appetizers. On the way there, we say hi to a few people from school. I stop to talk to Zoey, Mr. Mills's granddaughter, and wish her a happy birthday. She's new to our school, so I don't know her well, but she seems nice.

Minutes later, I catch Jace watching me with this sad look in his eyes. I can see the moment he tenses, and just like that, the gut feeling is back.

Jace walks toward me. "Come with me," he whispers, and he leads me through the double doors that take us to the backyard of the mansion. I'm so nervous, I don't even notice our surroundings. I just know that something bad is coming. Jace reaches for my hand and brushes his finger over the infinity symbol on my ring. He just keeps staring at the ring and playing with it, and my anxiety gets the best of me.

"What did you want to talk about?" I ask in a nervous tone.

He gives me a sad smile. "Later," he says.

He reaches for his phone and plugs his headphones in. I give him a puzzled look, and he smiles. He reaches over and puts the headphones in my ears. Nothing is playing at this point. He leans in and gives me a quick kiss before asking me to dance with him.

I blush and look down, avoiding his gaze. This is so like him, to make these big romantic gestures that I can never say no to.

He gently puts his fingers against my chin, tilting my head up. "Close your eyes," he whispers before he pushes play and one of my favorite slow songs comes on. He closes the distance between us, and my eyes drift shut. After a while, I feel the cold snowflakes falling against my skin, and I grin. But it is his laughter that brings me back to the moment. I open my eyes to find him watching me with a grin across his face—showing off his dimples—and there is this sparkle in his eyes.

I memorize every single detail—every single feeling about this moment. The cold. The few seconds of snow, just at the right time. His smile. That look in his eyes. It's almost as if I'm programming myself to memorize everything about this one happy moment.

As if it was my last.

CHAPTER 1

HEIDI

MAY 2018

"*J*ace," I mumble as I open my eyes.

Feeling disoriented, I realize that I'm lying face down on dirt and grass. *Snow . . . What happened to the snow?* I sit, slowly, and look up. The first thing I see is the moon. My head is spinning like crazy. At the sound of something howling, I frantically stand up and look around for my phone. I curse myself for having a black phone case.

"Ugh. I'm never going to find the thing in the dark."

I hear the sound of someone clearing his throat, and for a split second, I feel myself relax, thinking that it is Jace. I spin around—faster than I should—and see a tall dark-haired guy with bright green eyes, leaning against a tree right before me.

"Need help finding something?" he asks with a raspy voice, crossing his arms over his chest.

I take a step back. "Who are you?"

He shrugs and just keeps gawking at me. I haven't seen him at school before. He is the kind of person I would remember seeing. Something about him feels . . . different.

"I'm leaving," I say, and I feel stupid for even having to announce that. I should be running, but my still-spinning head is a huge sign I wouldn't make it far. I turn around and start to walk away slowly, and hope to God he doesn't follow me. *Ugh. I'm always making fun of people in scary movies who try to run and end up getting killed. Please don't let me become a cliché.*

I don't get far before I hear him again.

"Wrong way," he says.

I glance back, and he is at the exact same spot. He points in a completely different direction. I find myself questioning whether to believe him or not, but another howl coming from the direction I'd been heading makes me follow his guidance. I give him a short nod and start walking away. As soon as I'm far enough from his view, I pick up the pace, and with every step, I feel like something is behind me—until I'm out of the woods.

Somehow, I find my way out to where I can see the Mills estate. I keep walking, and I don't stop until I'm in front of the mansion. I stare at it—probably for longer than I should, considering that something is definitely not right. I look down at the long light-blue dress I wore to the ball, then back at the mansion. You can't even tell something happened here tonight. *His smile . . . the snow . . .* I look around, confused. Strange things happen in this town from time to time, but nothing like this. How many hours could have passed?

"My parents are going to freaking ground me for life," I mumble before I turn around and head home.

As I make my way down Eighth Street, it hits me that the Christmas decorations are gone. I shake my head and keep walking. I replay the night in my head over and over. The last thing I remember was Jace and me dancing. He'd have never let me go into those woods alone. When I get to town square, chills creep over my skin. I feel like someone is watching me again, and I start to walk faster. I'm pretty much running by the time I arrive at my front door.

I stop in front of my house and sigh. I reach for the doorknob and slowly turn it, thankful that my parents never lock the door. If I'm lucky enough, they're sleeping.

I slowly close the door behind me. The house is pitch black. *Yes!* I think to myself.

I go straight upstairs to my room. I open the door and wonder where this god-awful lavender smell is coming from. I look at the clock, and it is three in the morning. I think about calling Jace to find out what happened, but remember that my phone is gone. I'm definitely not taking the risk of waking up mom and dad just to use their phones. Without even turning the lights on or bothering to change, I just make my way to bed and lie down. My first thought is that the mattress feels weird, but I quickly dismiss it as me possibly being tired—even though I don't feel tired at all. And then, I turn around and see the shape of a body next to me. I scream bloody murder as I jump up and rush to turn the light on. A familiar girl lies on my bed.

"Rose?" I say. "Hey!" I yell at my cousin.

Nothing. She doesn't even move.

I start to tremble as I walk closer to my bed. I poke her arm once, then again—really hard. She just tosses and turns.

I turn around to go get Mom, but freeze in place when I see my reflection in the mirror. Barely recognizing myself, I take a few steps closer and lean in toward the mirror. My dress is covered in dirt and blood. My gaze goes to the gash on my forehead with dried-up blood surrounding it. The skin around it looks discolored. I lean even closer and lightly touch the gash on my forehead. I feel nothing, and that is when I realize that I must be having one screwed-up dream. This has to be a dream . . .

I poke at the gash on my forehead again. Harder this time.

"That is disgusting." It's the same voice I heard back in the woods, and I spin around to see that guy again. "You won't feel anything," he says as he yawns and sits on my bed.

I should be scared of him. I should be yelling or running, or both, but I feel oddly calm. And honestly, I'm just waiting to wake up at any second and make this all go away.

I glance at Rose, and she's in a deep sleep.

13

"She can't hear us," he says. His tone is dry and cold, but I can see concern in the way he's watching me, and my stomach drops.

"I'm not dreaming, am I?" I ask, and he shakes his head. I look back at the mirror and stare. "What happened to me?" I whisper, feeling the need to cry, but unable to.

Looking in the mirror, I see him walk closer and stand right next to me. His gaze holds mine through our reflections.

"You died," he says.

My knees weaken, and I lose my balance. When his arms inch toward me, I stop him.

"Get away from me," I say as I regain my balance.

He puts his hands up and steps back with this hurt look in his eyes.

"Who are you?" I ask frantically.

He lowers his head and runs his fingers through his dark hair before he looks back at me.

"My name is Zane, and I'm an angel," he says in a serious tone.

I just stare at him before I burst into laughter, and he gives me a confused look. When I manage to stop laughing, I watch him and tilt my head to the side. Maybe this is not real after all. "I've had messed up dreams before, but this tops them all."

"I didn't lie before. It's not a dream," he says.

Still laughing, I roll my eyes at him. "Do you mean you are a guardian angel? Because if so, you sure are doing a lousy job at it," I say as I point toward my forehead.

"I didn't say I was *your* guardian angel," he says in an annoyed tone.

My laughter vanishes. "Why are you here?" I ask.

"I was sent to help you."

"Help me with what?" I ask.

"You died before your time. You have a mission to fulfill before you can move on," he says, sounding even more annoyed than he did seconds before.

I frown as I glance back toward the mirror.

"What happened to me?"

He pauses for a while. "I don't know. Like I said, I'm not your guardian angel."

I turn around, cross my arms, and tap my foot on the carpet. "Don't you people communicate?"

He smirks and shakes his head. He looks like a completely different guy when he loses that serious look and cold tone.

"I hate that habit of yours," he says, and when I give him a puzzled look, he goes on. "The habit of making jokes when you are afraid, or sad, or stressed."

"You know me," I say, and he ignores me completely.

"To answer your question, angels do communicate, but we don't have all the answers. And I'm here as punishment and training."

I tilt my head to the side. "So not only do I get sent an angel that is not mine, I get sent one who doesn't know what he's doing. No wonder I'm dead!" I know I'm seconds away from falling apart. He's right. I always use humor to deflect the real stuff. I close my eyes for a split second. "If guardian angels are really real, where is mine?" I ask.

He sits back down on my bed. For the first time, I take a good look at him. The faded jeans, black T-shirt, combat boots . . . He doesn't look like an angel—at all.

"I wish I knew," he says, returning to his dry tone. "And for the record, I know what I am doing."

The snow . . .

"How long have I been . . . dead?" I ask.

He just sits there, staring at me, and I know he's not going to answer.

"Get out," I snap.

"But I am supposed to—"

"You haven't been very helpful so far. I don't even have proof that you're an angel, or that I am dead. Leave!" I order.

He puts his hands up. "Call me when you need me, and trust me, you will. I won't be far," he growls, before he disappears.

CHAPTER 2

HEIDI

The moment he is gone, I feel lightheaded. I crouch down in the corner of my room. A thousand questions run through my mind. What happened to me? What happened to Jace? How long has it been?

This can't be real. It just can't be! I sit here and stare at Rose. I hug my knees and just stay where I am and watch time go by. I'm in a trance-like state when the sound of my alarm makes me jump.

Rose rolls over, shuts it off, and goes back to sleep. Minutes later, there is a soft knock on the door. The door slowly opens, and my mom's face comes into view, and I lose it—or at least, I feel like I do. I want to cry, but there are no tears.

"Rose, honey. Wake up. Your mom is on her way to get you."

When Rose doesn't move, Mom comes in and walks toward the bed. I'm shocked at how much weight she's lost. Her hair is not done like usual. She wouldn't be caught dead in her natural hair color. In fact, I often joke that she practically lives at Shear Magic. She hates dark hair on her, but now, her hair is pitch black. I slowly stand up. I lose my balance for a split second before I walk toward her.

"Ro—" she starts to say as I step closer to her. I'm right next to her when she closes her eyes and takes a deep breath.

"Mom," I whisper as I reach for her. Only, my hand goes right through hers. I stare at my hand, confused—wondering why, considering that I was able to touch Rose's arm before.

I look back at my mom. She opens her eyes and looks toward the closet door, where she used to mark and measure my height while growing up. She wipes a tear away and rushes out of the room.

I follow her out. I feel stronger as I step out of my room. I keep following as she goes back in her room, crawls into bed, and closes her eyes. She doesn't get back up until my aunt arrives to pick up Rose, and she goes back to bed as soon as they leave.

Feeling like I am being watched, I turn around to find Zane standing against the doorframe. I roll my eyes and let out an annoyed grunt.

"Why are you here?" I growl.

He shrugs. "You need me."

"No, I don't."

He grins and volunteers the first useful piece of information since I first saw him. "Do you know why you felt weak when you sent me away?"

I shake my head. "How do you even know I felt like that?" I ask as I cross my arms.

"You're linked to the place where you died."

My eyes widen at hearing him say that like it's nothing.

"What?" he says. "You already knew you are dead. No big news there. Anyway. If I leave, you go right back to where you died, and I might not be able to find you or get you out, so I can't let that happen."

"I woke up in the woods. Isn't that where I died?" I ask, and he shakes his head. "I was told to go to that area for my next assignment. Another angel brought you to me. What I do know is that your body was never found, and it has been months. I can guarantee that if your body was anywhere in this town, you would've been found by now."

Annoyed, I blurt out, "Okay, so this angel brought me from somewhere. He should know where I am."

He raises his voice. "Trust me. I've asked. I was told it was not my place to have those answers. Point is," he continues, "we're both stuck here until you fulfill your mission."

I let out a frustrated sigh. "What is this mission anyway? Because this sure will go faster if you tell me everything I need to know."

"Can't," he says.

I give him a doubtful look.

"They didn't tell me, okay?"

I notice he is nervous and he can't make eye contact.

"Should angels lie?" I ask, and he looks like I've caught him by surprise. "Tell me the truth," I demand.

He sighs. "As a general rule, you need to find peace by finding out what happened to you."

He still can't make eye contact.

"What else?"

He shrugs. "I may have overheard that something needs to be repaired."

"Where did you hear that?" I ask.

"From the one who brought you to me."

"I'm guessing he orders you around?" I ask, and I notice that he has his hands clenched into fists. "Let me talk to him."

He bursts into laughter. "Oh, I don't think so."

I roll my eyes at him. I wonder why they would send me an angel after I died. Besides, I have yet to see wings. Angels should have wings, or at least I think they should.

I think back to the TV shows I watch—well, used to watch. "Are you some kind of creepy reaper?"

He laughs again. "Come on," he says, motioning for me to follow him, and his refusal to answer my questions irritates me more and more.

"I'm not going until you tell me," I say.

He grins, looking amused, and when I don't move, he says, "No, I'm not a reaper. And no one is even allowed to reap your soul until you fulfill your mission."

I give him a puzzled look.

"Let's face it. You're stuck with me. We might as well start by helping you remember what happened that night."

I sigh. As afraid as I am of finding out, I do want to . . .

I look back at Mom, still in bed. I get close to her.

"I love you, Mom," I whisper in her ear, and she opens her eyes again. I wonder if she can sense me here.

I walk back to my room with Zane following me.

"What are you doing?" he asks.

"Changing out of this dress."

He laughs, and I spin around to face him. "What?"

"No one can even see you. Why bother?"

"You can see me," I say, and he looks embarrassed. "Relax. I'm not trying to impress you, if that is what you're worried about. I just want out of this dress, okay? I need something that feels normal—and something clean. Please," I beg. By the expression on his face, he understands.

I walk into my room and go to my dresser, opening the top drawer. Everything is exactly as I left it.

Standing here, staring at my clothes, I ask, "Do you think they know that I died?" I glance at him, and he looks so lost. "My parents. I know my body was never found, but do you think they know it somehow?" I ask, being clearer this time.

I can see it in his eyes that he feels bad for me. "Your parents hope you're just missing. They haven't stopped looking." He pauses. "Close your eyes," he says, and I raise an eyebrow at him.

"Please," he begs.

I hesitantly close my eyes. Seconds later, I feel his touch against my forehead.

"Okay, open," he says, and his fingers linger against my skin for a moment longer. When he pulls away, he nods toward the mirror.

I look over, and the gash on my forehead is completely gone. I stand here in shock and stare at Zane.

"Thank you," I say. I glance back down at my dresser. "Do you mind leaving?"

"You won't be able to touch those clothes without my help," he says.

I give him a puzzled look.

"Try it," he says with a grin as he walks away and stands right outside of my room.

I do, and my hand goes right through it.

He smiles and closes the distance between us. "Now try again," he says, and this time, I can.

I turn around. "I was able to touch things without you around before," I say.

"I was here. You just couldn't see me."

I laugh. "Well, I'm not changing in front of you."

He turns and faces the wall.

"If you so much as peek at me, I swear . . ."

He doesn't say anything, but I can see the movement of his shoulders, and I can hear him chuckle.

I put my jeans on under the dress. I then unzip and remove the dress and put a tank top and sweater on. "You can turn around," I say as I go to grab my boots.

"You know you can't feel cold, right? Not that it is cold right now."

I shrug. "So? Maybe this is my favorite outfit. If I'm going to be stuck wearing the same thing forever"—I shake my head thinking of how unreal this is—"maybe I want this to be my permanent ghost outfit, okay?"

He laughs and shakes his head as he walks over to my closet. He reaches in, and when he turns around, he is holding a light gray sweater I got for Christmas last year. He throws it toward me.

"You might as well go with a real favorite, then." He winks before he turns back around and walks toward the door.

I put my sweater on.

"Zane?" I say, and he turns around to face me. "Won't people be able to see my clothes?" I ask, confused.

He laughs. "That would be entertaining, wouldn't it?"

I cross my arms and wait on a reply, clearly not amused.

"No," he says. "I have certain abilities. They won't be able to see anything that you wear, or hold."

I shrug and give my room one last look before I follow him.

When I walk by the kitchen, my eyes go straight to the calendar hanging on the wall—May 2018. I stumble back.

"Where have I been this whole time?" I say, raising my voice. Again, Zane says nothing.

I feel sick to my stomach.

"I want to see Jace," I say, and Zane freezes in place as I see fear in his eyes.

CHAPTER 3

HEIDI

"I need to see Jace," I say again when Zane doesn't say anything back.

He shakes his head. "You're not ready to see him."

The look in his eyes makes me feel anxious, and I start to wonder if maybe Jace is with someone else by now. Or even worse. I'm filled with fear at the thought that maybe something happened to him, too. I walk past Zane, making my way out the door. I feel weak as soon as I step outside. I look back, Zane takes a few steps closer, and I feel okay again.

"I told you, you need me close by in order to stay here," he says in a cold tone.

I wait as he approaches.

"Close your eyes," he says, and when I don't, he just shakes his head. He reaches for my wrist, and before I can pull away, he softly wraps his hand around it. Next thing I know, we are back in the woods in what seems to be the area where I woke up.

I wrap my arms around myself. "Why are we here?" I ask.

"To see if you remember anything."

I take a good look around. Nothing. I remember nothing. I just feel agitated and ready to see Jace, even though I'm afraid to. I look down at my ring and close my eyes, remembering when he was playing with it that night. I remember he looked tense.

"You remember something," says Zane.

"Not important," I say, and I swallow the lump in my throat and get the courage to ask, "Why am I not ready to see Jace? He is okay, right?"

He leans his back against a tree like he doesn't have a care in the world. "Because your emotions are going to be all over the place." He pauses. "Even more so than they are right now. I'm not dealing with an unstable ghost."

I raise an eyebrow at him and tilt my head to the side. I'm not even sure if I'm more insulted that he referred to me as a ghost or unstable.

He sighs and lowers his voice. "Look, at least give yourself a day to process, all right? I'll take you to see him then."

"Not like I have a choice," I say in a frustrated tone.

He actually chuckles at my reaction. "Come on," he says. "Let's walk back to the Mills mansion. Maybe you'll remember something."

I nod and start walking with him.

"Can I ask you something?" I say.

"Sure," he says. He doesn't mean that at all, and I doubt he will even answer it.

"Why are you being punished? Is that why you don't have your wings?"

He keeps walking without even looking in my direction. "I have wings. I choose when I want them to be seen."

"And the punishment . . . What did you do?" I ask.

He stops walking then and glares at me. It feels like those green eyes are piercing through my soul. If I even have a soul. "Do I have a soul?" I blurt out.

He laughs. "I thought we covered that when you asked me if I was a reaper." I give him a puzzled look, trying to remember that among the chaos that all of this has been since I woke up. He rolls his eyes. "Your soul is fine . . ."

We get to the back of the mansion, and of course, he doesn't think I noticed how he dodged that question, but I will ask him again soon enough. I stare at the mansion, trying to remember something—anything.

"The last thing I remember was Jace and me dancing in the snow, and laughing," I say.

Zane lets out a frustrated sigh, and I give him a sideways look.

"What?" he asks.

"Oh, nothing. I mean . . . I'm dead and can't remember what happened to me. I think if anyone here has the right to be frustrated, that would be me."

He leans his head down and runs his hand through his hair. "You're right. I'm sorry." He looks back at me. "Let's start over, okay? Maybe if we do something else to take your mind off it, your memories might come to you." He pauses. "Music store?" he suggests, and I actually smile at the thought of it.

Music has always felt like therapy to me, partly because I grew up taking dance classes, but mostly because music is Jace's thing, and I could've spent the rest of my life just listening to him sing.

I think about asking Zane if we can walk to the music store, but before I can even say anything, he is already reaching for my hand, and next thing I know, we are in town square, right in front of Havenwood Falls Music & More. We walk in, and I close my eyes for a split second. The store smells like . . . home. I've always loved living in Havenwood Falls, and this right here is one of my favorite places. I look toward the back and see the owner, Cecelia, talking to someone. Something about seeing the way she moves is so comforting—has always been. For a split second, watching her happiness brings a smile to my face. Her customer thanks her, and when she turns around, facing us, Zane tenses and abruptly blocks my view.

"What was that about?" I ask.

"What?" he asks, as if he doesn't know what I'm referring to. I roll my eyes at him.

I look around for a while, before I decide to just sit on the floor against the wall and people-watch. To be honest, I hope Jace shows up here. He loves this place. Zane sits next to me, blocking part of my view.

Soon, my mind quickly goes back to a much darker place.

I sigh. "Do you think it is best for my parents to keep thinking that I'm just missing or to know the truth?"

He stops to think about it. "Honest?" he asks, and I nod. "I think the truth is always best. It'll be painful, but it'll give them closure."

I glance down for a split second before looking back at him. "I agree. Is there a way to let them know?" I ask, and he looks into my eyes.

"I'll find a way, if that is what you wish."

"Thank you," I say.

It's weird, sitting here, looking at people and listening to their conversations, when they have no idea that I'm here. It somehow doesn't feel intrusive, though. I mean, who am I going to tell their gossip to? Zane and I end up spending the day listening to music and watching people go by. When dinnertime comes around, I can almost picture Mom and Dad sitting down to eat like they always do at six on the dot. When we finally leave the store, it's dark out. I stand in the middle of Town Square Park, watching the streets slowly grow empty as people head home. I look over at Zane. "What now?"

He tilts his head to the side and gives me a puzzled look.

"I assume neither of us needs sleep. What do we do now?" I ask.

He laughs. "We go back to your home until morning."

I feel like my stomach drops. I can't go back there. I can't take seeing that look in my mom's eyes. And my dad . . . I don't think I can take seeing him at all.

"You don't have to see them," he says, as if reading my mind. "I'll make sure it's clear before you go in."

I shake my head. "Why can't we just stay out? There are things we could be doing. Maybe go back to the woods, now that it is dark out, to see if I remember something."

He chuckles. "I don't think so. You're not ready for Havenwood Falls. Not yet, anyway."

I raise an eyebrow at him. "Care to elaborate?" I ask, and he just turns around and starts to walk away. I stay where I am.

After he takes a few steps, he turns back around. "You really don't want to go back to your home?" he asks, and I shake my head.

"Come on. I know a place."

I hesitantly follow him as he leads us through town toward the school, but we stop at the library.

"What? No magical transportation?" I ask, and he laughs.

"Don't get spoiled by my abilities. You won't have them at your disposal forever."

I roll my eyes at him.

We walk into the Victorian style manor that is the new library, and I close my eyes for a split second and focus on the scent of books. My mind becomes overwhelmed with memories of when I was little and Dad used to take me to the old library every week to pick out new books.

"Was this a bad idea?" Zane asks, and for the first time since we met, he sounds genuinely concerned. I don't answer right away, and after a moment, I realize there are tears running down my face. Something I couldn't do before.

Zane gives me a sad smile and shrugs. "Sometimes you just need to feel human for a while," he says before he turns around.

"Thank you," I say, following him up the steps.

Once we are upstairs, he turns around to find me sobbing.

"I'll be looking around if you need anything," he says uncomfortably.

I give him a short nod, and he walks into one of the rooms. Knowing I can't go far, I follow him in. I walk around, picking up book after book and putting them back, unable to find something that will keep my attention. My head is such a freaking mess, I know I won't be able to focus on anything. After a few minutes, I go to the side of the room where he is, and I see him sitting on the floor with his back against the wall, reading a book. Sensing me watching him, he looks up, and I slowly walk toward him.

CHAPTER 4

ZANE

I hold Heidi's gaze as she walks toward me.

"Can I sit with you? I don't think I want to be alone," she says.

I nod to the side, and she slowly sinks to the floor next to me.

"What are you reading?" she asks as she looks over.

Not once while she was alive did I ever dream about being able to have a conversation with her, let alone be sitting this close together.

"It's fiction. About angels," I say, and she laughs. The last time I heard her laugh like this, she was with her boyfriend, dancing in the snow. Right before I got pulled away. Right before everything went wrong. They kept me away and in the dark about her being gone until I was given this insane assignment.

She looks over at the book, and I watch her every feature as she reads over the lines, and I get lost in the moment. *I have to stick to the plan—get it together and detach.*

"Here." I hand her the book. "You read it. I'll find something else," I say as I get up.

"I'm sorry. I didn't mean to—I just . . . I read this before. Please stay," she asks.

I sit back down, but move over, putting some distance between us.

"How long have you been an angel?" she asks.

27

"A little over a century."

Her eyes widen for a split second. "What else would really happen to me if you weren't close by?" she asks. "I feel weak when I walk away. I know I can't touch things. What else?"

I tense. "You'd be able to see some things for what they really are."

She gives me a confused look, but I ignore it. She doesn't need to know about the beings that live here, on top of everything else. She would be a walking mess worrying about her family and Jace.

"When I touch people, can they feel me?"

"If you are intentionally trying to touch them and I'm close by, they might feel the energy, I guess . . . but no, you can't go around poking and hugging humans and make them feel that, if that is what you want to know." He grins. "And unless you are putting a great amount of energy into it, they will just walk right through you, even with me being near."

She looks away for a split second. She was obviously not amused by my attempt at a joke. "What will happen to me if I don't fulfill my mission? If I don't remember what happened or if I don't repair whatever it is that I might need to repair?"

I'm the one avoiding her gaze now. "You'd be stuck here. You'd never move on. You'd just watch people—your parents—get older. People would come and go, and you'd always just be here. That is, assuming I'm allowed to stay with you. Otherwise, you'd be stuck where you died."

I can see the horror in her eyes as she subconsciously touches her forehead, where her injury was.

She does that thing where she jokes to deflect from reality. "So much for sugarcoating the truth." She pauses, waiting for my reaction, and when there is none, she goes on. "What will happen to me if I do what I need to?" she asks.

I shrug. "I assume you'll get peace and all that good heavenly stuff." *And you'll be pulled away from me,* I think to myself and start to shake my head.

She giggles. "Are you sure you are an angel?"

"Why do you ask?" I say.

"There is this bitter tone when you talk about those things."

"I'm sure," I say. "Unfortunately," I whisper under my breath as I get up.

I pull another book out from the shelf.

"I miss Jace," she says in a tone that makes me feel a thousand emotions at once—none of which I should be feeling.

"I suppose it's normal for you to feel that way," I snap before I walk away without looking back at her, because if I do, I know I'm doomed. She'll end up stuck here, and it will be my fault.

CHAPTER 5

HEIDI

*W*ell, this ghost thing is going to get old fast. I spend the night reading books about ghosts of all things, to see if I can identify with anything at all, and also, to escape into someone else's world for a while. I sense Zane watching me every once in a while, but I ignore him, knowing that either he is a complete jerk or he is just not used to people.

When morning comes, I feel nervous like I've never been before.

I walk over to the window on the second floor of the library and watch people go by as they start their day.

"I'm not sure going to the school is a good idea. Maybe you should wait longer," Zane says, startling me.

I didn't even hear him move. I turn around and glare at him. He shakes his head, clearly frustrated that he's stuck here with me. I don't even have to say anything.

"Fine. Are you ready to go?" he asks.

"I could never be ready for this," I say, and I contemplate if seeing Jace is even a good idea at all, but deep inside, I know that I need to. I look back outside. "Just give me a little while before we go."

Zane backs away, and in an attempt to prepare myself to see Jace, I run just about every possible worst-case scenario in my head—the worst of all being that he moved on and is dating someone I know.

Zane doesn't make a sound until I tell him that I'm ready to go.

Going into the school feels like a nightmare. I walk a few steps behind Zane, mostly because I don't feel like talking or seeing his frustrated *I told you so* expression in relation to this being a bad idea. I'm not ready for this at all. The first familiar face I see is Gianna Augustine, and that is when it hits me that I won't be graduating with my class, or doing any of the things I was looking forward to. As the bell rings, I stand at the end of the hallway, feeling sick, and then stunned as people walk literally through me. With each step they take, as they walk through me, something strange happens. I capture a few split seconds of memories, all of them related to me in some way. I close my eyes as I see and listen to them talking to others about me. "Did you hear about Heidi?". . . "Hey. Did you see Heidi last night before she went missing?" And most of them saying, "I heard she ran away."

I look at Zane. I can't even tell if he is irritated or concerned, but without saying a word, he patiently waits until I'm ready to keep going.

"He is in art class," he says.

"How do you— You know what, never mind."

I take off in that direction.

When I go in, I spot Jace right away, but I can't make myself move past the doorway. I can feel Zane right next to me, watching my every move. Jace is sitting toward the back, alone, with headphones on as he writes on a piece of paper. A few other students are grouped together, working on different projects while they talk about the upcoming prom—yet another thing I won't be able to do. Not that it matters. All of that seems so small compared to the fact that I won't be able to be with Jace, or my family. I look back at Jace, and I still can't make myself move any closer.

"He is fine," Zane says. "Well, maybe not fine, but he will be. He's tough," he says with a confidence that throws me off.

I feel the need to cry the moment it clicks. I look down at my sweater. This is how he knew this is my favorite. This is how he knew me. I sigh and look over at Zane.

31

"You were his guardian angel, weren't you?" I ask.

He gives me a short nod.

"What happened that night?" I whisper to myself, and I'm surprised when Zane actually says something.

"I wish I knew." He pauses. "Actually, I wish I was around to stop whatever happened." He looks over at me. "I'd have done everything in my power to save you if I'd been around."

As he says that, he sounds like a different person. I look into his green eyes, and I see the regret. He meant every word. I look back at Jace. Two of his friends are in this class, but they won't even look in his direction.

"He's not alone by choice," says Zane. "A lot of people blame him. Some say you two argued and you ran away from home. Some even think he is involved with your disappearance."

I gasp.

"But you know he didn't do anything," I say.

"I wasn't exactly around, but it doesn't matter what I know or think."

I laugh, and he gives me a funny look. "I don't get it," I say. "We never fought. Not even once."

"Yeah. I know," he snaps.

I walk over toward Jace's desk and sit on the one next to it, facing him. *He looks so sad*, I think to myself.

When I look up, I notice Zane looking over at the other side of the room, where I spot a tall and pale redhead staring at Jace. I know I've seen her before, but for the life of me, no pun intended, I can't remember her name. She has always been reserved—that is about all I can remember.

"Elsie Brooks," says Zane.

She goes back to reading her book, but every once in a while, she looks at Jace, and not with a simple *I'm into you* look.

I look from her to Zane. "She knows something."

CHAPTER 6

ZANE

I walk around the desk and stand in front of her, blocking her view of Jace.

"So what now?" I ask her.

She has this look in her eyes. I've seen that look many times before. She's plotting something, and I know her. Once she puts something in her head, she goes for it.

"Now, we follow her," she says, nodding toward the girl. She sighs and sits back, where she can see Jace again. "Do you miss watching over him?" she asks.

I just stare at her, not knowing how to answer that. The best part about watching over him was being around her. Well, that was the best and worst part all at once.

"How long were you his guardian for?" she asks when I don't say anything.

I shrug. "Two years—maybe less . . . " Since her fifteenth birthday almost two years ago. I remember the day like it was yesterday. They snuck out that night, and I had the glorious job of keeping them safe.

She sighs again, looking at him. "This is so unfair."

"Tell me about it," I mumble.

"What did you say?" she asks, looking at me.

"Nothing. Go on . . ."

33

She looks over at her ring and starts to play with it. She doesn't look back up for a while. She just sits there quietly, which kills me.

I close the distance between us, put my hand on her shoulder, and take us back to the library.

"What the hell?" she practically yells as soon as she realizes where we are. "What did you do that for?"

"That was enough for the day," I say.

She turns around, grabs a book, and throws it against the wall. A guy who appears to be in his thirties looks up from his book, rolls his eyes, and goes back to reading it like nothing happened. Sometimes, being in a town full of supernatural beings has its perks.

"Really?" I ask in a sarcastic tone. "This is exactly why I pulled you out of there. You were getting too emotional. I'm not dealing with a ghost who is throwing fits."

"Fine. Then don't," she snaps before she takes off—fast. And farther than she should be going.

"What are you doing?" I ask. She is mad. I know her. She won't stop until it's too late, and so I'm forced to follow. "Are you going to stop?"

"Nope!" She yells back.

"Do you even know where you are going?" I ask.

She doesn't say anything, but I keep following her until we reach her house.

She stops at the front door and looks back at me. She nervously bites her bottom lip.

"Do you want to go in?" I ask.

"I don't know," she says. I know her emotions are all over the place. I can feel it in ways that I shouldn't be able to. "I miss them." She pauses. "I need someone . . . familiar."

I nod toward the house, hoping that is enough to encourage her to do what she needs to do.

We go in.

It's almost noon, and we find her mom lying on her bed, sleeping. There is a bottle of sleeping pills next to her. Heidi just stands there, watching her.

"I'm going to step right outside of the room," I say. "Give you some privacy."

"Okay," she says, still staring at her mom.

"Heidi," I say, and she looks up at me. "Talk to her. That will help."

"It won't be the same."

"I know," I say, before I walk out of the room.

I don't know how much time passes before I finally go back in. I find Heidi lying down next to her mom, pouring her heart out about how much she misses just being able to hug her.

"I saw Jace today." She pauses and closes her eyes before she rolls onto her back. "It's so unfair to know that all of our plans are gone. We won't go to prom together, or college. We won't get married. I don't even know what I'm really doing here. I can't remember what happened to me, and there is this mystery thing I need to repair. I just want to find out what happened to me, so maybe you and dad will have closure." She looks back at her mom and sighs. "Sad thing is that the only one I can have an actual conversation with doesn't even want to be here."

If she only knew just how much I want to be here. To the point where sometimes I wonder if her being stuck here is all that bad. I let out a growl. I can't be doing this. I can't punish her by keeping her here for my sake.

I back out of the room and sit in the hallway until Heidi comes out and says she is ready to go.

It's already getting dark outside, but we quietly walk back to the library. Once we are on the second floor, Heidi walks over to the window and leans against it, watching people go by. And as much as I want to tell her there is no place I'd rather be, I know I can't.

HEIDI

I look outside and zone out.

"Heidi," I hear Zane say right behind me.

I turn around, and I find myself face to face with him. To my surprise, he pulls me into a hug, and it doesn't take long before I feel tears run down my cheeks as I bury my face against his chest.

"I'm sorry this happened to you," he says as he awkwardly continues to hug me.

After a while, he lets go and steps away. He walks over to a bookshelf, grabs a book, and sits down on the floor. I realize that I missed contact more than I thought I did. I walk over and ask if he minds if I sit with him. He nervously shakes his head. I don't think he is used to all of this . . . human stuff. I sit next to him and lean my head back against the wall.

"You were human before, right?"

He tilts his head to the side. "Yes, but I honestly don't even remember it anymore."

"I miss sleeping," I say. "And food. Oh my God. I miss food! Cheesy waffle fries and a juicy hamburger," I say, and we both laugh. I lean my head forward and look at him. "What would happen if I ate?" I ask, still laughing.

"Well, you have no digestive system so . . . I have no idea."

I laugh even harder and shake my head. I reach over toward a bookshelf, grab a book, and start reading it. After a while, I lean my head on Zane's shoulder. He tenses, but he doesn't say anything, so I stay where I am and keep reading.

CHAPTER 7

HEIDI

J'm surprised when Zane agrees to go back to the school without any attempts to talk me out of it or give me a lecture.

We go a little later in the day, and it's lunchtime, so he takes us straight to the cafeteria.

The first familiar face I see is Zoey Mills. I get distracted watching her interact with Miranda, Jordan Woods, and a few others. I'm happy to see that Zoey fit right in with everyone else.

I sigh and look past them.

It's not hard to spot the redheaded girl, and from there, it's not hard to find Jace. She's still doing that thing where she keeps looking at him from time to time.

Zane chuckles. "With that intensity, I'm surprised she doesn't feel that she's being watched."

I ignore what he said, hoping I'm not starting to pick up his habits. "I want to try something I read about in one of those books at the library," I tell Zane.

He gives me a puzzled look.

"What?" he asks, and he looks like he is afraid of the answer.

"I want to possess Elsie to talk to Jace." I can hardly believe those words just came out of my mouth.

"Nope. Not a chance."

I laugh. "I wasn't asking for permission. Look, I need to find out what happened. I can't think of any other way. So unless you have a better idea?"

"I'll come up with something," he says in a rushed tone.

"Well, I'm tired of just ghosting around. I need to do something!"

He rolls his eyes at me. "Fine. But I'm kicking you out of her body the moment I deem it necessary. Possessions can be . . . addicting."

"Fine," I say. At this point, I'll say whatever he wants to hear.

"Fine." He glares at me.

Once he agrees, I realize that I wouldn't have gone through with it otherwise. I feel nervous like never before. I begin to wonder how it is going to feel, or if anyone will notice. What if I mess up?

Zane watches me curiously. "If you're really going to insist on this, you probably shouldn't overthink it," he says. I just roll my eyes at him.

I wait until Elsie gets up to go to the bathroom, and I follow her in. Zane starts to come with me, but before he steps foot in the bathroom, I put my hand against his chest to stop him. Talk about awkward. The nervous look on his face is priceless.

"What?" he asks.

"Don't be a creeper. You're not going in the women's bathroom. I got this. I'm sure you'll know if I need help."

He looks down at my hand still on his chest, and that is when I pull away and go after Elsie.

I find her staring at the mirror. She is brushing her hair, trying to control how wild it is. I step behind her. Close my eyes. And then, hoping that this will work, I take a step forward. I can feel her body jerk, and her head leans back before leaning forward again. This feels horribly strange. I look in the mirror. I feel like myself, but I see her. I look down at my—well, *her*—arms and hands, and watch her fingers as I move them around.

I take a deep breath. Breathing . . . I never thought I would miss this feeling so much. I look in the mirror again and tilt my head to the side. I run my fingers through my—her hair. This feels so weird.

Deciding that I need me—her to look more like me, I make a quick braid. I look in her purse to find eyeliner and lip gloss. I put it on and walk out of the bathroom.

Zane is right in front of the door when I open it. His eyes meet mine before he glances at the braid. "Was that necessary?" he asks.

My lips part to answer when his abrupt interruption startles me. "Don't talk to me. You don't want to sound—well, you don't want to make her sound like a crazy person, do you? Don't even look in my direction. I'll be with you. Let's go."

We go back to the cafeteria, where I spot Jace sitting alone. I slowly walk toward him, and I can feel her heart beating against her chest with every step I take. I'm standing right next to the table when I stumble back as the memories come in. From a large window at the Mills mansion, I can see Jace and me dancing. We are both laughing. When we stop, he reaches for my hand. He says something as I watch in horror, and then I run toward the woods. Jace stands there for minutes that feel like an eternity, before he runs after me.

I suddenly feel a jerk, and I find myself standing by Zane with Elsie in front of me. She quickly sits in front of Jace and puts her head down.

"Are you okay?" Jace asks in a concerned tone as Zane asks me the same question.

I put my hand on Zane's arm in an attempt to steady myself as I watch their interaction in silence.

"I don't know," she says, looking confused.

Jace notices the braid. I can see it in his eyes when he remembers how I wore my hair back when it was longer.

"Here." He offers her his drink, before things go dark and I find myself back at the library with Zane.

"You have got to stop doing that!" I snap.

"What happened?" he asks.

"Can we go back?"

He shakes his head. "What happened, Heidi?" he asks in a soft tone.

I look up at him.

"I saw her memories of that night . . . Jace said something that upset me. I ran into the woods, and after a while, he ran after me."

Zane doesn't say anything at first. "You saw her memories?" he asks.

I nod. "It happened the other day at school too. When people walked through me, I saw glimpses of their memories of me."

He rubs his forehead, but doesn't say anything.

"You don't think he would—" he starts to say before I interrupt him.

"Of course not! How could you even think that? You probably know him as well as I do." I pause. "But I need to know more. Can I do what I did with Elsie by possessing him?"

I can see the look of horror in his eyes as soon as I say it.

"Absolutely not. This memory thing, as far as I know, is not even common for beings like you."

"Okay, whatever. It worked. Maybe it will work on him, and I'll know more."

"Don't bother," he says. "You try to possess him, and I'll pull you out before you even get that far."

I cross my arms over my chest, and he chuckles. "You're not going to convince me by acting like you're upset. Not this time."

ZANE

I can't let her get hurt. I don't care what answers possessing him will give her. Nothing good can come of it.

I can see her frustration in her every move—in her every word.

She stares me down, waiting for me to change my mind. She's so hardheaded, I guarantee she's already plotting the next time she'll possess the girl. I shake my head and I can't believe I'm about to suggest this.

"I have special abilities that I could put to good use. To help you," I say, against my better judgment.

She crosses her arms and stares at me. "Like what?" she asks in a doubtful tone.

"I can influence her so that she'll talk to him and ask anything you want to know."

Her jaw drops. "Really?"

I nod.

She watches me curiously and then says, "He's not just going to talk to someone he doesn't even know. Are you going to influence him to answer with the truth?"

I shake my head. "I can't do that."

"Why?" she asks, and I ignore it.

"He'll talk eventually. He's been alone for too long. People always need someone to confide in."

I know the moment I say that, I said all the wrong words. I can sense the jealousy radiating off her. She's not even a jealous person under normal circumstances, but I know that look. I felt that many times before, even though I shouldn't have.

"I don't like this, and—" she starts to say before I cut her off.

I throw my hands up in the air. She's infuriating sometimes. "We'll try my way. If you want it to stop, or if it doesn't work, sure, go ahead and possess him." I won't allow it to happen, but she can think that for now.

CHAPTER 8

HEIDI

I spend the next few hours looking out the window, trying not to drive myself crazy. That gets old quickly. I turn to find Zane sitting on the floor, reading a book. My attention goes straight to the couple on the cover, making me chuckle.

"What are you reading?" I ask, and he quickly closes the book and stuffs it in the row of books next to him. As mad as I was over the whole discussion about possessing Jace, I have to keep myself from laughing. The sight of an angel reading a romance novel is just amusing. He ignores my question, as usual, and I don't press it. This is not the time to piss him off. "I can't stay here all day. Can we go to the music store?"

He stands up and reaches for my arm, but I quickly pull away. "I'd rather walk there, if that's okay."

He gives me a short nod.

On the way there, I can't help but ask, "Do you read romance books often?" I grin. He actually looks embarrassed, so I go on. "Not that there is anything wrong with that. I just—I don't know. Are angels allowed to read that?"

"I'm not aware of any rules against it," he says in a dry tone.

"Oh, okay." I look away as we head toward the store, and I'm caught by surprise when he goes on.

"I read them to understand you."

I stop and look at him with confusion, wondering what the hell that means.

"Humans," he says awkwardly. "I read them to understand humans."

I shrug, and we continue to walk. "Is it helping?" I ask.

"Nope."

I chuckle. "I didn't think it would. You know . . . you can ask me questions," I say. "If there is anything you want to know. Anything at all."

He abruptly stops walking and looks at me. "What does it feel like to kiss someone?" he blurts out, and after the shock that he actually asked something passes, I grin and close my eyes for a split second. I then look down at the ring on my finger and sigh.

"It feels like magic," I say. "The more you kiss, the more you want to keep kissing."

I can feel myself blush. I look up at him, and he has this intense, serious look.

"Come on," he says, nodding toward the store.

We go in, and again, I welcome the familiarity of the place. I see Glenn saying goodbye to a customer. I go to the spot where we were before and sit on the floor. I lean my head against the wall, close my eyes, and enjoy the music, the smell, everything about this place.

I can hear Glenn's voice. "Hey. Where are you? I came in early today just to train you. Call me when you get this message."

"I'm here! Sorry I'm late." I quickly open my eyes and see Jace rushing toward the back. I glare at Zane because I know what's coming.

"Don't you dare!" I warn him. He doesn't look happy, but he doesn't try to get us out of here.

I stand up and walk toward Jace as he puts his books in the back of the store.

"You work here," I say with a smile on my face. He always loved music, and I'm glad he's doing something he loves.

I look over at Zane. He's still sitting on the floor, watching me like a hawk, but he stays put as I follow Jace around like some crazy ghost stalker, looking for any sign that he may be thinking about me, or missing me . . . anything. Not that it will make a difference. Deep inside, I know that will actually make me feel worse, because nothing can change the fact that I'm dead.

When things quiet down, Glenn says he needs to go make a call, and Jace sits down behind the counter and grabs a music magazine. I stand next to him, with my back against the counter.

I glance at Zane, and he quickly looks away, pretending that he's not watching my every move. I then look back at Jace.

"I miss you," I whisper, feeling stupid for saying something he can't ever hear.

Out of habit, I reach for his hand, and I freeze in place as I get hit with a flash of memory. It's dark, but I can see it clear as day. Jace stands somewhere surrounded by trees. There is snow on the ground. I look from the ground to his hand, and it feels like everything is happening in slow motion. He is holding my phone, and when he moves it, I see the blood—my blood—on his hand, and I can feel the guilt he feels. I gasp as I look into his eyes—this time, back at the music store. Maybe it is shock, but for a split second, I feel like Jace is looking right at me, and then, I'm back at the library.

"What happened?" Zane asks in a concerned tone.

Words don't come out. I stand here, staring at a blank space. I can't think. I can't.

I feel Zane's hands on each side of my face. "Heidi. Look at me. Heidi."

I look up at him. I feel numb. I—

"What happened, Heidi?" His gaze holds mine in a way that I can't look away.

I feel my hands tremble, and when I start speaking, I don't even sound like myself. "I think I was killed. And I think Jace may have done it."

Zane stares at me, and the silence becomes overwhelming. He's not denying it. He should be saying there is no way. He knows Jace, like I do—or like I thought I did. Every bit of me begs him to tell me I'm wrong. That it's insane that I even think that, but he doesn't say a word. He just pulls me into a hug.

"I don't understand," I say after a while.

"What makes you think he did that?" Zane finally asks.

I sigh and try to get the courage to say it out loud. "When I reached for his hand—I got a glimpse of a memory." I'm filled with horror once again as I tell him exactly what I saw.

"Maybe he just found your phone," he says, and I shake my head.

"I could feel his guilt, Zane. It was weird and overwhelming. Why else would he feel guilty?"

Zane gives me a confused look. "Could you feel what Elsie felt when you possessed her?"

I shake my head. "Just her memories."

"I don't understand how or why you can pick up on those things, but he wouldn't have hurt you, Heidi. We'll find out what happened, okay?" he says in a soft tone. He continues to talk to me, and I just nod in agreement, but at this point, I'm not even listening to him anymore. I can't get that image or that feeling out of my head.

CHAPTER 9

HEIDI

I keep replaying Jace's memory in my head over and over again. Zane knows it, too. He's sitting on the floor and doing a horrible job at pretending to read a book. I can tell that by the concerned look in his eyes and also by the fact that he won't stop staring at me. By midnight, I'm restless. I can't spend another second here. I need to go and do—something.

"I have an idea," he says as he gets up. He extends his hand, and I put mine in his. Next thing I know, we are standing in the middle of Serendipity Dance Studio, where I've taken ballet classes since I was four. I stand here and look around. The glass windows from floor to ceiling allow for the moonlight to come through, making the studio look even more stunning than usual.

"I missed this place," I say.

"I figured," he says. "But I wasn't sure if bringing you here would be a good thing or not."

"I'm not sure either," I say. "It sucks I will never be able to dance again."

"You could still dance," he says.

I walk over to the window and look outside. "It wouldn't be the same. I danced because I loved to dance, but there was also something special about people admiring what you are doing."

"I am here, and I can see you," he says in a soft tone.

I turn around and look at him. Those bright green eyes stare right at me. I wonder once again why he is being punished. Saying things like this don't sound very angel-like, especially with the way he looks at me, and right at this moment, I'm not sure that is a bad thing. A part of me feels different—human, maybe—at being noticed. Or maybe I'm just going insane because I have no interaction with anyone besides him.

He holds my gaze for a moment longer, before he says, "Do you want to leave?"

I nod. "But I don't want to go back to the library. I have an idea, actually. Can you take me to the Mills mansion?"

He tilts his head to the side, waiting for more.

All I say is, "To the ballroom."

He takes me straight there. I remember being in this room that night as if it was yesterday. I just wish I could remember the rest of the night.

I walk to the middle of the ballroom, stopping under the skylight. I get on the floor and lie down. Zane approaches me. He looks down at me with confusion in his eyes.

"This is something I've always wanted to do," I tell him, and he chuckles. To my surprise, he lies down next to me and looks up at the sky.

I sigh. "What is it like being an angel?"

"Not worth the sacrifices," he says in a bitter tone.

I look over at him. "You must've had to give up something really important to feel that upset about it."

He keeps looking up. "I wouldn't say give up. You can't give up someone—I mean, something you never had."

I look back up at the sky again, afraid to know more, because I have a feeling that this has something to do with me. I mean, the things he says, and he was Jace's guardian for years before this punishment. He even cared enough to know my favorite things. But I know that I can't stay here like this, feeling trapped.

"I'm afraid of what will happen to me when I move on . . .

whatever that means. But I'm even more terrified of being stuck like I am now for eternity," I blurt out.

He turns his head to the side, facing me, and there is something different about the way he looks at me. "I wish I could promise you that everything will be okay, Heidi. I really do."

There he goes again. I let out a nervous laugh.

"Well, that sounds comforting," I say as he sits up, his back to me. *Ugh.* I have to know. "Zane?" I say, and he looks back at me. "I have to ask you something. It's more of a guess really. I just need to know," I start to babble.

"Go on."

"You know what it is that I need to repair, don't you?" I ask. He doesn't say anything, but I notice he tenses. "Your punishment and whatever it is that I need to repair are related, aren't they?"

I regret asking the moment I see tears in his eyes.

He looks away and lowers his head. "They are," he whispers. "But you don't have to worry about it. I'll make sure it's taken care of." He still avoids looking at me. "They're just trying to teach me a lesson. Make me realize there are consequences to everything I do, and that I should value what I am."

At this moment, my heart breaks for him. You can't force someone, angel or not, to do what their heart isn't into. And this also means there is a giant risk of me getting stuck here.

I can't even tell which one of us is made more uncomfortable by this conversation.

"Can we go back to the library?" I ask as I get up.

He doesn't hesitate.

BACK AT THE LIBRARY, I try to come up with something else to talk about, mostly to try to keep his mind off the conversation we just had. Unfortunately, my thoughts take me right back to Jace's memory, and then, something Zane said before about staying out at night pops in my head.

"What did you mean when you said that I wasn't ready for Havenwood Falls? I mean, I've lived here my whole life. I'm sure there is nothing I haven't seen."

He bursts into laughter.

"I'm glad you think that's funny." I keep staring at him, waiting on an answer.

"You should sit down," he says, making me feel uneasy. Just how bad can this be, considering everything else I've been going through?

He manages to stop laughing and sighs. "We're not the only ones around who are not human."

I relax. "Huh. I can't believe I didn't think of that before. So, there are other angels and ghosts. Why can't we go out there?"

He doesn't bother answering. I hate when he does that. He walks over to the bookshelf and picks up a book. I rush toward him and grab the book from his hand.

Looking up at him, I beg, "I need something to get my mind off Jace. Just please tell me. I don't care how shocking it is. Please, Zane."

He looks tense. "Sit down," he says.

I do. I sit on the floor of the quiet library, lit by nothing but the moonlight, and he sits in front of me.

"Do you remember the howls you heard on the night you awoke in the woods?"

I nod.

"Werewolves," he says.

I study his face, and he even looks serious. I burst into laughter. When I notice he's still not laughing with me, but just sitting there, watching my reaction, I stop.

"No way," I say.

He nods. "Vampires, shifters . . . you name it. Havenwood Falls is full of supernatural beings."

I give him a doubtful look.

"Everywhere you look. Everywhere you go. At school, I wouldn't be surprised if there are more supernatural beings than humans."

I grin at him. "Right," I say in a sarcastic tone. "Who? Give me names."

Zane scratches his chin and looks like he is deep in thought.

"Well," he finally says, "the Kasuns are wolf shifters. Julianna Fairchild comes from a long bloodline of fae, and Miranda—"

I burst into laughter, cutting him off. "You can stop. You're making this up, aren't you?"

He doesn't really give me an answer. He just shrugs and grins. He reaches for another book and hands it to me. "Read this. It will help keep your mind busy."

I slowly take the book from him and try to focus on reading it, which doesn't come easily.

When morning comes, Zane is ready to get us to the school, but I'm the one who doesn't want to go. I'm terrified. I'm afraid of seeing Jace. I'm afraid of finding out more.

CHAPTER 10

ZANE

*I*t kills me to see how much that one memory she saw is hurting her. She spent the last few hours pretending to read the book I gave her, while I sat here, helpless and wondering what in the world I am doing telling her the things I told her last night, and most importantly, telling her that I will repair something that I'm not sure I want repaired at all. I hate that she's part of a higher plan to teach me a lesson—that I am the "thing" she needs to repair, which just makes me angrier at being what I am. And at Fate for putting her in my path. Several times a day, I have to convince myself that letting go and devoting myself to my destiny is what I should be doing, but I find myself wondering over and over again how bad it would be if she doesn't move on. I could walk away from it all. But then I remember her words. This is not what she wants.

When it's time to go back to the school, I can see how afraid she looks, but there is no way he did it.

"He didn't do it, Heidi. We'll find out what happened," I attempt to assure her.

I know she wants to believe me, but she can't. I can tell by how tense she is. She sighs and bites her bottom lip.

"Just say it. What's on your mind?" I ask.

"Let's say he just happened to find my phone. Why the guilt?" she asks.

"Well, if something he said is what led you into the woods, it's only reasonable for him to feel guilty."

She looks at the floor as if she's thinking it through. Then her eyes meet mine again.

"Are you ready to go?" I ask.

I know she isn't, but she nods. As I reach for her arm, she closes her eyes, and then we're at the school, in Jace's class.

At the sight of Jace, she takes a step back and just stares at him. She looks terrified. I'm scrambling to figure out what I should even say at this point, or if I should take her out of here, when I feel her hand slip into mine. Our fingers entwine, and now I'm scrambling for what to say again, but for other reasons.

"We could go," I finally say, but she shakes her head.

"I need to find out that it wasn't him. It couldn't have been."

When she tries to let go of my hand, I hold on to her, and surprisingly, she doesn't pull away.

"Come on," I say. "Let's walk around. We can come back during lunch, when I can get Elsie to actually talk to him."

She agrees and looks at him once again, before we go toward the hallway. Still hand in hand, we walk around, and I find her watching a group of students who are standing around, talking about prom.

"What is it?" I ask.

"What are they?" she asks, and I give her a confused look. "Vampires? Werewolves? Humans?"

I laugh.

"I didn't think you were serious," she says. "But nice attempt at keeping my mind busy."

I laugh again. "Come on," I say as I lead her to the cafeteria, where we wait.

It's not until then that I let go of her hand.

"Thank you," she says.

I raise an eyebrow at her.

"For the angelic support." She smiles, and I tense.

"I don't think holding your hand like that classifies as angelic support."

"Oh," she says. "Are you going to get in trouble for that?"

I shrug. "It doesn't matter. You needed me. I was there for you."

Embarrassed, she tilts her head down, avoiding my gaze, and I know I need to stop saying things like that. For my sake and hers. I have to remind myself that if she were to stay stuck here for eternity—that would be an eternity of her blaming me for it.

When she finally looks up, I'm the one who avoids eye contact.

"Can I ask you something?" she asks.

"Sure."

"Is it really that bad, being what you are?"

I shrug, and stop to think about it. "For me? Yes," I say, and she probably thinks I'm a jerk for not appreciating the privilege of being an angel. "It wasn't always like that. I was proud of being an angel at one point."

"What happened?" she asks.

"Fate," I say in a bitter tone, and I leave it at that. And to an extent, it's true.

If only I had never met her, things would've been so much less complicated. The strange thing is I don't even know why *her*—after a century—why she had this effect on me from the first time I laid eyes on her. Why I was so filled with jealousy the first time I saw her and Jace kissing. Why I fell for her more and more every day—when I saw her dancing, when I saw her laughing, when I saw her just being her. And the worst part is that the way I feel has rendered this punishment useless. Every day that passes, I care more for her, and every day, I'm further away from being saved.

When I get out of my own head and look at her, I see that she's nervous again. I start asking her questions about school to distract her, but avoiding things that would make her feel sad, like her plans for prom, become nearly impossible. Before we know it, we hear commotion as people come into the cafeteria.

I spot Jace right away, and Elsie not far behind. I'm a little surprised when I see Elsie sit down at the same table as him. I look over at Heidi, and she looks even more afraid now. Or maybe it's not fear, but something else.

"Did you do that?" she asks.

"What?"

"Influence her to sit with him?"

I ignore the question. More and more, I notice how much I've been doing this. I hate lying to her; yet, I feel this undeniable need to protect her.

"Come on," I say as I stand, and when she doesn't move, I extend my hand to her.

She puts her hand in mine and gets up. As I lead her toward them, I can tell how nervous she is by the way she's holding on to me. Once we're close enough to hear their conversation, I listen for the right moment to cut in. Elsie is telling him about one of the math assignments she needs help with when I see *him*—the one who gave my punishment.

I quickly let go of Heidi's hand. My hands turn into fists, and I can feel my fingernails digging into my skin as he watches Heidi and me. I didn't think they would be checking in like this. They rarely do, and I don't want Heidi anywhere near him.

Heidi seems too engrossed in Jace and Elsie's conversation to even notice.

I look at her.

"Heidi," I say, and she looks at me. The entire time, I'm trying to keep an eye on him to make sure he doesn't get any closer. I'm not sure if this is good or bad, but he just watches from a distance. Seeing the pain in her eyes, I hate having to do this even more. "Heidi, I need you to do something for me."

"What?" she asks in a tone that breaks me.

"I have to walk away for a little while. I need you to possess Elsie until I get back. As long as you are possessing her, you're safe here."

The pain in her eyes turns into fear.

"I'll be as close by as possible. But I need you to do this, Heidi.

Please. And don't leave her until I am back. Can you do this for me?" I beg, and she nods.

"Promise no matter what you see or hear, you'll stay put until I get back."

"I promise," she says. I wait until Heidi slowly moves toward Elsie and possesses her before I walk away to meet the dominion angel.

CHAPTER 11

HEIDI

I stare at Jace and fight the urge to cry. He's going on and on about an assignment for class when I blurt out, "Do you miss her?"

I watch the blood drain from his face. He looks down at his food and leans back against his seat. His tone completely changes. "Of course I do."

We fall into silence, but not for long, mostly because I don't know how long we have. "I was at the Mills mansion that night. I saw her run into the woods. What happened?"

He looks up at me, and now he's the one who is on the verge of tears.

"Can we talk about something else?"

I just look at him, my eyes begging him to tell me more, even though I'm terrified of what that might entail. I absentmindedly pull her long red hair to the side and start to braid it. His gaze goes to my hands as I weave locks of my hair.

He sighs. "I can't talk about that night, okay?" he says as he pushes his tray away.

"Can't or won't?" I ask as I remove the rubber band from her wrist and put it around her hair.

"I can't." He leans forward and lowers his tone. "I heard the rumors. I didn't do it, if that's what you're getting at. Sheriff Kasun said I shouldn't discuss that night. That's all there is to it. And please don't ask me again," he begs.

I nod and leave it alone, knowing that I won't get anywhere without Zane's help. I look around for him, but he's nowhere to be found.

"She used to wear her hair like that," Jace says, pulling me back to the moment.

The way he says that raises goose bumps on Elsie's arm. "I'm sorry." I say.

He looks down at the table, avoiding my gaze. "Yeah. Me, too."

"Ask if he thinks you're still alive," I hear Zane next to me. I start to look his way when he stops me. "Don't. Keep looking at him," he orders.

I take a deep breath, and I notice how it doesn't feel the same anymore. Breathing has started to feel awkward.

"Do you think there is a chance she's still alive?" I ask, and he shakes his head. And that look of guilt is all over his face again.

"I wish that was the case more than anything else," he says, practically whispering. "But—" he starts to say. He then stops and just shakes his head, leaving me more confused than before.

"Maybe he'll talk more if outside of the school," says Zane.

I stare at Jace without saying anything. I start remembering the many times we were sitting here, making plans for after school. And now, I'm sitting here, across from the love of my life, wondering if he killed me.

Zane pulls me out of Elsie, but this time, I don't mind. I feel exhausted.

I see the look of confusion in her eyes before she asks, "Do you want to do something later today?"

And I know this is Zane's doing.

Jace raises an eyebrow at her.

"Come on," she says shyly. "What do you do besides school and work?"

"Nothing much," he says in a sad tone.

"Do you work today?"

He shakes his head, and I just stand here, feeling numb as I watch their interaction.

"How about the Burger Bar after school?" she asks, and he hesitates. "Just something to do. There's nothing to it. We'll go as friends. Maybe you can help me with my math homework."

He still hesitates, but finally agrees.

"I guess just meet me by my car after school," he says, and I feel the hint of jealousy creeping through. Maybe I don't need to know that bad—not if it's going to push someone new on him. And I know that's me being selfish, but I also know I can't handle seeing him with someone else.

When lunch is over, Zane and I stay in the empty cafeteria, and we sit where Jace and Elsie were.

"What's on your mind?" Zane asks.

He holds my gaze with those sad green eyes. I don't want to talk about it, but I find myself saying exactly what's on my mind.

"How much the thought of seeing him with someone else would hurt," I blurt out, and Zane gives me this sympathetic look, as if he can understand. Maybe those books are helping him remember human emotions after all.

"There is nothing going on between them," Zane says.

"Yet," I reply in a bitter tone.

Zane watches me with an intensity that makes me look away. "I don't think he could get over someone like you."

I'm caught by surprise, considering our conversation at the ballroom. Again, this doesn't seem like something an angel should be saying, and more and more, I start to believe that I will be stuck here forever, even if I do find out what happened to me.

I sigh. "I guess I can't expect him to be alone forever." His lips part to say something else, when I stop him. "Let's get out of here. Maybe we can walk around the school or something until it's time to go."

Zane gives me a wicked grin.

"What?" I ask in a suspicious tone.

"Come on," he says, and I follow him to the Spanish classroom.

~

"WHY ARE WE HERE?" I ask.

His grin grows wider. "To cheer you up."

"Ugh. I hated this class while I was alive. Why would it cheer me up now?"

He shrugs. "I know your teacher is not exactly a role model. He has said mean things to just about everyone in your class, and now, here we are. They can't see you. Let's say you wanted to play a few . . . hmmm . . . ghost pranks on him—no one would stop you," he chuckles.

I roll my eyes at him. "That's so immature. And again, are you sure you're an angel?" I laugh.

He raises an eyebrow at me. "Do you want to leave?"

I shake my head. "No!"

I can't believe I'm about to do this.

Zane takes a step back, and I stand here, looking at the teacher and students and pondering what I should do. After a while, I grin from ear to ear.

I look over at Zane and notice that he has been watching me with an intensity that makes me shy away.

"We need to make a quick stop by the art class," I say.

He follows me quietly as we go in. I grab a very small bottle of glitter glue, and then we go back. As Mr. Fernandez stands up to read something to the class, I walk over to his desk and put glitter glue all over his chair. When I look back at Zane, he's shaking his head and smiling. And when Mr. Fernandez finally sits down, after what's the longest lecture on earth, I'm laughing so hard it hurts.

"Sorry," I tell Zane. "I know this is stupid and immature, and—"

"You needed that laugh," he interrupts me. "It's good for the soul."

I smile at him. I then look back and watch as Mr. Fernandez stands up, and when he turns around, the entire class bursts into laughter. Even Brice Blackstone, who is shy and keeps to himself for the most part, can't stop laughing. It takes Mr. Fernandez a few minutes to figure out what's going on, which makes it even funnier.

"Well, I can't say that I'll miss this class." I look over at Zane. "Thank you," I say.

"My pleasure."

Zane takes me out of there before Mr. Fernandez can react. He says I would just feel bad later on if I had stayed, and I know he's right. I would never have done something like that when I was alive. We end up walking around the school until the last bell rings.

CHAPTER 12

HEIDI

I freeze in place when I see Jace's dad's convertible. I close my eyes and relive the memories of that night as if it had just been yesterday. His dad's convertible parked on my street . . . the drive to the Mills mansion . . . the Christmas decorations on the way. Jace wouldn't let anyone but me ever ride in this car, because his dad would kill him otherwise. I can't let Elsie ride in the car with him. I go toward them, and Zane lightly wraps his hand around my wrist, holding me back.

I look at him, and I feel like my soul is crushed. "I can't let her in the car with him. It's too—personal. This means something."

"It's just a car, Heidi," says Zane. "And even if you possess her, that is still not you in the car with him."

"Thanks for the reminder," I snap.

"I didn't mean it like that, Heidi, but—"

"I know. I know. It's not your fault. It's the truth."

When I look back toward Jace, it's too late. They're already gone.

Zane gets us to the Burger Bar, and right next to the car. The top is down, and they are both laughing. Genuinely laughing, like they are having fun.

"So, I was thinking," says Elsie. "Were you planning on going to prom?"

"Keep your emotions under control," Zane warns, but I can't. *Music*, I think to myself as I hear the radio's static, and then my and Jace's song comes on. His smile turns into a frown, and before the food even gets there, he tells Elsie he needs to get home.

"This is about Heidi, isn't it?" Elsie asks, and he nods without looking at her.

"I'm sorry," she says.

He punches the steering wheel with both hands. And when he looks at her, there are tears in his eyes—and he breaks down, crushing me even more. "It was all my fault. Everything that went wrong that night was my fault."

Her eyes widen. "What do you mean?" she asks in a nervous tone.

Jace shakes his head. "Never mind. I need to get you home. Where do you live?" he asks.

I look over at Zane.

"Make him answer her!" I order Zane, and as usual, he doesn't acknowledge what I said. Instead, he gets close to Elsie, blocking my view, and the next thing I know, she's giving Jace her address.

"What did you do?" I ask.

"She doesn't need to remember what he just said," he says, before I turn around and stalk off toward my house.

Zane follows me from a distance.

The house is empty, and I go straight to my old room and lay down on my bed, burying my head under my pillow.

I can feel Zane in my room, but he doesn't say anything. I feel annoyed, irritated, and scared. Mostly scared.

When I finally look over, I see Zane sitting on the floor under my window.

"I still don't think it was him," he says.

I sit up on my bed, looking at Zane.

"You know what scares me the most?" I ask, and he shakes his head. "I don't understand how it could've possibly been him, and I hope you're right because, from where I sit right now, it doesn't look good. And yet, I don't love him any less—and that is what hurts the most."

~

ZANE

I sit here terrified, because I don't know how to fix this. I can't fix any of this, and now time is ticking. They want me to be here next to her, getting answers, and they want it to happen soon, or I will be reassigned again—and she will be stuck who knows where. Either way, I hate the thought of never being able to see her again.

I stand, go toward her bed, and sit near her. "Tell me everything you remember about that night—until right before the moment your memory fails you." I was there for that part, but maybe this will help with her memory.

She hesitates, then looks down at her ring. She looks so sad that I regret asking, but maybe what I'm planning will help. She doesn't look away from the ring as she tells me about them being outside the Mills mansion, how he put the headphones on her, playing her favorite song on his phone while they danced. That is all she can tell me without falling apart.

"Come with me?" I ask as I get up.

She rolls her eyes. "You keep asking that like I have a choice," she attempts to joke.

She gets up and just stands there. "Where are we going?" she asks. I don't answer. I just take us to the back of the Mills mansion.

It's already dark out, and she looks around, taking in our surroundings. "What are we doing here?" she asks in a sad tone.

"I want to try something to help you remember. If at any point you want me to stop, just tell me."

She nervously agrees.

"Close your eyes," I ask her. I close the distance between us, putting my hand on her lower back and pulling her against my body. She tenses and opens her eyes.

"I want to recreate the memory to see if it helps you remember," I explain, and she closes her eyes again.

She leans against me, and I start singing her favorite song, 'Leave a

63

Light On' by Tom Walker, into her ear. She relaxes against me after a while, and we dance to almost the entire song before I stop and slowly pull away. Her eyes are still closed when I lean in and kiss her, just like Jace did that night—but that is not really why I kiss her. I've wanted to know what that would feel like from the moment I met her, and at this moment, knowing she will be pulled away from me soon, I know I would regret it for the rest of eternity if I didn't kiss her.

I ignore the burning pain on my wings as I savor every single move, every single second, of being this close to her. I don't stop until she pulls away. She looks at me, and I can see the confusion all over her face—or maybe it's shock. She just stares at me, taking me by surprise when she leans in and kisses me again. This time, her hand goes to the back of my neck, and I pull her even closer. Our kiss deepens, and we don't stop until she abruptly pulls away and spins around, facing the woods. I just stand here, watching her—knowing that I just made the biggest mistake. Yet I don't feel an ounce of regret.

CHAPTER 13

HEIDI

I run and I run, until I don't even feel the freezing cold anymore. It's not until after a while that I feel like someone is following me. I turn around and see the silhouette of a male figure.

"Jace?" I ask, scared.

He's not close enough, and at the sound of my voice, he stops where he is.

And the memory is gone.

I shake my head. I need to stop. I need to backtrack. The dance . . . the kiss . . . I need to remember what Jace told me. But nothing comes to mind. Nothing at all.

I look over at Zane, and he's just watching me, waiting for me to say something, and it's not until now that it hits me. "Are you going to be in trouble for kissing me?"

He shakes his head. "I had to—to recreate the memory," he lies.

I know this isn't true. I know he had been curious about kissing, and that felt like more. It wasn't a forced kiss to make me remember something. No one kisses like that without wanting to. And I should probably not have felt like I did when he kissed me, or when I kissed him. Unless I just crave human interaction so damn much, and that is why I felt . . . something. I sigh. I can't think about that right now.

"I need you to take me to Jace's house," I say.

He raises an eyebrow.

"I was just so close to remembering. I remember running in the woods, and someone following me. Maybe I will remember more if I see him."

"It's late," says Zane. "Maybe tomorrow."

I shake my head. "I need to remember. Please," I beg.

Zane lowers his head and hesitates, but next thing I know, we're in Jace's room. He's sleeping. His window is open, and his TV is on, giving me just enough light to be able to see everything. I take a look around, seeing how everything is exactly the same. There are still pictures of us on his desk, and on his wall. I go toward the bed and reach for his hand, hoping to pick up a memory. I stay here for a while, with my hand on his, until he becomes agitated and then abruptly wakes up. I look at my ring, and I recall that he bought it from Summit Jewelry. I remember someone at school joking about some of their merchandise being special—in a magical sort of way. I chuckle. I guess anything is possible. I slowly slide it off my finger, feeling a little terrified of how he's going to respond to what I'm about to do—if it even works.

"What are you doing?" Zane asks in an alarmed tone.

"I need him to see this ring," I say, hoping that my plan will work.

Zane nods, but he looks like he's in a daze, just going along with whatever I say. "Make sure you are not in contact with the ring."

I drop the ring on top of Jace's cell phone, which is next to him. At the sound of the ring hitting the screen, he quickly turns his bedside lamp on, picks up the ring and stares at it as I put my hand over his again.

His memories come flooding in.

We dance until the song is over, and when he pulls away from our kiss, he takes my headphones out.

He is tense. I give him a nervous laugh.

"Are you going to tell me what's going on now?" I ask. "I have a really bad feeling about whatever this is."

He reaches for my hand, and pulls it to his lips.

He then takes a deep breath.

"I don't even know how to tell you this," he says. Through his memory, I see the fear in my eyes.

I try to pull my hand away, but he keeps a hold on me.

"Just tell me, Jace."

He looks down at my ring as he tells me, "My dad got another job." He pauses. "We're moving away from Havenwood Falls." He looks into my eyes and sees the blood drain from my face. "We're moving to Germany," he says. "And Dad thinks that a long-distance relationship is too much while I'm finishing school."

He watches as I panic. He agreed with his dad because he didn't see it working any other way. I pull my hand from his, and I run.

He watches me go. Not long goes by before he texts me. Minutes, maybe seconds pass. No reply comes, and he becomes agitated. He paces back and forth, looking toward the area where I went, before he takes off running after me.

"Heidi, if you're still here, please give me another sign. Please," Jace begs, pulling me away from his memory.

I look over at Zane.

"Not a chance," he growls.

I ignore him.

"I need my ring back," I say as I reach for it and grab it from Jace's hand.

Jace closes his eyes as I do, and I get hit by another memory. Jace in the woods—the ground covered in snow. He reaches toward the ground and picks up my phone. I feel his panic as he looks around, searching for me, and as he screams my name before he realizes he needs help. I see Jace handing my phone to Sheriff Kasun and telling him what happened as the guilt becomes unbearable. He blames himself, but only for not stopping me and for not going after me as soon as I took off.

The memory is gone, and Jace just sits there, staring at his hand. Zane goes toward Jace and touches his forehead—within seconds, Jace is lying down, sleeping, and Zane grabs the ring and puts it on my finger.

I look up at Zane.

"He doesn't need to remember this, Heidi. That will hurt him more than you will ever know," he explains.

I keep watching Jace sleep.

"What did you see?" Zane asks, and while looking at him, I take off my ring again and place it on the bed before I get up.

∿

ZANE

She can't keep her eyes off him, even as she answers me.

"He was leaving Havenwood Falls," she says. "That is what he told me that night. His dad got a job in Germany, and they were moving. I was upset, so I ran." She looks at me then and smiles. "He didn't do it, Zane. It wasn't him," she says, and she looks so relieved.

"We need to go," I say in a rushed tone, before I take us to the library.

I feel overcome with anger. I rub my hand against my forehead as I pace back and forth.

I need to talk to the fool who sent me here, but I can't leave her.

"What's wrong?" she asks. Her mood has completely changed since we stepped foot back in the library. "Besides the fact that I died because I made the stupid decision to run into the woods. At night. In Havenwood Falls."

"Whatever happened to you wasn't your fault, Heidi," I say.

She looks down. "I made the choice—" she starts, but I interrupt.

"Look at me," I say. When she does, I can see the regret, and that just makes me angrier. "It. Wasn't. Your. Fault," I say again.

I leave out the part that I know this because it was my fault. The actions that led to her death were because of me, and I need to do something about it. That is the only way I'll be able to look at her again.

I clench my fists.

"I need you to possess Elsie again."

"What? Why?"

"I can't tell you that. But I need you to do this, and I don't know how long I'll be gone for."

For a split second, I see the terrified look in her eyes. "Where did you go at school when I had to possess her?" she asks curiously.

"I had business to take care of."

"Is that where you need to go now?" she asks, and I nod.

"Are you going to come back?"

"Of course," I say, but I can see the look of uncertainty in her eyes. It takes me by surprise when she closes the distance between us and pulls me into a hug.

"Please come back," she whispers. "I don't want to be stuck possessing her forever. If that's even possible."

I manage to relax. In times of need, she has this weird calming effect over me.

"That won't happen. I promise," I say, running my fingers through her shoulder-length hair.

It's the middle of the night when I take her to Elsie's house. Elsie is home alone and sleeping. Heidi possesses Elsie, and sits up on the bed.

"You'll be okay," I assure her before I leave.

CHAPTER 14

ZANE

*E*verything in me says I shouldn't get too far away from Heidi. So I go up to Elsie's rooftop and call out to him—to the dominion angel who punished me.

It doesn't take long before I hear him behind me.

"This had better be important," he says in an annoyed tone.

I turn around to face him, and there is an amused look in his eyes.

"All along . . . this was all because of me," I say, and he just crosses his arms over his chest and stands there with this attitude like he's better than the ones like me.

"Was all of this necessary?" I ask in a cold tone.

He raises an eyebrow, waiting to hear more, but by the grin on his face, he knows exactly what I am referring to. I could never understand how someone with his role can be so evil. Heidi didn't have to be put through this. They could've let her move on and punished me in other ways. He still watches me carefully, as if trying to assess what might be going through my head.

"You played with fate," he finally says. "You influenced the boy's family to decide to move, so that you could escape the burden of seeing her every day. I don't have to justify my actions when you are the one who started this mess. You've been breaking the rules ever since you met her, and it was about time someone noticed and handled your punishment."

I clench my hands into fists. "All I did was influence his family to move. She didn't have to die because of it!" I growl.

He shrugs. "Maybe she did. Maybe she didn't. You changed her path." He pauses and tilts his head to the side. "Did you really think that the boy moving and you not seeing her was going to keep you from feeling the way you do?"

"I don't—" I start to say before he interrupts me.

"Be careful. Angels shouldn't lie," he warns with a smirk on his face. "If it makes you feel any less guilty," he continues, "she didn't die that night."

"What do you mean?" I ask.

He chuckles. "The human girl didn't die until a few days ago. On the night when I brought her back and you were given your punishment."

"What happened to her?" I growl.

HEIDI

I lay here staring at the glowing plastic stars on Elsie's bedroom ceiling. Feeling restless, I decide to get up. I go to her computer and check on Jace's social media. She's already signed in. I click on his profile, and in a way, I get sad when I see he hasn't posted anything since I died. Well, besides post after post with my picture—asking people to share and to call if they recognize me. I start looking through our old pictures then —at town events, at school, at homecoming—and that's when I see Jace come up online. I nervously click on his name and send him a message.

Elsie: How come you didn't move?

It takes him a while to reply. I stare at the screen and feel my— Elsie's heart beat against her chest as I wait and wonder if he'll even bother replying.

Jace: How did you know?

Elsie: Small town . . . lol

Another long pause.

Jace: I begged my dad not to take the job. I said I wanted to be here, helping look for Heidi.

Elsie: And he stayed, just like that?

Yet another pause. This time, longer.

Jace: I was a mess. I don't think he felt like he had a choice. Look. I have to go, okay? See you at school.

And just like that, he's gone. I stare blankly at the screen for a while. When I feel like I can't take it anymore, I close the window and stare at the desktop picture with my mouth hanging open—a picture of Jace and Elsie. Only, it's not really her. She just edited her face over mine. I feel sick to my stomach. I shut off the computer and turn the light on to find there are more pictures on her wall—my pictures with Jace, replaced with her and Jace.

I can't stand to be in her body a second longer. I have no idea where Zane is, but hoping that he is at the library, I rush out the door.

I barely get across the street when I hear Zane's voice.

"Heidi!" he yells.

I stop and turn around. I look everywhere, but I'm unable to find him. Next thing I know, he's standing in the middle of the street, in front of me—well, in front of Elsie. I'm about to leave her body when I lay eyes on the guy behind Zane, and Elsie's memories come crashing in.

Elsie when she was about seven years old, playing with a boy twice her age. Elsie a few years later, crying over him after a motorcycle accident took his life and almost took hers too. And him coming to Elsie, his little sister, in what seems like a dream. He sits on her bed at night, watching over her as she sleeps. He promises her that he'll make her every wish come true. He says that he hates seeing her alone, and that if Jace is who she wants, he's going to make it happen.

Her memory morphs into mine. I'm running and running, crying over Jace's news, when I hear something. I stop, turn around, and see the silhouette of a guy about Jace's height.

"Jace?" I ask nervously. I want it to be him, but deep inside, I know it's not. He disappears. I frantically look around, and when I start to run back toward what I hope is the right direction to the Mills mansion, I feel something hit my head. Hard. Before my eyes close, I see him—the same guy who stands behind Zane right now.

CHAPTER 15

HEIDI

I don't remember leaving Elsie's body, but when I'm back to the here and now, I'm no longer in the middle of the street. I'm back at the library, sitting on a chair. Zane is kneeling in front of me, his eyes full of concern.

I sit here, in a state of shock, and it takes me longer than it should to notice that his wings are out. Beautiful, pure white wings that clash with his dark hair and green eyes in the most perfect way. He is breathtaking, and for a while, looking at him allows me to escape my reality. I'm completely mesmerized by him, and it's not until his wings vanish in front of me that I look into his eyes.

"I'm sorry," he says, and for a split second, I wonder why he is apologizing.

I slowly lean forward. "I remember everything, Zane. The guy that was with you—how do you know him?"

"He's an angel. One of the ones in charge. He gave me this assignment."

I'm so angry. I practically jump out of the chair and get as far away from him as possible.

"Please tell me you are lying," I demand. I know Zane is good, but I also know he doesn't care for being what he is. "Angels are supposed to be good," I say—more to myself than anything else.

I look at Zane and meet his curious and concerned gaze. "He killed me, Zane."

I can see the shock in his expression. Or maybe it's disbelief. So I go on and tell him about the memories. About how he's Elsie's brother who died in a motorcycle crash. The promises he made her and her infatuation with Jace.

Zane stands in the middle of the room, looking terrified. "This can't be true. A dominion angel wouldn't even be this young and definitely no . . . no!" he growls. "This is impossible," he says as he frantically starts to pace back and forth. "I have to talk to him."

I stand here, staring at him. I shake my head. "Then I'm going with you, because I'm not possessing her again."

We end up staying, but Zane calls out to the angel once . . . twice . . . when he calls out to him again and nothing happens, Zane loses it. In a blur of movements, he turns around and punches the wall with such strength that the bookshelves near him vibrate. Finally, he sits on the floor underneath the window and buries his face in his hands.

I sit next to him and wait until he looks up before I ask, "Is it possible that he isn't one of you?"

Zane just sits there, staring at the other side of the room as if he's in a daze.

"Zane?" I say in a low tone.

He doesn't say anything in return, but he does look at me with those sad green eyes.

"I don't get why he would put you through this punishment if he's the one who killed me," I say before I fall into silence and just sit here, with Zane looking at me in the most pitiful way.

ZANE

I can't even begin to understand how any of this happened. I slip my hand into hers and sit with my head leaning back against the wall, knowing that these are the last few moments we'll have together. She knows what happened to her, and there is no fixing me, but I can't leave her stuck here. When the sun rises, I'm going to tell her the one thing that's going to make her hate me forever—that I'm responsible for what happened to her. And then I'm going to call another Dominion to report Bryson before he comes near her ever again, beg for forgiveness, and do whatever I need to do so Heidi can rest in peace.

After a while of sitting in silence, Heidi leans her head against my shoulder. "And I thought humans were complicated," she says.

I chuckle. "Some of us were human before."

She looks up at me. "I don't know what's going to happen to me, and I'm guessing neither do you, but I need you to promise me that you're going to try to be Jace's guardian angel again. Someone needs to keep him away from Elsie."

I close my eyes and lean my head back against the wall. I want to tell her the truth about why I'm no longer his guardian, but I can't—even though she probably suspects it.

We spend the next few hours here, just sitting, and when the sun rises, before I can even call another angel—any other angel—she says, "Can you take me to see Jace? Even if it's the last time."

I nod and take her to his house. He's still sleeping. She sits on his bed, and I tell her I'll be right outside of the room. I watch her watching him. She doesn't take her eyes off him for one second. When I close the door behind me, there is an angel already waiting. I remember seeing her once before. She's one of the older ones.

"It looks like we have a mess on our hands," she says.

"How did any of this happen?" I ask in a frustrated tone.

"We weren't monitoring you, Zane. I'm ashamed to say that Havenwood Falls keeps us busier than we'd like, and you've always done the right thing or had the best intentions in mind. Even when doing something questionable, like influencing Jace's family to decide to move, you were trying to do the right thing. You can't blame yourself, Zane. Yes, you changed her path, but her life didn't end because of that. Bryson Brooks pretended to be a Dominion. His actions killed her—not your decisions."

"You already knew? For how long?" I ask.

"It's recent. Bryson was bragging to another about what he was doing to you. We believe it was done out of jealousy. Bryson told him about that night and about how he," she looks down for a split second, "played you." She pauses. "The angel he talked to came forward."

I can't even face her, but I know that I have to. I look up and meet her eyes with every intention of asking to see him. Before I even ask, she says, "He ran off. We have been unable to find him."

I clench my fists. "I don't want another assignment after this, unless it is to help locate him," I say, and she nods.

"What about Heidi? What happens to her now? What happened to her all along?"

She leans against the wall. "She was in a coma. She was kept right outside of Haverwood Falls so she wouldn't be found. Bryson wasn't sure what to do with her, so he basically just kept her in that state until she died."

My eyes fill with tears. "Where was her guardian angel? I've never even seen—"

She shakes her head, looking down toward the floor.

"Bryson?" I ask, and she nods. "He was the one. Only, he was never around Heidi much, and we didn't have reason to know that, because she was always protected." Of course she was always protected. I was always around. "He asked to watch over her around the same time you came along. I'm sorry, Zane."

She hands me a piece of paper. "She was buried at this address. Take Heidi there. That's all you need to do. She is at peace. She'll move on once you get there."

I nod once before I turn around and walk into Jace's room.

Heidi is standing there, still watching him, and when she hears me, she turns around and crashes into my arms. The pain I feel from seeing her like this is more than enough punishment for my part in all that happened.

I kiss the top of her head.

"Are you ready?" I ask when she finally seems to calm down.

She pulls away and walks over to Jace once more. She glances over at his table, and I see her ring there. She looks at him one last time before she walks back toward me.

I extend my hand, and Heidi slips her hand into mine.

I decide not to tell her about her guardian. She doesn't need any more reasons to hate my kind. But once we're out of Jace's room, I stop her.

"I was able to talk to another angel." I feel my hands tremble as I tell her what happened. "You didn't die until that night you awoke in the woods. You were in a coma under Elsie's brother's care. He was hiding you." She listens. She just listens without saying one word and without reacting at all. "I was given the address where you were buried."

"Where is he now?" she asks.

I sigh. "He is missing, but he won't be for long. I'm going to find him. He'll be punished for what he did to you. This I promise you."

Heidi looks at me, and I can't quite read her. Maybe she just feels as numb as I do. I look down, because this is not something I want to do. The thought of being without her presence is unimaginable, but I know how selfish it would be for me to keep her here for my sake. The thought of her having to endure watching lives go by as Jace moves on and her parents grow old, and not being a part of that, gives me the strength to do what I need to do. I close my eyes for a split second and wait a moment longer before I say, "Once I take you there, you'll move on. You'll be at peace."

She sighs, and after a moment of silence, she says, "I hate to keep asking for favors, but can you take me to see my mom and dad before we go?"

"For you, anything," I tell her before I take her to her house.

Her parents are in the kitchen, quietly eating their meal.

She watches them with a smile on her face. "I got so lucky to have them as parents," she says before looking at me. "That thing that you do with influencing people," she says, and I freeze. I have come to hate the reminder that I can do that. She bites her bottom lip and looks down toward the floor before she looks up at me again. "I don't want them to be alone, Zane. Can you make them—I don't know . . . maybe foster kids or something."

"Of course."

"You won't get in trouble for that, will you?" she asks in a concerned tone.

"I won't," I assure her. I would do this whether trouble was a consequence or not.

She looks at them once more before she closes her eyes.

"I'm ready," she says, but instead of taking my hand, she walks out of the house. On the front porch, she stops and looks back at me. "Once we get there, how fast am I going to be gone?"

"I honestly don't know," I tell her.

She gives me a sad smile and closes the distance between us.

"In that case," she says as she inches forward and gives me a kiss on the cheek, "thank you, for everything, Zane." She pulls away. "And so you know, because I know you were curious about it . . . that kiss was not bad at all."

She winks, and I'm the one looking away now.

CHAPTER 16

ZANE

*E*verything happens so fast. The address I was given is outside of Havenwood Falls and in a secluded area. I can feel the energy shift the moment we get to the exact spot where she was buried, and just like that, she's gone before I can say another word. She just vanishes in front of my eyes, and I feel the hole in my soul the moment that happens.

I stare at the dirt on the ground for what feels like an eternity. She's at peace now. This is how things work—only, this is not how things should've been for her. I know I need to leave, but I can't. I can't leave her here. What I am . . . my purpose . . . none of it matters as much as she does. I remember hearing a story decades ago, of an angel who did the unimaginable, but maybe it's only considered unimaginable because no one else has tried it.

I start digging, and I keep digging until I see the white sheet. I don't open it. I just cradle her in my arms, close my eyes, and focus on healing her—not for me, but for her. She should get to have the life she dreamed of—even if that means being with Jace. And as much as I'm filled with doubt that this will work, I know that I have to try. Her soul only moved on a few minutes ago. Maybe, just maybe, there is a chance. After a while, I feel weak, and I'm about to quit trying when I feel movement.

I carefully unwrap her then. Her eyes are still closed, but I can see the color slowly returning to her face. The cut on her forehead takes me back to the night when she awoke. I let my wings out as I cradle her—bringing her closer to my chest. I hold her for a while longer, just listening to her faint heartbeat and shallow breathing, before I take her to the Havenwood Falls Medical Center. I make sure there is no one around before I go up the steps and slowly put her down on the ground, next to the front door. I knock on the door, make myself unseen, and wait. A doctor with salt-and-pepper hair and blue eyes— Jasper Underwood—comes to the door and rushes toward Heidi. He picks her up as he calls for help. I follow them in, even though I know who he is, and I know he'll heal her.

He carries Heidi to the exam room and lays her down on the bed. He asks one of the nurses to get everything ready for lab work, and when she steps out, he looks in my direction. I know that since he's fae, he would've sensed me here.

I put my wings away. I don't even know why I do it, other than my knowledge that I've made far too many mistakes to be considered an angel. Not that I feel an ounce of regret. I'd have traded anything, my soul included, just to have her around again.

I make myself visible.

He gives me a curious look, and I wonder if he is trying to figure out what I am. I don't bother answering.

"She looks familiar," he says. "Who is she? What happened?"

"That is Heidi Bennett. She went missing on the night of the Cold Moon Ball. I don't know much of what happened," I lie—this angel thing is obviously not right for me anymore. He knows I lied too, but he pretends he doesn't. I suspect he's used to not asking too many questions around here.

"Did you find her?" he asks, and I nod.

"Outside of town. I brought her straight here." I pause. "I assume you'll ask the nurse to call her parents," I say. "If you can, ask them to call Jace Edwards too. She'll want him here when she wakes up," I say before I make myself unseen again.

He heals her more than what I had already done. I watch her

sleeping peacefully as he tells Rachel Freeman, a nurse with dirty-blond hair and blue eyes, to call the Bennetts and Jace Edwards. The nurse gives him a puzzled look when he says Jace's name, and then her eyes widen the moment she realizes who Heidi is.

"Don't call Sheriff Kasun yet," he warns her. "Let her family see her first without all the commotion. It's not like he'll be able to question her right now anyway."

The nurse nods and quickly leaves the room.

Minutes go by before her parents, Jace, and his mom rush into the medical center, and then to the room, guided by Jasper Underwood. Her mom and dad both cry on one side, and Jace holds on to her hand on the other side of the bed. After a moment of watching her, he pulls her ring out of his pocket and puts it on her finger. I approach her from Jace's side, ignoring the fact that I feel consumed by jealousy, and when I brush my finger against her forehead, she wakes up.

She slowly opens her eyes. "Jace?" she says.

By now, he's crying too. I take a few steps back as he leans down and kisses her.

"How are you feeling?" he asks.

I stand here, leaning against the wall with my eyes on her. I know this was the right thing to do, but it's weird seeing her human again.

"I don't know," she says.

The nurse asks everyone to step outside for a little while to do some lab work, but I suspect she does that to keep Heidi from being too overwhelmed.

When everyone steps out, the nurse looks at Heidi. "Try to get some sleep. They'll all be here, but you need to rest," she says.

Heidi nods and closes her eyes. When the door shuts, Heidi opens her eyes again and looks in my direction. For a split second, I feel like she's looking right at me. I chuckle, knowing how stupid that sounds.

While still looking in my direction, she grins in a way that's not quite like her.

"Hi, Zane. Miss me?"

I freeze in place. She chuckles as she slowly gets up, pulling the IV out of her arm. While I can't move at all.

She approaches me, without taking her eyes away from mine. She stops when she is inches away from me and rests her hand against my chest.

"What are you doing?" I ask.

She grins. "I assume there is no saving you anymore, so . . ." Her grin widens. She leans in and kisses me.

READ MORE ABOUT HEIDI, Zane, and Jace in *Blurred Lines,* coming May 2019.

ABOUT THE AUTHOR

Daniele Lanzarotta is the author of young adult and new adult paranormal/fantasy/contemporary novels, including the Academy of the Fallen Series, the Sudden Hope novels, and A Mermaid's Curse Trilogy.

Daniele is also a filmmaker and CEO & Founder of Elysian Nightfall Studios. She has recently worked on Virginia-based short films as the Second Assistant Director and Still Photographer. Daniele is currently working on the development stage for the adaptation of her novel, Sudden Hope, which she also plans to film in VA. She is also working on other film and writing projects.

She enjoys watching hockey, playing Rock Band, Guitar Hero, and spending time with her husband, two daughters, and the family dog.

Website: www.danilanzarotta.com
    Facebook: www.facebook.com/danilanzarotta
    Twitter: www.twitter.com/danilanzarotta
    Instagram: www.instagram.com/danilanzarotta

ACKNOWLEDGMENTS

I knew from the beginning that writing Avenoir was going to be a different experience. And it was. I quickly fell in love with Havenwood Falls and its characters. And I'm grateful to everyone who supported me along the way.

Thank you to Jocqueline Protho for introducing me to the Havenwood Falls world, and opening the door to this amazing opportunity.

Thank you to the readers. One of the many cool things about this project is that you got to know a little about Heidi even before my official first draft was done. Your enthusiasm and passion for the series made this writing journey extra special.

To the Havenwood Falls authors, it has been so much fun to collaborate with you. Thank you for answering questions and helping me find my way around Havenwood Falls and its residents. I'm lucky to be part of such an amazing group of authors.

Finally, I want to thank Kristie Cook for creating such an amazing world and for allowing me to be part of it. I learned so much from this experience. I can't begin to tell you how impressed I am by everything that you do, and I look forward to seeing Havenwood Falls grow more and more.

AVENGE THE HEART

MICHELE G. MILLER

HAVENWOOD FALLS HIGH

Avenge the Heart

MICHELE G. MILLER

A Havenwood Falls Young Adult Novella

ALSO BY MICHELE G. MILLER

From The Wreckage Series - Coming of Age Drama

From The Wreckage

Out of Ruins

All That Remains

West: A POV Novel

After the Fall - Austin's story (New Adult)

Into the Fire - Dani's story

The Prophecy of Tyalbrook Trilogy - YA Fantasy Romance

Never Let You Fall

Never Let You Go

Never Without You (Coming 2018)

Individual titles

Last Call (New Adult Romance)

Awaken the Soul, A Havenwood Falls High novella (YA Fantasy)

Avenge the Heart, A Havenwood Falls High novella (YA Fantasy)

CO-WRITTEN WITH MINDY HAYES

Paper Planes Series - Sweet Contemporary Romances

Paper Planes and Other Things We Lost (YA)

Subway Stops and the Places We Meet (Adult)

Chasing Cars and the Lessons We Learned (NA)

The Backroads Duet – Sweet Contemporary Romances

Love in C Minor

Loss in A Major (Coming July 27, 2018)

Nothing Compares 2 U, a 10 Things I Love About You novella

Visit Michele's website for updates
http://www.michelegmillerbooks.com/

For Mindy

IT HAS BEGUN

VIVIENNE

"*W*hy are you so glowy?" Zara asks in her faux British accent as she drops her ice skates on the wooden floor and lowers herself into the vacant seat across from me at Coffee Haven.

"Well, hello to you, too."

"Oh my gosh! You're pregnant!"

I choke. Thank God I hadn't taken a drink of my coffee. "What?"

"You are radiant, Viv. Like ridiculously so."

Careful not to crush the paper cup in my hand, I lean across the table and look my best friend in the eyes. "So, I'm pregnant?"

"Well, you are with Breckin . . ."

"And?" I bite the inside of my cheek.

"He's hot, and Breckin Roberts. And you're together twenty-four seven."

"My boyfriend is hot, so logically speaking, I'm pregnant." I return to my casual position. "It's happened—you've finally gone mad."

Zara's dark eyes study me intently. How much could I have changed since last night? I kick her shin. "Stop dissecting me. I'm not pregnant."

Her freshly manicured red nail taps her chin. "Are you positive?"

"Yes, I'm positive," I hiss. "You have to have sex to get pregnant.

I'm not having sex, Z. Plus, we've been together for three weeks. I might lose my mind around him, but I still have my morals. Give me some credit."

Her slim shoulders lift. "You're right, sorry. But seriously, you're—"

"Glowing," I interject and tug at the neck of my sweater. "I got it."

"Very well, backing off." She unwraps the frilly lace-edged scarf from her neck and looks beyond me toward the menu hanging above the counter. "I'm going to get a hot tea." Her eyes remain firmly set on my face until she's at my back.

Paranoia sets in. *Glowing?* I look at my hands, searching for the glow she speaks of. Nothing. I gaze around Coffee Haven, and no one stares back. The manager, George, chats up Zara as she orders. The gossip ladies are in their usual spot, getting their last batch of gossip in for the year over coffee and scones. Things are normal, for Havenwood Falls, anyway.

"So, where is lover boy? Is he not coming?" Zara asks when she returns to the seat across from me.

"To ice skate at the park? Do you know Breckin at all?"

Her booted foot nudges mine. "Evidently better than you do."

I look up, and there's Breckin, walking by the large picture window and entering the shop. He's dressed in his usual black, a slouchy beanie on his head, and the striped scarf I bought him for Christmas hangs loosely around his neck. He doesn't need those things: hats, scarves, gloves. He doesn't need the jacket or hoodie either. My angel stays warm all on his own, but keeping up appearances when you're a supernatural being is a priority.

His amber-flecked eyes catch mine the moment he's inside, and my stomach flips. He has that power over me. His name alone shoots tingles through my body. The sight of him lights up every nerve ending I own and tightens my core. Maybe I am pregnant. If anyone could get a girl pregnant merely by looking at her, it would be Breckin.

Zara draws a sharp breath. "Viv, you're flickering like those defective tree lights at Napoli's." She touches my hand, and the room turns sideways. "Viv?"

Everything goes fuzzy, and my head becomes too heavy to hold up.

∾

"Vivie?" Breckin's breath grazes my ear, his pine-and-snow scent bringing things back into focus. "Hey, are you okay?"

I blink. *What the heck happened?* I'm sitting at Coffee Haven, leaning heavily against a kneeling Breckin, while Zara clutches my hand like a vise. "Did I pass out?"

Breckin's warm hand cups my cheek. "Only for a moment. I walked in and you, well, you just kinda fell forward. I caught you before the table could give you a concussion."

"I fell forward?"

"Are you sure you're feeling okay? That was bloody freaky, Viv. You were—"

"Pale," Breckin interrupts. He reaches across the table and grips Zara's wrist where she still holds my hand. "Viv hasn't eaten today, and had a little sugar crash. She's fine, but maybe you should get her a muffin."

My jaw drops. He's using compulsion.

Zara's dark eyes flare, before Breckin releases her and she stands. "Let me get you a muffin. You should have eaten this morning."

"Chocolate chip," Breckin calls over his shoulder.

"I'm her best friend, Breckin Roberts. I think I know her favorite muffin."

His mouth twists in a subtle smile as he stands and drags Zara's now empty chair closer. "You all right?" he asks, pressing his lips to mine in a chaste kiss that leaves me wanting more.

"I'm fine." I take inventory of my body. Other than the pouting my mouth does at his leaving mine so quickly, everything seems normal. My heart beats, my pulse is steady, my vision is clear, my head pain-free. "The room just sort of flipped on me. I don't know."

I'm back at his side, cuddling into his warmth. *When did I move toward him? What the heck? Crap, I'm practically sitting in his lap. In the coffee shop.* I right myself. The gossip crew will have a field day with our display. Sure enough, Irene Beckett and Laverne and Sybil Carson watch with narrowed eyes.

Breckin squeezes my shoulder. "Have you felt okay this morning? Last night?"

"I'm fine," I say, more firmly this time. "What are you doing here, anyway? Yesterday you said it would be a cold day in hell before you spent an afternoon ice skating with a bunch of people in Danzan Park."

His brows raise, probably at my ornery tone. "I changed my mind."

"Why?"

Zara thrusts a sugar-topped muffin in my face, cutting off his reply. "One muffin."

"Thanks, Z," I say, taking the muffin from her hand. I'm not hungry, but who can resist the smell of a freshly baked chocolate chip muffin? I tear the edge off the top and pop it into my mouth. *Thank you, sweet creator of chocolate. So good.*

"Are we going, or what?" Zara picks up her skates. *I guess that's all the time my best friend plans on giving me to recuperate.*

I open my mouth with every intention of backing out, but Breckin beats me to the punch. "Yep, let's go." He stands and grips the back of my chair.

Evidently he's not worried about whatever happened to me when he walked in either. Or he's putting on a show for the benefit of onlookers, and Zara.

"You don't have to come with us, Breckin," I tell him, not for the first time since Zara and I planned this outing a few days ago. He's not big on public spectacles, which is a hard thing to avoid when you live in Havenwood Falls. He's humored me this break with all the town traditions he's allowed me to drag him to.

"Yeah, he does." Zara pins him with her gaze and crosses her arms over her chest. "If you keep finding ways to bail on hanging out with me, Breckin, I'm going to take it personally." A delicately plucked brow curves up, challenging him.

Breckin snorts. "Zara, if I didn't like you, you would know."

She swings her gaze to me. "See, this is why I like him. I like your honesty, Roberts. Let's go take advantage of the December sunshine and have some fun."

Breckin pulls my chair back, picking up my coffee cup as he does. He moves close as I stand and throw the oversized bag carrying my skates over my shoulder. "I told you I wanted you to have normal, remember? If this is your normal, then I'll enjoy it for you."

LIKE THE SQUARE, Danzan Park is full of families enjoying the last day of the year and the sunny winter afternoon. Zara and I have skated at the lake during Christmas break since we were little. It's tradition. When we were too young to come alone, our mothers packed hot chocolate and snacks, and froze their buns off for hours while we twirled around the ice. We liked pretending we were Olympic figure skaters, on our way to golden glory. It didn't matter that neither of us showed much promise; it was fun. It still is.

"I bet I can still spin faster than you," I taunt Zara.

She laughs and glides her way back, stopping next to Breckin, who isn't wearing skates, but is instead standing on the ice in his boots.

"No way. I was always faster," she tells my smirking boyfriend.

"In your dreams. Watch." I skate a small circle and pull my arms and one leg into my body, forcing a spin. The air whistles past my ears. Zara and Breckin's faces whirl by as my revolutions speed up. Around and around, her dark skin, his dark clothing. White snowcapped mountains, then other skaters. The scenery is a blur as I rotate faster and faster.

"Viv, if you break something, I'm gonna laugh." Zara teases, but there's an undercurrent of worry in her words.

Breckin tells me I need to slow down. I scoff. "I do not need to slow down." He growls. "Fine, I'll stop."

I force my arms away from the center of gravity, breaking the aerodynamics and slowing my spin down. Jutting out my foot, I stick my toe pick into the ice with a smile. Then I curtsy, sinking low and lifting my head to three very different faces.

Zara's olive complexion is pale, her mouth wide, her expression confused.

Breckin bites his lip and crosses one arm over his waist. He rubs at his jaw thoughtfully.

The third face I do not recognize, but his eyes cut through me like laser beams. He's beyond the frozen lake, among a crowd of people out enjoying the winter sun. His height and chiseled good looks make him stand out. I study him, my senses on high alert. *He doesn't belong here.* He's dressed for a fashion show—in a camel jacket and turtleneck sweater that look like they were tailored for his wide frame—not a day of fun in the park. *Who is he?*

Breckin touches my arm, and my attention snaps from the unknown man. "Are you dizzy? Because watching you spin like that made *me* dizzy," Breckin jokes, his fingers finding mine.

"You?" I ask. *The angel who flies like he has a death wish?* He chuckles under his breath, and I meet his handsome face with a smile. Then, because I can't help myself, I look around his frame and search for the camel jacket and sweater. The stranger is no longer there. I blink several times, certain I imagined him. "Not dizzy at all," I say breathlessly. "Also, did you freaking growl at me a moment ago?"

With a frown, Breckin looks over his shoulder, then back at me. "Why would I growl at you?" His smile is too wide to be truthful. "Let's go."

Go? I look for Zara. She's already pulling her skates off from where she sits in a pile of snow.

"Where are we going?" I ask as Breckin moves forward. He tugs on my hand, propelling my skates into a glide.

"To my place. We'll drop Zara off at her car behind the square first."

"Why are we—"

"Vivie," he interrupts, "did I tell you to slow down?" he asks, and I stare stupidly. "When you were spinning, did I tell you to slow down?"

"Yes?" My tone is questioning, which is crazy, because he most certainly did. I heard him.

"No. No, I did not. I *thought* it, but I didn't speak it. I also didn't growl at you. Not out loud. I know better." He hurries his steps, dragging me behind him like a sled.

He didn't speak?

"You heard my thoughts, Viv. You also spun inhumanly fast, and you lit up like the Fourth of July when I walked into Coffee Haven earlier. I was going to ignore the angelic glow until later, but the other stuff—" He glances over his shoulder again. "Let's go back to my place, okay?"

I bite my tongue, holding my thoughts as I remove my skates and we walk through the park back to Breckin's Bronco. Zara doesn't protest the abrupt end of our day. *What in the world did he do to her?*

"Are you sure you don't want to go to Rowan's party tonight?" Zara asks, poking her head into the vehicle once we arrive back at the square and she climbs out.

A loud high school party or a quiet night, kissing in the new year with Breckin? *No brainer.* "A Bishop party?" I ask.

"I know it's not normally our thing, but we're seniors. Plus, I don't have a boyfriend to ring in the new year with. Hopefully, I can find a willing participant later."

Oh, my poor boy-crazy friend. Does she resent the place Breckin has taken up in my life in such a short time? I look at Breckin, a silent *Should we go?* plastered on my face.

"Yeah, not happening. Sorry." His tone says he's far from sorry.

Zara rolls her dark eyes with a resigned sigh, like she didn't expect any different. "Whatever. You kids be good then. Keep all that snogging to a minimum."

Breckin's arm stretches along the back of the seats, his fingers combing through my hair. "No promises."

Zara closes the car door with a grumble. "God, I need to find myself a boyfriend."

"Happy New Year, best friend," I call out my open window while she unlocks her car. She flips me off with a laugh as Breckin drives off.

"Okay, let's take it back now." I spit out the words the moment we leave the parking lot. Shifting in my seat, I angle my body Breckin's way. He's so calm. *How is he so calm?* My nails dig into my palms, I'm that freaked. "How did I read your mind? What do you mean I spun inhumanly fast? How in the heck am I glowing? Oh! And, you used compulsion on Z!"

"Vivie, breathe."

"Breathe?" I use the dashboard to brace myself. "I'm pretty sure people are going to question why I'm suddenly a human light bulb, Breckin. Zara already did."

He takes my hand, his fingers weaving between mine.

"Am I a light bulb?" There's a note of humor in his question.

"I'm not what you are," I counter. He doesn't reply. His cheek dents inward, like he's biting it. His silence unnerves me. "Breckin? Do you want to tell me what's going on?"

His shoulders twitch as he pumps my hand in his. I've seen that move before. He's trying to control the angel within. That can't be a good sign.

"What's going on is we're going back to my house, where I get you all to myself for the entire night."

I smile in spite of myself. "You get me to yourself every night, Breck."

The boy lives at my apartment. At first, it was because of the threat looming from the reaper, Sebastian. Now he does it because my mother works nights and he can. Being apart from Breckin is rare, and thanks to our soul connection, that's a good thing. Neither of us handles forced separation well. It's beyond what is normal for two teenagers who began dating three weeks ago. Then again, we're not normal teenagers. He's part angel, and normal went out the window for me on the day I died. Well, died and was brought back to life by his angelic healing.

Breckin removes his hand from mine and adjusts the heater as we turn onto Eleventh. "Yes, but tonight I get you at my place, without having to worry about your mom coming home early from her shift." He holds his hand in front of me, testing the heat blowing from the vent. It's the sort of thing he does without even realizing it. "Did you call her today?"

Frustration wells up at his change of subject, but I indulge him.

For now. "Yeah, earlier, while I was waiting on Zara at Coffee Haven. She's enjoying herself."

"And she's with college friends?" he asks.

I nod. "A few nursing school friends she's kept in touch with, yeah. They get together every year for a girls' weekend in Vegas."

"She trusts you."

"She's never had a reason not to. She's a single mom, so I learned to be responsible at a young age." I catch his small smile out of the corner of my eye. He knows what I'm saying. He didn't have parents growing up. He had nannies, and he had Elias.

"Does she trust me?" he asks.

"You're a guy. Of course she doesn't trust you." I laugh. "But she likes you enough, and she likes Elias. When she left yesterday, she gave me 'the talk.'"

The car slows as we near Breckin's house. "The talk? Vivie, I don't want her to think—"

"She doesn't," I rush to soothe his worry. "Like I said, she trusts me. Breck, my mother got pregnant from a weekend tryst, and the guy disappeared. I've lived with that my entire life. I won't make the same mistake. She knows that."

Breckin sucks in a breath. We turn into his driveway and pull into the garage. It's not until he kills the engine and the garage door closes behind us that he speaks. "You know we're different than that, right? I could never walk away from you. Sex or not."

Talking about sex is awkward. How is it that Zara brought it up earlier, and now Breckin and I are discussing it again? *Note to self: if you can't talk about it without blushing, you should not be doing it.*

"Because we're soul bonded?" I ask, staring out the windshield at the impeccably organized garage wall in front of me.

His fingers touch my chin, turning my face his way. "What do you think?" he asks softly.

I unbuckle myself and wind a hand around his neck, bringing our lips together.

"I think you would never leave me because I'm your favorite couch pillow," I tease against his mouth.

"Something like that," he agrees, pressing his warm lips to mine again and again.

$$\sim$$

BRECKIN'S HOUSE is a mansion compared to the apartment Mom and I live in. It's not as overwhelming as the homes in Havenwood Heights, but the fully renovated and modernized Victorian is expansive and impressive. Since my first visit, we've always spent our time here on the basement level. It's ridiculous to call the space a basement. It has everything we need: bathroom, kitchen, pool room, television, fireplace, comfy sofas. There's even a guest bedroom. Plus, it's underground. In the two weeks since our fight with Sebastian, Breckin hasn't let up his guard. It's like he's worried the reaper told others about us—a Nephilim with a soulmate—and being in the basement eases that worry.

We settle on the couch and watch an action movie marathon. I scoot down low on the seat and prop my blanket-covered legs on the footrest. Breckin sprawls out lengthwise with his head on my lap—I *am* his favorite pillow—and his feet hanging over the opposite arm rest.

"Have you seen your father since that night?" I ask randomly, halfway into movie two during a commercial break.

His attention turns from the television, stilling the hand I've been running through his smooth angelic hair. He shakes his head in the negative as he turns in my lap. "I would have told you if I had."

"Would you?" I ask, twirling a chunk of his bangs around my index finger.

"Viv?"

I push at his head. "You changed the subject in the car, and you're not telling me everything. What are you worried about?"

He pulls himself into a sitting position and combs his fingers through his mussed hair. "I don't *know* anything. Yes, I'm worried. I'm worried that Hamon will try to take you from me. That another reaper will appear, that something else might want you, like Sebastian did."

His shoulders rise with a deep inhale. "Vivie, I'm worried I hurt you when I healed you, and we just don't know the repercussions yet. Then there's my eighteenth birthday and what that will mean for me, for you, for us." He scrubs his hand over his face, and his shoulders drop. "Elias is keeping things from me."

I pull my legs in and set my feet on the floor. My arms and hands reach for Breckin, drawing him close, until he's the one wrapping me in a hug.

"I'm sorry," I murmur into his neck. "You don't have to keep it to yourself. I'm part of this now. Let me in."

His hold tightens. "You're a high school senior. This is not what you need to deal with."

"So are you," I remind him, and he exhales. "I know, you're not normal, but guess what, Breck? Neither am I. Not anymore."

We separate, and my fingers go to my hair, twirling the ends nervously.

Breckin shakes his head with a grin. "No, you're not. You were glowing today, like an angel. I think my healing you did something. Changed you somehow."

"You saved my life and made me your soul mate, but the downside is I might be a human night-light?" When put in perspective, can I complain? So, I might glow occasionally. I could be dead.

"Elias trained me to control it, to mask it, when I was young. Maybe he could train you, too. We'll figure this out, but not tonight, Vivie." He gives my knee a squeeze, his amber eyes scanning my face. "Hey, you wanna go see the fireworks in a way you never have?"

I release my fear. He's so earnest. So worried about providing me with normal experiences, as though he's to blame for where we are now. "With you? Of course."

We take to the sky, leaving crowds and traffic jams to the humans. Every New Year's Eve Mount Mae Ski Resort has a torchlight parade down the blue square slope, Renae's Way. I've been many times, but never like this—never hidden in the sky, in the arms of an angel. From up here, the mountain appears like it's on fire. Skiers weave their way back and forth, the flames in their hands lighting the path, creating a radiance that steals your breath.

"It's pretty amazing, huh?" Breckin whispers in my ear.

"It's gorgeous," I agree. "This is why you love flying so much, isn't it? Everything is beautiful from up here. Lights look romantic, streets seem peaceful, the air is clean."

His wings stretch out, bringing us higher and moving us away from the slopes. "I used to love it because it cleared my head. Like running for you."

Like running *was* for me. Since the attack, I haven't been able to run. Haven't wanted to.

"You said used to," I point out, as below us the crowd erupts in a countdown.

His warm nose nudges the side of my face, pulling my attention from the ground to his eyes. "Isn't it obvious? I don't need to clear my mind the way I used to. When I'm stressed, I have you."

"Aw, of course you would say sweet things when I don't dare move."

Breckin laughs as a cannon pops in the distance. "I'll be sure to repeat myself when we're on the ground, then," he says, his leg hooking around mine tightly as he turns toward the north. Sparks ignite the sky, sizzling and popping in brilliant flashes.

"Happy New Year, Vivie."

Lifting my face to his, I smile as his eyes light up in a rainbow of colors. "Happy New Year, Breck," I say, my lips brushing his.

WHEN THE TRUTH HUNTS
YOU DOWN

BRECKIN

*W*e float to the ground with our mouths fused together. Vivienne's hands slip around my neck the moment our feet touch solid surface.

"I meant what I said earlier," I murmur against her lips. "We'll figure things out."

"Shh." Her fingers grip my hair.

With hungry mouths and searching hands, we celebrate the new year cloaked from the crowd in town square. Kissing her is like touching a live wire. There isn't a cell in my body that doesn't come alive when we're connected this way. Her soft lips tease mine, and the wildly erotic rhythm of our kiss has my hands drawing her closer and closer. I long to devour every part of this girl. When the last firework fizzles out and the crowd noise picks up, we part. My breathing is ragged, and Vivienne's lips are swollen, her flushed face owed more to our kissing than the cold.

"Ready to go back to my place?" I tug her crocheted hat over her ears.

She nods and glances around the square. Most people are packing up their chairs and thermoses and heading home, but a few linger.

"Hot chocolate and a roaring fire, right?"

"Of course. Anything for my human popsicle."

She slaps my side. "You know, I'm not nearly as cold as I thought—"

"Viv," I interrupt, as a spasm runs up my spine and along my wings. They're agitated. "We need to go."

Her spine stiffens beneath the hand I have at her back. She turns her head my way, her eyes both curious and concerned.

"Someone, some*thing*, is here." I have us cloaked from sight, but against another angel, it's useless. I grab Vivienne's waist and pull her in as I search the vicinity, looking for someone who shouldn't be here. Havenwood Falls has many supes to distinguish among. My powers aren't as sharp as Elias's, which makes pinpointing the exact nature or location of a threat more difficult.

Vivienne wraps her arms securely around my back, but I hesitate as a faint angelic shimmer catches my eye. It moves with the crowd away from our position, then stops as though it knows it has been spotted. The sea of people between us part, and there he stands: an angel with sharp, coffee colored wings.

"He's an angel," Vivienne says on a hitched breath, her fingers digging into my skin. "He was at the park today."

"Hang on." I jump into the air, my wings pumping as quickly as I dare when I have Vivienne with me. Her head tucks into my warm skin, and I hold tight while my mind contemplates what just happened.

"You saw the angel?" I ask, needing confirmation.

"Brown wings, cropped blond hair, marble-chiseled jawline?" She clings to me, her warm breath tickling my chest. "Yeah, I saw the angel."

Whoever he was, he doesn't seem to be following us.

"Breck? Where are we going?" Vivienne asks when I overshoot my house and keep heading north.

"I want to talk with Elias."

"Now?"

The changes happening within her line up like toy soldiers. "Right now."

~

We circle Ski-Ventures' hangar, and when I'm sure it's safe, I land on the gravel sidewalk to the front office door. Elias lives in the space above the office. Except for his usual spotlights on the property, the building is dark.

"I'm sure he's sleeping," Vivienne says, her hand tugging on mine. "Can't we call him in a few hours?"

"You know angels don't sleep, Vivie." She frowns. Why is she so hesitant? That isn't like her at all. "What's wrong?"

"Nothing." She kicks at the gravel, releasing my hand and turning in a circle. *She's full of crap.*

"I am not full of crap, thank you very much," she hisses. I nearly lose my footing as she rounds on me. "It's just that when you say we need Elias that means bad things are happening and"—she gathers her windblown hair and sweeps it to one side, twisting it around her hand— "well, I was kind of hoping we could start the new year without any bad things."

She's so beautiful, with her angry eyes and disgruntled pout. I can't stop my smile as I wait for her to stomp a foot. "Uh, Vivie, bad things don't exactly follow our timelines."

"Really, Breckin Roberts?" She snatches a rock from the ground and hurls it at me, hitting my shoulder.

"Nice throw."

"Don't be smug." She does stomp her foot this time. "I just . . . I don't get it."

"You read my mind again." I point out what she didn't realize on her own.

She stills. "I did?"

"Yes. I didn't actually say you were full of crap out loud." She grabs at her hair, her fingers returning to their nervous habit of twisting. "You also saw an angel who was cloaked."

"That's not unusual. I've been able to see you when you're cloaked."

I tuck my wings away and remove my shirt from my waistband,

pulling it over my head. "Elias and I assumed you saw me because of our bond. You didn't see him when he followed you just last week. So—"

She raises her hand. "Hold up. Why was Elias following me last week?"

"Because I can't follow you all the time. He helps out."

"That's creepy, Breckin. I don't want him following me around incognito. I don't need you following me around all the time either. If you want to be around me, just tell me."

I close the space between us and take hold of the collar of her jacket. "Vivie, I always want to be around you, but I can't. I need breaks." She has no idea how intense the emotions she brings out in me are. Or, maybe she does, but she's human. She's always dealt with feelings like these. Elias said my emotions as a Nephilim are half of what a human's are.

Drawing her closer, I drop my forehead to the top of hers. "My reactions to you are too strong. I send Elias to keep you safe when I can't."

The tips of her fingers brush my cheek. She's wearing fingerless mittens, and though her hands should be cold in this weather, they're warm.

"Why are your reactions too strong?" she asks softly.

I smile. It's an insanely human thing—to love. But I know no other word for what I feel.

"You know the answer to that," I tell her, unable to say the three words. Not yet.

She lifts to her toes and presses a simple kiss to my mouth.

ELIAS ISN'T HOME. He spends much of his time wandering Havenwood Falls, keeping an eye on things. He's been unusually jumpy the last few weeks. Even before the stuff with Vivienne, he was concerned about things going on in town. He ordered me to remain home over Thanksgiving weekend due to rumblings of demons and angels nearby.

"We'll wait," I say as I unlock his office and let us in. Vivienne drags herself through the door unhappily. "He doesn't have a fireplace, but I bet he has hot chocolate," I tease, touching her lower back as we walk inside.

Elias does have hot chocolate—the expensive kind, too. Vivienne squeals with delight when she finds marshmallows to toss in. This girl and her love of sugar. We settle on his large couch upstairs and turn on the television. Vivienne relaxes into the crook between my arm and shoulder, her back pressed to my chest.

"You're not freaking out as much as I thought you would," I say after a while, when she hasn't fallen asleep.

"You mean because I'm apparently developing superpowers and there's an angel in town who may or may not be after me?"

Crap.

"You're not developing superpowers, Vivie."

She lifts the arm I have resting over her waist and sits up. "But I may have another angel after me?"

I scoot into a sitting position, my back in the corner of the couch. "I don't know. That's why we're here."

"And the glowing, mind reading, super speed—"

"That would be your angelic heritage coming to life," a familiar voice says behind us.

We turn in our seats and find Elias standing in the doorway.

"I didn't expect to come home to find two teens crashing my place." His eyes are shadowed by his ever-present baseball cap, but they survey every aspect of the scene before him. A father's eyes, only they're narrowed in on me, like I'm the dirty teenage boy longing to spoil his precious princess. He's not wrong. I move my hand from her thigh. "It's past two a.m., Breckin. Shouldn't Viv be at home in her own bed?"

Vivienne stills, her eyes glued to the doorway even as Elias walks farther into the space. He just dropped a bomb and he's lecturing me on curfew?

"As you obviously overheard, we were waiting on you," I point out.

He rests his forearms on the back of a chair at a right angle to the couch, and I spy the twitching of his lips.

"Stop playing the menacing father figure, you ass. You'll scare Viv with that ugly scowl."

Vivienne grabs my shin as she whirls on the couch and faces Elias. "I'm sorry, did you just say . . . I mean . . ." She falters, her mind grappling with what he said when he walked in.

I pull my legs from behind Vivienne and sit beside her.

"What did you mean by angelic heritage?" I ask as politely as possible, considering I want to throw something heavy at his head. What has he kept from me?

Elias shrugs a shoulder. "I may have lied to you."

Shit. "May have?" I ask tersely.

"Okay, I lied to you."

Son of a— I inhale through my nose, slowly, deliberately. A fire smolders within my chest. Angelic anger ignited. My human temper isn't much better. Vivienne's leg touches mine from socked foot up to our hips. Having her near only stokes the fire.

Elias rounds the chair and perches on the edge. Removing his cap, he scratches at his bearded cheeks and levels his gaze on me. "Your father and I didn't technically fall, Breckin. We left."

"You *left* Heaven? Why?" I ask.

"Because," he sighs heavily, "we loved her more than we loved Him."

The world pauses. "Her?"

His watery blue gaze slides to Vivienne. "Phaedra."

Beside me, Vivienne gasps, and my arm snakes around her back automatically as recognition dawns on her face.

I catch Elias's nod in my peripheral view. "Yes," he says, his voice dropping lower than usual.

Her fingers toy with her lower lip. "You loved her more than . . . him?" she murmurs.

"Him." His brows lift as he nods again.

My fingers touch Vivienne's lower back, whether to ground myself or her, who knows?

"What am I missing?" I ask, my gaze going between the two of them.

I'm hit with a cacophony of emotions when Vivienne turns toward me. Every thought she seems to be having tries drilling its way into my head.

"Damn." Clutching my forehead, I clench my eyes.

"Viv, calm down," Elias says after a moment. More words and images hammer me. "You're projecting your thoughts to Breckin, and he can't take that all in. Take deep breaths, and calm down."

Her presence at my side disappears, and I open my eyes as she argues with Elias.

"I don't know how! What am I doing?" she asks desperately, her feet inching away from me.

Holy hell! I reach for her.

"Vivie, listen to him." I barely recognize my own voice. Blinking rapidly, like batting my damn eyes will diminish the thoughts bombarding their way into my head like a battering ram, I hold her gaze. "You're on overload."

Her hands wrap around mine. "Okay, okay. I'm breathing. I'm calming," she says with a grimace. "It's just, Phaedra was the first in our family to come to Havenwood Falls. My great great, I don't know how many greats, grandmother."

With that revelation, her thoughts turn down a notch.

"Tell me more about her," I say, maintaining eye contact with Vivienne and ignoring Elias's form now hovering beyond her left shoulder. "Get it out. It's helping."

"Oh." Her eyes widen. "Well, I don't know much about her. I've never known much about my family history. My mom's dad was a hippie who left the area not long after she was born. Her mom died when she was a teen, some strange illness. It's why she went to school for medicine."

I cock my head sideways as a rhythmic thumping slows within my body. No, not in my body—in Vivienne's. Her heartbeat. I hear it, feel it like it is my own. My wings shoot out, propelling me forward and into the coffee table as Elias and Vivienne are knocked back.

"Breckin?" Vivienne cries out, startled.

At the same time Elias curses, "What the hell!"

I pull the traitors tightly to my back and sidle away from the table, careful not to damage anything. When I'm in open space, they spring to full width again. They suddenly have a mind of their own.

"Your heart—" I gasp. It's racing again, from the shock of my wings appearing, I assume. I press my hand to my chest and glance at Elias. "I feel the beating of her heart."

Vivienne's hand mimics mine, covering her heart as she sinks into the back cushions of the couch. A small smile touches her lips.

"What about your wings, Breckin?" Elias asks.

"Did you hear what I said? I feel—"

"What about your wings?" His gruff voice asks for a second time. "You didn't sense me come home, and your wings are thinking on their own. Your father said you needed training."

My hand falls to my side. "*Hamon* implied I needed to be a better fighter. Since I have no intention of fighting for him . . ." I shrug.

Elias stalks me across the room, his face wild.

"Don't say that out loud," he warns. His gaze darts around. Does he think we're being watched? Listened to? "Your *father* was speaking of more than physical fighting. Your angel side needs to be stronger for what's to come."

"And what is that?" We both turn at Vivienne's cool voice. Whatever it was that caused so much chaos in her mind has left. She's poised, if a little unsure, as she rises to her feet. "It's time you tell us both the truth. What is coming, and what does it have to do with Phaedra?"

MADE FOR THIS

VIVIENNE

"*C*an you put those things away?" Elias asks Breckin with not a small amount of exasperation. "I'll get you a shirt."

Breckin nods and rolls his neck. His nose bunches up, like he's straining to hide the huge feathered appendages on his back. After a moment, they finally blink out of existence. Breckin rubs the back of his neck as he turns sideways to me. No wonder he needs a new shirt —the back of his is shredded, thanks to the unexpected appearance of his wings.

"Are you all right?"

My gaze slides from ogling his muscles and abs to his face.

"Huh?" I ask, a little breathless. *Oh, what this angel does to me.*

"Your cheek?" He brushes my skin tenderly with his knuckles, a knowing look working its way into his eyes.

"I . . ." My fingers circle his wrist. "Those weapons in your back pack a swift punch." What I meant as a tease erases the small smile I just saw light up his eyes. His face falls. "Breck, I'm fine. It was an accident." I move in and hug him tightly, my hands easily creeping between the torn pieces of cotton to touch his warm skin.

"Here," Elias says. Breckin's arm shoots into the air and catches the shirt tossed at his head. Kissing my forehead, he steps back and pulls what's left of his shirt from his body, replacing it with a new, slightly too big Havenwood Falls Ski-Ventures shirt.

"It's been a while since I've thrown away clothing due to unruly wings." Breckin laughs, but Elias isn't amused, and I'm worried.

When he's done, he takes my hand and draws me near once more, kissing my temple. "By the way, you have no idea what you do to me."

I pull my head back, my cheeks flaming. *This mind reading thing is going to be a pain in the—*

Breckin's finger touches my lips, as though he can stop me from thinking my thoughts.

Damn you! He laughs at my outburst and squeezes me tighter.

Elias returns to his chair, and we settle on the couch. Breckin clears his throat. "Okay, I think we need to begin with Viv's grandmother. Phaedra."

Elias nods.

Breckin repeats Elias's earlier revelation. Hamon and Elias were not forced from Heaven as they'd led Breckin to believe all these years. They'd left. "What you're telling me is that my father, the angel who hates mankind, was so in love with a human that he left Heaven to be here with her?"

I'm no expert, but the full-blooded angel in the room looks uncomfortable. His shoulders rise and fall before he speaks. "Phaedra wasn't human, Breckin."

"Phaedra wasn't human?" I repeat, like that will make it sink in. *That would be your angelic heritage coming to life.* I gasp as his earlier words sink in. "All of the changes . . . I'm not becoming like Breckin, I'm becoming . . ."

"Who you were meant to be," Elias finishes for me.

When I was little, Mom bought me a porcelain Christmas angel doll. She had curly platinum locks and large blue eyes, and held a candle in her movable arms. I plugged her in and watched for hours as her little arms opened and closed, and her head dipped from side-to-side. I twirled her curls around my chubby childish fingers and told stories about her angelic life. About the angel she loved who left her at my home while he saved people . . .

Sniffing, I pop out of the memory and focus like mad on keeping my thoughts in check. Breckin and Elias carry on a conversation that I've completely lost track of.

"I don't understand," Breckin says. "If Viv's ancestor is an angel, shouldn't she be like me? Wouldn't her mom?"

"It's more complicated than that." Elias looks between us. "I'd hoped Hamon would be the one to share the story someday. He's not exactly what you think, Breckin."

"You mean, he's not a fallen angel who abandoned his unwanted offspring to his best friend and only stopped by to threaten me with a future I do not want?" Breckin asks angrily. My heart crumbles at the vulnerability Breckin's showing. "If your story is meant to explain away his cruelty, I'm not interested."

Breckin pops to his feet, and I reach for his hand a moment too late as he pads across the room and disappears into the bedroom. I push up from the couch to go after him.

"Let him be," Elias sighs.

"No." That one word comes out with a defiance I didn't know I had. "Maybe that is how you've dealt with him through the years, but that's not how I will deal with him. Not when he's hurting."

"He doesn't know what he's feeling."

"Maybe not by name, but he feels something."

Breckin's explained his human and angel emotions to me. The way they push and pull for power. Sometimes he isn't sure which side of him is making decisions. He isn't one person, not in his mind. He is to me.

"You know, I don't care what side is struggling, Elias. He is Breckin. He's mine. My soul mate, my love. I can't let him hurt."

I'm barely around the coffee table when Elias's words stop me. "You are so like her. Probably the most like her of any of her offspring."

My shoulders stiffen. I look toward the doorway through which Breckin disappeared and will my legs to go to him, but my feet turn back toward Elias.

"You knew them? My ancestors?"

The rugged lines around his eyes soften as he nods. "Some better than others. Phaedra was soft and full of love. It was her downfall, Viv —her open heart."

Something damp trails down my cheek. I refuse to accept that I've shed a tear. "Are you saying it will be my downfall too?"

The barest of smiles cracks beneath his unruly beard. He needs a good trim. "Not at all," he says, looking beyond me. "I'm hoping your soft heart will save them."

"Them?" I turn toward where his gaze lingers and find Breckin leaning against the doorframe watching me. *Does he mean you?*

Breckin confirms my unspoken question with a slight incline of his head. "And Hamon," he adds, lifting a brow for Elias's verification.

"I kept things from you both, for many reasons. Viv, until Breckin saved you, there was no reason for you to know about your bloodline. Even after he saved you, I wasn't sure if you needed to know. I had no idea what his healing powers would do. The soul mate bond could have been the same as when humans bond."

"And now?"

"The changes you've noticed are angelic qualities. Maybe if you were a normal human girl, you'd still develop them, to a lesser degree."

If you were a normal human girl. My throat closes at the implication, the reminder that I am, in fact, not normal anymore.

"Breathe." I jump at Breckin's voice spoken so clearly in my mind.

I glare at him across the room as my pulse soars. "Geez, don't do that."

"That"—Elias laughs and waves his hand between us—"is what I'm talking about. You two hear each other in your minds. Your bond is strong."

My thoughts bubble up, trying to take over, and I push them back down. No way will I send this mess to Breckin to deal with. Breckin's wink tells me he knows exactly what I'm doing, but he's not writhing in pain, so while he might be receiving some of my random musings, I must be channeling most of it away from him.

"So Viv is part angel, but she's not a Nephilim?"

"No. Technically she would be, but Phaedra was stripped of her angelic markers before she had a child." Breckin and I share a confused look, and Elias scratches at his head as he explains. "Phaedra lived as a human with angelic blood that was . . . well, we never knew what exactly happened. I suppose you could say it was asleep all this time."

"And my healing Viv woke it up? That is what the reaper recognized in her almost immediately. He saw her angelic DNA," Breckin guesses.

Elias nods. "It makes the most sense."

"You lied to me. When Sebastian came after her, when we discussed her parents—"

"You discussed my parents?" It's my turn to be angry. Breckin's never asked about my father. "You know nothing about my parents. How could you discuss them?"

Breckin comes to my side and takes my hands. "Vivie, we were discussing your bloodline. Angels sense things, like DNA. You have a . . . different scent I never could identify. I thought it was because of our bond." He looks at Elias. "You knew, though. You knew she had angelic blood, and you lied about it."

Elias doesn't look guilty as much as he looks sorry. Breckin trusts him implicitly, and knowing Elias kept things from him can't be easy. I long to slink from the room to allow them time to discuss it all. Then it hits me. They're talking about things that pertain to me. This isn't about them alone. Not anymore.

With his eyes trained on my face, Breckin rolls his shoulders back and stiffens as he asks, "Does he know?"

Silence hangs before Elias's baritone answers, "He does."

"I'd like for you both to stop speaking about things like I'm not here." My gaze flicks between them. Elias opens his mouth, and I hold up my hand. "No. I am no longer a human girl; you said so yourself. Include me."

"Viv, I have watched over your line since the 1800s. That has been my job on earth, given to me by your father, Breckin."

"Oh, no." My eyes cross as the association hits me. "Hamon loved Phaedra. They weren't . . . they didn't—"

A strangled groan of denial dances through my head—Breckin's

MICHELE G. MILLER

voice. I sink back to the couch, my gut churning. Understanding dawns on Elias's face.

"You two are not related," he assures us. The knot in my stomach releases. "Phaedra married a human man, and they settled here in Havenwood Falls not long after it was founded."

"Why did you watch over her?" I ask.

"She was an angel without angelic powers. We knew she would be hunted once they discovered what she was."

The snarl of an angry animal echoes in my ears. My hand goes to my ribcage, the sting of an injury since healed returning. *Hunted.* "They?"

"The legions of damned," Breckin replies.

Flashes of white appear in my vision as the blood drains from my face. "I think I'm going to be sick," I murmur, getting to my feet.

Breckin's at my side instantly, one hand at my elbow and the other around my back as he ushers me toward the bathroom. I feel Elias's presence following us, but I close my eyes and breathe through my nose. The lid to the toilet hits the porcelain tank, and I open my eyes. Worried faces stare at me.

"Are you both going to hold my hair and watch if I throw up?"

Elias backs out of the bathroom, but Breckin remains. "Are you okay?" he asks, tucking my hair behind my ear.

I nod. "Just, give me a moment." I sit on the cold edge of the bathtub and lower my head between my knees.

Breckin's legs appear in my view as he kneels and takes my hands, rubbing them. "What happened?"

"You were right," I manage between deep inhales and exhales. "I don't want to deal with this stuff. I just want to enjoy our senior year. Maybe graduate high school, go to college, have a few dates with my boyfriend." I raise my eyes, looking up at him through a curtain of hair.

"Vivie." The two syllables roll off his tongue with such sadness, my limbs ache with it.

"Is the entire world like this? Angels and . . . and what? Demons? What else is out there?"

He gives my hands a squeeze and stands. "We're done for tonight. Let's go back to my house."

"Done?" my weak voice asks. We can't be done. I have far too many questions for that. Another dizzy spell washes in and prevents me from arguing. Once again, I close my eyes and breathe.

"There was an angel watching us tonight, and Viv saw him today, too," Breckin whispers in the hallway. "He could have followed us, but he didn't."

Elias grunts. "He could have been an angel passing by. Maybe he sensed you, or Viv, and became curious."

"Do you feel the difference?" Breckin asks, softer this time.

I remain hunched over on my bathtub perch, my head hanging low, my hair covering my face—my ears wide open. *Difference?*

Elias's whispered reply stops my breath. "Something is off."

I hold the air in my lungs, waiting for more. My heart slams against my ribcage, filling my ears and making them difficult to hear. I pick up bits and pieces as they fade further away.

". . . not Phaedra . . . not you either," Elias's deeper tone says.

Breckin mumbles.

Releasing my breath, I open one eye. They're no longer in the hallway outside the bathroom door. I stretch my legs in front of me, then pull them back in and stand. I poke my head out and don't see them. *Dang angels.*

The nausea has passed. Twisting my hair around my hand, I throw it behind my back, turn on the faucet, and splash water on my face. The dark shadows beneath my eyes and my sallow complexion stand out. I'm exhausted. Flipping off the light, I shuffle back toward Elias's living space. *Where did they go?*

I'm about to collapse on the couch when Breckin appears through a second doorway off the main space.

"Let me check—" he's saying over his shoulder when he turns and spots me standing there. With a smile he walks to my side. "Sorry I disappeared. Elias wants us to stay here tonight, considering . . . We were making the bed."

Considering an unknown angel was following us today? Considering

I'm different? That I'm part angel? Changing? I ask the questions with more than a little sarcasm in my mind, but Breckin doesn't hear a word, and I don't care to ask out loud.

"That's fine, lead the way," I say instead.

∼

BRECKIN TURNS his back as I slip off my pants and settle into bed wearing only my underwear and the long-sleeved shirt I had on under the sweater I removed. The bed is made with simple white sheets, a blue blanket, and a thick downy white comforter. The headboard is nearly hidden by a mound of pillows.

"Are you staying?" I ask Breckin as I shift and sort through the pillows until I find the perfect one.

"If you want me to."

Rolling to my side, I sigh. "What a stupid answer, Breckin Roberts."

A moment later, the bed sinks with his weight and the heat of my angel envelops me, folding and bending with my body until we are one. While one arm wraps under my shoulders and hugs my chest, the other remains at my stomach. He's careful not to touch the skin exposed by my being pantless. It's sweet, and I wrap my arms around his with a content sigh.

"Do you think Elias will tell us the story behind Phaedra and how they all came to be here if we ask?" I wonder out loud.

"I honestly don't know."

"Have you spoken to him about your father?" I ask cautiously. Breckin's fingers press against my skin in response. "He seems pretty adamant that there are things you don't know, Breck. Things you should know."

A low grumble plays in his throat before he speaks. "What I know is Hamon left me, Vivie. He left me here with a string of human nannies and Elias as family. I didn't meet him until I was ten. Did I tell you that? I have a hard time believing anything he says now could change my feelings."

Breckin likes to pretend he's not bitter. That Hamon, and what he did, or didn't do, does not matter to him. But it does, and in the darkness of night, he sometimes allows those emotions out. He swallows hard, and my body recognizes the tensing of his muscles at my back.

"He left paradise for her. He followed some angel to Earth, risking his eternity, but he couldn't be bothered to see his son."

My eyes burn. "Oh, Breckin." I attempt turning in his arms, offering comfort, but he tightens his hold and buries his face in my hair.

"It's not like Elias didn't try, you know . . . but I knew. I knew he was out there and not here."

Righteous indignation fills me. I understand his pain. I was a fatherless child, too, but Mom made it clear from early on that the man who left her me as a present was not someone I wanted to know. She was ashamed of herself, of that story, but the truth was she didn't know him beyond one night. And that one night changed her life. I understand that now, too. How one moment, one encounter, has the power to alter the course of your entire life.

I cling to him, holding him as tightly as he holds me until his emotions calm. His breaths slow and smooth out. His muscles relax. After a few minutes, he nudges the back of my head with his nose. I bend my neck forward, giving him access to my nape.

"Are you freaked out about it all?" His lips graze my skin with each word.

I pull my knees closer into my chest, and his follow, staying directly behind like a second skin. "Let's see, from an animal left you for dead, to a reaper wants you, to your angel DNA was suddenly woken up by my magic hands—I'd say tonight's news is easier to swallow than the other secrets you've shared with me."

A light huff of hot air tickles the baby-fine hair at my hairline.

"Are you laughing at me?" I pinch the arm he has wrapped around my stomach.

"With you?" he asks, as he plants another kiss on me.

I crane my neck, trying to look over my shoulder, and his mouth ends up at the shell of my ear. "You're not worried, are you?" I ask.

Breckin wiggles his arm out from underneath my body and rolls me over till we're eye to eye. The room is dark, with the exception of a sliver of light from the cracked-open door. *Did Elias, in a fit of fatherly protectiveness, tell him to leave it open?*

"Vivie." He cups my cheek. "I told you earlier, I will always worry about you, but tonight gave me hope I didn't have before."

"Why is that?"

"Tonight I learned the girl I gave my soul to, the girl I love, isn't human."

All but one word fades into a black abyss the moment he says it. Love. L-O-V-E.

"You love me?" My voice cracks. "I thought it was too soon and too ridiculous to say those words," I admit, my hand working up his chest until the beating of his heart is a song beneath my palm.

"Now *that* is a ridiculous thing to say."

His admonishment drags a light giggle from my lips. "I love you, too, Breckin."

His head slides closer on the pillow we share. "I know."

Our lips meet, brushing with the soft tentative first strokes of paint meeting canvas. We ease into the kiss knowing full well the fury that love and desire creates when our mouths connect. I love kissing Breckin. When we begin, his tender and easy hands sweep over my skin like a blind man reading braille. By the time we pull apart, my scalp stings from where he's tugged my hair through his fingers, and my chin is chafed from the light stubble on his. But it's only kissing. Two mouths moving in sync in a way that promises more. Eventually.

"You should sleep." He smooths my hair back and kisses me once more. A gentle peck.

"You know, if I'm going to acquire all these angelic powers, the least they could do is give me your never needing to sleep power."

Breckin rolls to his back with a chuckle. "My 'never needing to sleep' power? And who exactly do you think *they* are?"

I snuggle into his side with my face in the crook of his shoulder and chest. "I don't know. *They*. Whoever it is that doles these things out." I gasp and shoot into a sitting position. "Oh my gosh. I'm not human?"

Breckin pushes onto his elbow. "You catch on quick," he says through a wide smile.

"Am I? Could I?" I can't voice my thoughts quick enough. *Angelic powers.*

Breckin rescues me. "Vivie, why do you think I said I have hope now that I know you're not human?" When I don't move, his hand grasps the back of my shirt and tugs. I allow him to draw me back into his side. "Do you know what plagues me the most? It's wondering how I am supposed to live a life watching from afar as my soul mate lives hers."

Desolation returns to his tone, and I roll to my stomach and prop myself up on my elbows, whispering his name.

"I wasn't worried about it right now, but later . . . five, ten years from now, you were going to keep going, and I would be stuck here."

"You're immortal, aren't you?" I had wondered, but was too afraid to ask. His dark silhouette nods, and I take a deep breath. "You have hope now that I could be, too?"

I'm a logical girl. I read romance novels and like fairy tales, but I've never known much about supernatural beings. I've never studied the stories of angels, whether fiction or nonfiction. What would immortality mean? A lifetime with Breckin, but what about other things? Children? Mom? A normal life wouldn't be possible. What may seem like a gift feels like a possible curse.

He tugs my hair to regain my attention. "And you don't." It's not a question.

"Immortality," I say in a low whisper. "I don't know what that means. One moment I'm a girl . . ." The thought doesn't finish.

"Do you remember what Elias said when he first told us we're soul mates?"

I tuck up under his jaw and curve my body around his side.

Closing my eyes, I repeat Elias's words. "It's a powerful connection and most people consider it a gift from the maker."

"To fulfill the order of things," he finishes when I purposefully leave that part out. "We have a destiny, Vivie."

Breckin remembers Elias's comments on destiny, and I remember the reaper Sebastian's words the night he tried to take me from Breckin on the mountainside.

"Will she join you?" he'd asked Breckin, his electric blue eyes burning holes into mine. "Will she turn her back on her calling for you?"

Two words: destiny and calling.

Two parts: human and angel.

What if the two don't go hand in hand?

WITHOUT YOU

BRECKIN

"Festival of Lights?" I text Viv during English Lit the following Monday when we return to school.

From the moment we woke mid-morning on January first to the smell of bacon and pancakes at Elias's to the ride to school this morning, she's refused to discuss Phaedra.

When we returned to my house last Monday, we spent the day curled up on the couch in the basement with the lights out and the fire burning. I'd bring the subject up and she'd shush me.

"I want to enjoy our last day without my mom being home," she said between kisses. "She's going to want to spend tomorrow with me. Let's be in the now."

With her fingers digging into the hair at the back of my head and her mouth teasing mine, I had no power to resist.

Things have remained settled. No lightbulb Vivienne, no mind reading, no angels following us. We've had one week of normal. I knock my knuckles on the wooden top of my desk.

Her texted reply comes back twenty minutes later, right before the bell. "Yes?"

She's such a rule follower. She probably didn't remove her phone from her pocket until her teacher finished whatever their lesson was. I don't bother replying as the bell rings.

Weaving through the narrow halls of Havenwood Falls High is an adventure in supernatural species. I pick up the scent of every creature living among the humans. The perfume of teenage hormones and a hundred different blood types can be nauseating, but I've learned to live with it. My ability to hear things is more frustrating. There's nothing like sitting in class working on an essay test and picking up on a little supply-closet rendezvous between two of your teachers.

I catch Vivienne's laughter when I come to where our two hallways intersect, and I stop. Cocking my head, I determine she's still halfway down the hall. I lean against a bank of lockers and wait. Her lilting laugh tugs at my lips, and I search through the crowd to catch a glimpse of her shining hair. Instead, I find myself grinning stupidly at Kai Reynolds. The arrogant vampire lifts a brow and checks over his shoulder. He must spot Vivienne because when he turns back, his face clearly says *you're whipped, man* as he passes by. Tossing my head back, I acknowledge him, and he offers me a subtle nod in return. That's the extent of our friendship—nods and the occasional lazy comment about life.

Half the Kasun pack follows behind Kai, cutting up and jostling one another, and then Vivienne rounds the corner. At barely over five feet, Vivienne and Cressida Manos, the annoyingly cheerful mountain nymph she's with, were overshadowed by the rowdy wolves.

I wade into the sea of students and come up at Vivienne's side. "Fancy meeting you here."

"Breckin, hey." Vivienne's freshly coated pink lips spread into a wide smile.

Cressida's green eyes volley between us. "So, you two are really an item?" the junior asks as though she's surprised.

"We really are," I deadpan and take Vivienne's hand in mine. "Are you surprised this goddess gave me the time of day?" I ask the nymph.

Red flames to match her red hair color Cressida's cheeks. "No, no. I think you two are perfect together. Some might say a match made in heaven." She abruptly turns into the classroom on the right with a wink and a wave.

Vivienne's warm eyes pop wide. "Did she just—" Her steps slow.

A body bounces off my shoulder as students shove around us, cursing. We're an idle boat in the middle of a busy channel.

"Keep moving with the current." I tug Vivienne's hand.

"So, the Festival of Lights?" I ask to distract her from Cressida's little tease.

Vivienne frowns. "What about it?"

Her eyes cloud over as she mumbles beneath her breath. Her mind is in a whole other place.

Looking at the students around us, I take a breath and lean closer. "I thought we could go."

Vivienne huffs, once again slamming on her brakes in the middle of the hall. A white-haired guy skids to a stop before he runs into her back. Tarron Wilde, he's an elf . . . with witch blood. I shrug a silent apology for the roadblock as he meets my eyes, then steps around us.

"That was weird, right?" Vivienne asks.

"Nope, it's not weird at all. You're blocking the hall."

Her eyes look at me, but they aren't *looking* at me. "I mean, she winked. She called us a match . . ." Her fingers foray to the ends of her hair. Twisting.

At any moment now, the bell will ring for next period, and here we are, stuck in the main hall, with her fixating on Cressida's comment and me completely failing in my effort to ask her on a date. It shouldn't be this hard. Should it? Frustrated, I pull her hand and drag her toward an alcove a few feet away.

"Breckin," she hisses. "Geez, slow down."

I swing Vivienne around and tuck her against the wall, using my body to shield her from view. Her head tips back, her lips parted and no doubt ready to blast me for manhandling her. I swoop in and snag a kiss before she speaks.

"Vivie," I say pointedly. "I was trying to ask you out."

Her top teeth scrape her bottom lip as she blinks rapidly. "You were?"

Her confusion is adorable. "Yes, I was. I'd like to take you to the Festival of Lights tonight."

She gasps. "Oh my gosh, is Cressida an angel?" *Are you kidding me?*

I move back a step, and Vivienne's hand reaches for my shirt as she rushes to explain. "It's just . . . what she said . . . and that look she gave us," she continues.

"No. No, she's not an angel." I cringe at my too-loud words. The halls are quieter now. No doubt we're going to be late to our classes. "Viv, we can't talk about that kind of stuff here."

Recognition sets in. "Right." She releases me and straightens. "You're right. I'm sorry. My mind is thinking nonstop about everything. I snapped."

Her mind's going nonstop? "I've tried talking with you about everything for days now. You brush me off each time."

"Get to class." A voice of authority rings through the hall.

Vivienne's head snaps toward the voice. "Crap, I can't be late."

Yep, always the rule follower. We rush toward her next class along with the other stragglers.

"Did you not hear me at all?" I ask when the door to AP Calculus comes into view. I peek through the glass and breathe a sigh of relief. No teacher. "I asked you on a date," I remind her.

"You did?" Vivienne's nose scrunches, and her mouth twists in thought. *Way to make a guy feel good, Viv.* "Oh, you did! The Festival of Lights. I'm sorry, I promise I was half listening."

The bell sounds, and Vivienne yelps. Lifting to her toes, she presses a kiss to my cheek and leans closer to my ear. "Of course, I'll go with you."

I remain in the entrance as she hurries inside. Cressida's remark replays. We have to tell Vivienne about the other supernaturals in town. If the nymph picked up on it . . . *oh, shit!* Nymphs distinguish between the mortal and immortal. Vivienne *is* immortal.

"Where's Viv?" Elias asks when I walk into the Ski-Ventures office at the hangar after school.

"I left her at the library. She thinks she's sneaky, but I know she's trying to research the history of the town. She's not a good liar."

Elias steeples his fingers as he leans back in his cracked leather chair. "What does she want to know?"

"What do you think? You told her she's of angel descent. I imagine she's looking for her family history. Or maybe she's trying to figure out what else goes on in this town. A nymph made a telling comment today."

"A nymph? So Phaedra's blood is that strong? It offers Vivienne immortality."

"That's my guess. That's how nymphs work, isn't it? I could ask her what she sees in Viv. Viv suspected Cressida was an angel. We have to tell her about the other species before she asks too many questions."

Too many questions, especially when it comes to the supernatural side of town, can get you killed. Per the underground gossip channels, Roman Bishop's deceased wife, Jenni Ravenal, is a good example of that point.

"If other creatures have picked up on her angel side, then the Court may want to speak with her sooner rather than later."

"I thought you were handling the Court. I don't trust them, Elias. I don't want her dealing with that, if possible. Especially not with Roman."

"They won't hurt her, but she needs to control her powers as they come alive." His phone alarm sounds, and Elias stands. "We also need to speak with Rachel. We need to know who her father is, Breckin. I'm not sure Phaedra's grace can be that strong within Viv. There has to be something more."

Something good, or bad? "Why wouldn't it be strong? Is there something different about Phaedra? We need to know the whole story. *I* need to know the whole story, E. I need to understand about Hamon."

"Look, I have to make a flight. I have a group to pick up on Mount Sousa. The annual Silicon Valley pricks are back."

My father hates humans. Elias hates Silicon Valley humans. It's a group of douche-canoe guys who ski Havenwood Falls this time every year, dropping their tech money around town and hitting on women like they don't already have wives and kids at home. The Court obviously likes their cash or they wouldn't be invited back each year. There are strict rules and memory wards to keep people from remembering their visits to Havenwood Falls.

"Paul gave me stock advice this time," he mutters while I follow him out back to his helicopter.

"Nice guy."

"Well, it's better than the advice I got last year on how to 'have my cake and eat it too.'"

"I'll go out on a limb and assume he wasn't talking about actual cake?" I snort.

"No, he was not." Throwing his ball cap on, Elias stops and looks at me seriously. "You know Viv won't find anything at the library, don't you? Anything chronicling the supernatural events in town is probably kept with the Luna Coven."

"I know. She's being stubborn and pretending everything is normal. I figure I'll let her do her digging."

"Breckin, you need to watch her. I know you want to keep things as normal as possible, but if she changes too much, we'll have to come up with plans. And you're right—we do need to talk about you and your father."

"That's not what I meant." I don't want to discuss me and Hamon. I want to know about Hamon and Elias, and their past with Phaedra.

"I know what you meant, but he needs to tell you those things. He needs to be involved—"

"Soon," I cut him off. I'm not ready to involve Hamon. That means dealing with my birthday and what comes next. "I'm with her almost twenty-four seven. If things change—"

This time he interrupts me. "*When* they change."

He's right. When things change.

We take off at the same time, on different wings. Like a lovesick fool, I left my Bronco at the library in case Vivienne needed a quick escape. She's a horrible driver—her admission, not mine. Hopefully it'll remain in one piece if she takes it for a spin. Thankfully, the vehicle is parked at the street, exactly where I left it, when I return. As I walk up the icy, salted path to the large doors, I look over the building. This is the first time I've bothered to stop by since it was rebuilt after the fire last year that killed Jenni. It's impressive. The Gothic-Victorian design is appealing in a way one might not expect. I smile as I step into the large entryway and am greeted by two carved wooden gargoyles flanking the intricately designed balcony on the second floor. Everett Weston has a sense of humor.

"What's so funny?"

My gaze snaps from the grinning creatures to my grinning Vivienne. She moves with the grace of an angel—head high, steps quiet—and around her is a glow. It's subtle, much like the other day at Coffee Haven, but it's there. I flex my fingers, their need to reach for her deep-seated.

Vivienne halts and runs her hand through her hair, tucking it behind her ear as her grin grows. "That look is dangerous." Her voice is so muted I ask her to repeat herself.

She must be on a mission to kill me, because she closes the ten feet between us and steps into my space. Her chest brushes mine. "I said, that look is dangerous. You remind me of a wild animal looking for a meal."

Divesting her of her backpack, my arm snakes around her waist. "You wouldn't be wrong."

"No?"

I shake my head. "You're glowing, Vivie."

Her lips tremble as her eyes lower to the hands she placed on my chest when I drew her in. She flips her hand over, staring like she doesn't recognize her own appendage. The glow is already fading. "The library is boring alone. I was happy to see you," she says, her eyes meeting mine.

Her words are a balm to my soul. Each time she admits her feelings, I fear my chest will explode. I didn't grow up on feelings. Feelings are a weakness. Even Elias, as semi-normal as he pretends to be, says emotions are complicated. Giving her a squeeze, I breathe in the familiar ginger-and-mint scent she wears like a second skin and reluctantly step back.

"Remind me to show you something later, after the festival," I say as I weave my fingers through hers.

Her gorgeous head angles to the side. "Why later?"

"Because I have something else planned for right now. Are you ready to go?"

"Yep, I was sitting at the window in the other room waiting for you."

$\sim$

"YOU GONNA TELL me what were you smiling about when I found you in the foyer back there?" Vivienne asks once we're settled into my Bronco.

I glance at her sitting beside me. It's not more than thirty degrees outside and her coat is in her lap. Her body doesn't shake from the cold at all. I stretch my arm across the cab and touch her cheeks. They're red from warmth.

"You still haven't told me what you think about all this. About your being part angel," I counter as I start the engine.

"That's because I don't know." She tugs the sleeves of her sweater over her palms, a sign she's not ready to talk. I push anyway.

"What were you looking for in there?" I ask, pulling into the traffic on First Street.

"Looking for?" Her impossibly bad poker face emerges. "I have a paper due. I was doing research for my paper."

"No one goes to the library to do research anymore."

Her brows snap together, offended. "Sure they do. I like it in there. It's so peaceful and the fabrics and furniture—"

"Peaceful, huh?" I take the intersection at First and Main too fast, and my arm swings in front of Vivienne's chest instinctively as we go airborne for two seconds. "It's peaceful because no one uses it," I finish when all four tires are on the ground.

She bursts into laughter. "You just arm-seat-belted me."

"I what?"

Pulling one leg beneath her, she turns in her seat. "You're just like my mom. You threw your arm out to protect me. That's so sweet."

"Why are you talking like that? Stop, it's creepy."

"What? You don't like this?" she asks in a high-pitched baby voice. She might as well run her nails down a chalkboard, that's how appealing it is. She laughs harder. "Oh my gosh. You really *don't* like it. You should see your face; you look like you're going to puke."

Her head falls forward as she clutches her stomach, and I pull the Bronco into a parking spot at the edge of Miller Plaza.

"You think you're funny, don't you?" My grip tightens around the steering wheel.

She giggles. "Poor Breckin. You don't like baby talk?" The pouty face she makes is damn near impossible not to love, but that voice . . .

"Vivie, I swear—" I hiss, breathing through my nose. She mocks me, laughing harder with every word. When she doesn't stop, I reach across the seat and give her a tweak, right above the knee cap.

She jumps in her seat. I tweak it again.

"No." She slaps at my hand with a yelp. *Hello ticklish spot, thy name is karma.* I barely give her a moment to catch her breath from laughing at me before I'm halfway onto her side of the car and attacking her. My hands are everywhere—her knee, her thigh, her side. Her ribs are especially sensitive, and the moment I figure that out she's a goner.

"Uncle, uncle!" She's scooched so far down in her seat, she's nearly flat on her back with her legs pulled to her chest. Her feet kick at the air. "Breckin!"

Her hands have gone from slapping at mine to protecting herself.

"You done with the baby talk?" I ask firmly, my hands hovering above her.

Her blond hair is a tangled mess around her face, but I get one eyeball—one very narrowed *you are going to die* eyeball—through a part in the silken mess. I wiggle my fingers and move back in. She screams.

"Okay, I promise. No baby talk."

With a satisfied smirk, I offer her my hand and tug until she's sitting again. She huffs and straightens her twisted sweater. Blue eyes flick my way, a little side glance, and I catch her lips twitching with suppressed humor as she shoves her hair from her face.

Emotions swell within, and I grab her face and plant my lips on hers. Hard. My fingers curve around the base of her skull, sinking into her hair while my mouth parts hers for one satisfying, but fast, taste. I pull away as quickly as I attacked, so quickly that Vivienne's hands don't have time to make it past grabbing my forearms for support.

Thoughts spill from my mind. "I can't lose you."

Vivienne draws a sharp breath.

"I won't." I shake my head and touch our foreheads. "It would kill me, Vivie."

Her hands slip to cup my jaw. "You won't lose me," she says tenderly.

"You don't understand. I'm not willing to give this up. This laughter, this light. I didn't know what I was missing until my soul found yours." I close my eyes. God, that is so cliché. So trite, but how else do I convey the difference having her makes?

"Breckin, I get it. I do." Her hands apply the barest pressure to my skin, and I open my eyes and meet her gaze. "I grew up loved by a mother and friends. I didn't hide the way you have, but I think I understand what you're saying. Every time I see you, this bond grows stronger. That glowing I keep doing is all for you, obviously."

"Obviously," I mock playfully.

Her smile could sustain me for months. Our lips touch with a feather-soft brush before she looks past me. "What are we doing here?"

I release her reluctantly and move back behind the wheel of the Bronco. "Right. I'd kind of forgotten I drove here." We're in the shopping plaza across from the high school and medical center. "I figured we could get dinner for your mom."

Vivienne looks at the strip center and where we're parked. "Dinner from Sakura?"

"Oh boy. Your face is melting. Don't you dare get all mushy on me again."

"Whatever." She bends over and digs her cell from her bag on the floorboard. "I'll message Mom. She loves the moo goo gai pan from here. I can't believe you thought of her. How did you know I was supposed to bring her dinner tonight?"

I lift my brows.

"Right," she nods, "super angel hearing. You overheard me talking to her this morning before school, didn't you?"

"I might have," I admit. Vivienne bites her lip as her hands go to work, typing on her phone. I chuckle. "And because I see you slowly dying inside, yes, I did hear what she said about me, too."

"Ugh. You did?" Her butt slides forward as she cowers in her seat. "She's so embarrassing."

"She's not embarrassing. She's smart." With that, I grab my keys and jump out of the car. I feel Vivienne's eyes roll as I walk around the Bronco and open her door for her.

"You did hear the part where she warned me about boys like you?" she asks as she drops her legs out the door and hops down. "Is that why you're saying she's smart?"

"I heard the part where she said you were lucky to have caught a gorgeous specimen such as myself."

She pokes my ribs and laughs. "Yeah, I think what she actually said was that Breckin seems like he's the kind of guy who would have a massive ego. Are you positive you want to date a guy like that?"

The real conversation was more about how her mom worried Vivienne was cutting out Zara—who's driven her to and from school for years—for me. Her mother promised Vivienne that she did like me, and she admitted I was too charming and handsome for my own good—a smart observation. Then she warned her daughter of the pitfalls of going out with guys who could date whomever they wanted, and told her to not forget her morals or future.

"And what was your reply?" I ask with a grin.

"I said you would do, for now." She flips her hair over her shoulder haughtily and brushes by me.

I snag her from behind, my lips grazing the curve of her ear. "For now?"

Vivienne reaches up and grabs the back of my head, holding me so we're cheek to cheek. "Forever," she says, turning and pressing her lips to the edge of my mouth.

Snap. "Shit," I mutter.

Vivienne's head turns farther, her eyes going wide. "You seem to be having a hard time controlling those things."

"What makes you say that?" I shake my wings out, irritated to no end at their willfulness. The moment the itch hit my spine, I cloaked them. Thankfully, it's dark outside and the parking lot is poorly lit. Anyone watching us will have no idea I just ripped another shirt and flashed them with my wings.

"I thought I learned how to control this when I was twelve. See what you do to me?"

I return to the truck, willing my wings back in place as I reach for my leather jacket in the back seat.

"Mom replied she'd love to see us for dinner," Vivienne tells me through her laughter.

"Perfect. I'm starving."

"Hey," she says, taking my hand as I return to her side. "Afterwards, let's skip the festival and just stay in."

Stay in? This girl dragged me all over town for the Hot Cocoa & Cookie Crawl. She's repeatedly told me how much she loves doing town events—movie nights, festivals, art events—and now she wants to stay in?

"Is my surly attitude rubbing off on you?" I tease, running my thumb over the back of her hand as we head toward Sakura.

She bites her lip and turns her head. "Can't a girl just want a quiet night in?"

I tug on her hand, stopping her progress mid–parking lot. "You can want whatever you want, Vivie. I just want to make sure you're not saying no because you're scared of something, or because you think I don't want to go."

"What if it's a little of all three?" she asks. I cock my head, and she continues, "I know you don't love these events, I'm afraid the crowds draw more fallen who might be looking for us to the area, and I want to be alone with you."

"Tell you what, let's bring your mom dinner and see how we feel afterward. Okay?"

She agrees with a small smile, but there's an uncertainty in her eyes that wasn't there before she learned about her lineage. Another worry to add to her collection. I long to remove all her worries.

DON'T LET ME GO

VIVIENNE

*H*avenwood Falls Medical Center is my second home. Or third, considering I spent much of my time at Zara's when we were younger and Mom needed a sitter. Breckin and I enter through the break room door at the back of the converted house and unpack our take-out.

"So this is a hospital?" Breckin asks as he looks around the room.

"More like emergency clinic. If anyone is seriously injured, Elias life-flights them to a higher-level trauma center. Usually Denver or Colorado Springs, I think." I dig through the cabinets and pull three canned drinks from Mom's stash. "I would have thought you knew that."

Breckin waves off the soda. "I did know that, but I've never been in here. Or any doctor's office." He draws a halo over his head and grins.

My hands go to my hips. "Whoa, wait a minute. Are you telling me I didn't need all those shots through the years?" I ask. Breckin shrugs a shoulder. "Not fair." I pout.

"What's not fair?" Mom asks as she walks into the break room. "Hi, sweetie." Her hand smooths the hair back from my face the same way she did when I was five. She looks at Breckin.

"Breckin, good to see you again."

"Ms. Freeman." Breckin clasps his hands in front of him. The boy deals with angels, fought a reaper, and flies like a rocket through the sky, but my mother makes him nervous.

"Ah, Sakura—massive bonus points for this." Mom's face lights up as she takes a seat in one of the plastic chairs and motions for us to follow. "So, what's not fair?" she repeats.

"Oh, nothing important. I was just talking about something that happened at school."

"What have you two been up to this afternoon?" she asks between bites of snap peas and mushrooms. My gaze flicks to Breckin, then back. Mom's brow furrows. "Viv? You didn't go running, did you? I don't want you out there alone."

Breckin grunts his little over-my-dead-body grunt. It's been one month. Should I know the meanings of all his sounds already? "Don't worry. She won't be running alone anymore."

I turn on my boyfriend as Mom's eyes pop wide. "Excuse me?" I ask, taken back by his firm refusal.

He flashes an innocent smile, and I swear he turns up his angel glow. Is he trying to manipulate me by using his abilities? Dropping my spork in my chicken fried rice, I prop my chin on my fist and give him a stare down. My mother watches our interaction with a smile.

"Viv, we've talked about this," Breckin says meaningfully.

"Oh, I know what we've talked about. I'm just surprised you're sitting here in front of my mother, telling her what I will and won't do, like you have a say."

Mom purses her lips, and I expect her to butt in. Having a single mom growing up taught me one important lesson—don't take crap from guys. She won't scold my attitude if I'm sticking up for myself.

Breckin doesn't squirm. Not even an inch. "You don't think I know better than to tell you what to do?" His amber gaze focuses on my mother, and he graces her with another grin. "You raised a stubborn daughter."

"Don't I know it," Mom says pointedly. "I've never liked her running alone, so we have something we can agree on."

"Are you two ganging up on me now? Mom, I told you I wasn't

comfortable running anymore." She may not know about the attack that left me for dead, but everyone in town knows about Heidi Bennett's disappearance. It's been an easy excuse to use when Zara or Mom ask me why I stopped running. "And for the record, Breckin, if I want to run, you won't stop me."

"See, this is where you've read me all wrong, Viv. I would never try to stop you from doing anything you want to do. I'll just follow at your side."

"Like a stalker?"

"No, like a caring boyfriend who doesn't want anything to happen to you."

"You hate running," I remind him needlessly. *Why run when you can fly?*

"Not as much as I hate thinking of you getting hurt." *Again.* I hear the last word in my head, but whether he said it or it's implied, I can't be sure. My mind goes to the scene in the car earlier. *I can't lose you.*

His actions and words are a testament to the way he loves me. That one sentence is all that's needed to douse my irritation with him. If we were alone, I'd pull him close and . . .

"This is a non-issue, anyway," I tell them before my imagination gets carried away. "Like I've said, more than once, I don't plan on running outside anymore. Plus, my cross-country career is over."

"If it's a non-issue, why are you arguing with us?" he asks.

I toss a fortune cookie at Breckin's gorgeous head as Mom dissolves into laughter.

Crossing my arms over my chest, I slouch in my chair. "We brought you dessert for a midnight snack, but I'm not sure I want to give it to you anymore."

Breckin chokes on his own laughter. "She probably won't want it. How good can flan from an Asian restaurant be?"

"How good can—" Mom's mouth drops. "Have you never had the flan from Sakura?"

His top lip curls in disgust.

"Breckin isn't big on sweets. He ridicules everything I love as being too sugary," I explain while cleaning up my dinner trash. Mom's gasp fills the break room. The Freeman girls are known around town for their love of desserts. We're famous at the annual dessert crawl.

He shrugs. "Sorry, Viv's as sweet as I get."

My face heats up, and Breckin reaches across the table and touches my hand.

Mom has always known how to read me, but right now she's reading us, and her look speaks volumes. A dark shadow crosses her face before she shakes it off and smiles. "All right, that's enough sappy sugar out of you two. I need to get back to work."

WE FORGO THE FESTIVAL, return to my apartment, and work on homework with the television on in the background until ten, the official time Mom has ruled as Breckin's curfew at our place when she's not home.

What she doesn't know is that my boyfriend can fly. So, although he leaves at ten, it's only for the twenty minutes it takes him to drive his Bronco home, then return using his wings. I use that time to shower and get ready for bed, but I'm not fast enough, and Breckin is sprawled face down on my bed when I finish, his dark wings spread wide. The iridescent coloring shimmers beneath my ceiling fan light as they twitch and tremble about. Knowing how sensitive they are, I carefully brush my fingers along the edge.

Breckin heaves a euphoric sigh and turns his head on my pillow. "I've hidden them more since you've been in my life than ever before. They're dying to stretch out."

I love the sleek quality his feathers have. They're downy soft around his spine and along the underside, but the rest are like smooth ebony silk with amber-tipped edges.

"Well, I won't tell them no." I tease my fingertips over the feathers. Not even the promise of Breckin's shirtless skin can tear my gaze away from studying him. I chew on my lip thoughtfully. "Do you think I might get wings?"

His flutter, and I grin. "You like that idea, huh?"

143

Breckin pushes his chest from the bed, inches over and lifts his left wing. He pats the space beside him, and I crawl onto my stomach at his side. Once I'm settled, his wing lowers over me like a blanket. Its weight is heavier than I expected. I love it.

I rest my cheek on my folded hands and study his face while he tangles his fingers into the wet ends of my hair. "I'm not sure if I could physically handle seeing you with wings, Vivie."

My heart pumps a little harder and a little faster than before. The idea of having wings is both terrifying and intriguing. How will I cope with the changes as they come? At what point will I become less human and more angel? Or will I ever?

"Hey." He tugs my bottom lip down with the tip of his pinky. "Remember I said I wanted to show you something today at the library?"

My cheek rubs the back of my hand as I nod.

"Close your eyes."

I do as he asks, but can't help but laugh. "You want to show me something, but I have to close my eyes?"

"Mmmhmmm."

The sight of the back of my eyelids slowly changes from black to red, and my fingers shield my eyes automatically. "Breckin? What are you doing?"

My mattress moves under his weight as he shifts next to me. "Open your eyes and find out."

I crack one eye, then slam it shut. "Holy . . . what is that?"

All I saw was bright white through my fingers and cracked lid.

Breckin snickers. "Okay, open them again."

This time I'm greeted with a glowing white, but it's not blinding, like before. I blink a few times, getting used to the extra light, and push to my knees. The glow is Breckin. He's tucked his wings close to his back and rolled to his side, giving me the perfect view of his ripped abs, angel muscles, and celestial glow.

I'm in awe. "When you said I glowed, this is what you meant? What Zara saw?"

"No, your glow isn't half as bright as this." My face falls, and he laughs. "Don't be jealous. I've been an angel a lot longer than you have, you overachiever."

I'm drawn to him. My hands reach forward like they're beyond my control. I'm a marionette, and someone else holds the strings. His skin doesn't feel any different. It's warm, like always. The muscles, more defined than normal seventeen-year-old boys', jump and bunch at my touch, and Breckin sucks in air through his teeth.

His hand covers mine. "Do you feel the pull?" he asks through gritted teeth.

"To touch you?" I ask breathlessly, wetting my lips.

"That's the angel pull, Viv. My glow speaks to that part of you. Whenever you're around another angel who shines their light, you'll feel a closeness to them, but I think our soul mate bond makes ours more powerful."

The brightness fades slowly, and I smile, my mind forming the mental picture of him on a dimmer switch. I shake the random thought away. "Why do you think our bond makes it different?"

"I've been around other angels when they let their grace shine. Other girl angels," he says with an incline of his head to make sure I understand what he's saying. "It didn't affect me at all, but with you, I have a horrible time keeping my hands off you when you start glowing. It makes me feel possessive, and I'm gonna be honest—it makes me have thoughts I shouldn't be having."

"Breckin." I shove at his chest, but he doesn't budge.

"I'm just saying. It's, um . . . very tempting." He explains needlessly. My body still hums with the need to get close to him. Temptation is certainly a thing between us. "I showed you that because I imagine you will be a full-blown light bulb sooner or later, and we need to get it under control. When I saw you at the library this afternoon, it hit me. We can't let you evolve without help."

Evolve? Funny word for an angel to use. "What does that mean?"

"That means you are about to embark on angel training."

"Angel training?"

"Yep." He reaches for my arms and drags me back down to his side. "It's time we both get in shape for the things to come, Vivie."

He speaks with excitement, but my body registers the way he squeezes a little tighter. His birthday is four months away. Even if I'm in the clear since Sebastian is dead, and hopefully no one knows, or cares, about my existence and our bond—we still have Hamon to deal with.

HOLY GROUND

BRECKIN

*a*ngel training sucks.

Vivienne and I head to Elias's hangar every day after school and on Saturday and Sunday, to work on whatever he deems necessary. Most days, he separates us, sending me to lift weights or run while he works with her in private.

"Breckin, you distract her," he snaps when I complain about being sent away.

"I do not. I just want to help her. She said she's having a hard time finding that switch within. Maybe I can show her—"

"No." He's already turning his back to leave me behind.

"What is your problem?" I shout across the hangar. My voice echoes in the empty space. Elias looks over his shoulder, his icy blue eyes staring me down. "You know what, forget it. Do it your way. I'll go lift more weights, because that's going to help."

"What's going on with you and Elias?" Vivienne asks after a few weeks at the hangar. "Why are you so angry with him?"

It's Friday night, and we're sitting by the firepit on my back patio. January has remained uneventful. We go to school and we go to the

147

hangar, and we try to keep up with our classwork, too. When her mother doesn't work, Vivienne spends time with her, and I train with Elias on fighting. Honing skills that come naturally.

I poke at the burning wood, causing embers to fly. "I'm not angry with him."

Her knee knocks mine. "And you call me a terrible liar."

"What do you two do while he has me working out?" I ask. They haven't told me. Three and a half weeks of seeing him almost daily, and neither of them have said a word to me about what they talk about or work on up in his apartment. She's supposed to be learning how to control any abilities that come to life, but she still glows when I walk into a room after an extended time apart. "Why is it a secret? From me, of all people, Vivie."

Vivienne pushes up out of her Adirondack chair and stands in front of me, kicking at my legs. I angle sideways and she slips into my lap, her tiny frame resting perfectly against my chest.

"I wouldn't keep secrets from you." She touches my cheek.

"Then what—" I don't finish as a vision scratches across my mind. It's fleeting—a scene of Elias's stern face, his lips moving, but I can't hear his words—then it's gone, the scene sucked back like a black hole swallowed it.

I nearly toss Vivienne from my lap. "Was that you?" Her tired smile confirms it. "He's teaching you mental manipulation?"

"Sort of. He's been trying to teach me how to access my gifts, but all I seem good at is projecting thoughts or visions."

I use manipulation often. It's an easy fix for when humans stumble upon me accidentally being too nonhuman. I just touch them and give them something else to think about. It's a good power for her to have access to.

"You're not missing out on anything. I sit on his couch and meditate for hours on end, trying to find my angel side," she says as she leans back and meets my eyes. "Most of the time I get nothing but a horrible headache. Showing you that little bit wiped me out."

The resonant rumbling of a motorcycle fills the night, and Vivienne snuggles closer, a small groan leaving her lips.

"What's wrong?"

"They freak me out."

"They?" I lean to the side and peer down the road. A solitary headlight shines in the distance. Although it's built above ground level on a wall, the side patio to my house is open to the street. Our wrought-iron fencing provides security, but not privacy. There's no need for privacy when I can cloak myself if I don't want to be seen.

"Those motorcycle guys," she clarifies.

I tighten my arms and laugh. "Vivie, it's a motorcycle club, and they're not going to bother you."

"They're a gang! Swords of the Infernal Night—S.I.N.—that can't be good."

"And you're an angel who will kick ass with the best of us soon," I remind her, brushing her hair with a kiss. She scoffs as though I've overestimated her future abilities. "It's only one bike, anyway. Stop fretting."

The biker moves in graceful slow motion as he nears the intersection of Fairchild and Eleventh. He plants his feet, shifting on his bike seat while his head swings toward us. Jack Peters. He idles through the intersection and stops even with us. Vivienne's fingers clutch at my shirt until the fabric is taut across my stomach.

"Peters?" Jack's not one to stop and speak. Ever. He nods a silent greeting, and his head tips from side to side. My gaze flicks to Vivienne in my lap. *Shit.* Gripping her hips, I push her to her feet and stand behind her. "Something going on?" I ask cryptically.

"What is she?" he asks, his voice deep for a seventeen-year-old.

I rub her lower back, willing her to remain calm. "Part angel, and that's not yet public knowledge."

He shakes his dark head. "There's something else there, Breckin." He turns back to the road. "By the way, there are fallen ones hanging around. And damned," he adds before he pulls his feet from the asphalt and takes off. The rumbling from his engine bounces between the houses.

Vivienne spins in my arms, bumping into my chest in her haste. "What was that, Breckin? He knew what I was? Wasn't that Jack

Peters? I've never seen him talk to anyone. I've seen him stop by the firehouse when his dad is working and I'm at Napoli's, but that's it. How in the hell does he know I'm anything other than human?"

Her questions come at me in rapid succession.

"Viv, take a breath." My gaze roams the sky. *There are damned hanging around.* I fight the urge to hide her inside.

"Take a breath? Jack Peters knows what I am," she spits out each word. "He mentioned the fallen. Does he mean your dad? More reapers?"

"No. Reapers aren't fallen, remember?" My angel side knocks at my back to be let out, paranoid about what could be watching us.

"What did he mean by damned?" her voice shakes.

Have I not explained angels to her better than this? "There are angels on earth who work for Heaven—they carry out the Creator's divine plans. Then there are the fallen, the ones who were either cast out or defected, and those who left but don't align specifically with either side. In that sense, Elias is considered fallen. And last, there are the damned. They are the ones who aligned with Hell." Hamon is a bit between fallen and damned. He lures humans into sin, which is to Hell's benefit. I always assumed he'd aligned with Hell, but Elias says Hamon is more of an independent contractor. An angel angry with God and mankind for reasons I've never been made to understand.

Her eyes grow wide with my explanation. "And how does he know about me?"

"Jack's not human, Viv." I take her hand and lead her to the back door.

She tugs back. "He's angel, too?"

I exert a bit more force on her hand, and she follows again. "He's not."

"Not an angel. So, he's something else." We step inside, and I lock the door, draw the shades, and turn to find Vivienne with her arms crossed, her hip popped, and her face screwed up. She means business. "What is he?"

"He is a hellhound. They have excellent senses, especially when it comes to angels and demons. Or the dead." She sways slightly on her feet, and I take her by the shoulders. "Viv, I wanted to fill you in sooner, but Elias wanted you to establish control of your abilities first."

"Fill me in on what?"

"Angels are not the only supernatural beings in Havenwood Falls. There are more. A lot more."

I settle Vivienne on the couch in the basement and go to the kitchen to make her a hot chocolate. While the milk warms, I send Elias a text letting him know about Jack's comment. There are other angels in Havenwood Falls, but Jack specified the damned. He meant the ones we'd want to be on watch for. They might be hanging around and keeping an eye on me for Hamon. Or they could be passing by innocently. There's also the off chance they're looking for Vivienne. The options are numerous, and I'm not taking any chances.

Vivienne's lying on the couch, her head resting against the back cushion, when I lean over the back with a large mug in hand. "Extra chocolate, extra marshmallows."

A wobbly smile greets me when she tips her chin up. "You know me well."

Taking a seat on the end, I pick up her feet and put them in my lap. "So, I'm gonna go out on a limb and assume you have questions."

Her blond brows lift. "You think?"

Where do I begin? This town was founded on the idea that supernaturals and humans could live together peacefully. There are wards and rules, but for many species, this place is the closest thing to living freely they will ever find.

"Ask me whatever you want, and I'll answer truthfully," I say when I can't come up with the right opening.

She blows across the top of her mug. "You say supernatural and I think unicorns."

"You're such a girl, Vivie."

"No unicorns then?" Her smile is disarming. It's the smile of a fragile girl who has no idea what she is about to learn exists in the world.

"There are a lot of shifters here. Wolves, mountain lions, bears, dragons, and yes, unicorns."

The mug lowers from her mouth. "You're not kidding, are you? Shifters? Like people who change into animals? They change into dragons?" Her eyes grow wider with each question she asks.

"They do." The library comes to mind. "Remember my smile at the library?" She inclines her head slightly as she takes a sip of her drink. "There were carved gargoyles decorating the foyer. Everett Weston designed the place. He is a gargoyle."

Vivienne chokes, a dribble of chocolate dripping from her lip. "A stone statue? That hot man is a—"

My jaw scissors as she catches what she's said. "Hot man, huh?" I ask, and Vivienne's mouth opens and closes twice as I explain Everett. "Obviously, he isn't a stone creature. A gargoyle is a protector. Everett is part of the Spiritual Assembly of Protectors, which means he can take on divine assignments. That is the only reason I give you his name specifically. We would consider him an ally if we needed one."

"Meaning there are gargoyles that are not allies?"

"Vivie, there is good and evil in everyone, human or otherwise."

"This is so insane," she mutters, and I agree.

This is insane. Humans hide in a bubble, thinking they're the only intelligent species on earth. That good and evil is as simple as black and white. That they are the ones who make the rules, when in truth many of the residents in this town could destroy everything with little more than a snap of their fingers, or a shot of fire from their lungs.

"I'm not sure how much trouble I could get in for telling you this."

"Trouble from whom?"

"The Court of the Sun and the Moon."

"The Court—" Vivienne leans over and puts her mug on the coffee table. "You should probably start at the beginning."

Explaining everything I know takes time. The Court, the wards, the creatures. I stay away from naming names, although she asks, preferring to stick to the basics.

"Elias has worked with the Court several times when there were issues with angels in the area. Because of that, he's been able to keep them from digging into your origins further."

"But I'll have to meet with them eventually?" She chews on the edge of her nail when I nod. "And the magical tattoo thing?"

"That won't be an issue for you. The Court uses the tattoos as a way of registering and keeping track of supernaturals. As angels, we're exempt."

"Why are angels exempt?"

"We're superior. There's nothing the Court can offer us. With vampires, the tattoos allow them to walk in the daylight; with shifters, apparently the tattoo keeps them safe from each other when hunting, among other things. I don't know all the specifics, but those are the basics. Angels are born with more power and abilities than they can offer."

"How have I lived in a town my entire life and never noticed vampires or nymphs? How does no one know?"

"You and half the population. That's the whole point. That's why there are wards to keep the town hidden, and memory spells."

"What about when Sebastian grabbed me at the school? How was his presence covered up?"

"Elias. He went by the school while you were recovering and made sure no one remembered a thing."

The night goes on like this. Vivienne asks questions, and I answer them as best I can.

"I assume you and Elias aren't the only angels here?" I give her foot a squeeze. "Well, you, Elias, and me."

"They come and go, but yes, there are others. Most don't live here like we do. They're here to fulfill a purpose, like guardian angels. There is one, Cecelia—"

"From the music store?" Vivienne's hand goes to her chest. "She's an angel? I should have known. She looks like you would picture an angel to be."

"Vivie, *you* look exactly like what an angel should look like." My palm rubs up her shin. "I still can't figure out how we didn't connect before I healed you. I can't imagine how I never fell for you before."

Vivienne shifts and climbs onto my lap. "For the record, you are way hotter than that gargoyle."

"Yeah?" I grip her hips, reveling in the feel of her weight.

Our lips connect with a light brush as she smiles. "Totally."

"I should get you home," I murmur, glancing at the time, but Vivienne has other ideas.

"I think I should stay for a while," she says, drawing my bottom lip into her mouth and sucking lightly as her hands tangle in my hair, holding me in place.

I dive into her mouth, and her taste is my undoing.

BRAVE

VIVIENNE

*H*avenwood Falls High is a zoo for the supernatural. I still struggle with accessing my angelic side, but my nose no longer struggles with identifying the many creatures I've lived among my entire life. The Kasuns are wolves. They were the first people I unequivocally identified. It happened out of the blue. I walked into the cafeteria for lunch one day, my gaze fell on Kase Kasun and his crew, and *bam,* I just knew. I nearly dropped my soft drink in my haste to get away. Now whenever Breckin and I see Willa, Kase, or one of their pack members, Breckin makes absurd comments about throwing things, just to see if they'll play fetch. It's his way of calming me around the shifters, because my mind can't help but envision my attack last December. I'd assumed it to be a random animal, but Breckin's revelations have brought to light other possibilities. Elias says the sheriff—also a wolf—swears he checked around, and no shifters were to blame. At least now, with my super senses, I'll know when something comes at me.

I'm LATE. Convincing Elias and Breckin to give me a day with Zara was no easy feat. I search for Breckin as I jog across Eighth and hurry down Main toward Callie's Consignments, certain he's lingering nearby. The sun is on full display today, warming the temperature to above normal for late February.

Callie's is huge. Elegant furnishings are strategically placed throughout the store with antique décor complementing the settings. Much of the first floor is filled with clothing and accessories. Most of the items are vintage, which is why my British-obsessed best friend loves the place. Taking a quick glance around, I don't spot Zara.

"Z?" I raise my voice slightly.

"Pretty complexion and dark hair?" I spin at the heavily accented voice, chills dancing up my spine.

"I'm sorry?" I ask, as a dark-haired woman appears from behind the large armoire near the far wall with pillows in hand. She's beautifully exotic, and a bit of a mess with her long dark wind-blown hair and casual plaid shirt over tight jeans. I've never seen her, but something about her has my skin jumping. She's not human, that's for sure.

"Your friend, the one with the dismal British accent?" she asks. Biting my lip at the woman's grimace, I nod. *That's Zara all right.* "She's in the dressing area."

The unease the stranger awoke settles when I move out of her eyeline and step into the dressing area. It's like a gypsy caravan in here. Rich, colorful fabrics cover the walls. Thick carpets are layered on the floor. I'm jealous of the luxury displayed every time I come in here. And it changes constantly. Callie excels at finding unique pieces. If only Mom and I could afford it.

"Z?"

"I wonder if I can find something that says Jane Austen meets Titanic?" Zara ponders through the thick dressing room curtains, ignoring any type of polite greeting. "You know, lace and bead work. Not too frumpy, though."

I take a seat on the vintage couch and sift through the stack of clothing draped over the armrest. "Are these all your things?"

I may be late, but she obviously began her shopping expedition early.

Zara's head pokes out. "Callie really needs trolleys in here. I could barely hold all of that."

"Trolley? You've been reading more slang dictionaries, haven't you?"

"Perhaps." She winks and parts the curtains dramatically. "Take a look at this? Opinion?"

"Opinion? Gorgeous. I love the empire waist and the fabric gathering around the neckline and sleeves." She looks like she stepped out of Regency London.

She does a little twirl in front of the huge gilded mirror leaning against the wall.

"I swear Callie has someone in London to find these things just for me. Even the peacock-blue color is my favorite." When she's done admiring herself, her gaze finds me. "Did you meet Nikita?"

"Who? Oh, you mean the girl out there? Kinda, I guess."

Zara smooths her hands along the skirt of her dress and turns from side to side. "She's Callie's cousin. From New York. Gorgeous, isn't she? She's visiting."

"And you found this all out how?" I ask, impressed with her investigative skills. Maybe I should ask her to look into the history of Havenwood Falls for me.

"I asked her, silly. Callie was walking out when I came in. Nikita— killer name, isn't it?—offered to watch the store for a few minutes. She has this dark, bad-girl vibe to her. I'm totally intrigued."

"You? Miss Jane Austen wannabe, crumpets and lace lover, finds the hot rocker chick intriguing?"

"You know I find anyone new to Havenwood Falls interesting. How often do we get fresh blood here?" Her laugh fills the dressing area. "Anyway, did you not find anything to try on?"

"Prom isn't until May, Z." And though Breckin asked about it, I can't seem to muster up the enthusiasm for it. Our future is so unknown. "I'm not shopping until I have a date." I'm not sure why I lie to her.

Her dark eyes roll. "Um, you planning on breaking up with Breckin between now and May nineteenth?"

MICHELE G. MILLER

"Of course not, but . . ." But his eighteenth birthday is in April, and I still don't know what that means. Will I have my soul mate come May or will I be a complete and utter mess? "I'm just waiting, okay?"

Zara ducks back behind the curtains and proceeds to model four other dresses of similar styles before she moves on to the casual clothing stacked by my hip. I take snapshots on my phone so she can get the "social media view" before making decisions about everything. She's not a diva, but the girl is serious about her clothing. She wants to be a buyer for a fashion line in L.A. or New York. Now that I know there are memory wards on the town, I wonder if she'll ever return to Havenwood Falls once she leaves.

Nikita is nowhere to be seen when we're ready to check out, and my intense feelings are gone.

∼

After dumping Zara's purchases in her car, we walk to Napoli's for a late lunch. It's a little after two, and the square is bustling. Residents tend to come out of the woodwork when the sun shines in the middle of the winter. Especially after the dreary weather we had this past week. We're nearing the fountain when a fire ignites up my spine, and a groan escapes my lips.

"Viv?"

I stop walking, and my arm reaches behind my back, straining to scratch an itch that isn't an itch. As quickly as it came, the sensation disappears. Zara's brows drop low over her eyes.

"Sorry, I was attacked by an itch." I feign scratching as we continue.

"So, anyway, I was closing last night and guess who came in after his shift at Shelf Indulgence and totally flirted with me?"

I trip over my feet as another pain rends through my back. *What in the ever living hel—lo, angel at five o'clock.*

Propped against a tree, just off the path through the square, is a tall, dark, and uncharacteristically handsome guy a few years older than us.

158

Behind him are a set of wings that remind me more of a crow than an angel. Almost flat at the top, where Breckin's are rounded, they form the letter T with his body. From tip to tip, the span probably matches his well over six-foot height. The feathers are long and cream with brown specks. They're not beautiful at all, nothing like the inky iridescence of Breckin's.

My back hums with the stir of a thousand nails prodding my skin at once as my gaze roams up his dark chest and our gazes lock. His fiery, reddish-brown orbs study me as I study him, and my heartbeat picks up. Somewhere, in the back of my awakening dread, I hear Zara saying my name. Does no one notice the shirtless angel in their presence? I tear my eyes from his and look around.

"Viv? I swear, where are you today? You've been—"

"Well, well, what do we have here? A baby angel all alone?" I whirl around at the accented voice behind me. "What is your name, precious?"

"—barely paying attention to me all day." Zara drones on, seemingly unaware of the angel before us.

He's cloaked.

The angel turns his head thoughtfully, and the riot of short dreadlocks covering his head flop haphazardly. "Do you want me to show myself for your friend?"

Turning, I thrust one arm through Zara's and reach for the cell phone in my pocket. "C'mon, Z. I thought I saw someone."

We take two steps before a growl sends chills through my body, and I'm jerked back. The cell I'd just fingered flies from my hand to the ground.

"Didn't anyone tell you to never walk away from your superiors, precious?" His grip on my bicep is crippling.

"Hey, let my friend go! Who are you?" Zara rushes forward, her fingers trying to pry his hand away, to no avail. The angel grips her wrist, his lips moving slightly before he shoves her.

"What did you do?" I ask him frantically, as Zara walks away.

"I thought we could use some alone time." He smiles. Then there's a flash, and two seconds later, I'm falling to my knees and rolling on the ground. We're in the alley between the buildings around the square, but we moved so fast, I didn't even feel it.

"What are you?" He sniffs as I scramble back. My knees sting, and I look down at my torn pants, blood coloring the fabric.

Wiping the debris from my torn-up palms, I gain my footing. "Who are you?"

"I am Zeke, my little half-breed." He pushes closer, knocking me into the brick wall at my back. "Who created you?"

"I don't know."

"You don't know?" Zeke laughs. His hand touches my throat, the sharp tip of his nail scratching my skin as he draws it down along my veins, outlining the V of my shirt. "I think I'll take you with me and see what we can find out about you." His face moves closer, and I tense as his tongue touches my cheek. "I'd like a taste of this pretty skin."

Ignoring the wet scrape of his tongue along my skin, I draw a deep breath, then jerk to the side while coming around and grabbing Zeke's head from behind. Using all my strength, I slam his face into the wall, then I take off at a sprint. His growl ignites my terror, but I don't dare scream. What if a human saw us? I don't want anyone to get hurt because of me. Where did Zara go?

I bounce off Zeke's chest. Shuffling back, I turn and run the other way. In a blink, he's before me again. He's transporting. I can't get away.

"I'm nobody. I didn't even know I had angel blood." I snap my jaw shut. *Stupid Viv.*

His orange eyes light up. "You're the girl," he says. "The soul mate."

My vision blurs, then clears. I have nowhere to go and no real power over this strong creature, but I'll fight to keep myself and Breckin safe. I allow him to close the distance between us, then kick at his thigh. The bone in my shin cracks, and I drop to the ground.

"You are weak." Zeke stands over me. "We can make you strong. You and your soul mate. Think of everything you could have."

"I don't know what you're talking about." Pain shoots along my leg, burning with a fire that should have me writhing. When Sebastian attacked me, I could barely speak from the pain.

"You think we don't know who you belong to, beautiful?" His booted foot steps on my thigh, and I wince. "We have plans for you and your little Nephilim."

He cracks a dark smile, then stomps his leg down on mine. His heavy boot snaps my femur, and each fracture and splinter within the bone grates in my ears. My scream could wake the dead.

Zeke laughs and licks his lips. He looks at me like I'm his favorite dessert, and my stomach roils. It is his lust that holds his attention when another angel appears in a blink behind him with a blinding sword and punishment written on his familiar face.

The blade slices Zeke's head clean off before he knows what's hit him. I push backward as Zeke's body disintegrates into nothing but embers falling onto my body. Heat stings my cheek, and I swipe the ash away, feeling ill.

I look up at the avenging angel who swooped in to save me. He doesn't look happy. "You should be healing. Can't you heal?"

My head answers with a slight shake from side to side when my voice refuses to speak. The sword disappears, then he's on his haunches sliding his arms beneath my knees. I bite my lip, tasting blood, as I try to keep from screaming. My vision blurs.

"Put your arms around my neck and hang on."

I comply, locking my fingers around his neck and trying not to press too close to his skin. My gaze focuses on his large wings. Up close like this, they're varying shades of grey outlined in white. Like someone took a white marker and traced the edges of each and every feather. They snap out, and we shoot into the air. Unlike Zeke, who seemed to transport us from one spot to the other, we fly. But we fly at a speed Breckin has never dared, and we arrive at Breckin's house before the contents of my stomach can evacuate via my mouth.

My limbs shake as he stalks toward the glass doors that open to Breckin's back patio. *Where is my angel?* No sooner do I have the thought than an agonizing scream reaches inside my head.

A growl I recognize as Breckin's fills the backyard. He lands at full speed, his feet hitting the deck and skidding as his wings stir up the snow.

"What did you do to her?" Breckin runs for me, his face twisted with pain. "Vivie? I'm sorry . . . I should have been there. Are you all right?" His hands reach for me. "Give her to me," he orders boldly.

The arms holding me tighten. "Open the door, and we can lay her inside."

Heat rushes from the house when Breckin opens the glass door. He slaps his arm across the threshold, blocking our entrance. "If you did this, I will kill you. Father or not."

Hamon doesn't respond, and Breckin drops his arm, so we can pass. Hamon's arms shift beneath my legs as he turns sideways to fit me through the door. The small amount of jostling makes my leg explode with pain once again. Tears overflow.

Breckin winces as his hand goes to his temple.

"What's wrong?" I ask through gritted teeth.

Breckin smooths his face somewhat. He can't hide the creases around his tight lips and narrowed eyes. He's in pain. My gaze remains pinned on him as he follows closely behind Hamon, pointing us toward the same bedroom I woke up in the last time an angel tossed me around.

"She's not healing. You need to heal her," Hamon says brusquely as he sets me carefully upon the guest bed.

"Of course I'm going to heal her." Breckin pushes by his father. His hands go right to my leg, ripping my jeans from ankle to thigh. He lowers his face to mine, kissing my lips as his hands graze over my leg. He presses his cheek against mine. "Vivie, babe, I need you to try not to project so much. I can't think."

I lift a hand to his silky hair, needing that connection. "Oh, God, no wonder you look like you're in pain. I'm sorry."

That's why he was screaming my name before he even arrived. He must have felt my pain from far away.

Breckin smiles. "Don't be crazy. I'd project, too."

Sitting back, he grabs my leg and closes his eyes. I focus my breathing, reeling back all my thoughts to keep him from feeling them. It only takes a moment for the light to emanate from his hands and my bones to mend. There's a muted click, like two building blocks being snapped back in place, then the heat is gone and the pain is no longer, and I burst into tears.

"Viv?" Breckin grabs my shoulders and draws me into his chest as he perches on the edge of the bed.

My nails scratch at his bare back as I try to hold him tighter. Zeke's face, the wicked smile he wore right before Hamon appeared—his plans for me were not noble. Another moment and who knows what would have happened? I lift my head, wiping my running nose and the deluge of tears on my sleeve as I look for Hamon.

He's retreated closer to the bedroom door, his arms crossed over his chest. His face may be neutral, but his eyes take in everything. I want to hate him for the father he is to Breckin, and yet he saved me.

"Thank you," I tell him, though the words don't come out. He must read my lips because he nods.

"Breckin, Hamon?" Elias yells, the front door slamming shut behind him.

Breckin looks toward the door, and Hamon waves him off. "Take a minute."

The moment the door closes behind Hamon, my face is in Breckin's hands. "Who is Zeke?"

"I don't know." I manage between shaky breaths. "He was in the square, just watching us. I felt him, and then he appeared before me and grabbed me." I relay everything that happened up until the moment he arrived on the porch. "Oh gosh, Zara. She was with me—"

Breckin holds me down when I try sitting up. "I'm sure she's fine. He probably just sent her off. We'll find her and make sure."

"I dropped my phone."

A half smile appears. "If that's all you lost, I'm happy to buy you another." His thumb brushes my cheek. "Your pain rushed in so suddenly. I had no idea what happened. I just knew something was wrong. I don't . . . Hamon just appeared?"

"He did."

There's a knock at the door.

"Breckin?" Elias pops his head in.

"Yeah, come in. She's fine." Dropping a kiss on the top of my head, Breckin peels himself from my arms. "You're a mess. Let me get a washcloth."

"How chivalrous of you to remark on my looks after what I just went through," I say with a frown. Breckin grimaces, and I fall into the pillows behind my back. My gaze strays over Elias's shoulder. "Where's Hamon?" I ask.

Elias looks at Breckin before he answers. "He didn't want to bring any more attention here than he might have already, so he left."

"Any more attention?"

"I told you we're in hiding here," Breckin says as the water turns off in the bathroom. "Hamon has kept my existence a secret for almost eighteen years. Or so he says."

"Breckin." Elias's warning tells me this isn't the first time they've had this discussion.

"I don't understand. He's barely visited Breckin in all his years here, but he happened to be close enough to swoop in and save me today?"

"He was hunting the hunter," Elias explains.

Goosebumps break out across my skin as Breckin returns to the side of my bed and hands me a cloth. I swipe at my face with the warm material as he uses another to wipe my knees. Every cut and scratch on my palms is gone, and my legs are perfect, too. His healing is effective, and I'm grateful.

"Is that what he said?" Breckin asks Elias after a moment. "Are we sure he isn't behind this attack? Maybe striking her was done to weaken me."

"Is that what you think of me, son?" Our heads swivel to the door to find Hamon standing there.

"Back so soon?" asks Breckin, snidely. Clearly his distrust for Hamon runs deep.

Hamon just smiles a smile so similar to his son's, I don't know how

Breckin doesn't recognize it. "I was halfway out of town when I realized it was time for you to stop hiding and me to stop running."

WALK ON WATER

BRECKIN

$\mathcal{A}$s if the emotions from hearing Vivienne's terror weren't enough, my father now wants to show up and make amends? Vivienne's hand slips into mine, pumping twice.

Trying to maintain a calm façade, I ask, "Is your being here a danger to Viv?"

Hamon's gaze flicks between us. "It is. It's a danger to both of you."

I step forward. "Then leave."

"Breckin." Elias lifts his hands.

"Don't. My first priority is her, Elias. You know this." I suck in a deep breath and look at my father. I hate calling him that. "I will not go with you in April. I will not choose to join your fallen. I'm not aligning with them."

Hamon huffs. "Did you make this decision because of her? Your soul mate?"

"No, I made the decision a long time ago, but she is my main concern now. I'm not you, Hamon. I want redemption."

"My son, you do not know me well enough to say whether you are like me or not. In fact, I would say you are much more like me than you realize."

Elias remains still. His body tenses as his gaze volleys between

Hamon and me. Behind me, Vivienne squirms on the bed, but her hand doesn't leave mine.

"What if you had lost her today?" he asks. His amber eyes hold me hostage, and my hand tightens around Vivienne's as a precaution. "What if she was ended and you were forced to continue on, knowing you were not there to save her?"

"I would bring armies of terror down on those who took her from me," I say unequivocally.

He tips his head and turns. "Then we understand one another," he says as he leaves the room.

I pull my hand from Vivienne's and hurry after him. His long legs carry him through the house and out the back door with haste. I hesitate to speak. My mind is at war with the pros and cons of him being here. He hasn't offered me answers for seventeen years. Why would today change anything? Then the vision of Vivienne in his arms assaults me, and I need to know. "Why?"

His wings snap taut, and his muscles flex, ready for takeoff. At the last moment, as his knees give and he jumps into the air, he turns his head. His amber eyes meet mine, the hint of red glowing like wildfire. "Because you love her."

"NOTHING I DID WORKED." Vivienne's talking to Elias in the bedroom as I reenter the house. "Maybe it was my fear that kept me from reaching inside."

"Or maybe we were wrong. You might not have access to your angel the way Breckin does, or the way a full-blooded angel does," Elias counters.

"He transported. You told me angels had different gifts, but I didn't—" Her voice drops, then picks up again in low murmurs. I don't push my senses to catch her words. I give her her private fears, knowing she'll tell me if she wants me to hear them. Instead of returning to her side, I take a seat on the couch. There are fallen lurking around town, Vivienne was attacked, and Hamon saved her. *Because you love her.* Did he truly save her for me?

~

VIVIENNE REFUSES to do anything that could harm an innocent after her brush with Zeke. She cuts off Zara and everyone else. To help smooth things over, I use compulsion, keeping her friends busy with other things when they approach her. The lying and seclusion takes a toll.

"Is this how you felt?" Vivienne asks as we're driving away from school one afternoon.

"Is what—" I stop my question when I catch the longing gaze she has focused on a group of students screwing around in the parking lot. It's drizzling and cold, but that doesn't stop their laughter and playfulness. "Did you want to go with them?"

The group is mainly seniors, piling into cars and heading to the Burger Bar for after-school shakes and fries. The closer we come to graduation, the more they seem to be doing that. Like the reality of the end is upon them. Vivienne shakes her head, and I press the brakes.

Throwing my arm over the back of her seat, I turn to her. "Viv, nothing will happen if you want to be with your friends. Elias explained the event with Zeke. It was a one-time deal."

Her head swings my way slowly. "You can't lie to me anymore, Breck." *Damn it.* Soul bond connections are annoying. "I can't protect myself, I can't protect others, and I can't protect you. I'd rather go home."

Weeks pass this way. As my senses and power strengthen rapidly, Vivienne makes no progress with hers—other than those connected to our bond.

At the end of March, two weeks before my birthday, I drop Vivienne at her apartment after school.

"Why's Elias here?" she asks, climbing out of my Bronco.

I school my features. "Because he's going to stand guard for a few hours while I set things up."

"Set things up?" Her brow arches. "What things?"

"You'll see. Just do your homework and get ready for a date. Elias is going to bring you to my place at seven, okay?"

VIVIENNE ARRIVES with Elias at seven on the dot and doesn't make it through the door from the garage into the house before Zara mows her over.

"Z?" Vivienne looks for me over her best friend's shoulder as they hug.

"Surprise! Your Romeo of a boyfriend here planned this whole thing. God, I feel like I haven't seen you in weeks."

Vivienne forces a smile as Zara draws her toward the living room. "I see you every day at school."

"Well, it doesn't feel like it. This house is amazing, Viv. Breckin gave me the grand tour. No wonder you two spend so much time here instead of hanging out with the rest of us. We should totally have a party." Zara looks back at me, and I shake my head. I catch her whisper, "Convince him."

I grill cheeseburgers, while Vivienne and Zara use the deep fryer I bought to make fries. We sit around the table and talk about people at school, college, television shows, and celebrities. Mostly the girls talk and I nod, or frown when they bring up how hot certain actors are.

I'm taking a bite of my burger when I bite into something sour. "Ew. Viv, did you put pickles on my burger?" I pull off the bun and tomato and find four offending pickle chips.

She stops with a fry mid-air. "Of course I did."

"Of course you did? Why do you say it like that? Are pickles a burger requirement?" I tease.

Zara and Vivienne give me identical *are you an alien from outer space* looks. "Your boyfriend doesn't like pickles, Viv?"

"I didn't know. We've never . . . gosh, yeah I guess I never noticed him not eat them." She reaches over the table and plucks the pickles from my food. "There."

"There?" I ask incredulously. "I can't eat it now. It's contaminated. I'll have to make another."

"You're kidding, right?" Vivienne asks, gaping.

I get up from the table. "Nope. I hate pickles. Hate."

"Breckin, you've never once offered me your pickle."

Zara giggles, and I close my eyes, counting to five before I dare answer her.

"What are you talking about?" I ask, a little worried about their answer.

Zara huffs, like she can't understand why they need to explain this to me. "It's common knowledge that the pickle-challenged should offer the pickle-lover their pickle whenever they have one," she says with superiority.

For crying out loud. I rub the back of my neck.

"Whenever we go to the deli or Burger Bar, you get a pickle on your plate, and you've never offered it to me. I can't believe I didn't notice."

"And I'd be a little scared of you if you had," I mutter as I make a new cheeseburger.

Something hits my shoulder, and I turn to find a fry on the floor at my feet. I mentally add pickles to the long list of things Vivienne is crazy about, along with sweets, Napoli's pizza, and all the coffee drinks that taste like pure sugar.

At the end of the night, Operation Cheer Vivienne Up is a success, and for the first time in weeks, she falls asleep with a slight smile.

MY DEMONS

BRECKIN

"*B*reckin?"

I'm lying on Vivienne's bed the next night while she showers when Rachel walks into the bedroom. Thankfully, I was already cloaked. She invited me over for a movie and dinner, her famous grilled cheese sandwiches, with pickles on the side, and tomato soup, but as far as she knows, I left the apartment twenty minutes ago. Which I did, but I'm back as usual, still refusing to leave Vivienne unprotected at night.

I draw my wings closer to my spine as her mother stands in the doorway. Her eyes scan the seemingly empty room.

"I know you're here. You come back every night. You can show yourself."

My heart leaps to my throat. *Shit. Is she playing me?* I shift into a sitting position and wait for her to check under the bed or open the closet, but she doesn't. She steals a glance at Vivienne's closed bathroom door, then cracks a parent's smile.

"I'm not exactly sure how it works, but I know you can hide yourself from sight. I'd like to assume that's what you're doing right now and that you're not in the bathroom with my daughter, because that would cause issues between us." She walks farther into the room. My stomach hits the floor, and my wings bristle. What exactly does

171

she know? "I've kept quiet because I knew you were protecting her, but I think we should talk, angel."

I drop the cloak, and she jumps as I appear. Her palm slaps at her chest, her audible gasp telling me she's startled, though the glint in her eyes says she's not surprised. It doesn't matter. I can erase this entire scene from her mind whenever I want. If she's holding something back—if she knows something—I want to know what it is.

"You knew?" I ask.

"That our town is full of things we don't speak of, or that you're a Nephilim?" Her gaze lingers on my dark wings. I don't respond, so she continues. "I have a journal, handed down from generation to generation. I know my family's heritage. And I know my daughter is different since meeting you."

Whoa. That's a revelation. "You have a journal? Viv's never seen it?"

"Of course not. If she were like the rest of us, she wouldn't have the need to know, at least not until she was older. What happened, Breckin?"

"I don't know what you're asking me."

"Yes, you do." She sits beside me on Vivienne's bed. "I was a headstrong teen. I'd lost my mother, and I never had a father. I was lost, then I came upon the journal in my mother's things as I was packing them away. Six generations of women starting with Phaedra. The angel." Rachel rubbed her hands together nervously. "None of them displayed the angelic attributes. Phaedra kept the journal on herself, her daughter, and her granddaughter, Lola. Then Lola took over, and it must have been passed down after that. Each woman kept notes. They all lived in this crazy town and knew of different aspects of it, but they kept it to themselves, preferring to live like an unknowing human.

"When I found the journal, I became obsessed with what it meant. I grew up friends with Rose Howe—"

The Howes are witches. Rose's daughter, Scarlet, is a junior at Havenwood Falls High and belongs to one of the only integrated social groups at the school, electing to hang out with both wolf and dragon shifters, and a fae. It caused a scandal at the beginning of the school year among some of the supes.

"Rose and I would sneak through her mother's books looking for anything we could find about awakening my angel DNA, but I imagine magic like that was locked away. So I tried other ways to figure out how to tap into what I am. Nothing worked, and eventually I left this town. I should make it clear to you that everything I'd learned about the supernatural here—my friendship with Rose, anything about this town, our heritage—it all disappeared from the journal, and from my memories, once I left Havenwood Falls. It wasn't until I returned that the journal was restored and my memories returned. There I was in Denver, with no background and nothing but vague memories of my life. So, I went to school and moved on."

I waited for the *until* in her words, but the water turned off in the bathroom. Rachel frowned.

"Breckin, since you started coming around, things have been different. When Viv and I are together, I feel a tug in my chest. I love my daughter, but it's not that sort of tug. It's a feeling like something is trapped in there, trying to claw its way out."

I run my hand through my hair, thinking. With the knowledge that we can erase her memories if this backfires, I close my eyes and project my thoughts toward Vivienne. *Your mother knows about me, and you.* Something heavy hits the floor followed by Vivienne's muttered curse. Confident she heard me, I fill Rachel in.

"On December eighth, I spotted Viv injured on her normal running trail up on Mount Alexa. She was bleeding heavily from an animal attack, and I didn't think she was going to make it."

Rachel's eyes tear up.

"I healed her, and as far as we can tell, that healing woke the angel within." Vivienne opens the bathroom door. She's chewing on her bottom lip as she looks at us sitting on her bed. Me with my wings in plain view. "It wasn't just her angelic blood that awoke that day, Rachel. There's something more between Viv and me, something stronger. We're soul mates."

"Why didn't you tell me?" Rachel stands and moves toward the bathroom doorway, pulling Vivienne from her rooted spot and hugging her. "I thought we shared everything."

"Everything?" Vivienne leaned back. "In my mind, telling my mother, whom I assumed was as normal as I once was, that I was evolving into an angel and I had a half-angel soul mate, sounded like something that would land me a trip to the looney bin."

Rachel's forehead creased as she shook her head. "Viv, you nearly died and you kept it from me?"

"And you apparently knew my boyfriend is an angel and you elected not to tell me."

"Wait—" I speak over their bickering, standing as a question knocks at the back of my mind, looking for an answer. "How *did* you know about me?"

How does one journal, a young witch, and some strange feelings add up to uncovering my secret? How did she make that leap?

Vivienne steps from her mother's embrace and comes to my side as Rachel smiles.

"Elias is your guardian and your father is Hamon," she says, like it's obvious. "Phaedra wrote about them both."

My palms prickle with excitement. She wrote about them? I could get the story from someone who would have no reason to lie to me, no reason to sugarcoat things. "Can I see it? Can I see the journal?"

Vivienne's hand touches my lower back.

Rachel shrugs one shoulder. "Sure, I don't see why not. There is one other thing, though. Another reason I was suspicious." Her fingers go to her collar, playing with the fabric as she looks at Vivienne. Nervousness exudes from her pores. "There was one other time when I felt that strange tugging I described to you."

Her words hang in the air.

"I felt it when I was with Vivienne's father."

ELASTIC HEART

VIVIENNE

When Breckin sent me the message saying Mom knows we're angels, I knocked a shampoo bottle onto my toe. He had to be teasing. Toweling off from my shower, I throw on the clothes I wear to sleep and open the door to find them sitting on my bed. Breckin's wings are on full display, and Mom is not on the floor in shock. When did this become my life?

Why didn't you tell me?

Um, hello? Why in the hell did you not tell me about the journal, about the angel genes, about our family's connection with Hamon and Elias, and finally . . . *the odd feelings you had with the man who gifted you me!*

Breckin chuckles, and my gaze snaps to his face. His mouth is taut. He's laughing in his head—at me and my flurry of thoughts. I pinch his nonexistent love handle.

Where do I begin with her?

"What do you mean you felt the same sensation Viv gives you with her father?" Breckin asks, and bless him for saying something because my mouth feels as though it's filled with sawdust.

Mom clasps her hands over her head and pushes her hair back with a deep sigh. Her blue eyes plead with mine when she faces me. "I'm sorry I didn't tell you."

"Tell me what?" I ask, punctuating each word.

"I didn't go after him. He found me in a bar. Nothing special, but when I saw what he was, I didn't walk away. I'd hoped—"

Anticipation sends a wave of electricity across my skin. I'm antsy and itchy and altogether uncomfortable about what she might say.

"He was an angel, Viv."

"That's impossible." I turn to Breckin. "Isn't that impossible?"

"I . . . uh, I don't know. I've been told not all Nephilim have angelic traits, but considering . . ." He trails off.

For weeks now, Elias has told me that the easiest way to tap into my angel side was when my emotions are high. If there's ever the perfect time, this is it. The porcelain angel from my childhood returns to my memory. No wonder she got rid of it one year without warning. It must have freaked her out watching me stare at it so obsessively.

"Viv, sweetie?" Hands touch my arms, and I slap them away.

"Don't," my voice says, but I'm not here. I'm floating above this scene. My emotions are too frantic to process. My father was an angel. My mother knew. She lied to me.

"Vivie?" I turn my face into the heat that is Breckin's touch on my cheek. His snow-and-pine scent comforts me. "Clear your thoughts. This is just another hurdle we'll figure out together." I blink twice, and his face comes into focus. "Hey, you," he says with a smile.

My bottom lip trembles at the tenderness.

"We've got this, Viv." His brows lift like he's verifying I'm all right.

"Yeah. Yeah, I'm okay."

He leans closer and brushes a kiss near my temple. "I'm going to call Elias."

I'm cold the minute Breckin leaves the room. I walk around my bed and look out my window. A light snow falls, the white flakes sparkling as they hit the ground. I'm so ready for spring.

"What was his name?" I ask, keeping my gaze outside. "Was it Sam, or was that a lie too?"

Her reflection in the glass moves closer. "That was the name he gave me."

"And he showed himself to you? That's how you know he was an angel?"

She moves closer. "Viv, sit with me," she says softly as her hand closes around mine.

We move to my bed, and I climb into the middle and sit cross-legged while she pulls one leg up and hangs the other off the side. There are dark shadows under her eyes. She slept today, but working nights takes its toll on her. Or maybe the tired look has more to do with me lately.

"You're not a child anymore, but I still hate admitting my failures to you. I was alone in Denver. Sure, I'd made friends, but I was unhappy. I had no family. Your father cozied up to me one night at a bar when I needed someone to talk to. He was charming and gorgeous, and I felt drawn to him. I did try to walk away, but he followed after me.

"That was when I saw what he was. We'd been dancing, and that tug I told Breckin about, it wouldn't stop. I remember the ache still. I thought I was having a heart attack at twenty-two."

I bite the inside of my cheek and rub my palm over my own heart. "I know it well," I tell her. "When I'm away from Breckin, I can't get back to him quick enough. The angel side of me fights to be with him. I have no power over it."

Her eyes shine. "You're not supposed to be that in love at seventeen," she says with a hint of sadness. "You're your own person now. You don't need me anymore."

"That isn't true. I'll always need a mom." My free hand covers our clasped ones. "I just need a mom who will be truthful with me."

With a sniff, she continues, "That feeling scared me, Viv. I ran from him and hurried to my car. I was about to start my engine when he appeared in the parking lot. He was searching for me, his head turning every which way, and that's when I saw his wings. He turned, and they shot out of his back, these massive black wings with midnight blue and deep purples streaking the shiny feathers. I got maybe fifteen seconds before he disappeared"—she snaps her fingers—"poof. Like that.

"For some reason, I didn't freak out and hightail it out of there. Something deep inside me knew that him being an angel wasn't so out of the ordinary. I went back inside. I went back to the bar, sat down, and waited. Soon enough, he showed up. After a few drinks, I took him home with me."

When a child asks how their parents met, they expect to hear some funny tidbit followed by a love story, or something about sparks igniting and eyes never straying again . . . they don't expect to hear the sordid details of a one night stand.

"No wonder you gave me so many safe-sex talks growing up."

"He didn't use his powers against me, Viv. He may have used his charm to get me to dance and to get a few kisses, but once I saw his wings, I wanted that moment with him. I'm ashamed to admit it excited me."

"Well, I would say you got excitement, about nine months later, right?" I say, not kindly.

"Viv?" Breckin knocks on the frame of my bedroom door. "Sorry, I talked to Elias, and we're thinking you two should come over to the house for the night."

"Yeah, we can do that," I reply, not giving Mom the chance to argue. She rubs her palms down her thighs and stands with me, giving me a nod of consent.

THIRTY MINUTES LATER, we're parking Mom's car in Breckin's garage next to his Bronco. Mom and I have lived in our little two-bedroom apartment forever, and seeing the open awe on her face as Breckin walks us through his beautiful home hurts my heart. She loves beauty as much as I do, but money is scarce.

We stop at the staircase to the basement. Breckin touches my back. "Want to take her downstairs? I'll be right there."

"So this is where you two spend all your time?" she asks as I flip the light switch and lead her into what has become my safe space.

"There's a bathroom and bedroom over there, a full kitchen." I point everything out for her. "I'll put our bags in the guest room, since I'm sure that's where he wants us."

"Is his house warded or protected somehow? Is that why he wanted you here?"

"Us, Mom," I call over my shoulder as I drop our bags on the large bed. "He wants us here. And I don't know if it's protected. He's always brought me down here. I think having only one way in or out, and it being underground helps him feel like he can better protect me."

"And can he? Protect you?"

"I will, or I'll die trying," answers Breckin as he descends the staircase with Elias at his back.

Mom stiffens. "Can you die? I mean differently than a full-blooded angel?"

The idea is a knife through my chest.

"He won't die," I say. My head held high, I look at Breckin like I'm ordering him to survive whatever comes our way. Death is not an option. I want forever with this angel. He winks, and a thrilling surge of tingles run up my spine.

Feeling slightly mollified, now that I've made my position clear on his leaving me, I introduce Elias. It's a silly formality, because they've known each other around town for years, and he's watched her and our family line since before either of us were born, as Breckin explained to her on our drive here. She said she already knew, because of Phaedra's journal.

"So I understand you are the reason I've made it through life relatively unscathed?" Mom asks, her voice shaking. "I have to admit, once I knew I had my own guardian angel, I was a little more careless with myself."

The gruff angel flashes a half smile filled with emotion before he motions toward the couch. "Shall we?"

Breckin and I exchange looks. What did he and Elias speak about before they came downstairs? Breckin sits in the oversized chair closest to the fireplace, grabbing my hand and pulling me into the space next to him, as Mom takes the couch and Elias takes the other chair closer to her.

"We should let them speak," Breckin whispers as his arm goes around my shoulders and tucks me into his side.

Their body language is uncomfortable times one thousand as they settle into their seats. Mom presses a hand to her throat, her forehead wrinkling as she studies Elias.

"I would like to read Phaedra's journal," Elias finally says, scratching the beard at his jaw.

"Of course."

As if that agreement from my mother was all he needed, Elias relaxes. His shoulders fall, and he sinks back into his chair.

"Rachel, we need to know about Viv's father. I'm sure it's not easy to talk about, but if he was an angel . . ." He trails off, a wave of emotions once again sweeping over his features.

Rubbing her arms and tucking her legs up beside her, she begins. "We met at this bar in Denver . . ."

Elias listens intently to the almost word-for-word retelling of the story she gave me in my bedroom at the apartment. Breckin's attention to her story tells me he didn't listen in on us after he left my room to make his phone call. His fingers play mindlessly up and down my bicep as he listens, making my eyes heavy. Like Elias, he remains silent, but his expressive face gives me all the clues I need to know what's playing in his mind. There are too many unanswered questions for his liking.

"And you never saw him again?" Elias asks when she finishes.

"I did not."

"Viv's birth was hard on you," Elias states rather than asks.

That nudges me from the sleepy spell Breckin's caress put me in. "It was?"

Of course Elias knows. He watched over us.

Mom's wide gaze shifts to Breckin and me like she forgot we're here. "It wasn't easy, but you were worth it."

Her soft smile says so much. The pain, the uncertainty . . . the love she feels for me is worth it all. My arm tightens around Breckin's stomach. I know the feeling well.

"It makes sense. I'm unaware of a human living after giving birth to an angel's child, but you did. That part of you that holds Phaedra's blood must have protected you."

"Wait," Breckin says. "What does that mean for Viv? Will having kids be difficult for her?"

Mom chokes as Elias releases a throaty growl. "Is that a concern right now?" he asks with a scowl.

I'm shaking my head and sitting up, but Breckin has apparently lost his mind. "Well, at this moment, no, but since we're discussing it . . . it's something I'd like to know. I wouldn't want to put her at risk."

I hiss his name as the mom glare hits me from across the room.

"You do know the sure way to keep her from risk, don't you, Breckin?" Elias asks tersely.

"I'm not sure if I remember. Will you remind me?"

Mom gives a dainty snort, breaking the tension in the room, and I shove Breckin sideways. Elias shakes his head with a light laugh.

"We don't need to discuss any of this right now. No concerns. None at all," I reiterate, giving Mom a serious look. "I'm barely adjusting to the idea of not being human, let alone the idea of having little angel babies someday."

Breckin's jaw drops. "You don't want to have little Breckins with me?"

"Breckin," Elias snaps. "Can we please be serious here?"

"I am being serious. I have every intention of marrying this girl and having a big, happy, normal angel family someday."

My eyes roll because he's being ridiculous, but it's also ridiculously sweet, and I do want that. I want a future with him.

We'll have one, he says in my head.

Elias and Mom share an unreadable look. Parent looks, I suppose. This wasn't the future Mom and I dreamed about over the years, but it's the one presenting itself. If we make it through the next few weeks.

"So, what about the feeling Rachel described?" Breckin asks, getting back to the real point of our meeting. "It sounds similar to the tug between Viv and me. Could it—"

"We don't have souls, Breckin. You know that." Elias steeples his fingers. "Maybe it was some other bond, though? I'm not sure."

Mom clears her throat. "I feel it now." She meets Elias's blue eyes and tilts her head, her hand once again going to her throat. "I've felt it since the moment you walked in."

ON MY OWN

BRECKIN

*E*lias jerks backward like he's been slapped. His jaw drops.

"It's not romantic in nature," Rachel rushes. "It's just . . . gravitational. It's strongest when I'm around Viv, but I've felt it around Breckin, too."

"What?" I sit forward, nearly knocking Vivienne to the floor in my haste. I shoot her an apologetic grin and turn back to her mother. "Why? What? Why?"

Vivienne squeezes my thigh. "You said those words already."

Elias blows out a deep breath and stands to pace the room.

"In all the years I've been around you on and off, Elias, I've never felt it. Same with Breckin"—she looks at me—"I didn't notice anything until the last few weeks. I thought maybe it was because you were around more often. I know you're an angel, so I didn't think much about it."

"Viv's angel side is trying to talk to yours," Elias says. He stops pacing, his gaze meeting each of ours. "You share the same makeup. She knows it's in there, and she's talking to you."

Well, shit. "That's horror movie kind of stuff," I say with a cringe.

"No, Breckin, that's celestial kind of stuff. Angels were created as brothers and sisters. We call for each other naturally." His mouth twists, then he looks to Rachel again. "Maybe you're feeling this tug to Breckin and me because of Phaedra. We were . . . close."

Her name drips with pain every time it leaves his lips. What exactly is their story? And how does Hamon fit into it?

"Okay, but wait." Vivienne holds up a hand. "I hear what you're saying, Elias. Mom and I share the same blood, so my angelic side talks to hers. I guess I can see where maybe it's waking hers up, like Breckin woke mine. And hers is trying to get to you two because you're you, and well, Breckin has Hamon's blood. You were all connected." She ticks off each point on her fingers, her forehead creased. "But what about my father? Why would she have felt that way with him? Especially way back then, when her gene was still asleep. Where's the connection?"

Elias nods thoughtfully, taking in her points. "I'm not sure we're going to have all the answers. Everything is speculation here. It always has been."

Could there not be some Angel 101 book lying around that would tell us how this all works? They were created, they fell, they're cut off. Those are the only absolutes I've ever known. Hell, even us thinking we're soul mates may not be accurate. Maybe the bond we share is something else. Maybe it wasn't my healing Vivienne that changed her —maybe Death did. There is no one who can tell us for sure what we want to know. Elias goes by what he's seen through centuries of living, much of which he's never adequately described to me, because he says there is no way to adequately describe the creation of the world and his place in it before he came here.

Rachel rubs her arms as she stands. "Let me get the journal for you."

Elias's gaze tracks her movement across the room, his face blank. Once she disappears into the guest bedroom, he turns to the fireplace and stares into the flames with a deep frown.

I move to his side and watch the fire with him. "If her father is an angel, why didn't she show any signs? Hell, she's got the blood of two angels within . . . shouldn't she have developed some gifts?"

He massages the back of his neck. "I understand Phaedra, but—"

"Why?" I hiss a little harsher than intended. From the corner of my eye, I catch Vivienne stand. Her brows reach her hairline, lifted in question, as she joins us. She hates being left out of these things. Lacing my pinky and ring finger with hers, I ask Elias the question I probably should have asked weeks ago. "There isn't an age to our angelic blood. You've told me that before. It doesn't pass down the way traits do in humans. It doesn't get weaker the further you are from the original DNA, right?" The wrinkles at the edge of Elias's eyes deepen, and I forge on. "So my child, and his, and his, and his, forever and ever will always bear Hamon's blood. Why was Phaedra's any different?"

Vivienne shakes her fingers free of mine and moves in front of Elias, putting her back to the fireplace. He's a good half a foot shorter than me, but he's still a head taller than her. Add in his bulky build next to her diminutive frame, and he looks like he could swallow her whole. Her delicate hand touches his arm tenderly. "Elias, I can tell the history you've kept from Breckin is painful. I'm sure you had a good reason for it, but now we need to know. You know we do."

He remains silent.

"You said she was stripped of her angelic markers. What does that mean? How does that even happen?" Vivienne asks.

His look is all the answer I need, but Vivienne can't read him the way I can.

"It was God, Vivie," I say as Rachel returns to the room. "The Creator punished her. There is no other way to strip an angel of their power. They're divine. Even the fallen and damned don't lose all their abilities. They just use them for the wrong purposes."

"What did she do that was so bad?" Vivienne's face mirrored Elias's. Pain. The kind of pain that embeds into the marrow of your bones and siphons you dry. He turns away, his head dropping.

"She never would tell me," he confesses, the rasp of his voice scratching across my heart. *Why so much pain?* Even Vivienne swipes at the lashes beneath her eyes as she looks from me to her mother.

"Actually," Rachel says, speaking with the subdued tone of a medical professional who has relayed diagnoses—both bad and good

MICHELE G. MILLER

—hundreds of times to overwrought families. She holds out an accordion style binder. "I keep everything in here. The original entries are tattered and difficult to read, but along the way, they were rewritten. I suppose to preserve the words. She wrote it all in there."

Elias barely glances up as he takes the binder into his hands. "Thank you."

For the longest time the only sound in the room comes from the soft flames of the gas fire. I break the silence. "Go."

Realizing he has been the focus of three pairs of eyes, Elias straightens.

"Go on upstairs and read it. We can talk more tomorrow."

With a murmured goodnight, Elias leaves, taking the steps two at a time and closing the door at the top. Vivienne leans against my back and yawns. It's three in the morning.

Reaching behind my back and pulling her arm around my waist, I rub her forearm.

"You two should probably get some sleep," I suggest. Rachel laughs softly. Clearly, a seventeen-year-old telling her to go to bed is humorous. "Sorry, I don't mean to be disrespectful."

Rachel's already waving my apology off when Vivienne butts in. "Sure he does. Breckin has a thing with being overprotective. You'll get used to it, Mom." She stretches to her toes and kisses my cheek. "I'm gonna brush my teeth, then you can wash up," she tells her mother.

"Thank you for that, Breckin." Rachel's voice pulls my gaze from watching Vivienne's backside walk away.

"I feel like I'm the one who should be thanking you"—I smile and jerk my head toward the bathroom—"for that."

She gives a huff of laughter. "You love her."

"More than anything." I can't express that sentiment strongly enough. "It sounds stupid, doesn't it? We're teens."

"Well, you're not exactly normal teens, though, are you?"

"No, we aren't. I grew up knowing about Heaven and Hell. The real stories. And Viv . . . well, she's pretty focused."

"Breckin, you don't have to justify yourselves. I can see how much you care for each other. I appreciate the way you protect my daughter,

186

especially now. It was my biggest fear when I became pregnant. It's why I remained in Havenwood Falls after I came back. I wanted to protect her from him."

Which reminds me. "How did you make your way back here? You said your memories were gone." As angels, or half angels, the wards don't work on us, but Phaedra's gene wasn't active in Rachel before Vivienne's came alive. No one recognized the Freemans for the angel gene they had within.

Rachel nods. "The wards . . . yes. I have two theories on that. My best answer is your uncle, as Viv likes to call him. Elias watched over me back then, right? Perhaps he compelled me to return when he saw my predicament?"

That makes sense. Elias would have wanted Rachel here, where he felt it safest for her.

"And second," she says, ticking off each thought on her fingers, "in the journal, Phaedra wrote about a promise she made to three witches to protect and watch over a canyon. A canyon that became the seat of Havenwood Falls much later."

Seems like Rachel has had the answers to Vivienne's quest for the history of her family and this town all along. "So you think maybe her promise to them forged a bond between your family line and the magic here?"

"Perhaps." She rubs her arms. "Breckin, there are things in that journal . . . explanations Phaedra made that will affect Elias and Hamon. For the better, I think. I—"

The lock on the bathroom door snaps, and Vivienne walks out. "Your turn."

Rachel looks at me and smiles. Whatever she intended to say fades as she pats Vivienne's head and grabs her things before heading into the bathroom.

When the bathroom door clicks closed, Vivienne grins. She pulls on the sleeves of her nightshirt, tugging them over her palms. The mischievous gleam in her eyes awakens the angel, who's behaved so well tonight. The taste of her minty mouth is permanently etched on my tongue. I long to draw her close and dive in.

187

"So, where are you going to be while I'm in there?" she asks, pointing toward the guest room.

I've been by her side every night since the week I healed her. That's over one hundred days of feeling her heart beat while she sleeps.

"I guess I'll be setting up camp on the couch here."

"This couch?" she purrs, her hand skimming along my side and around my back as she circles me and moves around to the front of the couch. "This very wide couch that I already know from personal experience can fit two people comfortably?"

"Vivie?"

With a wink, she scurries into the other room, returning with pillows and a blanket. Tossing the pillows on the couch, she tugs at me. When I resist, she pouts prettily. "I want to be with you."

The angel takes the bait. Snatching her close, my fingers press into her hips. "Me, too, but your mom—"

"Will be fine. We're just laying here. Sleep, nothing more."

She has no idea how difficult that is. While she sleeps, her soft body pressed up against mine, I lay awake imagining all the things that I want to do to her.

"Breckin," she gasps, her eyes wide. "Do you really?"

"Do I really what?" I ask, confused, then it hits me. "Crap, you heard my thoughts, didn't you?" The apples of her porcelain cheeks stain pink as she nods. "I'm sorry—"

My apology dies as a vision of the two of us together pops into my mind. My spine vibrates with the need to release my wings as Vivienne's skin shines in the moonlight. We're on a beach, the waves lapping at our skin as our mouths, then bodies, come together in pure bliss.

"That's what I see"—she cups my cheek and the vision dies—"someday, Breck. Just us. We don't have to rush this, because I know it will happen, and it will be divine perfection."

Divine perfection. That is what we are. Souls destined to meet, angels destined to love. We come from the fallen and the damned, and yet we've been given *this.*

I brush her lips carefully. "Someday."

THE DARK OF YOU

VIVIENNE

"*D*o you feel a vibration within your chest? Like a pulse, humming with energy?"

I clench my eyes tighter and dig deeper. Imagining invisible fingers, I peel away skin and muscles in search of the missing piece. It's a game of Operation, my mind visualizing the tweezers picking through my body. She's there, somewhere within my makeup, but I can't reach her.

My head falls back to the couch, a deep exhale leaving my lungs. "I can't."

Breckin's hand rubs my knee. "How do you read my thoughts, or project your feelings to me?"

I rub my temples. "I don't know. That just happens. I don't control it."

"Vivie, we need to get to her. I need for you to be able to protect yourself. We have two weeks." Frustration coats his words.

"Do you think I don't know that?" I snap. Breckin leans forward with a low growl. He digs his fingers through his hair angrily, and I grab at his arm. "Sorry. I know you're trying to help. Why are you so grouchy about it this morning, though?"

. . .

I woke on the couch alone, the basement nearly black without windows to allow the morning sun. My mind struggled to place where I was, until I turned and saw Breckin's faint silhouette hovering over me. The fireplace burned on low behind him, and my heart slammed into my ribs at the haunted look he wore.

"Breckin?" I pushed to a sitting position and turned around. The guest bedroom door was closed. "What are you doing?"

"I need you to work on your abilities." His tone was serious.

"Okay. I have been working on them, but if—" He shakes his head before I finish, so I clamp my jaw shut.

"No, Vivienne. We need to work harder. I need you to access your power, if you have any."

"If?"

"Why aren't you feeling them? You are the blood of two angels. Obviously, it's in there—we've seen glimpses of it. You have to pull it out and take control."

"DAMN IT." He scrubs his hands over his face. We've been at this for more than an hour. He's attempted explaining the feelings until he's blue in the face, and I've concentrated so hard, my head wants to explode. Still nothing. "I had a . . . I guess it was a vision, last night."

His fingers bear down on his forehead like he can rub whatever image he sees out of his mind, and I purse my lips to stop from interrupting. My leg bounces as my nerves crank into gear.

"You were screaming. That's not even the right word. It was piercing. Your terror ripped me open and wrenched my heart out. There was so much . . ." His jaw clenched. "I just need you to be able to protect yourself. What if I can't be with you all the time? What if another Zeke shows up?"

"Who's Zeke?"

I spin at Mom's voice.

"No one." There's no reason to upset her. Breckin is upset enough for twenty overprotective mothers.

"He was a fallen who attacked Viv last month," Breckin says.

I throw him a dirty look as Mom walks around the couch and sinks to the edge of the chair, brows raised.

"Hamon killed him, but not before Zeke broke her leg in two places. I healed her," he further explains.

Anger mixed with fear burns in her eyes. "I thought you were protecting her."

"Mom." I wrap a hand around Breckin's thigh. "I forced him and Elias to let me go that day. They've followed me every second of every day since this whole thing began. I needed a day. I thought it would be fine."

Breckin ignores me and meets her gaze. "You're right, Rachel. I shouldn't have let her out of my sight. I won't make that mistake again, but even with me at her side . . . If we're attacked, she needs her own strength."

The urge to throw something hits me. I know I need my own strength, but maybe I don't have any. Maybe the glowing, and the speed, and the sensing other creatures were all flukes. Maybe I'm a lemon. The angel who would never be.

"Is there something after her? After either of you?" Mom asks.

Breckin's mouth opens, then closes as his head tips up. A moment later, the door opens from upstairs, and Elias comes down into the basement. His hair is a tangled mess, like he spent the night ripping his fingers through it. He snaps his attention to Mom, stopping in front of her, pages gripped in his hand.

"You took her to the Court?" Anger and accusation color his words. Breckin leaps to his feet and grabs at Elias's arm, but the older angel shrugs him off. "What did they do to her, Rachel? What did you have them do?"

"Elias." My voice isn't half as scary as his when I jump in front of him. Mom shrinks back in her chair, her face pale and eyes wide. "You have no right to speak to her that way."

The man who has always shown such care and calm around me looks like he wants to snap a few necks. I worry I'm one of them as his blue eyes scan my face. Our stares clash for what feels like a full minute before he shakes his head and slides back.

"Tell your daughter what you did."

Mom touches the back of my leg, nudging me to the side so she can stand. With her fists clenched at her sides, she holds her head high as she says, "I did what I thought I had to do to protect her."

The world spins.

"When I found out I'd become pregnant, the reality of what I'd done hit me. I had no idea what type of angel Sam was. I had no idea what she would be. I ran home, to Havenwood Falls, and I went to Rose for help."

Okay. I breathe in, then out. *Rose Howe, the witch. That's fine. She mentioned her friendship last night. Breathe, Viv.*

"And Rose brought me to the Court. I don't know who they were. They didn't let me see them, because I'm human. I don't know how Rose convinced them to speak with me, but she did. They felt the darkness."

"He's aligned with Hell?" Breckin asks as I stand there shocked.

Mom blinks. "Yes, they said he wasn't an angel of Heaven, but was damned. A demon of Hell."

I can't hold my temper. "Demon?" I gasp. "You said he was an angel. You saw his wings."

She's a deer in headlights as she looks between us. Clearly, she has no idea. She was a stupid young woman who slept with an angel in the hopes of awakening her own angelic gene. Apparently, she didn't have the sense to consider consequences, or protection, at the time.

Elias's hand falls on her shoulder, and I want to slap it off. *Don't comfort her. Look what she's done.* Tears blur my eyes.

"Viv," Elias says softly. "What the Court meant was fallen angels who align with Hell are no better than demons. They may be born of Heaven, but if they choose Hell, the darkness and corruption turns their insides to ash and flames. They're damned. They lose all chance of redemption."

My stomach cramps. *Does that make me . . . ? Am I . . .*

"The reaper," Breckin murmurs. With a curse, he stalks to the kitchen and slams his hand on the white marble countertop so hard, I'm afraid we'll find a crack later. "Sebastian knew she was different.

That night up on the mountain, he asked if she would join me or if she would turn her back on her calling. I assumed he was insulting me and saying he thought I was damned, because I'm Nephilim. That he was asking if I would turn her to Hell. But, that can't be . . . reapers can read our alliance. That's their job. Sebastian knew I had no plans of turning to Hell. He knew I wouldn't swear allegiance to Hamon."

Elias sucks in a breath. "The reaper used that knowledge to align himself with Hamon. That's why your father killed him."

Their explanations and line of thinking feel like a merry-go-round. I can't keep up. "You're saying Sebastian was actually asking if you would turn me away from Hell? He thought I was aligned with Hell, that Hell is my calling?"

Panic weighs me down. Elias and Mom speak at the same time, but my eyes lock on Breckin's, needing him to tell me what he thinks. His hands cup my face and draw me closer as he shakes his head. "Vivie, we can't trust anything he said, but the fact that he asked which way you would turn tells us he didn't know. I think that's why he wanted you so badly. Your allegiance isn't chosen."

My throat burns with unshed tears. "Sure it is." I cover his hands and press my forehead to his. "I choose you. I choose us."

"And I choose you. It doesn't matter who your father is."

"But is that why I'm not evolving?" I pull back and turn to Elias. "Would my father's blood stop Phaedra's?"

"No, it's all still celestial blood. You may have an affinity for darkness, thanks to his choice, but you're still part angel. The Court could have affected it, though," Elias says.

The Court. We're back where this began. Mom brought me to the Court, the true governing body of Havenwood Falls, as Breckin had explained before.

Elias waves the journal in his hand. "Rachel, you wrote in the journal that the Court said they would try to help her. What exactly did you ask of them?"

"I asked if they could help hide her. I knew about the memory wards on the town, and how they have spells to protect different species. I figured they had to have something that would keep her safe.

Keep anyone from knowing she is part angel. They took a sample of my blood, then they made me leave the room."

"I've never scented another angel gene in her . . . for the Court to hide it from us, they would need a lot of magic. They took your blood? They covered her parentage. It had to be a blood binding. I need to speak to them, find out who was there and what happened."

He's halfway up the stairs before Breckin runs after him. "E, wait!"

I shoot Mom a glance and take off after Breckin.

"What does that mean?" Breckin asks as I catch up to them by the front door.

Elias looks at me as he answers. "They probably bound your angel DNA up in your mother's blood. Covered it. Shifters and other creatures think you're human. We didn't notice, and I've been around you your entire life. It means that the reason you can't access your angel side could be because it's trapped within their spell. Breckin may have weakened the spell when he healed you, but your DNA is still tied up."

"Can that be reversed?" Breckin asks.

Elias waits for a beat before answering, "Most magic can, so I would think so, but there's a price."

"What price?"

"If your father is looking for you, Vivienne, or if the fallen or damned who know him find you—they will sense his blood in you. You won't be able to hide."

WAR OF HEARTS

BRECKIN

*I*t's been hours since Elias left. Vivienne and Rachel alternate between pleasant conversation and full on World War III battles, sending me from the basement to the first floor of the house. I wander the empty rooms, doing my best to keep my thoughts to myself.

Vivienne's father makes no difference to me. Fallen or damned, she is mine and she is good. My father, though . . . something Elias said downstairs nags at me.

"The reaper used that knowledge to align himself with Hamon. That's why your father killed him."

It meant little in the moment, with everything being thrown at us, but now . . . now I want to know more. Elias has pushed for me to talk to Hamon for weeks. I pull my cell phone from my pocket and pull up the number I have for him. My fingers hover over the keyboard. *What do I say?* I type out a text.

Thank you for saving Vivienne. We should talk.

It's not groundbreaking, but it's something. I've never reached out to him myself. Elias has been our connection my entire life. I didn't even have a way of reaching him until a year ago, when Elias was dealing with something for the Court and worried about me having no one if something should happen to him. At the time, I figured having no one wasn't much different than having Hamon. Maybe I shouldn't be so quick to judge anymore.

The binder Rachel handed Elias last night with Phaedra's story is nowhere to be found. I search drawers and closets, thinking he stuffed it away for safekeeping. The story has me curious. I could ask Rachel, but Elias's adamant refusal to tell me the entire story without Hamon present prevents me from doing so.

I rejoin Rachel and Vivienne downstairs, and we mindlessly watch television and wait in silence for Elias to return with news from the Court. Hamon never responds to my text.

It's after dark when the sound of Elias's truck pulling into the driveway has me charging upstairs. His face is ragged when he meets me at the back door.

"What's wrong?" My muscles flex at the stress rolling off him.

"Vivienne needs to come with me. The witches have agreed to undo the spell."

"So, there was a spell? What did they do?" I ask as Rachel and Vivienne's footsteps sound on the stairs. For a moment, I worry Elias won't speak. I'm so used to secrets between us, but this involves all of us.

Scattered thoughts invade my mind. *Vivienne.* She's flipping through every emotion possible with no filter. She doesn't have the control to keep them to herself. My wings strain against my skin, always yearning for her, as Elias blows out a deep breath.

"Yes, there was a spell. We can discuss it later. I need to take her now."

"Now?" Vivienne asks as she stands beside me. She wraps her arm around mine and leans into me. Rachel takes a spot on her other side, her face a mask of worry.

"Why the urgency, Elias?" I demand.

"I spoke to your father earlier, Breckin. There are things . . . We've been planning for issues to arise because of you, for years—"

I swallow the little moisture left in my dry mouth. "Issues because of me?"

"There's so much you don't know. The legions of damned would like more than anything to get the son of Hamon in their clutches. They know you exist now. There's been movement."

Zeke. Jack saying there were damned hanging around . . . "How?"

Elias's gaze lands on Vivienne, and she leans closer. "Sebastian didn't have to speak to many. He put the bug in someone's ear, and it moved through the chain. Hamon coming here to help you when he did, it brought attention to Havenwood Falls."

"I don't understand. Hamon is one of them. He works with the fallen. Why would they want Breckin? Why was it necessary to keep him in hiding all these years?" Vivienne asks.

"He works with the *fallen*, Viv. Not the damned," Elias points out. "There is a distinction. And we hid Breckin to protect him."

"From what?" Vivienne pushes.

Elias looks over his shoulder, and my gaze follows. Is he expecting something? I step forward, subtly shielding Vivienne. "Hamon's not who you think he is—"

"Stop." I draw away from Vivienne's grasp. "You keep saying that, but you never say more. I have seventeen years that say he's exactly what I think he is, E. If you want me to change my opinion, it's time you tell me what's going on."

Elias tosses his head back and sighs.

"Breckin," he says my name low. When he looks at me again, it's with all the understanding of the father he's been. He knows my struggles. He's been here for them. And he's been with Hamon since the beginning. Literally. He bridges the distance between us and clasps my arm affectionately. "He was trying to keep you safe, but by doing so, he forfeited his right to be what you needed him to be. He knows this. In the beginning, when you were born, I tried to get him to stay, but he was set on revenge."

"Revenge?" *Against whom?*

His hand squeezes my bicep. "Look, we don't have time to discuss this right now. I told Addie Viv and I would be at the meeting spot by now."

"Wait." Vivienne finally speaks up. "Addie? Addie Beaumont is a witch?"

Elias and I merely look at her, and she holds her hands up in surrender.

"We need to go," Elias says again.

"Fine. Let's grab shoes and coats and go. We can discuss Hamon on the way." I turn, but Elias stops me.

"Only Viv and I can go."

My gaze meets Vivienne's before I turn to Elias with a laugh. "I'm sorry?"

"You're not going."

"Like hell, I'm not going. You are not taking my soul mate to have some crazy ritual done by witches without me there."

Elias steps closer, his stocky physique making up for his lack of height when he stands in my face. His features harden. "You are not going."

Bad idea. The feeling screams at me. This isn't smart. I can't let her go. I step back, and Elias steps forward. He holds my gaze, his eyes silently telling me to calm down.

"I don't like this."

"I know you don't." He looks at Rachel and Vivienne, who are both standing there with different expressions. Vivienne watches me, her teeth tugging at her lip. Rachel's crossed her arms over her stomach, her mouth in a straight line. "The coven doesn't have to do this, Breckin. It's a favor. You know I won't let anything happen to her."

The vision I had while Vivienne slept replays. The darkness punctuated by her screams. "Give us a sec?" I ask.

Taking Vivienne's hand, I lead her to the office in the back of the house. It's the only room on the first floor that provides privacy, besides the guest room. Shutting the massive doors behind us, I lean against the wood and watch her.

"You think I should do this, right?" she asks after a moment.

"I don't know what other choice we have. If those witches did something to your blood that affects your angel side, we need it removed. I need you at one hundred percent." *All this time I've wondered why our soul bond didn't click sooner. Was it this spell?*

Her mouth twists. "What if this is me at one hundred percent?"

Before she can blink, I've grabbed her and twisted her around until she's pressed to the door and I'm hovering over her, my arms caging her in.

"Do you remember the first time we stood this way?" I ask, recalling the fear in her beautiful face that night.

She tugs my hips closer as she smiles. "You accosted me in the bathroom at Burger Bar."

"That I did." My lips brush her forehead. "Do you remember what I said?"

"You said you've got me."

I smile at her breathy tone as she repeats my words.

"I do. If you don't evolve fully, then I've got you, Vivie. We'll leave if we have to, go into hiding. No one will take you from me."

Our gazes hold in a moment of silence. She sees clear through me —through the layers of walls I've built around a heart that's never known love—and touches the very core of who I am. *I am hers.* I stroke her cheek. *And she is mine.*

"Hey, I was thinking." She tips her head back against the door and bats her pretty lashes. "How would you like to be my prom date?"

"I thought we weren't making plans." I tried asking her about prom a month ago when the posters began popping up in the halls at school. She refused to plan. She wanted to wait until after my birthday.

Her arms tighten around my back. "I changed my mind. Let's make plans. If we make plans, it means everything is going to work out."

"Everything *is* going to work out," I promise as my mouth descends on hers. We kiss until Elias shouts our names, then I kiss her some more. Memorizing the shape and feel of her lips beneath mine. The satin of the skin at the back of her neck. The ginger smell of her hair. "I love you, Vivie," I tell her, before I walk her outside and watch her drive away with Elias.

RISE

VIVIENNE

J'm blindfolded and sitting in the middle of a ritual circle in the wilderness alone. Well, not alone—with witches. Real witches. Oh, at night. Because it wouldn't be scary enough without adding the nocturnal animal sounds. A twig snaps to my right, and I jerk to the left, nearly toppling over. *Get a grip, Viv.* Murmurs reach my ears. Are they doing the spell now? I pull my knees closer to my chest. Addie said to sit here and be still. And no matter what, I'm to keep my mouth shut. Message received.

The steady rush of the waterfalls in the distance gives me a slight reference point for my location. Finally, when I'm unsure if I can take another minute in the dark, goosebumps tease my arms as the snow-muted crunch of footsteps approaches. There's a dim glow through the dark blindfold I wear. Candles? They're witches; surely that's it. A bitter aroma permeates the air, burning my nose, as voices chant. No introductions then? Okay.

"Lie back, Vivienne," someone says.

I do as they say but my mind can't stop wondering who these women are. Cressida is a nymph, the Kasuns are shifters, Jack Peters is a hellhound. Which of my classmates are witches? *Rose Howe!* Is Scarlet Howe a witch like her mother?

Little they say or do makes sense to me. Where's Elias? He blindfolded me the moment we were out of Breckin's sight, saying it was a requirement of the witches. I tried following along with his turns as we drove, but it was impossible. We weren't on the road long and the falls are near, so we're either off a street in Havenwood Heights or off Alverson Road. Addie met us when we got out of the truck and walked us through the grass and woods before telling Elias he'd come far enough. He'd pumped my hand for courage, then let go, allowing Addie to guide me the rest of the way.

A cool hand takes mine, and I flinch when something sharp pricks my finger. Addie warned me beforehand, but it doesn't lessen the shock.

"Sanguinem dimittere eam."

"Ea sanguis revelare."

"Revelare in sanguine suo."

A sharp pang hits my chest and spreads through my torso as my limbs twitch uncontrollably. The voices continue.

"Potestatem dimittere."

"Angelus revelare."

"Virtutem revelare."

Behind the words I can't understand are more chants. Constant and musical, the soft words lull me into relaxation, even as the pain in my chest grows. My back arches off the frozen ground as my spine pops. I bite my lip and suck in air. The chanting accelerates, becoming louder. Phrases like "light of the moon" and "power of the sisterhood" reach my ears, and I focus on them, instead of the inferno igniting my skin.

I grit my teeth. My ears pop, and a million sounds infiltrate my senses. And still the fire burns.

I slap the ground with my hands, searching for something to hang onto as the taste of the air coats my tongue and the aroma of the forest overwhelms my nose. And still the fire burns.

Writhing at the heat, I curl into a ball on my side. The witches' chants no longer reach me. My mind is focused on one thing, and that's the undeniable need to escape.

My hands long to claw at my skin. I want to rip open my chest and flee. I want to go home. I want to . . . I scream and kick at the ground.

Fight it, angel.

The voice is so clear, so divine, I still as tears fill my eyes.

Fight the darkness.

"Custodire a malo suo."

I thrash on the ground, curling into myself more when Breckin's scent hits me. He's on my coat and in my hair. Snow and pine. I inhale deeply and see his face. Breckin's words fill my head as a growl competes with his voice. A cold sensation trickles up my spine and over my shoulder, dousing the fire burning my insides.

The witches stop chanting.

"Custodire a malo suo," the main voice stands out once more. She repeats the phrase twice more. I whimper and fall into darkness.

"VIVIENNE?" I jerk at Elias's voice. "Viv?"

Heat washes over me as I open my eyes and look to the right. Elias stands in the open door of his truck, watching me. My breathing hitches. I'm in his truck. How did I get in his truck?

"Shhh." He cups the side of my head, my wet hair clinging to my face.

"What?" I ask on a shaky breath. "Where's Addie? What happened?"

"How do you feel?"

I blink once more, then shake my head. "I'm . . ."

A knife slashes through my chest, and I turn, gripping the dashboard as an agonizing feeling of brokenness invades my soul.

"Breckin," I gasp, black spots filling my vision.

Elias chuckles lightly and touches my arm. "Of course, let's go home." His face morphs from one to two, and I sway in my seat. His grin disappears. "Viv?"

A crunch so sickeningly painful and gloriously satisfying all at once fills my mind. The scent of smoldering embers fills my nostrils. "Oh, God . . . something's wrong, Elias."

Vivie!

His voice is as real as my own, and when he screams, I'm thrown forward, slamming my head into the dash, as my back is torn apart by a pair of wings.

Elias curses, catching me as I tumble from his truck and stumble forward. "What the . . . I have . . . those are . . ." I grab his arms for balance. My shock at having wings is crippled by the terror coursing through my veins. "Breckin?"

Vomit rises in my throat.

Elias steadies me. "What is it?"

"He's . . . he screamed. There was a horrible sound." The wings in my back toss about frantically. Elias's fingers dig into my skin as I straighten. "I'm gonna be sick," I manage on a gasp as the fracture of bones reverberates through my mind. My gut churns, though somewhere within me there's an odd rejoicing at the pain.

A light illuminates the darkness, and it takes a moment for my mind to process that it's coming from Elias's cellphone.

"Can you control those?" he asks as he shuffles me back toward his truck.

"Control them?" *Is he kidding me? I have freaking wings.* The beat of a bug's wings tickles my ear. My tongue catches the taste of the spray in the air from the falls. My angelic abilities are working at full speed. The dizziness comes in waves, ebbing and flowing through my body. Through the cell, I hear Breckin's voicemail pick up, and my wings go berserk again.

"He would have answered," Elias says, pocketing the phone and looking around. His head tips to the sky.

"Elias!" A shout comes out of the black night sky.

"Hamon," Elias mutters low. He grabs me and pushes me back, his body blocking mine a moment before Breckin's father lands.

"Are you two okay?" Hamon asks. In his hand is the glowing sword he used to end Zeke. "They have Breckin. The house was ransacked. He's here . . . I smell him."

A sudden anger invades my being, and Hamon's face snaps in my direction. His blue eyes narrow, and the sword wavers.

"Hamon, it's all right. It's her. It's Vivienne." Elias speaks in the voice of an adult soothing a child. He holds one arm in front of him while the other holds me tucked behind him. "He's not here."

Nothing Elias says makes sense. *Who's not here? Who's he?* I push at Elias, surprised when my strength moves his arm.

"Who has Breckin? What happened? My mother was at the house! Is she okay?" I toss the questions at Hamon as I unsteadily step out of Elias's shadow.

"Viv," Elias's warning halts my steps.

Hamon's face is at once handsome elegance and righteous fury. My gaze flicks to his fist wrapped tight around the hilt of the glowing angel blade, and my jaw tightens. His knuckles flex and relax while he watches every move I make. Somewhere within, an old sadness surfaces, and my throat tightens. *Is that Phaedra's blood?* My head whirls.

"Hamon, put the sword away," Elias says in that same warning tone.

Hamon looks between us. His eyes touch on every part of me, from my shoes to the tips of my new wings. The perusal stirs up the flame of rage inside my chest. Rage and sadness—the two are at war within me. A broken sob escapes my lips.

"I can feel them." I clutch Elias's shoulder and turn him to face me. "Phaedra's blood and my father's—it's like two creatures sharing my body. Is that normal? They're in my head, in my chest."

With a pleading look at Hamon, Elias takes my hand. "You'll learn to control them. I promise. I'll help you," he says.

"It worked, then. Her mother had her blood bound?" The angel blade disappears behind Hamon's wings before he steps forward. My body fights to both step closer and move farther away from him. "How did she know?" Hamon asks Elias as his eyes search my face.

"I don't think she did. She went to a friend, who took her to the Court. A member of the coven told her he was damned, but I don't think she knew who he was."

205

Hamon throws his head back.

"Is this your idea of divine intervention?" he shouts angrily at the sky.

"Are you talking about my father? About . . . Sam?" It takes me a moment to remember the name of the angel who fathered me. "Did you know him?"

"Know him?" Hamon spits the words out in a growl, and my muscles tense. I want to punch him. *Why do I want to punch Breckin's father? What is wrong with me?*

"Vivienne, your father—"

"Your father betrayed Heaven. He betrayed us. He is the reason Phaedra was killed," Hamon interrupts Elias. "He's the reason Breckin has remained hidden all these years."

My head shakes as bile once again burns the back of my throat.

"Your father has your soul mate, Vivienne. And I don't think he plans on giving him back."

JOURNEY (READY TO FLY)

VIVIENNE

"*T*hat's enough, Hamon," Elias says through clenched teeth. "What her father did back then isn't our main concern right now. Rachel was at the house. Did you see her?"

"I didn't go in. I saw the shattered glass, then I caught *his* scent." He jerks his chin my way. "I followed it."

My legs carry me forward, away from Elias and Hamon as they argue back and forth. Mom has to be all right. I would know if she wasn't. *Wouldn't I?* I clench my eyes closed and beg for her safety as Hamon's accusations overwhelm me. *My father took Breckin? He betrayed the angels behind me, killed Phaedra?* All these connections between my family and Breckin's—it's part of the plan . . .

"In human terms, it means we were matched to fulfill our destiny."

"Destiny?"

"C'mon, Viv. Don't tell me you don't believe in destiny? That people are put in places to make things happen, or sometimes bad things happen to good people because they need to learn a lesson that will bring them to something better?"

"I don't know what I believe in. Maybe things happen for a reason. Maybe it's coincidence."

"We're not a coincidence, Vivie."

Drawing a deep breath, I ask over my shoulder, "Where is he?"

Elias and Hamon are studying me when I turn around. What a sight I must be, with my half-shredded shirt, damp hair, and disobedient black wings. I roll my shoulders back and stretch my tiny frame taller.

"Where would he take Breckin?" I ask Hamon.

A cold mask slams down over Hamon's eyes. "That is not your concern. I will deal with it."

I ignore his refusal. "Elias?"

Hamon takes one step my way, his wings expanding to their full size. The white trim around the feathers glows in the darkness. "Did you not hear what I said, daughter of Andras? I will find my son."

Living in Colorado, we're taught that most predators will not attack unless provoked. There are many sayings—don't poke the bear, let sleeping dogs lie—it's common sense. Hamon just poked the bear. My hands shake as the fuse to a frenzy of emotions ignites. *Be still,* I order the wings dancing at my spine. They listen and snap back at attention. Taking three steps forward, I move into Hamon's personal space. His presence has the two halves within me at war. I better understand my internal conflict now. The desire to hurt versus the desire to comfort. Andras, his enemy, and Phaedra, his . . . what? What was she to Hamon? Judging by the pain written on his face when he mentioned her being killed—I would say she was his love.

I catch Elias's subtle move forward as I sniff. "I am the daughter of Rachel Freeman. I am a daughter of Phaedra. I am not the daughter of Andras. I will never be his daughter. If he is who you say . . . if he has Breckin, he is nothing to me. And if you think you can order me away from *my soul mate*, you are mistaken." My voice shakes, and I ball my hands into fists. "I may be tiny, but I am not useless. Help me find him, Hamon."

Elias speaks up. "Viv, you can't fight. You're not strong—"

I suck in a breath, ready to argue, but Hamon speaks first. "No," he says with a half smile. "Breckin is her mate. She's right. She can be of help."

"Breckin wouldn't want her involved."

"And I wouldn't forgive myself, or you, if something happened to him, and I wasn't involved." I focus on Hamon, sensing his agreement. "I felt his pain. I will feel it again, and when I do, I will follow after him. If you know where to find him, you'll save us the headache, and my bond with him may help us."

"They'd take him to Amartía."

My dark side, my father's blood, leaps at the word. *Uh-mar-tea-uh*, I pronounce the word mentally, and the darkness jolts again. Muted shouts echo at the outer reaches of my mind. A searing pain burns through my shoulder, and I scream out loud. Elias grabs for me, and my wings slap him away. He reaches a second time, and the appendage slaps him again.

"They're hurting Breckin," I say between shallow breaths. "He's being—" Another bone shatters, and a low guttural sound rips at my heart.

"Elias, you need to go to the house and find Rachel. Make sure she is all right and see if they left anything. Vivienne and I will head for the nearest tomb and await your call."

"You're going to need me, Hamon. You can't go down there without backup."

"I have backup." He points to me. "And you've lost enough."

"Hamon . . ."

"Don't argue with me. Stay here. More of the damned could come in search of Breckin. Or Vivienne, if she was the one they were after. You need to alert the Court and maybe call in a few favors to keep things safe here, but don't come after us. This isn't their war, Elias. This is ours."

Breckin's agony has faded to a dull throb in my mind as Hamon wraps an arm around my waist and pulls me close, pressing my cheek to his chest. My wings don't fight his touch as they brush his forearm, but I'm too spent to care.

"I can't fly with you any other way with your wings like that," Hamon apologizes.

"Just get me to Breckin. That is all I care about."

We shoot high above Havenwood Falls, then hover there amongst the hanging clouds. "Can you tuck your wings close to your body?"

"I don't know." All the times Elias and Breckin worked with me on pulling my abilities out of my body—they never told me how to put them away.

"You breathe, Vivienne. It's an order from your mind. It's not difficult."

"Says the man born this way," I grumble as Hamon's eyes widen.

"Vivienne, it was in a fight with Andras and his army that Elias had his wings irreparably ripped from his back. Do you want to get to Breckin, or not?"

My stomach roils at the picture of Breckin's beautiful ebony and amber wings laying discarded and bloody on the ground. Inhaling deeply through my nose, I close my eyes and focus on my wings' movement. I search for the strand of control, the fiber connecting my wings to my brain. When I sense a line of energy moving, I follow it, riding it like a wave until I'm in the middle of my wings. It's an odd sensation. Like I can see down to the molecular level of my being. The luminescent outline of ebony wings, like Breckin's, and yet different. They're dainty, smaller at the base, tilting up like the letter V, before jutting out near my shoulders and angling toward the sky. Mentally I reach for the edge of my left wing and pull it toward my body. Then I reach for the right.

"Good job," Hamon says before he takes off at high speed.

Flying as an angel isn't the same as flying as a human. Hamon moves at twice the speed that Breckin ever did, and yet it feels like everything is passing slower. The wind rushes over my head and body, rustling my wings—which have miraculously stayed close—and jostling my legs about. I focus on my body, willing every muscle to remain still. It's surprisingly easy, and somehow my usual fears of heights and falling is gone.

"Will you tell me about Phaedra?" I ask after a few minutes of flight.

Hamon rolls his neck but he doesn't answer.

"Will you tell me about Andras then?"

Still no answer.

"Do you want to save your son, or get revenge?"

He gives a low harrumph. "Can't I have both?"

I sure hope so, but . . . "What if you can't?"

What if there's only one option here? From every hint that Elias has tried to put down about Hamon, I feel as though I know his answer, but I don't want to be wrong. Breckin is my only choice. He needs to be Hamon's, too.

"Vivienne—"

"You can call me Viv," I interrupt. "Vivienne is a mouthful, and no one uses it."

We bank left, and I draw in a breath.

"Very well, Viv." The nickname is strange on his lips. "There's something so formal about his enunciation. "My entire existence on earth has been about finding Andras and ending him."

The control on my wings slips, and we deviate from our course. The minor break in our aerodynamics causes turbulence, and Hamon's arm tightens as he slows. I draw my wings back into my spine with a curse and an apology. We level out, then dip toward the ground. The city below us is covered in lights. We circle the city before dropping lower.

The moment we land, I push away from him and look around. A cemetery? The lights of the city are miles away but easy to see. We're in Denver. In a cemetery. What is this Amartía place? Hamon said we'd go to the nearest tomb . . .

"Anything?"

I spin around, expecting Hamon to be speaking to me, but he's on his phone. *Elias! Mom!*

"She's fine." Hamon sighs into the phone as his gaze keeps constant watch over our surroundings. "Elias wants to speak with you." He holds out the phone, and I eagerly snatch it from his hand.

"Elias? Is my mom—"

"She's fine, Viv. She's here. Breckin hid her."

"Can I speak with her?" My grip tightens on the cell phone as their voices mingle through the line.

211

"Viv, sweetie?"

"Mom!" Tears flood my eyes, and I blink them back. I will not show Hamon my tears. "What happened?"

"I'm fine, hon. We were silently watching television when Breckin jumped up. He ordered me to go through the doorway in the game room and lock myself in the safe room. I didn't hear a thing until Elias showed up. I didn't know he was gone. I'm sorry. I should have made him come with me."

"No, no . . . it's not your fault." It's just like him to run into the fight instead of hide from it. "I hope you know why I had to go with Hamon, though. I need to help find him, Mom."

"I know." Her voice is filled with emotion. "Please be careful, Viv. I love you."

"I love you, too."

The phone is shuffled, then Elias returns. "Viv?"

"Yeah?"

"Trust Hamon, okay?"

I glance over my shoulder at Breckin's father. They look more like brothers than father and son. It's a bit disconcerting. As is the sadness I feel every time I look at him. The bitterness that accompanies my sadness isn't so bad. I can work with that side of my blood right now. "Are you sure?"

"Breckin is like a son to me, Viv. I would not have let Hamon take you and go after him if I was not sure. Trust him."

Trust the man who hurt my angel. I'll try.

We hang up, and Hamon faces me. He shoves his hands into his pockets and cocks his head to one side. He probably heard everything we said. Good. Let him know I don't trust him.

"I will not let you use Breckin for revenge," I say as I slap his phone into his chest. He yanks his hand from his pocket and takes the phone.

"I have no intention of using Breckin for revenge," he says as his other hand wraps around my wrist. "I plan on using you for revenge."

BREATH

BRECKIN

*A*martía. Elias told me about the home of the more dangerous
fallen and damned when I was younger. An underground
world where the wicked come to play. The only playing I've witnessed
is the playing they've done with me. Every bone in my body has been
snapped twice since they found me at the house. The feathers from my
wings are scattered about the floor in the dark cavern they've kept me
in. The healing process is agonizing. The slow repair of each hairline
crack in my bones drains my energy.

They know how to keep me down.

They mention Hamon's name, so I lay here and I wait for him,
knowing that is why I was taken captive.

I also wait for Vivienne, because the moment I arrived, I knew.

The vision I had—the one with her screams in the pitch black and
the scent of ashes—that vision happens here.

FIGHT ON

VIVIENNE

$\mathcal{M}$y body tenses, and my wings shoot out. Is he betraying me, the daughter of his enemy, to save his son? I can't fault him. What wouldn't I do to save Breckin?

Hamon takes a step closer, and I stand my ground. I will not cower before him.

"He's here," Hamon says. I arch a brow and search our surroundings. "Your father, Vivienne. He will be down there, in Amartía. Since word of my involvement with a Nephilim in Havenwood Falls spread, he's had the damned ones looking for answers."

"Zeke?" I ask.

"And others."

"So, what? You're going to hand me over in exchange for Breckin?"

His careless shrug stings. Not that I expected much out of him, but he did save my life, twice. Why bother if I meant nothing to him? A rising panic presses in.

"Breckin won't let you do that. He won't leave me with the damned."

"Not merely the damned. Your father. And I doubt Breckin is in much of a position to fight it, Viv." He looks from side to side, then jerks his head toward the left. "This way. Let's go."

Even if I could fly on my own, I wouldn't fly away. I need to get to Breckin, and Hamon is my ticket in. So I follow.

It's dark, but it's easy to ascertain the age of the cemetery. We pass crumbling monuments and tombs with every step. The air is ripe with a rusty soil scent. In the distance, a statue rises above the rest, an angel with its wings silhouetted by the moon. I keep my eyes on the angel until we've passed by.

"Tell me the story about Phaedra." He doesn't reply. "You refuse, Elias refused, my mother refused. It must be one heck of a story if no one will tell it."

He inhales sharply. "It doesn't matter."

That draws a laugh from me. "Doesn't matter? Isn't that why we're all here?"

He stops, and his eyes glow in the moonlight as he looks at me. *That's right. I do know a little about the past.*

Walking again, he sighs. "There were four of us. Me, Elias, Phaedra, and Andras. Angels were created to be companions, much like humans were created. We weren't made to bond with one another, but after a while Andras, Elias, and I became true brothers. And Phaedra was loved by us all."

"Loved?" I ask. Romantically? Or platonically? The pain I've picked up in their voices when they mention her lead me to believe there is at least some of the former.

"She tolerated us. We were cocky angels who constantly competed to be the best. You wouldn't know it, but Elias is ridiculously competitive. Phaedra kept us from finding too much trouble."

"I always thought the whole point of angels was worshiping God."

He huffs. "Sort of. We've existed for eons. We do not count the passage of time as humans do. I couldn't tell you how long I've been on earth, let alone in existence. The Creator's intent changed when He created man. Angels were given free will, same as humans, but until man was born, we did not find a need to express it."

I can't stop the awe from creeping in as I look at Hamon. I'm talking to an angel who lived in the heavens. I've never dug into my religious beliefs. A higher power, sure, but what all that entails . . . I'm still uncertain. Or I was, until Breckin flew into my life.

"The four of us were assigned as lords over Creation. Dominions. Our job was to oversee the tasks of other angels. Andras grew bored of that task. The more we watched mankind exercise their free will, the more jealous he became. Many angels felt the same. We watched as man sinned again and again and were forgiven. It did not seem like justice."

"And that was when the heavenly wars began?" I ask, knowing some of the concepts of the Fall from art and reading.

"Yes. Like wars on earth, it was monstrous. Brothers and sisters fought one another. I was forced to end the existence of angels I'd known my entire life. Andras fell with the others, pushed out by the Creator, forbidden from ever returning."

Hamon's words hang in the air between us as we turn down a path going deeper into the cemetery. A grassy knoll rises to our left, and built into the knoll are a line of crypts. We stop before the third one. A surge of elation rises within my chest coupled with a sinking fear. The air is thicker here, dense with a blanket of despair. My wings pull tightly against my spine, as though they fear this place.

I study the crypt made with large stones and an arched door. A name is carved across the top, but years' worth of lichens and moss obscure it.

"What is this?" I step closer to the black iron double doors.

"The way to Amartía."

"A crypt? In a public cemetery?" That can't be safe.

"Only those without loyalties to Heaven can enter unexpected."

"But then . . . how do I get in?"

Hamon moves to my side and wraps a hand around the gate.

"You have his blood, Viv," Hamon says as he tugs the gate open.

Swallowing my fear, I enter the crypt on shaky legs. There's nothing to see in the pitch of night. My angel vision allows for outlines of walls and a black door before us. Hamon waves his hand, motioning me forward, so I go. An unfamiliar symbol consisting of lines and circles is etched into a piece in the center of the iron door.

"The mark of Amartía. The mark of the damned."

Hamon touches the mark, and the door clicks, then swings open.

"So you *are* damned then?"

He flashes a small grin. "No, I am expected."

If I had to imagine the scent of Hell, this would be it. Smoke and ash billow out from the entrance. Red embers litter the path before us.

"Go in, Vivienne," Hamon says, leaning over my back.

My wings wrap around my shoulders at his nearness. "You don't have to do this, Hamon."

"Do what?" He nudges me in the side, and I cross the threshold.

"Don't turn me over to him. Breckin will never forgive you."

"I'm not in the business of buying my son's forgiveness."

Biting my lip, I walk forward until I stumble down a step. My hand touches the steaming wall, an ember burning my skin.

"Amartía isn't a fixed place. There's dark magic at work here. If you were to enter from another crypt, you might find yourself in a garden, or a mansion."

But we get a black cave of fire and brimstone? Lovely. I take the steps carefully, going deeper and deeper underground. A breeze passes by, and I can almost imagine the scent of pine and snow. It makes my chest ache. His painful scream haunts me, and I grasp onto anything to keep from fixating on what he may be going through.

"So, Andras fell, then Phaedra fell, too?"

"Fell? Phaedra? Never in a million years would she fall from grace. Phaedra refused to believe that Andras couldn't be brought back around. He'd been led astray by consummate liars, turned by the master of deception. She swore she could make him see the error in their ways."

I come to a stop at the bottom of the staircase and wait for Hamon's direction. There are two paths. One glows with light at the end of a long stone-and-root hallway; the other is like the path we've just come down—embers and darkness. A smile trembles on his lips.

"That way," he says smoothly, pointing me toward the darkness and fire.

"She had a soft heart." I speak my thoughts out loud, and Hamon grunts.

"She did. She left without telling us. She just disappeared."

To save her friend. Elias hoped my soft heart would save Breckin and Hamon. That I would be their path to redemption. But how?

"So you left Heaven to go after her?" *Because we loved her more than we loved Him,* Elias had said.

"We did, but time on earth moves differently than in Heaven, and when we found her, Andras was long gone. She was heartbroken and would never tell us what happened—only that he refused her offers to return."

How painful that must have been. For all of them. They left Heaven to save their friend, and look what happened.

"Elias and I were punished for leaving without permission. When we attempted to return to Heaven, we were locked out. Elias has waited for the call to return home all this time."

"Elias, but not you? Because you align yourself with Hell and don't expect to return to Heaven?" The question is bold.

"I lost my faith. I've wandered, but I do not align with Hell. I align with Elias."

I clutch my stomach as it dances. We must be close. "Why did you lose your faith?"

"Do you ask this many questions of my son?" He sounds as though he admires me. As quickly as I think it, I brush the thought away. If he admired me, we'd be doing this differently right now. I don't reply.

"Phaedra could never let go of the idea that Andras would come home, and I could never let go of my anger at his turning. I parted ways with Elias and Phaedra. I always came back, but never for long. It was while I was away, near the end of the 1800s, that Phaedra was stripped of her grace. Without her wings or any abilities, she settled into a near-human life in Havenwood Falls. After that, Elias and I took turns watching over her and fighting those who threatened us . . ." He stops speaking and pushes in front of me.

"And then what happened?"

Hamon rounds a corner, and his hand shoots back and wraps around my arm as burnt embers flutter by my face.

"Then he came home and found his best friend had lost his wings and his one true love had met an untimely death," says a voice in the distance.

A snap resounds as darkness becomes light, and in the middle of a cavern filled with black stalactite is an angel with dark curls and perfect olive skin. His wings are shades of blue, purple, and black, like Mom described. This is my father. Andras. At his feet, with one wing hanging at an odd angle and covered in blood, both fresh and dried, is Breckin.

Hamon has to physically restrain me as my wings stretch wide. I am fury. Every atom in my body that makes me human fights to get to Breckin. His name is a broken scream so loud, there's no doubt the rest of the fallen and damned know we're here. Breckin's wings spasm against the ground. They cover him like a blanket, protecting him, but the discoloration and blood covering his skin tells me they aren't enough.

"Careful," Hamon whispers against my ear as he holds me.

Andras tips his head back, his pale blue eyes closing halfway, as he takes a long whiff of the air. My insides go cold. "Very smart, my brother, using my daughter to find me."

"I am not your daughter." I buck at Hamon, my head slamming into his jaw. "Let me go."

Hamon's fingers dig into my arm. His hold is like steel bands trapping me to his side. I scream and fight, but he does not budge. "He will shred you to pieces and not give a single damn, Viv. Bide your time."

I settle, if only because fighting does me no good, and take deep breaths.

"I figured it was only fair, *brother*, since you have my son, that I return the favor." We step farther into the cave. "Do you notice anything about her? Anything familiar?"

Hamon pushes me forward, and I fall to my knees, still unaccustomed to the weight of my wings on my frame. Twenty feet away, Breckin shifts, and I'm hit with a wave of emotions and thoughts like a hammer to the head. I gasp, curling into a ball on my hands and knees as my stomach turns.

"She's Phaedra's?" Andras asks.

"She is. Her gene was so hidden in her line, it wasn't detectable. Not until my son woke it up."

The cavern shakes with Andras's laughter, and I lift my head so I can follow their conversation, wincing at the barrage of feelings Breckin sends my way.

Hamon has moved closer, closing the gap between himself and Andras. They're both standing at ease, as though this is a normal conversation between two old friends. My gaze shifts to Breckin's prone form once more.

Breck? Can you hear me? I'm getting you out of here.

If he hears the thoughts I'm projecting his way, he doesn't comment.

"So the Creator saw fit to give me a daughter of Phaedra's?"

"No. The Creator saw fit to give my son a daughter of Phaedra's," Hamon counters. His arm goes behind his back, and he reaches for his angel blade.

My muscles go taut, and I push up from my hands to kneel, ready to run for Breckin.

"Do you think I did not plan for you to show up?" Andras asks, and a door slides open on the wall behind him. Two of the damned appear. I recognize the one from that day at the park immediately. Cropped blond hair, brown wings. He smiles at me as he walks to Breckin's side. The other is dark like Andras, with spotted wings.

"Do you want to do this, Hamon? You could join us. You've lived on the edge for so long. He will not call you home."

"I have wanted nothing more than to avenge her death, Andras. Whatever happens to me doesn't matter . . . as long as you're gone."

Hamon hurls himself into the air and straight for Andras with a warrior's cry.

Vivie.

Breckin's voice snaps my attention back to where he lies. Beneath his wings, his head moves slightly, and his eyes appear just under their cover. I bite my tongue to keep from crying out as his golden gaze holds mine.

Those wings are sexy as hell.

My cry escapes, but Andras and Hamon's shouts cover the noise. The two hovering near Breckin are focused on the fighting and miss his movement.

Are you all right? I ask. His wing looks repaired. I dig around in my mind, searching for any pain he's having, and can't feel a thing.

Seeing you here has improved me vastly. Can you . . .

Breckin's thoughts turn to an audible shout as I'm thrown into the wall. My head smacks the ground, and everything goes hazy. Blinking rapidly, I use the stone wall to stand and take in the scene. Breckin is in a battle with both the dark and blond damned, while his father and Andras play cat and mouse.

"Do you know how surprised I was to find that you, who has always hated humans, had a son with one?" Andras drawls. "The reaper was happy to betray you and tell us of your son. The Nephilim with the human soul mate."

Hamon's low growl rumbles the cave. "The reaper paid for his greed with his existence."

"So I heard. I expected as much. You kept your son in hiding. You knew your enemies would go after him if they knew. And her—" Andras's gaze flicks to me. "What a lovely gift she is."

"You betrayed us," Hamon shouts.

"*He* betrayed us, Hamon. I left of my own free will."

"And took Phaedra with you. You knew she'd come after you, you knew she'd never give up, and you didn't care. She loved you enough to risk her salvation for yours."

"That was her choice."

They fly at each other at blinding speeds. The blade Hamon holds could end Andras's life with the right swipe, and I can't help but wonder if Hamon is choosing not to make that move. Then I see the smaller dagger in Andras's hand. The eerie blue is the same as the sword Hamon uses. Their fight is even.

A deep growl turns my head back to Breckin, and I run for him as he flings himself around the dark one and twists his body. Bones crack, and a knife falls to the ground. It doesn't glow, so it's not an angel blade, but it still draws blood.

"Breckin, watch out!" I warn as the blond grabs the knife and slices it across Breckin's rib cage. Breckin falters for a moment too long, and the blond's arm goes up at the same time as the dark one rises to his feet once more. Knowing he can't fight two at once, I launch myself into the air and hurtle toward the blond, taking him to the ground.

"What's your name?" I ask through gritted teeth as the blond and I wrestle around on the ground.

He flips me easily, and my wings protest the weight as he pins my arms above my head. "Jarrod, little hellcat. Why, are you asking me on a date?"

"No, I just wanted to know the name of the one I'm about to kill."

His white smile falls, and I buck my hips, tossing him forward, rolling and flipping until he's beneath me. My elbow smashes into his face, a sickening crunch telling me his nose is broken. It buys me a moment, but it's not long enough, and I'm thrown to the side.

"Your wing, Viv," Hamon shouts. I turn his way as I roll away from the blond, and Hamon points at his side.

With his focus on me, Hamon barely has time to move when Andras comes behind him. Andras's blade catches his side, and he grunts but whirls around and lands a kick to Andras's legs. Everything happens so fast. As our fathers trade punches, Breckin falls to the ground when the dark one he fights bashes a rock into the back of his head. He rips at Breckin's wing, bending the bottom half until it snaps, and once again the pain invades my body.

"No!" I cry out as something smashes against my gut, and I bend forward from the force.

"Vivienne. That's your name, isn't it?" Jarrod asks as his fingers grasp my hair and yank my head back. He looks down on me, his pretty white smile so out of place in this violent, desolate cavern. I reach around, my hand going to my back where my wings meet my spine. "Such a pretty little half angel. I'm glad I know the name of the princess I get to break."

His face lowers to mine, his wicked grin reminiscent of Zeke's in that alley, and my body tenses as my hand closes in on what Hamon told me to look for.

"I am not a princess, Jarrod. Try to break me, and I'll avenge what is mine."

My arm swings around, and with all the strength of two angels and a girl who wants her soul mate and heart returned to her, the glowing dagger Hamon hid among my feathers slices across Jarrod's throat from ear to ear. Darkness pours from his throat, sending the former angel to the ground in a pile of ashes, and I gag at the sulfur scent burning my nose.

SUNRISE

BRECKIN

*a*shes hit my face, and I raise my head to the sight of Vivienne standing, a dagger twirling around her fingers.

"And what is your name, dark one?" she asks, looking my way, and the pressure at my back releases.

"This isn't my fight," the one I've been fighting says, raising his arms and backing away.

"Oh, I believe you made it your fight when you attacked what's mine."

Damn, the electricity that explodes every time I see her blows a fuse. Angel Vivie is badass.

The coward runs for the wall, disappearing through a doorway, and I grit my teeth, praying Vivienne doesn't follow. She watches the door for a moment longer than necessary before she finally turns to me, and her entire face changes.

Gone is the badass angel warrior with gleaming black wings.

"Hey," she says, falling to her knees and pulling my head into her lap. This is *my* Vivie. My delicate little human. "Are you all right? Can you heal yourself?"

Her hand skims over my wing. Her scowl and furrowed brow tell me it looks about as good as it feels. When she swipes at the liquid seeping from a cut over my eye, I take a deep breath.

"My avenging angel." I lift a hand and tangle my fingers in the ends of her hair dangling over my face.

"That's right. You awoke me. Now I get to avenge you." She smiles, and I groan as the crackling of my healing bones echoes between us. She flinches, and I know she can feel my pain. "It's okay, Breckin. I've got you. You're safe."

I blink, trying to keep my heavy eyes open. I get them both—the badass angel warrior and the delicate girl. For eternity.

"Watch out," Hamon shouts, and I turn in time to see Andras flying our way, an angel blade in his hand. Vivienne collapses on top of me, her dark wings covering us both as Hamon screams and bodies collide.

A whispered "I'm sorry, brother" reaches me before the scent of death and ash. Vivienne jerks up enough for me to see Hamon on his knees over what's left of her father before my eyes close.

I WAKE at home in the upstairs master suite with Vivienne tucked in at my side, one ebony wing covering me. Protecting me. Everything after seeing Andras fall is a blur. Vivienne and Hamon supported me as we hurried through the halls of Amartía and back to the cemetery. I have no memory of how we returned home.

I reach for Vivienne's wing and stroke the feathers. She lifts her face off my chest and smiles.

"You know you're supposed to put these things away occasionally."

Her lips purse. "If only I knew how."

I scratch at her feathers, and they shiver, making me smile as Vivienne releases a little groan. "I know all the right spots to scratch. I'll teach you if you're nice to me."

She shifts and rolls farther onto my chest so her wings spread out before me. "How nice?"

All the dirty thoughts run through my mind—and into hers—but they're interrupted by a knock on the door. "Breckin?"

The door opens. Vivienne slides to my side, her face red as I sit up, surprised to see him here. "You're still here."

Hamon looks between us. "I thought you both might like answers."

"Yeah, um . . . we'll be down in a minute."

He closes the door, and I glance out the window for the first time. It's daylight. "We're missing school, huh? It is Monday, isn't it?"

Vivienne climbs from the bed. "It is. Obviously, I can't go like this. We can miss a day or two after everything."

I throw on a shirt as I watch her move about the room. If I thought her beautiful before, it's nothing like what I feel now. She radiates so much light, I want to shield my eyes. And her wings . . .

"What happened with the Court?" I ask. I missed so much.

"They reversed the spell." She shrugs. "Elias sat me in his truck, then BAM, everything hit. The spell was like a belt, holding it all in, and once it was released, I gained access to it all. I don't even need sleep anymore."

"The one ability you really wanted." I wink. "But your father—"

"He's wasn't my father, Breck. He was just a fallen angel who damned himself, then slept with my mom. I have no feelings toward him. Maybe I will someday, but he would have killed you out of spite."

I grab her hand as she moves to the door and pull her into my chest. "I'm still sorry."

Vivienne tucks her face against the side of my neck, and we stand that way for a long time.

WE CONGREGATE IN THE BASEMENT, because every meeting of importance happens in the basement. I tried not to look at the broken glass and shredded furniture on the first floor as I walked by. At least downstairs everything feels normal. Well, everything except for Hamon standing here, and Rachel, and Vivienne with her wings. I make a mental note to ask her how her mother dealt with seeing those for the first time.

As if watching television, a vision flicks through my mind of Rachel's shocked face as Vivienne returned with Hamon and me. I look at Vivienne leaning against the counter in the kitchen.

Wow. Your abilities have magnified, huh?

She tips her head and arches a brow. *Think of how much fun this will be.*

Trust me, Vivie, I'm making a list.

"How are you feeling?" Elias asks me as he takes a seat across from Rachel.

"One hundred percent." Hamon and Elias share looks of relief. "Andras liked to talk. He filled me in on who he was, who you all were. And he told me about Phaedra."

"Her story is all there in the journal." Elias points to the table. "We agreed you two should read it."

Hamon takes a deep breath. "Breckin, you should know that I never intended to turn you toward Hell. All these years, I've done what I had to do because I was searching for Andras. I hid you here with Elias and stayed away to keep you safe. I knew if he ever found out about you, he would come for you. My allegiance was never to Hell."

"So it was all lies then?"

"Yes, to protect you. To get into Amartía. To find where Andras was, and to keep other angels, fallen or damned, away. If they feared me, they'd stay away from you." He grips the back of a chair and takes a deep breath. "I made things difficult on you because I needed you to be as strong as you could be when the inevitable happened. The last few months, things unraveled. The more ambitious of the fallen followed me everywhere once they caught wind of Vivienne's existence —thanks to Sebastian. The human with an angel soul mate was a huge draw for the dark side."

"Is the only reason you agreed to save her from Sebastian because she was a descendent of Phaedra's?" I ask.

"No. I had no idea who your soul mate was. When I spoke to Elias, he didn't say her name. I knew who Vivienne was, as a person, but I didn't know she was yours." I'm skeptical, and he senses it. "I

227

saved her for you, Breckin. I know what it is to lose the person you love."

"Were you and Phaedra a couple, then?" Vivienne asks, straightening from her spot leaning on the counter.

"I loved her enough to make her mine, but she couldn't stop feeling guilty."

"For what?"

"She could never forgive herself for causing me and Elias to leave Heaven. Just like with Andras, her concern was our salvation."

Vivienne crosses the room and touches Hamon's shoulder. "You have to forgive yourself." He draws back. "I didn't read the journal, but my mother told me about it. Phaedra wrote a lot about you and your quest to find Andras. Elias alluded to the same. You are not to blame for her death. She chose to stay here because she loved you two. That was her choice."

Hamon's finger grazes Vivienne's cheek, his eyes softer than I've ever seen them. "I'm sorry I scared you last night."

Scared her? My back prickles to attention. "How did you scare her?"

Vivienne laughs. "Your son is a little overprotective, if you haven't noticed," she says as she holds her hand out for me to take. "I may have told your father I would not let him use you for revenge. And he may have said something about using me instead."

I breathe through my nose and will my wings to remain away.

"It was the only way to find him. Amartía allows angels with undefined loyalties in, but the dark magic makes it like a labyrinth. The only doors open to you are the ones they want open. I've always had one—"

"The long hall with the light at the end?" Vivienne asks.

"Yes. You opened the other. The hall that led us to Andras. I used you to get my revenge."

Elias had tried to tell me to talk to Hamon, that he wasn't what I thought he was. In five months our lives, both Vivienne's and mine, have become unrecognizable. Everything has changed.

"What now?" I ask, my gaze moving around the room. To the father who was never present, but always protected me. To the uncle who stayed loyal to his friend, even when it cost him dearly. To the woman who held secrets to protect her daughter from potential harm, and to the girl who lit my soul on fire. "What happens when my birthday comes?"

I'd lived with the idea that I would have to make a choice to serve Heaven or Hell on my eighteenth birthday. I expect the answer I've heard on numerous occasions, but instead Hamon looks to Elias. "We'll do whatever normal people do on birthdays."

Vivienne's eyes go wide.

"Does that mean you're staying in town?" My heart picks up speed, and Vivienne shushes me in my head.

"I'd like to remain and see my son graduate. If that's all right with you."

My words stick in my throat, so I nod.

"Have you ever had a chocolate cake, Hamon?" Vivienne asks. "We'll definitely need a chocolate cake for his birthday."

Rachel and Elias laugh as Hamon looks at my girl with a confused expression.

I give her hand a squeeze. "Chocolate on chocolate," I correct my sugar addict.

"Well, of course. Only the best for you."

VIVIENNE and I are tangled up together on the basement couch later that afternoon. Hamon and Elias went with Rachel to the apartment to help her pack. The Freeman girls will be moving in with me, as will my father. It's all in the interest of safety and sanity.

I look at Phaedra's journal sitting on the coffee table.

"Phaedra lost her grace because when she was called back to Heaven, she refused to go. She didn't go after Andras on her own. She was sent by God, on a mission. She was sent to redeem him. She could have returned and lived out her eternity in splendor, but she chose an uncertain future because she could not bear the thought of leaving Elias and Hamon." I'm thinking out loud, still putting the pieces of the past together.

Vivienne's wing flutters about, and I reach around to stroke it. She's like a kitten crawling up on my lap every time she wants to be petted. "I can't say I blame her," she says.

"I think that's why I found you," I say thoughtfully. She looks at me expectantly. "Phaedra was sent to redeem, and when she didn't go home as called, she was stripped of her powers, but she maintained her immortality. Why didn't the Creator just make her human? Be done with her? Why did your mother come across the one angel who was the downfall of her ancestor, and instead of walking away or being scared—she had his child? Why are we soul mates? There was a plan, Vivie. Our destiny."

"Perhaps," Vivienne says with a smile. "I guess we'll never know, unless we're called back."

Being called to Heaven. That's a possibility I haven't allowed myself to ponder. My fingers brush through her hair. "You're not mad or resentful, even a little, for what has happened since we met?" I ask.

"Not at all. I would rather have this adventure with you, wherever it takes us, and know I'm with the one I love, the one my soul loves, than live a normal life and never have the love we share."

I kiss the top of her head. "I love you, Vivie, but you know we won't get very far on that adventure if you don't put those wings away."

She props her chin on my chest and looks up at me. "You keep saying that, but you haven't told me how to do it."

"Well"—I shift her on top of me— "the key is to relax." My hands go to either side of her spine and run along the edge where the wings meet the skin.

"Will you help me with that?" she asks, sliding up my chest until we're face to face.

"It would be my pleasure." My lips land on hers, coaxing and teasing as my fingers play upon her skin.

With a sudden jerk, Vivienne gasps and slaps at my chest. "Breckin, that was too naughty of you."

I withdraw the mental image with a laugh. "Sorry, I told you we were gonna have some fun with that."

EPILOGUE

VIVIENNE

Aren't you glad we don't have to have graduation in the cemetery like Sun and Moon Academy? Breckin's thoughts make me giggle as I sit among my fellow Havenwood Falls High graduates on the football field.

What is with that, anyway? It's obviously related to the supes, right?

I wish I could see his face as he laughs within my mind. *Of course. They have all sorts of strange customs there.*

Mayor Stuart wraps up her speech—something about the world of possibilities open to us, but in a fit of boredom, Breckin has kept my mind occupied with thoughts the entire time, some of them totally inappropriate for the occasion. I'm still floored by how much he hates human traditions.

Not all of them, Vivie. I liked prom, he reminds me mentally.

Prom. Yeah, that he liked. Dressing in a tux, indulging Mom with picture after picture, enduring dancing and chatting with kids from school—all knowing what he had planned afterward. Candles, flowers, slow dancing in the moonlight away from prying eyes, and . . .

The clearing of Breckin's throat in my head is akin to ice water being thrown on me. *Are those appropriate thoughts at this time, Miss Freeman?*

I huff, *You brought it up first.*

He laughs, and I swear I hear the sound outside my head as well as within.

When Principal Friske begins calling names for us to receive our diplomas, I tune Breckin's suggestive musings out. One by one I watch as kids I've known my entire life walk across the stage for the last time as Havenwood Falls Dragons. In the short months since I learned of the supernatural side of this town I've identified a host of species. Gallad Augustine, a witch. Macy Blackstone, a witch hunter—who dates Gallad. Love *really* is complicated for those two.

Are you feeling nostalgic?

Get out of my head, Breckin Roberts! I look back at the rows of seniors behind me as my row stands and works its way toward the front.

I can't help it. You're projecting all these crazy emotions. Something like a caress floats across my mind.

His mental touch causes my wings to spasm. They're eager to stretch. I've learned to shelter the appendages, but they don't appreciate long periods of confinement. The first few weeks of school after they appeared were hell.

I'm sad, Breck. How many of my friends will leave town and not return?

Hey, it's the closing of this chapter, but we are about to write something even more amazing, Vivie. We have so much to look forward to.

After the party, I remind him sternly, thinking of the traditional graduating class bonfire and camping party by the river we're to attend tonight.

Yes, after the party. I'm only looking forward to it because I can't wait to roll town square.

Again, I giggle. *So, you're not looking forward to sleeping with me in a tent all alone after months of having our parents under the same roof watching our every move? You're more interested in throwing toilet paper into trees and bushes and making a complete mess of the square? Should I be worried?*

Ahhh, Vivie. You have no *idea how much I'm looking forward to sharing a sleeping bag with you tonight.* My wings twitch again, and heat sweeps my body as he continues his soft words in my head. *Even more, I'm ready to fly, aren't you?*

Ready to fly.

Breckin and I planned a getaway after graduation. Just us, endless flight, and the world. Surprisingly, it was Mom who was on board with the idea first. Hamon and Elias weren't exactly thrilled. Poor Breckin —those two are the most overprotective father figures I've ever seen. It's comical, considering our soul bond, to watch the eons-old angels lecture Breckin on gentlemanly behavior. Eventually, with Mom's help, they came around. We're still unsure where our purpose lies. Hamon has switched his own purpose from avenging Phaedra to helping us figure out ours. If there is something we're meant to do, a reason for our bond, he'll figure it out. Of course, maybe we're supposed to live as normally as possible—go to college, get married, have a family one day. We'll discover our purpose, but right now, it's one day at a time.

"Vivienne Jane Freeman." Principal Friske calls my name, and I step onto the stage. Out in the cheering crowd sits my family. Mom— the woman who raised me by herself, always knowing that I might become something *more*. Elias—who gave up his wings trying to protect Phaedra, and gave up his freedom to protect Breckin. Then there's Hamon. Living with him has been eye-opening. He's fierce and loyal, and has taught Breckin and me a wealth of knowledge about our angelic abilities.

I shake Friske's hand and, like my friends before me, turn to the crowd and give a little jig. I did it! I survived high school at Havenwood Falls High.

We survived. Breckin butts into my head. Pushy angel.

Our gazes lock as I come down the steps of the stage and find him near the back of the senior class. Zara sits not far behind him, and we share a smile before my focus returns to Breckin.

Am I ready to fly? Breck, we're gonna soar, I promise.

The amber in his eyes flashes. *You've got that right,* my *angel.* The resolve in his tone is as strong as mine.

We will soar. Two half-angel soul mates destined to be. Tomorrow is filled with uncertainty, but the unknown no longer fazes me. I have Breckin at my side. Our eternity starts today.

ABOUT THE AUTHOR

Michele writes novels with fairytale love for everyday life. Romance is central to her plots, where the genres range from Coming of Age Fantasy and Realistic Fiction to New Adult Romantic Suspense. She is the author of the bestselling From the Wreckage series, a Havenwood Falls author, and co-writes the Paper Planes series with author Mindy Hayes. Mindy and Michele also write clean contemporary titles under the pen name Mindy Michele.

Having grown up in both the cold, quiet town of Topsham, Maine, and the steamy, Southern hospitality of Mobile, Alabama, Michele is something of an enigma. She is an avid Yankees fan, loves New England and being outdoors, and misses snow. However, she thinks Southern boys are hotter, Alabama football is the only REAL football out there, and sweet tea is the best thing this side of heaven and her children's laughter!

Her family, an amazing husband and three awesome kids, have planted their roots in the middle of Michele's two childhood homes, in Charlotte, North Carolina.

Website: http://www.michelegmillerbooks.com/
   Email: authormichelegmiller@gmail.com
   Facebook: https://www.facebook.com/AuthorMicheleGMiller
   Twitter: https://twitter.com/chelemybelles
   Pinterest: http://pinterest.com/chelemybelles/
   Instagram: https://instagram.com/chelemybelles/

ACKNOWLEDGMENTS

I'm so grateful to the people who support me through the book process and life:

My husband and kids deal with me forgetting laundry, dinner, carpool, emails, and the list goes on. How they put up with me I'll never know!

My amazing crew of readers, bloggers, and friends on Facebook and "in real life" keep me sane. You make this solitary life a little less solitary, and a lot more lifelike.

My core reader group on Facebook, Mindy and Michele's M&M's: Thanks for being a sounding board when needed, book pimps when needed, and friends always.

To Jo Pettibone: Thank you for walking with me from day one with Viv and Breck and being the best Alpha a writer could have. You talked me off the ledge a few times with this one. I'm so lucky to have you!

To Mindy: Thanks for having patience with me, and allowing me to write Avenge the Heart while you tried to plot Loss in A Major. Co-writing isn't much fun when your co-writer is busy with other projects. I'm grateful you indulge me. xoxo

To the Havenwood Falls family: This group continues to grow, but their generosity, creativity, and enthusiasm for this project astounds me. I'm so lucky to be able to write, and collaborate, with these amazing creatives. Many of the characters and places I mention in both of my Havenwood Falls books were created by others in this amazing group.

More specifically, thanks to these ladies for creating and sharing your characters with Viv and Breckin in Avenge the Heart:

Randi Cooley Wilson: Nikita

R.K. Ryals: Jack Peters and Cressida Manos

And of course, a final HUGE thank you to Kristie Cook for creating Havenwood Falls and making this all possible. A year into this journey, I am still in awe of your business savvy and ingenuity.

CURSE THE NIGHT

R.K. RYALS

HAVENWOOD FALLS HIGH

Curse the Night

R.K. RYALS

~ A Havenwood Falls Young Adult Novella ~

Fist of the Furor

City in Ruins

The Standalone Embrace Yourself Series

The Story of Awkward

An Introvert's Tale

Contemporary Romance Reads

The Singing River

Hawthorne & Heathcliff

The Best I Could

Sex & Such

Capture the World

For those who find strength in differences and confidence in being yourself.
Let your light shine.

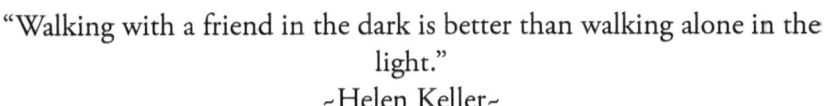

"Walking with a friend in the dark is better than walking alone in the light."
~Helen Keller~

PROLOGUE

JACK PETERS

*N*o matter the time of day, the clubhouse was rarely empty. Unconscious bodies littered the space, the forms sprawled across the floor, the threadbare sofa lining the walls, and the pool table resting in the center of the room. Half-naked women spooned with men in leather vests sporting a sword-impaled skull and patches. Empty beer bottles and specially mixed brews from Sanguine Elixirs dripped sticky liquid onto scarred hardwood floors. Blood, alcohol, and God knew what else.

I snorted. The prospects were going to hate cleaning up the mess.

Club SIN. That was the name I called it in my head. The place where the Swords of the Infernal Night congregated. A motorcycle club on the wrong side *and* the right side of the law. One percenters. And my dad was their leader. I was the prodigal son, the tattooed jackass he hoped would take over for him one day.

Maybe I would.

Picking my way around the bodies, I walked toward a door at the back of the room, my stride full of purpose and determination.

I knew he was in there, and I knew he was awake. He always was.

The door made no sound when I opened it.

Inside the room, a man sat at a long mahogany table, his head bent over a stack of papers, his fingers twirling a knife. I watched it spin on the wood.

"Pops."

Liam Peters looked up, his hard gaze finding mine, the sunglasses he always wore pushed up on top of his head. My father was light where I was dark, his sandy hair a little too long, his face covered in scruff. Tattoos lined his arms. His chest and shoulders were broad, filling out the leather cut he rarely removed. Havenwood Falls' finest nearly untouchable outlaw. He and his business partner, Tychon Savage—or just Savage, as everyone knew him—were the epitome of good and evil. For them, there was no line separating the two. They *were* the line.

"Pops, I need your help."

CHAPTER 1

CRESSIDA MANOS

FIVE DAYS EARLIER . . .

"*W*hat is a four-letter word for 'being connected to someone'?" Paris asked, her pencil poised over the page of her open book, the front cover folded under the back. Light poured in through a large picture window overlooking Main Street, the glow highlighting the stained concrete flooring, light yellow walls, and multicolored display cases lining the interior of my family's art business, Apex Art Studio. It was early June in Havenwood Falls, the ease of summer already sinking into the bones, comfortable and unhurried. A peaceful respite before Midsummer's Night Terrors, a festival held in the square on the Summer Solstice.

Wet clay covered my hands, my fingers working the lump on the potter's wheel. I was responsible for the handmade pottery the customers painted—the pieces we didn't have shipped in—and I loved it. The entire creative process was soothing. Hypnotizing.

"Is that the only hint?" I asked, pressing my thumb into the center of the lump, my gaze ficking to the dark-haired, dark-skinned girl sitting cross-legged on the floor next to my stool.

Named after the place where her parents met and where she was conceived, my best friend Paris Francine Callahan was fascinated with crossword puzzles and had been since the day we were introduced in elementary school. Paris was human—an important distinction in Havenwood Falls, where a substantial portion of the population was supernatural—and shy. Extremely shy. Even though she was stunning enough to grace the cover of Vogue. I was the plain one out of the two of us, all five foot one, redheaded, pale-skinned, button-nosed, freckled inch of me.

"One of a matched pair?" Paris added, reading. "Third letter is a T."

"Mate." The word slipped off my tongue too easily.

Paris penciled it in. "It works. How did I miss that?" She glanced up at me. "How did *you* get that?"

I kept my gaze locked on the vase forming before me. Having a mate was common in the supernatural world, depending on the species. I was an oread, a mountain nymph, and while we didn't mate or bond, I knew enough supes who did. As for Paris, she was completely oblivious to Havenwood Falls' supernatural side. If she suspected something was off, she never mentioned it.

There was a rumble down the street, the sound of revving motorcycles getting louder as a group of men in leather vests cruised past our shop window.

Paris set her book aside and hugged her knees. "Do you think they're dangerous?"

I was too close to finishing the vase to look away. "SIN? No doubt."

SIN, or Swords of the Infernal Night, was Havenwood Falls' local motorcycle club. The club kept to itself, which was why it was rarely a topic of conversation in town. It was no secret they existed. They owned a delivery company, Cerberus Delivery Inc., and their trucks were the main means of delivering goods from outside town to businesses and individuals in Havenwood Falls. The sister of the club's vice president also owned Silk, an exclusive nightclub. But no one discussed them or their businesses, especially Silk's private clientele. I knew more than I should, because my father tended to talk too much about work at home. Not only did Cerberus—more commonly referred to as CDI—deliver unique goods to my father's business, but many of Silk's well-off clients liked buying expensive jewelry.

What *was* a secret—to the mortals anyhow—was that the leader of SIN, Liam Peters, and his business partner, Savage, were shapeshifting hellhounds. Most of their club members were supernatural. Maybe even all of them.

"The dangerous part is kind of hot," Paris admitted. "Though I wouldn't want to find out how dangerous," she rushed to add. "It's like wanting to eat an entire plate of chocolate. Tempting, but no."

Paris was diabetic, which played into her reserved nature. Her mother was overly protective, and Paris wasn't fond of testing her blood sugar or giving herself insulin shots in front of people.

"Why, Paris, are you into bad boys?" I teased.

She snorted. "As long as they're more 'rebel without a cause' and not Hannibal Lecter."

Finishing the vase, I glanced at her. "So, you'll warm the bed of a heartbreaker with a rap sheet, but not a serial killer. Noted."

Neither one of us had warmed anyone's bed. We were both going into our senior year at Havenwood Falls High in the fall, and neither of us had even been kissed. Paris was too shy, and I was always friend-zoned.

The studio door opened, and my sister, Leda, walked in, her brows arched. Pulling her key out of the lock, she shook it at us. "Why bolt the door when you have the closed sign up?"

The door being locked wasn't a bad thing, but it annoyed Leda when she had to dig for her keys instead of being able to just walk in.

"We're keeping rapscallions out." I gestured at her. "Case in point."

"Rapscallions?" Leda laughed, her gaze passing between us. "You two say the weirdest things. That word is seventeenth-century old."

"Tell that to Dad."

"Yeah, well, Dad's . . ." Her sentence trailed off, but I knew what she left unsaid. Dad's age predated the word. At six hundred ten years old, he predated a lot of things. "Can you catch the shipment for Apex out back and put out new inventory before we open on Monday?"

"Wasn't that supposed to come in yesterday?" Standing, I rushed to a paint-stained, industrial-sized sink built into the wall at the back of the room. The clay on my hands turned the water tan as it circled the basin to disappear down the drain.

I was a study in disarray, my unruly red hair bunched on top of my head, my body hidden by a light blue button-up shirt, overalls, and an apron. I was the complete opposite of my sister. She was tall where I was short, slender where I was skinny, blonde where I was redheaded, and elegant where I was laidback and disorganized.

Leda's heels clicked on the concrete floor, her red shoes complementing her black dress pants, black suit jacket, and red blouse. Her fingers sparkled. Rings were an everyday fashion accessory for her, and she had easy access to them. Not only did my family own the art studio on Main, but we also owned a jewelry store, Summit Jewelry, on the corner of Eighth and Main, next door. Like my sister and I, the two stores couldn't be any more different. While Apex was a chaotic, colorful shop that smelled like paint, Summit Jewelry was an elegant store with shining hardwood flooring, hanging chandeliers, and a showcase floor full of glass cases.

"Dad got word of a rare jewel he wanted at an auction outside town. He won the bid on it, and CDI was kind enough to wait the extra day to deliver. For an added fee, of course. I've already got the shipment for the jewelry store and locked up Dad's new prize. The jewel is pretty, I'll give him that, but it probably cost us a fortune." Bitter humor colored Leda's voice. "I'm headed back to the store. Make sure they don't break anything."

Tucking my hands into the pockets of my apron, I turned to Paris. "Want to help?"

"SIN is out back? As in now?" Her eyes went wide. Paris worked part time at Apex, but her hours rarely coincided with shipments.

"It *is* their delivery company."

She launched to her feet, instantly towering over me, and touched her hair nervously.

Leading the way, I opened a door at the back of the studio and stepped into a storeroom. Another door led into the alley, and it stood open, no doubt courtesy of my sister.

A boy I instantly recognized but had never met ducked into the space, wheeling a stack of boxes in front of him. He was tall, at least six feet two, and while that was intimidating, it was nothing compared to most hellhounds. He had a lot of room to grow. The white short-sleeve T-shirt stretched across his torso was mostly hidden by a plain leather cut, which meant he wasn't a part of the motorcycle club, but —if the rumors I'd heard were any indication—he also wasn't opposed to it. He was ripped, his muscles straining against the fabric as he unloaded the boxes. A thick chain tattoo wrapped his left arm, starting somewhere beneath his sleeve and circling down to his forearm. Other tattoos I couldn't make out peeked at us from under his right sleeve. Dark hair, cut close to his head but left longer on the top, fell carelessly onto his forehead, bringing attention to the expensive sunglasses covering his eyes.

Paris inhaled sharply behind me, trying desperately to make herself as small as possible, even though I made a terrible shield.

Jack Peters. Middle son of SIN's leader, Liam Peters. Although I didn't *know* him, I recognized him easily. He was seventeen and a rising senior at the prestigious Sun and Moon Academy, and we had a lot of the same acquaintances. I'd say friends, but I wasn't sure he had those. He was as elusive as his father and his father's club.

"Hi," I greeted him cheerfully. Jack didn't respond. I wasn't even sure he looked at me.

"You need help moving this stuff into the store?" a deep, raspy voice asked, and I nearly jumped out of my skin. Paris squeaked.

A man entered, his large body completely stealing whatever oxygen and space was left in the room. This man, *everyone* knew. While I was used to CDI and their deliveries, I'd never actually met the head of the motorcycle club. Sightings of Liam Peters in town didn't count.

Liam surpassed his son by several inches, his massive build filling out a leather cut plastered in patches. Sunglasses shielded his eyes, his chiseled jaw covered in scruff. He wore his sandy blond hair a little long, his obvious tattoos far outnumbering Jack's.

"That'd be good," I managed, backing me and Paris into the studio. Paris's fingers dug painfully through the back of my overalls.

"They're massive," she breathed.

"Shh," I hissed, lightly kicking her.

"Isn't that Jack Peters?" she asked, nodding at the younger man, completely ignoring my attempt to shush her. If only she knew how well hellhounds could hear.

Liam and Jack unloaded boxes along the wall, an awkward silence falling.

"Do you think they kill people who can't make conversation?" Paris mumbled.

I jabbed her with my elbow, and while I didn't have the hearing hellhounds did, I didn't miss Liam's faint chuckle.

Too much time passed, all of it in silence, the sound of boxes thudding the only noise in the room.

"What's takin' so long?" a petulant voice called, followed by feet stomping into the studio.

Now *this* voice I was used to. Cade Peters. The youngest son of Liam, and a literal pain in the rear on a *good* day. He often rode along on deliveries, and he was really good at driving me crazy. Full of confidence, he strutted across the room, his sunglasses resting securely on his nose. I just hoped he didn't remove them. It wouldn't affect me if he did, but it would hurt Paris. If a human or a non-immortal supernatural peered into a hellhound's eyes three times, it was a death sentence. Hence the sunglasses. It was also the reason all the Peters boys attended the Academy rather than Havenwood Falls High.

Cade barely spared me a glance, but he gave Paris his undivided attention. "What's up, Manos? Who's the friend you got there?"

"Nope," I said, nose scrunched. "You can take your fourteen-year-old hormones to someone else's door, Peters."

My words did nothing to deter him. After a wholly appreciative once-over—this would be impossible for anyone else while wearing shades but was somehow completely possible for a Peters—he glanced at my potter's wheel. I slid in front of it, arms crossing. The last time he appreciated my art, I lost two vases and a really awesome unicorn. Kids loved the unicorns. And the dragons.

"Whatcha workin' on there?" he asked, attempting to dodge me. At fourteen, he was already taller than me, but I was quicker. "Ponies and rainbows?"

"Depends. You interested in ponies and rainbows?"

Again with the Liam chuckle.

Cade scowled. "The only thing I like to ride, Manos, is—"

"Cade," Liam warned, the rumble of his voice enough to make both Paris and me jump. "What have I told you about respecting ladies?"

"Really, Pops, that ain't no lady, that's just Cress—"

Jack popped him on the back of the head, having come up behind him too quick for any of us to see. When Cade tried to protest, Jack popped him again.

"*Isn't* a lady," he corrected. "And be glad it wasn't Pops." His voice was as deep and raspy as his father's.

"Sorry, ladies," Liam said, finishing up with the boxes. "He hears crap from the boys and thinks it's okay to repeat it. He doesn't have the best examples at home. Least of all a motherly one."

"Melaina—" Cade began.

"My point exactly," Liam mumbled, cutting him off. "Excuse us, ladies."

I followed them to the storeroom, pausing at the door to the alley. Jack lingered, stopping just short of walking out the door.

"You've got . . . stuff," he touched my cheek lightly, the heat of his fingers startling me, "here." He dropped his hand as fast as he lifted it, and I hated that I couldn't see his eyes.

"Oh." I touched the spot, my fingers brushing over dried clay. "Thank you."

He left, climbing on a motorcycle in the alley. Liam straddled a Harley nearby. Cade hopped into the passenger side of a delivery truck, a burly man in a CDI uniform peering out at me from the driver's seat.

"Your dad has some expensive taste in jewelry," Liam told me, pulling on a helmet. "That was a nice rock we dropped off at Summit. Tell him if he needs another *special* delivery, to let us know. I told your sister the same thing, but you look like you may be better at delivering messages."

"Leda isn't a huge fan of Dad's odd tastes in antiques," I admitted. Leda wasn't a fan of the *money* she knew Dad spent on things that fascinated him, and Dad had a very large collection of things that fascinated him, everything from vintage watches to Persian rugs.

"I gathered that," Liam replied, flashing me a knowing grin.

His motorcycle revved, and they were off, the bikes escorting the delivery truck down the street. My fingers brushed my cheek. I could still feel the heat of Jack's touch, and it unsettled me. Were all hellhounds that warm?

Closing the door to the alley, I locked it and reentered the studio.

"That was exciting!" Paris called, her voice echoing from a small restroom near the utility sink, the door cracked.

"You missed them leaving," I told her.

"I had to pee. You know I always have to pee when I get nervous." The toilet flushed, and the sink turned on.

I dug through a desk drawer at the front of the studio.

"They weren't anything like I thought they'd be." Paris exited the bathroom. "Except the youngest, which is weird."

Box cutter in hand, I went for the boxes. It was going to be a long afternoon, but it was the first Saturday in months we didn't have paint-and-sip reservations. Or a birthday party, for that matter. Which made it perfect for doing inventory.

Paris went for the price gun. "All those rumors about Jack Peters— do you think they're true?"

If only she knew. Havenwood Falls was full of rumors, and most of the time when it came to the supernaturals, if it wasn't the truth, it was close enough. Jack's reputation preceded him, and while it wasn't as bad as his father's, his was certainly headed in the same direction. It would scare any sensible person away. He was the kind of guy girls snuck out to spend a night with just so they could say they did, the kind of guy other guys hit up for favors they knew no one else would do, and the kind of guy who had no problem crossing lines.

He was the kind of guy a girl should stay far, far away from.

"Yeah, I think most of them are true," I replied. Pulling ceramic figurines out of the first box, I set them aside, then collapsed the cardboard. My cheek still burned, and I swiped at it.

"What are you . . ." Paris began, then leaned toward me. "I think you may have gotten yourself with your fingernail or something. There's a pink spot on your face."

I stared at her. "What?"

"It's barely noticeable. I wouldn't have seen it if you didn't keep rubbing at it."

"Do you have your phone?" I asked. I had a cell, but I rarely carried it on me. The service was so bad in Havenwood Falls, it was practically pointless.

Paris dug a phone out of her blue jeans pocket and handed it to me. I clicked on her camera icon, using the self-image feature to look at my face. There, on the bridge of my cheek, was a tiny pink spot, smaller than any of my freckles. A very small burn.

"Really, I can hardly see it," Paris assured me.

It wasn't the pink spot that bothered me. It was knowing how it got there in the first place. Jack Peters had *burned* me.

I probed it carefully before returning Paris's phone. "Guess I did get myself somehow. It'll go away."

Returning to the boxes, I cut a new one open, my thoughts scattered. I wasn't sure what disturbed me more—the burn, or the little part of me that didn't want the burn to heal.

CHAPTER 2

JACK PETERS

*T*he best part of riding my motorcycle was the wind. The vibration of the bike and the freedom were part of the euphoria, too, but it was the wind that made me feel like I was flying. As if I could shut my eyes and suddenly take off into the air. As if I could escape who and what I was. Not that I hated being me. Out of all of Liam's sons, I was the one most like my father, which was exciting and terrifying.

"You're super droll today," Cade called out after we'd pulled into the delivery company's parking lot and switched off our engines. My fourteen-year-old brother jumped out of the passenger seat of the truck, a goofy grin plastered on his face.

I pushed the kickstand down on my bike. "Droll?"

"I heard it from Cressida. The chick from the art store."

Our father, Liam Peters, sauntered toward us, and even though his eyes were hidden by his sunglasses, I knew he was amused. "The pixie?"

"She's an oread, a mountain nymph, Pops," Cade huffed. "She's expanding my vocabulary."

Liam snorted. "Then learn how to use it correctly, son. Otherwise you just sound stupid."

I laughed. "Is that what was happening today? You were getting an education?"

Liam removed his fingerless riding gloves and slapped them against his jeans. "If you've got a crush on that redhead, I need to teach you better flirting skills."

"Whatever." Cade started to brush past us, the heat pouring off his skin nearly scalding.

Face hard, Pops took Cade by the shoulder, stopping him. "Girls aside, you've got to get a better grip on your emotions. If someone were to touch you right now, they'd get burned. Jack isn't droll; he's calm." With his free hand, Pops pulled his sunglasses down the bridge of his nose, his red-tinted eyes peering at Cade over the brim. "You can't play with romance if you have to worry about killing someone."

"Romance?" I chuckled, because I knew doing anything else would only embarrass Cade further. Pops wasn't subtle. He treated his sons like members of the club rather than his children. "The nymph is too old for you."

Cade pouted. "By three years. Age is just a number."

Climbing off my bike, I slapped my brother on the back. "Cressida Manos doesn't date."

"What?" Cade's features relaxed, his skin cooling. "Where'd you hear that?"

I honestly couldn't remember where I'd first heard the nymph wasn't into dating, but it was common knowledge among our graduating class, both at Havenwood Falls High and Sun and Moon Academy. It was also common knowledge that her older sister, Leda, was into girls. Considering Cressida's dateless high school record, it was assumed she was, too. But judging from the startled look she'd given me when I brushed the clay off her cheek at the studio, I was beginning to doubt that.

The memory brought a smile to my lips. I was used to the way girls reacted around me, both the shy girls and the flirtatious ones, but Cressida hadn't come on to me. She'd reacted to the touch, a blush riding high on her cheeks, her green eyes wide and unnerved. Up until that moment, she'd been too focused on keeping her friend's voice down and my snarky brother in line to pay me any attention. Maybe that's why I'd let my guard down, singeing her face. Thing is, I didn't know why I'd done it, and Pops would have killed me if he knew.

Cade threw me a disgruntled look. "She just needs the right guy. You wait and see—I'll wear her down."

"More like scare her off," I mumbled as my brother trotted off, determination etching his brows. Ah, the joys of crushing on someone. I hated what the future held for him. Girls didn't want romance from guys like us. They wanted a good time and a good story to go with it.

"You've got to stop comparing us," I told Pops when Cade disappeared into the clubhouse across from the delivery company. "I read in some magazine that comparing your children only causes dissent and mistrust."

Liam pulled his sunglasses off. "When did you start reading parenting magazines?"

"I was looking for an article about an archeological dig in South America. The parenting shit was just in there."

"And you read it?'

My lips twitched, and I grimaced in an attempt not to smile. "Someone has to. It wouldn't hurt for you to check that stuff out every once in a while, Pops."

He smacked me on the back of the head, hard enough to get my attention but soft enough I knew he did it out of affection. "I'm trying to make you boys tough. The world doesn't work like those articles."

"Maybe not, but could you use Savage as your example next time? Dealing with Cade's sulking is enough to give me indigestion." Savage was Pops's best friend, his business partner, the vice president of SIN, and a fellow hellhound. He'd always been a part of our lives, enough like family we'd called him uncle as children. Which was why using him as an example of an "exemplary hellhound" would be a lot better than telling Cade he needed to act like me. Cade respected Savage. He resented me.

Liam rubbed the bridge of his nose. "How'd you end up so much like your mother?"

"Luck."

Pops smacked me on the back of the head again, and I backed away, laughing.

"Your mother would have made a damn fine club president if she'd been born male."

"Is that a hint, Pops?"

Liam cocked his brows. "Just a suggestion, son. You know Taemin isn't cut out for the life. Your older brother is better suited for hacking computers than he is running a motorcycle club, and Cade is way too hotheaded."

"I'll keep that in mind."

Pops and I were good at this game. He knew how to get under my skin, and I was becoming a pro at evading his expectations. Scary thing was, I knew I'd like running the MC because, as much as I pretended I wasn't like my father, there was one thing we had in common: for us, being in power felt good.

CHAPTER 3

CRESSIDA MANOS

*M*onday came too quick, my cat's fluffy tail hitting me in the face minutes before my alarm went off. Kittypatra McSlinky, Slink for short, was a needy pet, especially in the morning. Her way of garnering attention included countless minutes nibbling my toes under the comforter, followed by wagging her butt in my face.

I shoved her aside gently. Oreads didn't require much sleep, but that didn't mean I didn't like sleeping.

Slink pawed at me, and I ruffled the hair between her ears. The tortoise-hair cat wasn't just my pet; she was my responsibility. I was the only one in the house who liked her. Mom was of the "your cat, your problem" mentality. Dad referred to her as "that damn cat" because she had a thing for clawing his expensive suits when he left them hanging in the laundry room. Before Leda moved out, she and the feline spent every morning in a hissing match because Slink liked peeing in Leda's brand-name shoes.

"You're just misunderstood, aren't you, you little cutie?" Slink rolled over, and I ran my fingers down her soft belly, her purr vibrating against my palm.

Mom and Dad were already gone when I finally made it downstairs, my hair clipped up and my trusty, worn cut-off shorts paired with an equally worn sweatshirt. Even though it wasn't sweatshirt weather—temps generally averaged in the upper seventies in Colorado in June—I didn't feel cold or heat the same way most people did. I wore the sweatshirts and oversized clothes so I didn't have to wear a bra, the upside to being flat-chested. The people in town assumed I was cold-natured. The key to fitting in with humans was maintaining a consistent image. And I hated bras.

After dumping cat food in a bowl by the refrigerator, I grabbed a granola bar from the pantry, slipped my feet into a pair of polka-dotted red rain boots, and hurried out the door. The morning was misty, the cool wetness like gentle tears on my cheeks. Even clipped up, I could feel my hair frizz. As an oread, traveling by foot was quicker than standard human transportation, especially in the mountains where our house was located, just far enough from town to feel at home among the rocks. Oreads could jump impossible distances, fall from crazy heights, and run extremely fast. We were like Olympic high-jumpers on steroids. My parents owned a car, because not having one when we lived out of town would look suspicious, but we didn't need one.

Running, I eyed a drop-off in the distance, dodging trees and foliage as I sped toward it. Lungs filling with sweet, damp air, I jumped over the side of the cliff, laughing as I fell. The wind pounded me in my face, my toes curling to keep my boots from falling off. I landed hard—hard enough to kill a human—but my feet and body absorbed the impact like a sponge. Mom would kill me if she saw me, but my favorite part of being an oread was the falling. Most people feared falling, but I lived for the exhilaration of it. I lived for the freedom.

Breathing hard, I crouched, laughter rolling out of me, the sound echoing through the mountains. The laugh bounced back at me so clearly, it was as if it came from someone else, as if I was laughing with a friend rather than alone. An oread could echo her voice from anywhere. It made having an imaginary friend as a child so much easier. I'd spent hours talking to myself as a kid, asking questions and then echoing back a reply.

My laughter still ringing on the breeze, I broke into a run, the world blurring past me. At the edge of town, I slowed, carefully making my way down the back roads until I reached the south side of town, where Tenth Street intersected with Petran Road. A large parking lot full of eighteen-wheeler trucks and two large buildings loomed on one side of the street. The building closer to the trucks was a massive, metal warehouse with a loading dock at the back. Double glass doors on the front were etched with the figure of a three-headed, ferocious hound. Cerberus Delivery, Inc.

Motorcycles lined the building opposite the warehouse. This building was smaller, the exterior redbrick with a thick wooden door, the SIN logo hanging above it. The sword-impaled skull stared back at me, and I found myself fascinated with the image. As if it could see things in me I couldn't quite understand. Maybe it could.

The door to the building flew open, and Cade Peters marched out, his expression sour. I groaned inwardly. I passed the CDI warehouse and the SIN clubhouse every time I volunteered at the local animal shelter, but it was always too early for me to run into anyone. We Manoses were early birds.

"Come on! It's summer, Pops!" Cade roared.

Two women followed him out the door, each of them with mussed hair, hastily pulled-on clothes, dangling purses, and smeared lipstick.

"Better not to argue, honey," one of the ladies said, her hand vanishing into her purse. A cigarette appeared in her fingers, and she stuck it between her lips before drawing out a lighter.

Men in leather cuts, all of them too large for their own good, stumbled out after the women, all of them grumbling.

"It's too early for this shit," one of them said before climbing onto a motorcycle. He pulled a helmet off the handlebars and shoved it onto his head.

"Should have laid off the liquor," a familiar deep voice replied, amused. Jack Peters ambled over to his brother, gravel crunching beneath his combat boots, while he pulled his leather cut on over a plain white T-shirt.

"Tell your dad he's supposed to let us know this shit beforehand, so we can," the guy groused.

Jack laughed, the deep rumble so beautiful, the air drank it appreciatively. No one should look or sound that good. It was a crime against humanity. "Pops likes catching people off guard."

Cade glanced up, his gaze passing over me, and I stumbled forward, pulse quickening. *Not today, Peters. Please not today.*

"Yo, Manos!" Cade shouted. He ran toward me, and if I wasn't so worried about the mortals in Havenwood Falls, I'd have taken off like lightning. "I thought I smelled coconut."

Spinning, I smiled brightly, because no matter how irritating and moody he could be, I still liked Cade. "You're up early."

His black hair caught the sun, the rays tinting it blue in the light. Cade was a contradiction. Taller and broader than humans and most supernaturals, he was still shorter and lankier than typical hellhounds. I knew this because my dad spent a good deal of time drilling my sister and me about supernatural creatures. As we were my parents' only children, Dad was hell-bent on making sure we knew how to protect ourselves from anything.

"Why? Do you pass here often?" Cade asked, a grin splitting his face.

Why couldn't I keep my mouth shut? "Nope," I answered too quickly, the lie obvious. I was terrible at lying.

Cade perused my figure, and I was suddenly glad the Peterses all wore sunglasses. I wasn't sure what it was Cade saw in me. Most of the time I couldn't figure out if he was giving me a tough time or if he had a crush. A tough time made way more sense than the crush thing. I wasn't anything like the type of girl the Peters men hung out with.

"You headed to the studio?" Cade asked, sinking his hands into his blue jeans pockets, his shoulders hunching up to his ears even though it wasn't cold outside.

"What's with the getup?" Jack Peters sidled up next to Cade, his presence swallowing his younger brother's. Because of their size, hellhounds appeared older than their actual ages. Up until a certain point. Once they reached adulthood, however, they seemed to quit aging.

My reflection stared back at me in his sunglasses, and my cheeks heated. "It's comfy couture. You should try it. It's all the rage in summer."

Jack glanced down. "And the rain boots?"

"We're going to get showers today." Oreads were also good at predicting the weather.

In unison, the brothers glanced at the sky. Blue. No clouds.

I grinned. "Mid-afternoon, right after lunch."

"Really?" Cade whistled. "You're full of surprises, Manos."

"It's nothing special," I said, shrugging. "My parents and sister can do it, too. They're better at it."

"Does it ever hurt?" Jack asked suddenly, genuinely.

My gaze flew to his face. "What?"

"Smiling like that. Every time I see you around town, you're grinning."

"That's just Cressy," Cade reassured.

"Cressida," I corrected. I hated, hated, *hated* it when people shortened my name.

"Cress," Cade teased.

"Cressida." Still smiling, I shook my fist at him.

Cade pulled down his sunglasses, a mischievous glint in his red-hued eyes. "Ressy . . . Ida . . . Sid."

It was taking everything I had not to hit him.

"Put your sunglasses back on," Jack demanded, the command sobering the mood.

Cade glared at him. "It doesn't affect oreads."

"That doesn't mean you should take them off." Reaching out, Jack replaced his brother's sunglasses. "You'll get in the habit of removing them."

"God, you sound like Pops," Cade mumbled.

They were kind of cute when they argued, sort of like puppies yipping at each other. "You guys." Stuffing myself between them, I took them each by the arm. "Haven't you ever heard that fighting before breakfast is really bad for digestion?"

Cade and Jack froze, and the moment grew uncomfortable. They had biceps of freaking steel. It was like being wedged between two walls.

"Is she for real?" Jack whispered over my head.

Cade shrugged, dislodging my hand. "Maybe she didn't get the memo." He glanced down at me. "Girls don't touch Jack."

"What?" That had to be the most ridiculous thing I'd ever heard. Especially considering the number of ex-lovers he had in town. I laughed and made it a point to pat Jack's arm. "That's not what I hear."

Slowly and deliberately, Jack carefully peeled my fingers away from him. "You need permission first."

His skin suddenly warmed, and I yanked my hand away, cradling it. "Hey, now!" My fingers stung.

Cade's mouth fell open. "Did you just burn her? Like, seriously?"

Sticking a few of my fingers in my mouth, I sucked on them. "What was that for? That hurt!"

"Seriously," Cade barked out a harsh laugh, "after all of the lectures from you and Pops about controlling this and controlling that, and you go and burn someone."

Jack took a step back, creases forming between his eyebrows. "I—"

"What's with the commotion out here?" Liam Peters appeared behind his sons.

I stuffed my hand behind my back, so quickly I'm sure it looked more awkward and telling than genuine.

Cade nodded at his brother. "Pops, Jack—"

"Was just telling me that he doesn't think it's going to rain today, but it's definitely going to happen." Words spilled out of me, so fast they ran into each other. "likereallygoingtohappenandit'sgoingto"—I took a deep breath—"you know, rain."

Liam's gaze dropped to my arm, and I tucked my hand farther behind my back. Damn hellhounds and their ultra-heightened senses.

"Is that so?" Liam asked, his mouth tightening. "You would know, right?" He nudged his son, and I couldn't help but wonder what his eyes looked like right now. If his voice was any indication, Liam was angry, and he was having a challenging time holding it in. "Listen to the oread, son. They know a thing or two about the weather."

I started backing toward the road. "Hence the rain boots." Nervous laughter escaped me. "They're really good for puddle jumping." My mouth needed to close now. Like, really.

Jack snorted. "What are you? Twelve?"

I couldn't tell if he was playing along because he didn't want to admit he'd burned my hand, or if he was really being sarcastic. I chose to believe he was playing along.

Tapping my chest with my non-throbbing hand, I flashed a smile at the group. "In my heart, I am. Gotta go! I'm late!"

Without a single glance backward, I hightailed it to the end of Petran Road, heart pounding. My breathing was labored when I finally stopped, not from exhaustion but from nervous excitement. In the distance, Danzan Park spread out before me, the large grounds on the southeast corner of town and near my destination. At several hundred acres, Danzan Park was a place full of countless fun outdoor opportunities. There was a playground, a picnic area, dog park, disc golf course, public pool, soccer fields, basketball courses, ice rink, skate park, and a spacious area for concerts and festivals. There was also a lake. I spent a lot of time walking dogs there.

Lifting my wounded hand, I studied it. Despite the redness of my fingers, the burns didn't hurt anymore. The spots weren't bad enough to blister, but they should have felt more uncomfortable than they did. Adrenaline, maybe? Some weird hellhound pain-numbing magic? Or had Jack only meant to scare me?

"You're later than usual," a female voice called out.

Dogs of all shapes and sizes jumped up on a chain-link fence, tails wagging and tongues lolling. Some of them raced around the pen barking while others rested in the grass.

Isa Hilton, Havenwood Falls' resident veterinarian, approached me from the side of a nondescript stone building. A sign hanging from a post in the yard read *Havenwood Falls Animal Shelter.* I had volunteered at the shelter for a couple of years, even fostering Slink before deciding to adopt her. While I didn't get the chance to volunteer as much as I had in the past, I made it a point to come once a week.

A much nicer building close to the shelter had a manicured lawn and paw-shaped stepping stones leading up to a shining glass door. A sign near the road read *Havenwood Falls Animal Hospital.* Both buildings were owned and operated by Isa. Isa was the most interesting human I'd ever met. With dark hair and wide-set eyes, she was beautiful, her features a strong testament to her mother's Korean roots. Her height, she once told me, came from her father.

A tattoo, a yellow sunflower wrapped by a thorny black rose, peeked out at me from her wrist, her white lab coat obscuring most of the design. The tattoo was Court-issued. All the supernatural creatures in Havenwood Falls were required to have one—mine was a charm bracelet tattooed around my ankle—which was why Isa was so fascinating. Although she was human, she had telekinetic powers. *Strong* telekinetic powers.

"The kittens in the back need worming." Isa paused in front of me, a pen poised over a day planner in her hand. "We had an unexpected drop-off last night—two beagle mixes that need dipping. Other than that, it's just the basic duties."

I scrunched my nose. "None of the other volunteers came in this morning, did they?"

Isa sighed. "It's so much harder to find good volunteers during the summer. Why is that?"

"Vacations, sleep, parties, hookups, more sleep . . . geez, I have no idea what the allure could be. I much prefer cleaning up dog poo and worming baby kittens."

Isa shook her pen at me, her megawatt smile revealing a dimple in her cheek. "Sad thing is, you actually mean that when you *should* be doing all that other stuff, except maybe not the hooking up."

"Well, I guess you don't need the extra help th—"

Jerking me toward the shelter, Isa whopped me on the rear with her day planner. "Go. Scoot. I won't say another word."

Chuckling, I walked into the building, my nose taken hostage by the overwhelming odor of bleach and flea control products. Opening cabinets in the cramped back room, I found the kitten wormer, made my way to the cat room, and got to work.

It was after lunch when the rain began, the sound soft on the shelter's roof. Because I'd known it was coming, I'd retrieved the dogs from the outside pen and was leaning against the wall, listening to it pelting the windows, when the uneasiness suddenly hit me. A dark, strange sensation, sharp and painful, bloomed in my stomach, and I doubled over, my head spinning. As quickly as it appeared, the pain and dizziness left me, but the uneasiness remained.

"What?" I mumbled, clutching my abdomen. For most, occasional pain and lightheadedness were a normal part of life, stemming from a host of causes, from malnutrition or disease to a menstrual cycle.

But I wasn't most people, and I certainly wasn't normal.

Oreads didn't get sick. Not ever. We could get injured, but we did *not* get sick. If we died, it was because someone or something deliberately killed us. Which meant whatever had happened to me wasn't remotely close to normal for my kind.

"Hey, you okay?" Isa walked in, snapping an umbrella shut behind her.

I straightened, startled. "Yeah . . ." I shook my head, clearing it. "I just . . ." Just what? "You know, I don't know." Forced laughter leaked out of me. "I'm good." A cold sweat broke out on my brow and, for a moment, I forgot where I was and who I was with. "What did you ask me?"

Isa blinked. "I asked if you were okay."

What did she mean, was I okay? *Something* had just happened, but for the life of me, I couldn't remember what it was. Had I been in pain?

I laughed softly. Whatever. Oreads didn't get sick. "Why wouldn't I be?"

"You were doubled over just now," Isa said gently. "Are you sure you're okay?"

Doubled over? "No . . . I wasn't." Was I? "Everything's good," I promised.

Isa studied me, her dark eyes searching my face, unconvinced. "Okay, I'll take your word for it. We have a mange case boarding at the clinic. I have him isolated, but we're going to need to replace some things after he's back at home. We need to be extra vigilant about washing our hands, so it doesn't spread to the shelter."

"Okay." My thoughts strayed, Isa's words droning on in the background, as comfortable against my ears as the rain pattering against the windows.

Was I okay?

CHAPTER 4

JACK PETERS

"*W*hat the hell were you thinking?*"

Pops's voice rang through my head as I drove my bike through the night. The sun had set hours ago, and although most teens would have had to check in with their parents by now, things worked differently at my house. For one thing, we lived at the MC clubhouse, a place of excess and sin on a difficult day and money and underhanded business deals on a good one. Once I proved I could control my hellhound-given powers, Pops quit keeping tabs on me. Having no rules was supposed to teach me how to get around the law. My recent mess-up hadn't left Pops in the best of moods.

Cressida's shocked face haunted me, her disbelieving look mingling with Pops's angry words in my head. Still, she hadn't ratted me out. Even after she realized Pops knew what happened, his heightened hearing having caught our exchange, she hadn't ratted me out. She'd protected me. That meant a lot to guys like me.

Why did I burn her?

Pulling my motorcycle to a stop outside Havenwood Falls Cemetery, I cut the engine and stared off into the night. Even with my sunglasses on, I could see everything in the dark. A hellhound's heightened senses included night vision. We also didn't sleep much, and if we did, we preferred sleeping during the day.

The cemetery loomed before me, its arched entryway covered in climbing white roses and draped in white wisteria. Water dripped in places from the afternoon rain showers, the *drip-drip* loud in the stillness. Most visitors found the place lonely and sad, but for me, cemeteries felt like home, welcoming and full of love. A place where souls passed through. A place of goodbyes and new beginnings. There *were* hints of anger and loneliness, too, but mostly it was a place of beautiful memories, the serious stuff having been left outside the cemetery grounds. Most souls didn't take bad memories with them in death. In some cases, they forgot their past lives entirely, their spirits prepared for the crossing over. The souls that did take the past with them had some serious anger issues. Either that, or they'd been through some deep shit in life.

Climbing off my bike, I crouched inside the cemetery's entrance, my fingers digging through the damp soil, knuckle deep. Overwhelming warmth flowed through me, calming my troubling thoughts. Cemetery grounds were watered in tears. Grief was one of the strongest forms of love, a release of love so uninhibited, so unrestrained that it was refreshing. I'd cried when my mother passed away, every tear a drop full of the overwhelming affection I'd felt for her.

"Do you know how weird you look when you do that? Especially from the sky."

I didn't look up. I didn't have to. Breckin Roberts and I tended to run into each other often at night. As a Nephilim, part angel and part human, he liked flying when the world was asleep. At six feet two, the recently graduated senior and I were eye to eye, his golden brown hair and amber eyes completely opposite from my soot-colored hair and red-tinted irises. But we had a lot in common. Both of us kept to ourselves, more aloof than social.

Breckin leaned against the cemetery's entryway. "Something's troubling you."

I glanced at him, a small smile playing on my lips. "How are you and Viv these days?"

Vivienne Freeman was Breckin's soul mate, and there'd been a lot of adventure in their lives recently.

Breckin studied me. "Your changing the subject is only making me more curious."

Rising to my feet, I faced him, all pretenses gone. "You and Viv were at Havenwood Falls High. What do you know about Cressida Manos?"

Whatever Breckin expected me to say, it wasn't that. "The mountain nymph?" He stepped away from the entryway. "Red hair. Overly cheerful. Yea high." He lowered his hand, holding it about a foot below his chin. "Little bitty thing."

"That'd be her."

Breckin chuckled. "So *not* your type, man. She's too . . . well behaved. And sweet enough to give anyone a cavity. Seriously, the ultimate optimist. What's up with that?"

"My brother has—"

"No excuses."

"Damn you, Breckin." Grimacing, I ran a hand through my hair. "I burned her. Twice."

Breckin froze. "You what?"

"I burned her."

Silence fell between us, Breckin's incredulous stare making my skin crawl. Being what he was, he knew more than most about how hellhounds worked and the personal rules we liked to follow. A rogue hellhound with no respect for humanity was dangerous.

"You're serious," he said finally, a chuckle escaping with the words.

"It's not funny, man."

"Oh, no, yeah it is. For you to falter like that . . ." He laughed harder. "Cressida Manos, Havenwood Falls High's most likely to be everyone's friend. Damn, I wasn't expecting that."

I glared. "That's what's bugging me. I don't even know her, so I can't figure out why she's getting under my skin. She didn't even do anything."

Breckin started to speak, but I stopped him. "Hellhounds don't do the whole bonding, mating, soul mate thing, so don't even suggest it."

He knew we didn't, but somehow, I felt like it needed to be emphasized. Especially since he was currently glowing with soul mate love.

Breckin shrugged. "Maybe you just like her."

"I don't know her."

"Attracted to her?"

"Have you seen her?"

"That's harsh, dude." Breckin's brows furrowed. "But I see your point. She dresses like she just got out of bed and has no seductive qualities at all. Don't you hellhounds prefer femmes fatales?"

"I don't think this is attraction."

"Don't you only burn when you're angry?"

"That's my point. Something's off."

Breckin grimaced. "I don't think I'm going to be much help tonight, buddy. I'm out, but if you need—"

I waved him off. "Yeah, yeah."

He grinned, backing up before lifting into the sky. I looked away, my gaze dropping to the ground. I knew better than to watch him take flight. With my vision, an angel's wings were bright enough to temporarily blind me.

Talking with Breckin always helped organize my thoughts. Burning Cressida shouldn't have happened, not unless something about her was off somehow. Which begged the question: what was wrong with her?

CHAPTER 5

CRESSIDA MANOS

"*H*ave you been to the jewelry store today?" Mom asked when I entered the house later that night.

Kicking off my rain boots, I inhaled the scent of pizza, a special kind only Mom made with sautéed cashews and water chestnuts on a bed of spinach and grated parmesan and provolone cheese, all of it placed carefully on flatbread and spread with a secret sauce, the ingredients of which Mom refused to divulge. It might sound funny, but my mother's food somehow tasted like the mountains. Like fresh wind blowing down into a ravine or a chilly rain on stone.

"I volunteered at the shelter all day, since you were at the studio. Was I supposed to stop by the store?"

Mom stepped into the foyer, a spoon in her hand. She tasted the sauce on the end, and then offered it to me. "Too salty?"

Barefoot, her auburn hair pulled back from her unlined face, my mother, Theia Manos, looked more like my older sister than my six-hundred-year-old mother.

Licking the spoon, the wonderful flavor exploding on my tongue, I shook my head. "Just right. Don't do a thing to it."

Mom smiled. "Just what I hoped to hear." She reentered the kitchen, banging cabinets open in her haste to finish dinner. "Don't worry about the store. I just wondered if you'd seen the new jewel your dad bid on."

Slink's furry body curled around my ankles as I walked into the kitchen. Full of stainless steel appliances, whitewashed cabinets, and lots of greenery, both fake and real, the kitchen was my mother's favorite place to be. The entire back wall was a display case full of pottery and art projects shoved among rock collections and hanging ferns. Greenhouse-inspired. Magazines would eat it up.

"The one CDI delivered this weekend?" I asked, hopping onto a wrought iron barstool. I'd been in charge of the Apex shipments, but Leda and Liam had both mentioned a special jewel delivery. Dad got a lot of special deliveries.

"That's it. You should see it." Mom's gaze went distant, her blue eyes sparkling. "It's mesmerizing." She peered at me. "It reminds me of your eyes, actually."

"So it's an emerald?"

If there was one thing mountain nymphs loved more than rocks and art, it was precious stones. Anything that came from the earth called to us. We understood stones much better than we understood people. And yet, we were people persons. Go figure.

"Like no emerald I've ever seen. For once, I can't fault your father for this purchase."

I laughed. "What about Leda? Is she giving him a tough time?"

"No, not after seeing it. I think she's just as mesmerized as the rest of us. Speaking of, I think Leda may have a girlfriend. She's been a little off lately. Primping more than usual. Gone longer than normal on her lunch breaks."

"That's great, right?"

Mom set a bowl of sauce on the bar, and I dunked my finger into it. She swatted me with her spoon.

"Maybe. You never know, especially with new relationships. No more sauce until . . ." Mom's words trailed off, her eyes narrowing. "What happened to your fingers?"

I snatched my hand away, shoving it under my leg. "Nothing. A little red paint I couldn't wash off." The burn I'd gotten from Jack was still there, less red but unhealed. Oreads could survive falls and heavy blasts and could heal decently fast when our skin was punctured. Not as fast as some immortals, but decent. But Jack's burn was lingering longer than usual. Maybe because he was a hellhound?

"That didn't look like paint."

"You don't trust me?"

Mom blew out a breath. "That is the worst thing ever a child can ask a parent."

I grinned. "Why?"

"You know why."

My laughter filled the kitchen, echoing off the cabinets. "Seriously, it's all good."

The front door opened, and Dad walked in, his wiry five-foot-nine-inch frame and shocking white blond hair filling the space with a brightness only Dad could manage.

Hanging his suit jacket up by the door, he loosened his tie, then tousled my hair. "What did I miss?"

"Your daughter being petulant." Mom opened the oven and shoved the pizza inside. "You've got twenty minutes until I pull this out."

Dad gave Mom a quick kiss, then rushed up the stairs to change clothes. I sat back, watching Mom as she patted her flushed cheeks, her gaze on his retreating back. I envied their relationship. It was such a beautiful love, over four hundred years strong, the kind I hoped to find someday.

Dad returned in an old sweat suit Mom and I were forever trying to get him to throw away. It was so old, it had holes in places that definitely shouldn't have holes.

"Did you bring the stone home?" Mom asked, retrieving the pizza before setting it on the table.

I moved to the dining room, settling into a seat on the right side of the table while Dad took the head.

"I left it at the store. I feel like it's safer there."

Safer?

Mom tucked the dress she wore under her legs and sat down, her mouth falling open. Dad liked showing off the things he bought. In some cases, we endured hours-long history lessons before being forced to weigh the jewelry in our hands while looking at it from every possible angle.

"Are you worried about theft? Here?" Mom asked.

Dad's brows furrowed. At six hundred ten years old, Dad normally didn't look a day over forty, but tonight he looked older somehow. Troubled. "It's just a feeling."

Mom studied him, frustration evident in her gaze. "Better safe than sorry, I guess. Maybe tomorrow?"

Dad glanced at her, a suspicious glint in his eyes. "Tomorrow? To the house? Why?"

"Why not?" Mom asked.

"You can come by the store to see it."

Our heads shot up, my gaze clinking with Mom's, like two wineglasses before a toast. An awkward, very bad toast. Dad was treating Mom like a customer. A nosy, not appreciated customer.

"I know, but—" Mom began.

"Come there," Dad said firmly and loudly, startling us both. Dad rarely got agitated, and he never raised his voice.

"Okay," Mom replied meekly. "I didn't mean anything by it."

My stomach churned. "If you'll excuse me." Pushing my chair back from the table, I looked at them both. "I think I'm done. It was great, Mom." Truthfully, I'd not even touched the food, my appetite spoiled by their dissent.

My parents barely spared me a glance, their gazes locked on each other. Clutching my stomach, I sped up the stairs, Slink on my heels. My parents weren't the type to argue, and when they did, it wasn't over something as small as a jewel. After four hundred years together, they could read the mood too easily to fight over small things.

"What was that about?" I asked aloud, shedding the clothes I'd worn at the shelter only to replace them with another sweatshirt and a pair of cotton shorts. In the bathroom next to my bedroom, I splashed my face with water, brushed my teeth, and then crawled into my bed.

For some reason, my body felt heavy. Not so much tired as burdened. As if I was trying to pull myself out of quicksand.

Something was off.

My fingers suddenly burned, and I looked down at them warily. Had Jack Peters realized the same thing?

CHAPTER 6

JACK PETERS

A few hours before dawn, I pulled my motorcycle back up to the cemetery. I'd made three trips around town, keeping to the back roads before looping back to the gate, my thoughts a chaotic mess of questions I couldn't answer.

But I knew someone who could.

Cutting off the engine on my bike, I relaxed on the seat, my body beginning to adjust to the silence when the hairs on the back of my neck suddenly stood on end, my eyes, ears, and nose alert to something out of place in the graveyard.

Hellhounds were natural protectors of the dead, of passing souls and those seeking entry into the underworld. While I'd been trained to deal with the dead, and had been forced to on occasion, I'd never had to deal with living trespassers in the Havenwood Falls cemetery. Visitors came in and out at all hours of the night—especially the vampires—but the feeling I got now wasn't coming from a visitor. It was from an intruder, and he was desecrating something. The dead didn't like their graves messed with.

With silent footfalls, I followed a path through the human cemetery to an arched tunnel that went under Blackstone Road, the passageway leading into an older section of the cemetery reserved for Havenwood Falls' supernatural families. This part of the property was a hodgepodge of different tombs. Some of them were protected by metal cages to keep the dead from rising. Others were covered in runes and magic symbols. Mausoleums dotted the front section, and glass balls and crystals hung from the trees, some of them clinking together in the night. Wind chimes—a recent addition by relatives of the deceased—hung from a post near a grave, and the breeze played music with the hollow pipes as I ducked out of the tunnel.

A familiar figure crawled in the dirt near an older tombstone unmarked by runes, magic, or metal, a trail of curly red hair flowing down her back.

"What the hell," I murmured, stepping forward. It was almost as if I'd conjured her with my thoughts. Except I hadn't expected to see her doing this.

Cressida Manos kneeled before the gravestone, her fingers covered in paint, her hands trailing streaks of neon colors over the stone. Small empty bottles lay strewn in the dirt around her. She giggled as she worked, completely unfazed by the mud coating her legs and bare feet.

"What the devil are you doing?" I demanded.

Cressida glanced up, but rather than be concerned or surprised by my presence, her giggles grew, her finger rising to her lips. "Shhh, I'm making them pretty."

My mouth fell open. "Who?"

"The dead." Plastering more paint on the stone, she hummed under her breath. "I thought they needed a little color."

"You thought?" Gripping her by the shoulders, I dragged her backwards. "Does this grave belong to your family?"

I knew it didn't. I knew all the graves in both sections of the cemetery by heart, but I was curious about her reply.

She twisted out of my grip and crawled away, mixing the paint on her hands with mud as she went. "It's nice to help out strangers. Don't you ever feel charitable?"

Something about the way she moved, her face full of unhinged glee, made me uneasy. She seemed like a completely different person. As if she were possessed. "This isn't charity. It's vandalism."

Laughing, she pushed herself to her feet, hugging herself, the gesture spreading paint and mud to her clothes. Streaks of it ran down the side of her face. She looked like a part of the earth, rising like fire and vengeance, and for the first time, I saw beauty.

I was insane.

"Vandalism?" She swayed on her feet. "Coming from the son of an outlaw, that's rich. Be a good boy and fetch . . . or, you know, something. Isn't that what dogs do? Can't you go to hell from here? I bet they have a nice big playground just for your kind."

I snorted in disbelief, my gaze locked on her face. Her green eyes were wild and unfocused. I didn't know much about Cressida Manos, but the things I'd heard and the few times I'd encountered her personally didn't match up with the girl I was facing now. This wasn't the girl who'd tried to protect me from getting in trouble. There was something evil about the girl I was facing now, and it triggered the hellhound inside of me.

"Yeah," I sneered, "there's a whole obstacle course for dogs down there. We heel, fetch, roll over, play dead, and occasionally, we breed."

My words caused her to freeze, her shocked gaze swinging to mine, her hand flying to her mouth. "Oh." A small giggle escaped, her palm turning the laugh into something like a sneeze. "Oh! You have a sense of humor. If a little misguided." She wagged a dirt-crusted finger at me. "You're funny."

I didn't laugh. "And you're drunk."

"No," she giggled louder, "not possible." She hiccupped. "I don't drink." Stumbling toward me, she rose up on her tiptoes, lifted her head, and breathed into my face. "See? Nothing."

She smelled like green apples and toothpaste.

"It's hard candy." She lost her balance, her hands shooting out, her fingers wrapping around my forearms. "It's good for focusing." Dropping one of her hands, she fished in the pocket of her cotton shorts before offering me a plastic-wrapped lump. "Watermelon or apple?"

Rather than accept the candy, I yanked my sunglasses off, stuck them on my T-shirt, and shook her loose before framing her face with my hands. Her head looked tiny sandwiched between my large palms, and I forced her to look at me.

My skin started to heat, and I struggled to keep it cool. No more burning. My control was better than that.

"What is this?" I asked.

Cressida stared at me, her eyes locked on mine, and it was like watching someone hit a light switch. The sarcastic, amused smile on her lips faded into a painful, confused frown. Her gaze widened, her lips moving silently. The same two words over and over until, finally, she managed a weak, "It hurts."

"What?"

"Your stare."

I released her so fast, we both stumbled backwards. "I thought oreads weren't affected by a hellhound's eyes." My mind raced. Burning her would be nothing compared to hurting her with my gaze. My dad wouldn't just be disappointed, he'd be furious. "Oreads can't be affected by a hellhound's eyes. You're immortal, right? Tell me my eyes can't hurt you. Tell me." Even I recognized the desperation in my voice. My dad wouldn't be the only one I'd have to deal with if I hurt someone in Havenwood Falls. I'd also have to deal with the Court.

"What are you talking about?" Cressida asked, bewildered. "Why are you here? What is this?"

I looked up to find her spinning in place, a completely freaked out expression on her face.

"What's going on?" She held her hands up, her eyes taking in the mud and paint. "What am I doing here?"

If I was confused before, it was nothing like the confusion that slammed me now. "What do you mean, what's going on? You were vandalizing a tombstone."

Cressida jerked her head toward me, her green eyes dull. "I wouldn't . . . I couldn't . . ."

I nodded at the grave.

She glanced at it, at the paint-smeared stone, and her hands started to tremble. "I wouldn't."

I took a step toward her. "You just did it. Are you telling me you don't remember?"

Her face filled with panic, and her breathing deepened, her thudding heartbeat calling out to the beast in me. It didn't help that I was still upset over the eyes thing.

"I'm telling you I didn't do it!" she cried, her voice shaking as badly as her hands. Her gaze dropped to her feet. "Where are my shoes? Why don't I have shoes on?"

Her fear and confusion engulfed me, twisting my pounding heart, and I reached out, smoothing her wild hair away from her face. "What kind of paint is that?"

She shied away from my touch. "What?"

"The paint," I repeated. "What kind is it?"

Taking a deep breath, she squinted at the empty bottles on the ground. "Acrylics."

I fought back a laugh. Even deranged and out of her mind, this girl didn't know how to properly break the law. "Well, that's fortunate. I don't think you've been here long enough for it to dry, and the stone was already damp. Help me clean it off."

Leaving her briefly, I went to my motorcycle and removed a bottled water and an extra white T-shirt I'd grabbed earlier in case I stayed overnight at the cemetery.

Returning, I threw her the water. "I'll scrub, you pour."

Catching the bottle easily despite her trembling hands, she twisted the lid off. Together, we kneeled before the headstone, my body completely dwarfing hers. I'd met her sister the day we made the delivery at Summit and Apex, and I didn't remember Leda Manos being this small. Or this ruffled.

Cressida dumped water onto the stone, and I scrubbed at it with the T-shirt, the paint coming off easier than I'd hoped. The nymph's heartbeat slowed as we worked, the work calming her, the thudding less prominent, less panicked.

"You think you can talk now?" I asked.

Leaning back, she glanced at me. "I don't know what happened. I didn't do this."

The girl who'd been painting the tombstone when I found her and the girl I was talking to now were two completely different people, despite sharing the same body.

Sighing, I met her gaze. My sunglasses still hung from my shirt, leaving my eyes naked, but she didn't shy away from my stare. The other girl—the strange, wild version of Cressida—had been hurt by it. "I believe you."

She froze, her throat working hard, swallow after swallow, and I knew she was trying not to cry. "Something is wrong with me."

That I couldn't help her with.

"At least you won't get in trouble for this," I said, perusing our handiwork.

Setting the water bottle down, she fisted her hands, her gaze roaming over the cemetery. Silence fell between us.

"Why are you here?" she asked finally.

Despite the mud, I sat back, feeling the damp ground seep in through the bottom of my jeans. I was already wet from the knees down. "I guess you could say I have a thing for hanging out with the dead."

"I've heard that about hellhounds." Cressida nodded, the movement so resolute it was like she was giving herself permission to do something. "Should we start over?" she asked.

Ah, so that's what she'd been talking herself into. "Start over?"

She offered me her dirt-covered hand. "Cressida."

I didn't take it. "I know your name. No need to reintroduce ourselves."

She glared. "It's a new start."

"Why?" I asked. "I don't think there's anything wrong with the old start."

For a long moment, she stared, and then—after coming to the same conclusion—her face changed, a smile stealing her unease. "I guess not." She gestured at the tombstone. "Thank you."

"Don't sweat it. Dawn'll be here soon. You need a lift home?"

"No, it's quicker for me by foot."

"Even without shoes?" Apparently I didn't know as much about oreads as she did about hellhounds.

"Even without those."

Standing, I brushed myself off. "All right, then. I guess that's my cue. Stay safe, nymph, and try to stay out of trouble. If you find out what happened tonight, please feel free to find me and let me know. The curiosity is killing me. You owe me that much. Deal?"

She gave me an absent look full of turmoil. "Deal."

Her unsettled expression made the beast in me bristle, and I groaned inwardly. I much preferred breaking the law to having the protector in me piqued. Once the protector inside of me was interested, I was screwed.

I had a bad feeling about tonight.

CHAPTER 7

CRESSIDA MANOS

*F*ollowing Jack Peters out of the cemetery, I watched as he straddled his motorcycle, giving me a final curious perusal before revving his engine and taking off into the night. He made an impressive figure in the dark, as impressive as he did in the daylight. It was comforting being near him. Somehow, I trusted him. After tonight, all the rumors about him seemed less like truth and more like conjecture. Then again, I'd overheard stories from his former one-nighters, and they'd been too detailed to be entirely false.

As soon as Jack was out of sight, I started shaking again, my body trembling uncontrollably. My hands fisted, my jaw clenching to keep my teeth from chattering, the tears I'd been holding back slipping down my cheeks. I stared at the cemetery's entrance, a whimper escaping my lips. What happened to me? Why had I come here?

Dread rising like a raging inferno inside of me, I left the grounds, making my way warily into the mountains and up the pass toward my house, faster than any human, but slower than normal for me. Even at night, eyes were everywhere in Havenwood Falls. Shifters prowled, vampires who found it hard to sleep paced into the late hours, and creatures who preferred the dark did gods knew what, as long as it didn't violate Court rules.

The sun was preparing for its trek across the sky when I made it home, and I rushed to rinse my feet with an outside water hose before sneaking inside. According to a clock hanging above our mantle, it was half past four in the morning, and I hurried upstairs, shedding my clothes in the bathroom before stepping into the shower. Water sluiced over my skin, steam rising, the liquid washing away the paint, mud, and shame. Time passed, my skin wrinkling in the water, my head hanging. Not all of the paint came off of my skin, and after finally stepping free of the shower, I dug a bottle of turpentine out of a small wooden desk in the corner of my room, a towel wrapped around me as I scrubbed at my hands.

"This is crazy." I whispered.

Slink jumped onto the desk, knocking the turpentine over, and I jerked off my towel to soak it up.

A light in the hallway switched on, and I dove for my dresser, pulling on an oversized old T-shirt and another pair of cotton shorts just as the door swung open.

"You okay in here?" Mom asked, entering. "I smell turpentine." I didn't have to look at a clock to know what time it was. Mom's schedule was a well-oiled machine, steady and unchanging, which meant she'd been busy in the kitchen while I spent an eternity shedding my shame in the shower.

I nodded, the towel on my head falling off in the process. I caught it. "Yep, all good."

She studied me, her brows arched, and even though there wasn't a hint of accusation in her gaze, my heart beat like a drum inside my chest, each thud full of guilt and terror.

It was suddenly too hot in the room, and I pulled at the collar of my shirt.

"What have I told you about—" Mom began.

I lost it. Completely lost it. "No, no, no! I take it back. I'm not good. Not good at all. Do you know what I did last night, Mom?" Wringing my hands, I paced the room. "I vandalized a tombstone with acrylic paints. Actual acrylics. Like that's a cool thing to vandalize anything with. In the middle of the night. In a cemetery." Pausing, I blew out a breath. "In the middle of the night. In a cemetery." Because I felt that was worth repeating.

Mom's eyes widened. "Cress—"

I slapped my forehead. "I don't even know how I got there. It was in that old part of the cemetery. The section for supernaturals." My words spilled out, along with all my burdens. I'd never been good at keeping things from my parents. "Ican'tevenrememberdoingitbut-Iwasthereand—"

Mom stepped toward me, her hand flying to her chest. "Mercy, Cressida, slow down. What is wrong with you? Did you have a bad dream?"

"No, Mom, I'm telling you I—"

"I never heard you leave the house, and you know how light a sleeper I am."

"Yeah, but, Mom, I—"

"Did you go to sleep as soon as you came up from supper? It's not good to doze off on a full stomach. Gives you bad dreams."

Frustrated, I moved past her to my small bathroom, swung the door open, and pointed at my discarded muddy clothes. "When did my nightmares suddenly involve mud wrestling?"

Mom gasped.

"There's something wrong with me," I told her. "I don't remember going to the cemetery, but I remember being there. I don't remember painting anything, but I remember seeing the tombstone with the paint on it."

I sounded like a crazy person.

Mom brushed past me and picked up the clothes. "Aren't you a little late for April Fools' Day? You're not making sense, sweetheart. Do you think you could have just gone outside? Everything is a little muddy after the rain."

My lips thinned. This was unbelievable. "Are you saying I sleepwalked? Can oreads even do that, Mom? Like, seriously? Can we? Because up until now, I rarely sleep, and I very rarely have any dreams at all."

Mom lifted my clothes, sniffed them, then lowered them again.

I scrunched my nose. "What are you doing? Trying to see if I rolled in something dead while at the cemetery?"

"Checking for alcohol or drugs. Even oreads can get drunk and high."

"Not funny, Mom."

She squinted at me. "Were you alone at the cemetery?"

I hiccupped, one violent hiccup after another, as if my body was vehemently trying to keep me from revealing the fact that I'd been with Jack Peters, bad boy extraordinaire. There was no way Mom would believe there'd been no drugs or alcohol involved if I mentioned him. Even though I was pretty sure he didn't do that kind of thing.

"Sure," I replied, hiccupping.

Mom circled me, sniffing. "This isn't like you. If anything, coming up with outlandish stories was more Leda's thing when she was your age."

My hiccups stopped. "This isn't a story!"

"Then why isn't anyone from the Court showing up at our door? You know if something was wrong with you, the tattoo and the wards in the town should have picked it up."

My whole body slumped. She had a point. "I don't know. Maybe I have some rare oread illness that hasn't been discovered yet. Something the tattoo or the Court's spells wouldn't know to pick up. Like when that virus got past our viral protection software last year, and we had to buy those new computers for the store." My eyes went wide. "I could be dying, and we wouldn't even know!" Rushing to the standing full-length mirror next to my closet, I pulled down my lower eyelids. "I should see a doctor, right?"

In the mirror, I watched Mom roll her eyes. *Seriously* roll her eyes. "Oreads can't get sick, Cressida." She peered at my reflection. "Have you taken a sudden interest in theatre? Is it like this weird obsession Leda suddenly has with the harp?"

I frowned. "I don't think you're hearing me, Mom."

Mom shook my clothes at me, mud and all. "Oh, I'm hearing you. Oreads have strong constitutions, and while we don't always have dreams or sleepwalk, it's not unheard of. But we *don't* get sick. If this is going to become a habit, we'll start bolting the door."

Ugh! I couldn't believe Mom wasn't getting it. Was her disbelief because I was *too* good a daughter? Is this what you got if you never broke the rules?

"Why?" I asked. "So I won't sleepwalk off a mountain? It's not like the fall would kill me."

"Smart-aleck behavior doesn't suit you, darling." Mom cradled my clothes and walked toward the door. "It's after six. Didn't you want to get some art in before the studio opens?"

I sighed, completely defeated. "Are you and Dad okay at least? Last night was weird."

Mom frowned. "We're fine. There's oatmeal on the stove. Brown sugar and butter, just like you like it."

She closed the door behind her, and I fell onto my bed, my gaze on the ceiling. Slink jumped onto my stomach and kneaded me with her paws. I was learning a very important lesson this morning. Sometimes being a supernatural in a supernaturally protected town could be a real pain. Especially if whatever was happening was completely impossible for an oread and somehow undetectable by the Court.

Pulling my pillow out from under my head, I stuffed it over my face and screamed. Had I been dreaming? I mean, could it be possible I had been sleepwalking, and then woken up when Jack found me?

The pillow fell to the bed. That made more sense than being sick.

I glanced down at Slink. "Why can't you be a talking cat? You know, like that one in the Japanese anime you watched with me the other day? A little ancient wisdom would be nice."

Lifting her paw, I pointed it at me, and made my voice echo, all childlike, off the walls. "Your mother is a six-hundred-year-old oread. You're getting nothing from the ancient wisdom department."

I hated it when my fake-talking cat was right.

CHAPTER 8

JACK PETERS

*T*he first thing Pops always did when he wanted me to do something was pretend he gave a shit about the stack of books and DVDs I kept stuffed on a crooked shelf above my desk

My bedroom at the MC clubhouse was a perfect square of chaos. Discarded clothes, loose change in a collection of empty grape soda bottles, a box full of pocket knives, stacks of magazines, and posters of half-dressed women were scattered everywhere: the floors, the walls, and under the bed. The posters hung like wallpaper, the pictures courtesy of the club. Not that I didn't appreciate them.

Pops stood at my desk when I walked in, a towel draped around my neck. I ran the rough fabric through my hair, soaking up the excess water in the strands while Pops ran his fingers down the titles on my shelf. All of them were history books and documentaries, texts and videos ranging from European to American history to stuff about forensic anthropology and archeology.

"Indiana Jones was a badass," Pops mumbled. This was his way of making himself feel better about my taste in literature. I should probably throw in a couple copies of porn.

"You didn't come in here to discuss the Pax Romana or the importance of overseas exploration," I said, yanking the towel off my neck and replacing it with a black band T-shirt. "What's up, Pops? If you're interested in that sibling-comparison article, it's the fourth magazine down." I kicked at the stack next to my bed.

Liam massaged his forehead. "Sometimes I wonder if you came from my loins."

"Does the club know you talk like this?"

"This sparkling personality is reserved specifically for you."

"I'm honored. Really."

Pops grinned. "We're doing a run tonight out of town. Nothing too serious, so I'd like you to ride along. Observe."

I stared.

Pops cleared his throat. "You can't prospect until you finish school, but it wouldn't hurt for you to ride along on some of the less serious runs."

The finishing school thing was Pops's rule for his sons. It didn't apply to others. The general rule—outside of Taemin, me, and Cade—said anyone eighteen and older could prospect, high school diploma or no.

"Did you get this approved?" I asked.

"We voted on it in the last meeting. Minor stuff only."

I sat on the edge of my unmade bed, the black comforter trailing on the hardwood floor at my feet. "Pops—"

"Give it a shot, Jack. You don't have to make any decisions now, and you can always prospect after," he hooked his thumb at the shelf of books, "you're done playing Indiana Jones. You do realize I lived through part of this shit, right?"

Lowering my head, I snorted back a laugh, my hand rubbing the back of my neck. Pops was three hundred fifty years old, which was young for a hellhound. It wasn't like he was in a hurry to hand over the presidency. His outlaw days began in the golden age of piracy. He was forty-eight years old when he first met the famous Blackbeard. Pops especially liked telling that story when he was drunk. Repeatedly, as if it was supposed to get better with each telling. Truth was, I loved hearing it, but there was no way in hell I was telling him that. Liam Peters knew how to tell a story.

"Run tonight," Pops reminded me, moving to the door. "We ride at six o'clock sharp."

My thoughts drifted to Cressida and the weird night we'd spent in the cemetery. The shirt I'd used to clean the tombstone was safely tucked under my mattress, a freakish souvenir, the reminder causing a bud of unease to unfurl in my gut.

"I'm not sure tonight's good for me, Pops." Damn the protector in me. For some reason, I didn't want to be too far away from Cressida Manos.

"No school. No commitments. No excuses," Pops said firmly. "Six o'clock sharp." He left, leaving the door open behind him.

Standing, I pulled a cell phone I rarely used out of the drawer next to my bed, stuffed it into the pocket of my jeans, and followed Pops out the door.

The main room of the clubhouse closely resembled a tavern. A large area with scarred hardwood flooring, it was an open space with a long bar off to the side. A pool table rested in the center of the room surrounded by random tables and red-cushioned, metal-backed chairs. A jukebox sat against the side wall, a worn old couch sagging next to it. A big flat-screen television was anchored near the ceiling facing the room, and old neon beer signs hung along the walls. Two doors, one closed and the other propped open, led to a meeting room and a kitchen.

The smell of bacon wafted through the open door, and I grinned when a dark-haired woman in a tight dress and stiletto heels sauntered out of the kitchen, a plate of food resting in her hands.

Melaina Savage was everything a man could want in a woman and everything a man should be afraid of. The three-hundred-year-old sister of the MC club's vice president and a fellow hellhound, Melaina was the owner of Silk, a nightclub in town, and the only consistent female presence my brothers and I had following our mother's death.

Offering me the plate, she studied me, the red hue in her hazel eyes hidden by special contacts. "Don't think just because I'm feeding you right now that this shit's going to become habit."

I accepted the plate sheepishly. Melaina only showed up this early in the morning if Pops asked her to come. If it was possible for a hellhound to tuck his tail between his legs, I'd do it. "I'm man enough to admit I'm scared right now."

Her brows arched, amusement flirting with her red-stained lips. "What's this I hear about you burning the Manos girl?"

"Oh, shit," I groaned. Knowing Cressida was giving me all sorts of grief.

Melaina thumped me on the forehead with her manicured nails. "When did your daddy start letting you cuss like that?"

I laughed, backing away to shovel food in my mouth before I lost my chance to do it. "There ain't a single clean-mouthed Peters in this house."

"*Isn't*," Melaina corrected. "You're one of the smartest people I know. Don't let people think you're uneducated when you're not."

"Yes, ma'am."

"Now, about the Manos girl . . ."

I kept eating, taking my time swallowing before answering. "It was an accident."

Melaina's face hardened, her eyes blades of hazel steel. "We don't have accidents like that, Jack. We do well staying off the Court's bad side here in Havenwood Falls, and we want to keep it that way. We keep the bad business out of town and the good business in it, and we sure as hell don't abuse our powers."

"Maybe you should be talking to Cade."

"He's still learning," she pointed out. "While you're on the verge of becoming a member of the MC."

Appetite gone, I offered her the plate. "It really was an accident."

Her gaze softened. "You have a bright future ahead of you, Jack. Stay straight, okay? If you've got woman problems, just let me know. If there's one thing I know, it's women."

"Not this one," I mumbled under my breath. "I don't think anyone would understand this one." And that was an understatement. I knew a lot about women, too. Well, physically anyway.

Sudden interest flared in Melaina's gaze. "That sounded like a challenge."

"Nope," I said, shoving the plate at her. "Stay away from this one, please."

Her gaze dropped to the dish in my hand. "I know you haven't forgotten where the kitchen is."

I frowned. "Boy, you sure know how to melt a man's heart."

She laughed. "I don't melt men's hearts, sweetheart. I burn them. Figuratively speaking, so you don't get any ideas."

Her warning reminded me of Cressida, and I took a step toward Melaina, my gaze holding hers. I hadn't put my sunglasses on yet, and I was glad of it. "I promise not to make any more mistakes. Leave the Manos girl to me."

"I'm not that vicious, honey. Follow the rules, and I've got no interest in your love life."

A relieved sigh escaped me.

"I have to say, though, this is the first time I've seen you this torn up about a girl," she said thoughtfully. "I always figured you for the love-'em-and-leave-'em-type, like your daddy."

"This chick isn't one of my girls."

"Hmm," Melaina mused. "Guess that says it all right there." Heels clicking on the floor, she headed for the exit. "You know where to find me."

A chuckle escaped me, my gaze following her affectionately. "Hey, Melaina." She glanced back. "Thanks."

She winked, shoved the door open, and disappeared into the light beyond. We gave each other grief, but the club and the people connected to it were family. All of them.

CHAPTER 9

CRESSIDA MANOS

Coffee Haven was bustling with early morning fatigued visitors when I took my place in line, my hands disappearing into the pockets of my shorts, the oversized shirt I wore so long in the front, it covered the shorts completely.

"You could try harder, you know?" Leda pointed out, taking her place in line behind me. "I swear it looks like you came to town in a sleep shirt and nothing else. It's embarrassing."

"It's comfortable." I rose up on my tiptoes, leaning in close to her ear so I could lower my voice. "And no bra."

Leda huffed in disgust. "There are people in here who can hear you, you know?"

I shrugged. "If they're that interested in what I'm wearing, they need to find a hobby."

Shoes thudded over hardwood floors, and I let my gaze wander over the room. Other than the art studio and animal shelter, Coffee Haven was my favorite place to be in Havenwood Falls. With historic built-in features, including a long marble counter, and strategically placed plants and crystals, Coffee Haven was a beacon of positive energy. Willow Fairchild, the shop's owner and a powerful empath fae, also displayed local art, everything from paintings to sculptures to photography. The large picture window in the front pulled in tons of natural light, creating a sense of warmth that chased away the recent shadows in my brain.

Sitting in their usual spot, the town gossips mingled over coffee, their heads bent close together. Irene Beckett, a retired schoolteacher and one scary old woman, eyed me curiously, the big glasses covering most of her face magnifying her gaze. Despite being a mortal woman, Irene knew entirely too much about the supernatural happenings in Havenwood Falls, but for some reason the Court let her knowledge slide. I wondered whether that was due to respect or fear.

"You're being judged," my sister hissed. "It's the attire." Leda tugged on the hem of her red blazer, the suit jacket a perfect match to her knee-length skirt. "We should go shopping together."

I threw her a look. "I'll stick to the oversized, marked-down stuff at Callie's Consignments. It's much more comfortable than the fancy stuff you get."

She blew out a breath, sending wisps of blond hair flying around her face, the strands falling artfully from her twisted updo. At least her hair listened to her. My hair was going through puberty, completely obstinate and hard to deal with.

"Hey, have you seen Dad this morning?" I asked her.

We moved forward in the line.

"Yeah, why?"

"There seemed to be some tension between him and mom last night. Like, not normal tension. They were arguing about jewelry. That jewel that was delivered the other day. The emerald. Dad even raised his voice about it."

Leda frowned, concern etching her brow. We might have been total opposites in appearance and personality, but we had one thing in common: family was everything. Oreads were a tight-knit species, friendly, accepting of each other—even though we liked to tease—and very close.

"That doesn't sound like them," Leda mumbled.

"Yeah, it wasn't like them at all. It was weird."

Leda squeezed my shoulder gently, the subject of my clothes completely forgotten. "I'll keep an eye on them."

A bright-eyed Willow Fairchild greeted us when we finally made it to the counter, her turquoise-blue gaze searching our faces, her silvery-blond hair highlighting blemish-free pale skin. A bright blue, sleeveless summer dress hugged her slender frame.

Pointing an elegant finger at me, she narrowed her striking eyes. "A tall caramel macchiato with an extra shot of syrup," her finger rose to my sister, "and a tall chai latte."

"Never fails," I said, grinning. Willow always made coming to the shop a personal experience. "How's the little one?" Willow had given birth to a daughter on the first day of school last year.

"Little," Willow replied, working on the order. "She's just starting to walk, and it's taking everything I've got not to wrap her in bubble wrap." She finished one of the orders and set it on the counter. "Caramel macchiato, extra syrup. How about the Manos family? I'm feeling some anxiety in the air this morning."

My stomach clenched. "Nothing we can't get past."

"Hmm." Willow set the second order on the counter. "Chai latte."

Leda pushed a twenty-dollar bill toward her. "I've got both of ours."

Accepting the money, Willow rang up the sale and offered Leda the change. "I would try meditation," she suggested. "Or something personally relaxing. Anxiety isn't good for your health."

"Thanks." Grabbing my coffee, I moved out of line, Leda on my heels. "What are you feeling anxious about?" I asked her once we were away from the crowded front.

Leda pulled the tab on her cup and blew on the steaming liquid. "Nothing."

"Liar." Pushing the shop's door open, I waited for Leda to brush past me. "Mom said something about a new girlfriend."

"What?" Leda spun, mouth opening and closing, a cough bursting out of her lips. "I think I swallowed a fly." Her words came too quick, muffled, and overly eager. She rubbed her throat. I wasn't the only Manos bad at lying.

My lips twitched. "You know flies are born in poo and garbage, right?"

Leda coughed harder. "Seriously, Cressida."

"Just trying to make you feel better."

"I'm reveling in your sisterly warmth and affection." Lifting her cup, she saluted me. "I'm off. No rest for the weary."

"Said no oread ever," I chirped, watching her walk away. She was definitely thinking about someone, and even though I knew she was worried about what I'd said about our parents, I didn't think it was Mom and Dad she was thinking about. Pedestrians eased around me, and I leaned against a lamppost near the coffee shop to get out of their way.

In the distance, the rumble of a motorcycle rose on the wind, and I stiffened, my hands clutching the warm biodegradable cup. The rumble grew louder, and I knew even before the bike came around the bend that the rider was Jack Peters. Maybe it was instinct, or maybe I knew he wouldn't be able to let our night at the cemetery go that easily.

Pulling his motorcycle to a stop at the curb, Jack straightened, his sunglasses-covered eyes searching the area. His leather cut rested over a black T-shirt that hugged his biceps and revealed more of the tattoos on his arms.

I nearly strangled my cup, my eyes glued to him as he lifted his head and inconspicuously sniffed the air. His chin lowered, his face turning my way, and I fought the urge to hide. There was something predatory about Jack Peters.

After removing his helmet and kicking down his stand, Jack climbed off the motorcycle, checking the street before jogging across. Pedestrians stared at him, some of them students from my school, and I sunk as far into the lamppost as I could get.

"You aren't easy to find," Jack said when he was within earshot.

"I didn't know you were looking."

He came to a stop next to me. "I figured we should talk."

Through the window of Coffee Haven, I saw Irene Beckett press her face against the glass, her mouth moving so fast, the gossips next to her—Biddie Half-Moon and Laverne and Sybil Carson—didn't stand a chance of keeping up. This was going to be all over town by nightfall.

"Not here," I murmured, wincing at the grin and little wave Irene Beckett threw my way. "Let's meet at the studio."

"I'll walk with you," Jack offered.

I froze. "You don't need to move your bike?"

"It's just down the street, Manos." He grinned, the smile wicked. "Why? Are you afraid of being seen with me?"

Pushing away from the lamppost, I marched down the sidewalk. "Depends on who you ask. Your reputation precedes you."

"Ah," he fell into step beside me, "so you're worried people will think you're sleeping with me."

It was a statement rather than a question, the ease with which he said it speaking volumes, and embarrassed heat flooded my face. "I didn't mean—"

"Don't even try to remove your foot from your mouth," he said, amusement coloring his words. "It would only be a problem if I was ashamed of it. There's nothing wrong with what I do. Considering I'm walking with a potential criminal at the moment, I'd say we're even. Except," he nudged me, "people don't exactly know you have a wicked side, do they?"

"I don't have a wicked side."

We approached Apex Art Studio, and I ducked past the window of Summit Jewelry to keep from being seen from inside. Jack kept walking, completely nonplussed.

"I think you're ashamed of me," he teased.

Sliding my studio key into the lock, I entered the space, letting him brush past me before shutting and bolting the door. "Why would I be ashamed? Technically, we don't even know each other."

"Says the girl who needed me to get her out of trouble last night."

"Can you just stop? That wasn't me. I don't know what that was." I switched on the overhead lights and inhaled the scent of paint and disinfectants. "I told my mother."

Jack pulled off his sunglasses, his red-hued gaze locking with mine. Alone, he seemed so much larger than he'd seemed out on the street. Dangerous, even. "Wow, you commit a crime, and then you admit it to your parents." He shook his head. "Who are you?" Sarcasm dripped off his words.

I was too caught up in my own thoughts to care. "She didn't believe me."

That got his attention. "What?"

"Apparently, if you're a good enough daughter, it's hard to convince people to believe you're bad." Crossing my arms, I closed my eyes and inhaled deeply. "There's also the fact that oreads don't get sick and that neither my tattoo nor the wards alerted the Court. Final deduction: I was sleepwalking."

Silence fell, and I opened my eyes to find Jack studying my face. "She really didn't believe you?"

"Even after I showed her the muddy clothes."

"Wow, I think I'm doing something wrong with my life. I sneeze too loud, and I've suddenly got a dozen fingers pointing at me."

"Must suck for you."

"I hear the condescension in your voice, and I choose to ignore it." He glanced around the studio, his gaze passing over the yellow walls, unpainted pottery, and empty canvases. "I thought this place didn't open until one?"

"I work on personal art when it's closed."

Sipping on the coffee in my hands, I peered at Jack over the rim of my cup. Without his sunglasses on, he looked less menacing somehow. More boy than beast. Or maybe he was just growing on me.

"Do you think you were sleepwalking?" His question came out of nowhere.

I let my gaze drop to the floor. "It's not unheard of with oreads. Mom says, anyway. So it seems the most logical explanation."

Jack swore under his breath, the words "not fucking likely" audible through his growl. "Look, I'm going to be out of town tonight. Do you have a cell phone?"

My gaze shot up. "Yeah, why?"

"Give me the number." Pulling a phone out of his pocket, he handed it to me. "Service sucks in this town, but texts seem to work better."

"No, they don't."

"Just put your number in, Manos."

I pulled up his contact list and added my name. "Why are you doing this?"

He took the phone from me, and then pressed the number I'd just added. From a desk in the corner of the room, my phone began to ring. I usually left it at the studio hooked up to the charger and didn't bother with carrying it home.

"Now you have my number."

"Why are you doing this?" I repeated.

Jack tucked his phone back into his jeans. "You don't really know any hellhounds, do you? Not too personally anyway, right?" When I didn't respond, he leaned forward. "You were in trouble last night, and it triggered something. The hellhound in me wants to protect you. Once that protective gene gets sparked, it's a bitch to try to ignore." He grimaced. "Lucky me."

"Oh, gods!" I gaped at him. "We're not like bonded now or something, are we? Because from what Dad's told me about your kind, I didn't think you did that. I'm not sure how much you know about oreads, but we're really not all that into—"

Reaching out, he placed his fingers against my lips. "We're not anything. Feeling the need to protect someone has nothing to do with . . . that. Hellhounds are essentially bodyguards when the need arises. If we bonded with everyone we protected, things would get a little awkward."

He dropped his hand, and I sucked in my cheeks. This whole thing was still awkward. Very, very awkward.

"Is that what you do?" I asked. "I mean, when you're not in school? You're a bodyguard?"

He laughed, the sound harsh. "Not exactly. That's more my Pops's thing right now. I do odd jobs for my father's delivery company, and I bide my time."

"Until what?"

"Graduation."

"Oh." Speechless, I moved away from him, keeping myself busy by collecting the supplies I needed to work on a new piece of pottery.

Jack watched, his gaze tracking my movements.

I pulled the studio apron on over my clothes. "Do you want to try?"

He backed toward the door. "Nah, I should go. Look, just keep your cell with you tonight, okay?"

I watched him leave, an odd hollow sensation forming in my chest. It almost felt like . . . I missed him. Which was weird and completely . . . I mean, was it weird?

My cell phone dinged.

Racing to grab it off the desk, I opened my messages.

Keep the phone with you, Manos.

Adding his number to my contact list, I hugged the phone, a smile playing on my lips.

"What's wrong with you?" I asked, slapping myself gently in the face. "It's just a message. A stupid, overbearing, completely dictatorial message." Staring at it again, I fought a smile. "Just a message. Get a grip."

My mouth, brain, and heart weren't even remotely communicating with each other.

A guy had asked for my number. I grinned like a fool.

CHAPTER 10

JACK PETERS

*E*vening came too quickly, the anxiety I felt over the Cressida situation stealing the hours in the day. I'd barely gotten a chance to check in with her when six o'clock rolled around. Pops gathered four of his men, sending his VP, along with his most trusted club members, on a more difficult run while the rest of us straddled our motorcycles, helmets on and engines rumbling.

We hit the road at six sharp. A delivery truck preceded us, and I fell to the back of the group as we rode out, my tires eating the asphalt beneath me. The mountains loomed before us, starkly beautiful in the late afternoon. Like sleeping giants curled into a fetal position.

Silence and wind. That was the tale of the road. Stark, lonely, and beautiful. The sun began to set as we cruised forward, streaks of orange, pink, and purple blooming across the sky like fireworks. Riding with a club was all about rank—the higher your seniority, the further up the line you rode. Being a potential prospect, I was nothing more than a hang-around, but I didn't mind pulling up the rear.

I enjoyed the trip, letting the wind massage my scalp, its chilly fingers pulling the cobwebs out of my brain. As a minor, I should have been wearing a helmet, but breaking the law wasn't something my father sweated, especially when I appeared old enough to be without one. An accident wouldn't kill me either, and I enjoyed the wind, so I didn't always follow the rules.

My father once told me being on the road was a lot like being married. Exhilarating, unexpected, and full of unseen obstacles. Navigating it was like making love to a woman. How far you made it depended on how much of yourself you were willing to give up. Pops was a philosopher at heart.

The roads were steep and winding, the darkening horizon a bruising wall of trees and cliffs, meadows and valleys. For me, it was all about the ride. I didn't need a destination. There was something beautiful about not knowing where I wanted to go.

A little over two hours later, with miles and miles of road and Havenwood Falls behind us, we entered Montrose, the roads growing bumpier as we pulled through intersections, under lights, and past a group of warehouses, each more run down than the next.

It was after eight o'clock when we finally pulled into a parking lot. A group of men, all of them in leather cuts, waited on us. They straightened when we approached, a couple of them throwing cigarettes to the ground before grinding the butts into the asphalt.

Pops waved me to the side, and I parked away from the group, leaning back on my bike to wait. I was a bystander, a long-distance observer, only along for the ride. Participating in business was an earned privilege.

Pops dismounted, removed his bike gloves, and shook hands with a burly, bearded man. The guy smelled like a human, fear and adrenaline rolling off him in waves, the scent of drugs permeating his clothes. It was a wretched smell, and one of the reasons most hellhounds didn't indulge in much outside alcohol and weed.

I laughed under my breath. If only Cressida could see me now. Our lives couldn't be any more different. The people we called friends and the family we shared our homes with were nothing alike.

Why do you care? The question echoed in my brain, and I massaged my temples.

After a brief meeting in the parking lot, Pops disappeared into a warehouse, his head bent near the bearded guy's, the two of them in deep discussion. I could hear every word they said, but I tuned out the conversation, because the less I knew about my father's business dealings, the better off I was. Especially if I chose not to prospect with the MC.

Time passed, and I climbed off my bike, making my way into a barren field next to the parking lot, the beast in me restless.

Pulling my cell phone out of my pocket, I texted Cressida.

Jack: Everything okay?

Her response was quick.

Cressida: All good.

I dropped the phone back into my pocket, hooked my thumbs in my belt loops, and looked up at the sky. A blanket of stars stared down at me. When I was a little boy, before my mother died, she'd told me the stars were a minefield of explosives. That if a person could touch them, they'd immediately detonate and dissolve. Stars, she said, weren't meant to be handled. They were only meant to be enjoyed. Now that she was gone, they didn't look the same. Sometimes I wished I could touch them, to see how many of them I could destroy. Not because I wanted to get rid of the stars, but because I wanted to prove my mother was right.

Laughter rolled into the night from the parking lot, and I shook myself, digging once more for my phone to check the time. I really needed to start wearing a watch. An hour had passed.

The beast in me howled, feeling caged and helpless. This part of being a hellhound bugged me. Not that I didn't want to care for people, but once I got worried, it literally consumed me, turning me into an obsessive creature hell-bent on keeping someone safe.

I texted Cressida again.

Jack: What are you up to?

Five minutes passed with no response, and I began to pace the field, kicking at the dirt and rocks beneath my combat boots.

Jack: Did my message go through?

Another ten minutes. Still no response. The hairs on the back of my neck stood on end, the hellhound within howling. He didn't like not knowing how she was. *I* didn't like not knowing how she was. Although I referred to the hellhound within me as "he," the beast and I were one and the same.

"Let's ride," Pops called.

My bike had never felt so good. I'd also never been so tempted to eschew tradition and ride ahead of the group. We may be outlaws, but Pops had drilled responsibility into every single one of us so deeply, we'd become one with the word. A well-oiled machine.

The itch to get home must have been strong for all of us because we rode faster going back in than we had coming out. I wondered if the way I felt now was the same urgency people felt when hellhounds were after them, when the hounds of hell were on their trail. Literally

Slowing at a traffic light, we pulled to a stop, and I dug my phone out.

The screen blinked, a message waiting, and I scrambled to open it.

Cressida: I'm in trouble.

My heart skipped a beat.

Jack: Where are you?

She didn't reply.

The light turned green, and we took off. My pulse raced, and I counted my breaths to keep my skin cool and my temper under control.

Guilt ate at me, and I didn't know if it was because my beast wanted to protect Cressida, or if it was because I was starting to really care about her.

Her too-slim body, unruly red hair, and small face filled my thoughts, and I scoffed. There was no way I was interested in her. Was I? The way she smiled, and the way she'd tried protecting me when I burned her also raced through my brain, and I sucked in a breath. Was I?

Worry ate away at my gut, her message ringing in my head. *I'm in trouble.*

CHAPTER 11

CRESSIDA MANOS

Tall, lean, and intimidating, Deputy Tate Kasun studied me, his dark eyes sparkling with humor despite the police station's low lighting and the absolutely insane position we were both in.

"I feel like this is one of those television shows where, at any moment, someone is going to jump out and say this is all a prank." He tapped a pen in front of me. "Cressida Manos, of all people."

"I'm guessing it wouldn't help to say it wasn't me?" I posed it as a question.

Tate leaned back in his chair, pulling at the collar of his uniform, his foot tapping the station's hardwood floors. "I think what we have to remember here is how absolutely brilliant your life of crime is. Not only did you get the spray paint from your own family's store, you paid for it. *Paid* for it. I can't decide if you are the most honest criminal I've ever brought in, or the least logical."

I pouted. "This doesn't feel very professional, Deputy Kasun."

"My sister would agree, but then she'd probably have a lot to say about you sitting in this chair right now."

A member of my graduating class at Havenwood Falls High, Willa Kasun was Tate Kasun's younger sister and a shapeshifting wolf. All of the Kasuns were. My life was becoming canine-complicated, from getting caught by a hellhound in a cemetery to being arrested by a wolf while graffitiing two businesses in Miller's Plaza. The worst part? I couldn't remember committing the crimes. Unless you count the part where I came to covered in incriminating evidence and holding empty spray cans while outside a business in a halo of flashing police lights.

Weren't there reality shows less dramatic than this?

The door to the police station flew open, and my parents walked in, both frowning. Tate and I stood simultaneously.

My dad's eyes fell to my hands. "Really, Tate, handcuffs?"

Tate shrugged. "If you're going to have an interesting story to tell at school, you might as well go big."

Did I mention how much I loved Tate Kasun? Except maybe the whole "he arrested me" thing. He was much nicer than his jerk of a brother, Conall.

My gaze flew to my mother. "I told you I did it!"

Interest piqued, Tate glanced between us. "Is that a confession?"

"No!" I sputtered, my eyes flying anywhere and everywhere to avoid his gaze. The room blurred, the tan-colored walls and wooden blinds giving the place a warmer feel than any police station had the right to have. "I just meant that . . . that . . . ugh!"

Mom approached me, her auburn hair pulled away from her face. A loose button-up tunic, the buttons haphazardly done up, rested over a pair of khaki slacks.

"I'm telling you something is wrong with me," I told Mom before she could reach me.

She closed her eyes, inhaled, and then opened them again. "Talk to us, Deputy."

Tate remained standing. "I got a call from some locals who said they saw someone vandalizing property, and I found your daughter spray painting the outside of VIP Nails and Long & Associates CPA. Not only are there witnesses, but I caught her in the act, and so did my dash cam. You can't get better evidence than that." He glanced at me. "Fortunately for your daughter—"

"Cressida," I inserted.

"Not now," Dad warned me.

I pinched my lips together. Father's Day was right around the corner, and I wasn't exactly making this year a brilliant one.

"Fortunately for your daughter," Tate continued, "both Dao Pham and Brian Long are willing to not press charges, as long as she promises to clean up the graffiti." He sighed. "I've already notified the Court."

We all knew what that meant. Because I was a supernatural, any crime I committed would be reviewed by the Court of the Sun and the Moon. Consisting of the leaders of the Old Families, the Court's main purpose was to maintain peace in the town, especially among the supes, while ensuring the town's supernatural secrets were protected. This was the reason the supernatural residents were required to sign into the Court Registry and receive a tattoo.

"Because she's a minor and because Pham and Long are willing to waive the charges, I doubt she's going to have to stand before a formal review, but I'd expect to at least hear from Addie or Saundra Beaumont."

My father nodded. "Does this mean she can leave with us now?"

Tate made a show of undoing my handcuffs. "I have no reason to hold her." Nodding at me, he added, "Make sure you show up tomorrow morning to clean up those storefronts. I don't care how long it takes you. You got lucky this time."

Rubbing my wrists, I looked at him. "What if I *want* to talk to the Court? What if I think something is wrong with me?"

Tate's eyes narrowed, lips pursing thoughtfully. "I can put in a request, but I don't doubt they'll be contacting you themselves."

"Wait a minute," Mom protested. "I told you, Cressida, if it was anything worse than sleepwalking, we'd know by now."

It wasn't that Mom wanted to avoid the Court, but everyone in Havenwood Falls had a healthy dose of fearful respect for the Court members. Unless conditions warranted, it was better to remain under the radar.

"Sleepwalking?" Tate asked, surprised.

"Oreads can have vivid dreams," Mom told him.

Tate laughed. "Who knew your mind was so full of mischief, Cressida?"

Dad threw him a look.

Tate cleared his throat, his fingers pulling at his shirt. It looked like it was suffocating him. "Well, then, that does it. I'll finish filling out the report, and if you want to avoid charges, make sure you show up at Miller's Plaza on time."

"She'll be there," Mom promised, resting her hand on my back, not so gently urging me toward the door. We'd barely cleared the entrance when she turned on me. "Cressida Gwen Manos, I swear to th—"

"I feel like swearing might not be the best idea at the moment," I interrupted. Mom glared, and I took a step back. "But then again, if it makes you feel better."

Dad pinched the bridge of his nose. "What were you thinking?"

"I wasn't," I protested. "I'm telling you, it wasn't me!"

"Then how do you explain what just happened? They told us they had you on video."

We were so caught up in our heated debate that none of us saw or heard the motorcycle pull up to the police station.

"Hey," Jack's deep, familiar voice inserted. "Everything okay?"

My parents' horrified gazes slid slowly—ever so slowly—to the leather-vested biker on the sidewalk. Relief and dread filled me. Relief because I was glad to see him. Dread because I wasn't quite sure how to explain him to my parents.

Dad spoke first. "What's this?"

Jack pulled off his sunglasses, his gaze finding my face.

"Is this the trouble you meant?" he asked, nodding at the police station.

I tilted my head. "It happened again."

Mom's eyes widened, her gaze flicking between us, her body frozen.

"I . . ." She paused, shook her head, and covered her eyes with her palms. "I'm going to remove this hand, and when I open my eyes,

316

we're going to be back at home and this is all going to be a bad dream."

Silence.

She dropped her hand.

I forced a smile. "Surprise?"

Mom took a fortifying breath. "You're still here. He's still here. *We're* still here."

My father's absolute refusal to move or speak completely freaked me out.

"Breathe, Dad," I prompted.

His face turned red, the flush so unexpected, I stumbled away from him, the move taking me closer to Jack.

In a deliberately low, menacing tone of voice, Dad gritted out, "What. Is. This?"

I bit my lip. "You know how I told you I painted that tombstone in the cemetery?"

"No," Dad answered.

"Yes," Mom replied.

They looked at each other.

"What? Why didn't you tell me this?" Dad asked.

Mom's hands found her hips. If she'd touched any other spot on her body, I wouldn't have worried, but her hips were a bad, bad sign.

I waved my hands at my parents, garnering their attention before their trivial debate turned into a full-blown argument. If I thought introducing them to Jack was scary, seeing them fight was even more terrifying. "This is Jack Peters."

My parents didn't return the introduction.

Dad offered a tight smile. "I've heard of him."

Sure he had.

I suddenly wanted to do the whole "cover my eyes and take a time out" thing my mom was so fond of.

"Jack's the one that found me painting the tombstone in the cemetery," I revealed. "Before he helped me clean it up." Mom's lips parted, and I rushed to add, "In my defense, I *did* tell you what happened."

Mom snorted. "Not everything."

"Minor detail."

Stepping toward Jack—who was now standing next to his bike—Mom perused him, her gaze rising up, up, up until it finally landed on his red-hued eyes. "Doesn't look minor."

A muscle in Jack's jaw jumped, and I could tell he was trying very, very hard not to laugh.

"And here I was worried about you," he hissed.

My head shot up. "You were?"

"Okay," my dad scrubbed his face, "why don't we go home, sit down, and talk some things over? I think I need a full detailed description and a drink before," he glanced at Jack and winced, "I can process this properly." Gesturing at Mom and me, he added, "You and you, come with me. You," he pointed at Jack, "stay here."

"Yes, sir." A smile escaping, Jack's gaze dropped to my hip and the outline of my phone. I patted the pocket of my shorts. Even though Tate had arrested me, he'd let me keep my phone. I'm sure part of that had to do with the handcuffs and the victims not pressing charges.

It was going to be a long night.

Trailing after Mom and Dad, I slipped my phone out, quickly typing two words before pressing send.

No matter how much I tried to hide my unease with humor, I couldn't shake the fear that gripped me.

There was no way I was sleepwalking.

CHAPTER 12

JACK PETERS

*C*ressida: **I'm scared.**

Those two words did me in, my gaze locked on the phone in my hand, on the scratched-up screen, and the words I couldn't let go of. Despite being nothing more than letters on a backlit surface, Cressida's text was packed with emotion.

The drive back to Havenwood Falls after the out-of-town run had been trying enough knowing Cressida was in trouble, but to find out she'd committed another crime—albeit minor compared to the stuff I'd done and to the shit I knew my father was involved in—made my head hurt with niggling questions and doubts. Sleepwalking, my ass. Still, it was a relief knowing she was okay, that she'd been dragged in by Tate Kasun, the more easygoing of the Kasun crew, and that her parents had cared enough to rush over.

A voice in my head, one all hellhounds were familiar with, tossed warnings out at me like bread crumbs. Looking at it from a logical standpoint, Cressida's mom was right. It really did look like she was sleepwalking, going into town and committing crimes she'd never attempt if she was awake, as if sleep removed all of her inhibitions and set her free from the expectations and rules that normally regulated her life.

Only one problem with that scenario: Cressida *liked* the rules. It didn't take knowing her well to gather that. She enjoyed being Cressida, following a set schedule and carrying her portion of the weight in life and work. I didn't think sleep would change that.

Slipping onto my bike, I rode through the maze of roads, down one street and up another, until I glided into the MC parking lot. Lights shone brightly from inside, the glare spilling out into the night. Music spilled out with it, the occasional shout and "hell, yeah" carried away on the breeze as men and women weaved in and out through the door. The smells of alcohol and sex were ripe on the air.

I lounged in the shadows, watching and waiting. I wasn't in the mood for a party.

My younger brother stumbled into the night, high on life and too much sugary soda—Pops was lenient, but not when it came to alcohol —and I snorted back a laugh as he cocked his hip against the corner of the building and reached for his pants.

"You piss on the side of that building and Pops is going to tear you a new one," I called out.

Cade squeaked, fell against the brick, and then pushed himself away, running his hands down his clothes as if nothing out of the ordinary had happened.

"Holy shit, Jack!" he fumed. "I'm not the only one who pisses out here."

"You want to make a bet on that, or would you rather find out what scrubbing brick during the summer at dawn is like? Trust me on this one. Been there, done that."

Cade sniffed. "What are you doing out here anyway?"

"Not much for celebrating tonight."

"Whatever." Cade's expression went from nonchalant to pissed off. It was like that a lot lately. Fourteen was a hell of an age for hellhounds. "I don't get it. You get to do shit with the club Pops wouldn't even dream of letting me do, and instead of reaping the rewards, you sulk in the dark."

"Don't start," I warned.

Cade ignored me. "They even have your favorite grape soda. And because it's you, I bet they let you have the alcohol."

"And that's why Pops hasn't let you do much for the club yet. By the time you get your bike, you need to learn control and realize how little half of this shit," I gestured at the party, "matters. What matters is the brotherhood, not what you can reap from it."

Cade looked away, his sunglasses picking up the glare from the security lights near the company warehouse. No matter how much we tried to get along lately, my brother and I spent more time arguing than seeing eye to eye.

Changing tactics, I rubbed a hand along my jaw. "Talk to me about Cressida Manos."

Cade's head jerked my way. "Dude! Why?"

By the way he bristled, I could already tell this conversation wasn't going to go well, but I forged on. "Some weird shit is going down with her lately, and I'm trying—"

"You don't get to hit that," Cade interrupted. "She's nowhere close to the kind of girls you hang out with anyway."

I scowled. Was my reputation really that bad? First, Cressida was worried about walking down the street with me, and now my own brother was warning me away from a girl my own age. "I'm not hitting anything, and if I was, I don't need your permission. Right now all I care about is protecting her."

The anger on Cade's face momentarily wavered. "From what?"

"That's what I'm trying to figure out. She was arrested tonight."

Cade gawked. "Cressida Manos? Arrested? No way!"

"Yeah, I didn't get there in enough time to find out why, but I have an idea."

Pulling his sunglasses down, Cade peered at me over the rim. "Are you talking with her? Like, as in fully checking her out? As in interested in her for more than a tumble in the sheets?" Sometimes he didn't talk like a fourteen-year-old.

This was it. "And if I am?"

Cade kicked at the gravel at his feet. "Damn it, this isn't fair, bro."

I laughed, the sound harsh. It took everything I had not to tell him how ridiculous I thought his crush was. Then again, maybe that's why it annoyed me so much. At only fourteen, he'd noticed Cressida's charms, while everyone else overlooked them simply because of her outward appearance and her too-bubbly personality.

"Look, I stumbled on her at the cemetery the other night, and something about how desperate she seemed really got to my beast, okay? You know as well as I do, once the beast is interested, there's no backing down. So, can you do me a favor? If you notice anything unusual, let me know."

"Is it just the beast?" Cade asked quietly. "Is this really just a protection run?"

And here was the real reason for approaching my brother. Hellhounds didn't like dealing underhanded with their own families. No matter what kind of shit we got involved in with the club or outside of it, we stayed honest with each other.

"It's not just the beast," I admitted. Something about Cressida had sparked my interest, and out of respect for my brother and his wide-eyed crush, I wanted to lay it all on the line.

Cade shrugged. "It's none of my business."

Grunting, I turned to walk away.

"Wait," Cade called. I paused, my back to him. "Thanks for being honest."

I'd just seriously complicated our relationship, but at least I hadn't lied. At least I wasn't hiding anything.

CHAPTER 13

CRESSIDA MANOS

There wasn't anything more terrifying than my parents when they combined forces, allied together against one common enemy.

The way they stared at me now turned my blood to ice. I didn't often think about how old my parents were. I mean, it's not like I set an alarm every morning to remind myself that they'd lived for over six centuries.

Tonight, I saw the age in their eyes, and the history that we rarely discussed—like the fact that they'd lived in Paris during the whole bloody guillotine era—was right there in their gaze, all sharp steel and fire.

"So, before we get started, are we mad that I got arrested or that I am acquainted with Jack Peters?" I asked, standing uncertainly in the living room. They sat on our coffee-colored couch, elbows on their knees, fingers steepled.

I was dead.

"Let's start with Jack," Mom began.

"Let's not," Dad mumbled.

My parents had never looked at me the way they looked at me now. Sudden panic squeezed an overly excessive confession out of my mouth, each word tumbling out one after the other, all in one breath.

"I am not doing drugs." For some reason, I felt like that was an important distinction to make right off the bat. "'Cause, you know, I don't want you to get the wrong idea or anything. I also don't drink. So, the whole me painting stuff at night thing has nothing to do with alcohol. And if you think Jack Peters has anything to do with it just because he showed up all friendly-like tonight, he doesn't. I swear. Really. I've maybe known him a few days."

I held up two fingers, three, and then dropped them all together. "Well, I mean, I've known *about* him for forever, but we haven't been friendly. *If* we're even friends." My brows furrowed. "Actually, I'm not sure what we are, except that he helped me clean paint off a tombstone. Oh!" I held up my hand. "He *did* ask for my number. Which is kind of like a move, right? I mean, guys don't ask for your number if they don't want to talk to you. Or at least, I wouldn't think so. So, maybe he's interested. Which would be kind of nice . . . I mean . . . nah, maybe not."

Mom and Dad stared at me, horrified.

My pulse quickened, and logically, I knew I needed to shut up, but the words kept spilling forward. A flood of complete humiliation. "I'm not having sex, if that's what you're worried about. I mean, I haven't even—"

"That's enough!" Dad roared, storming to his feet.

I froze, my mouth opening and closing like a fish desperate for water, before tentatively asking, "Too much?"

Mom massaged her forehead. "A little too much."

Dad began pacing the living room. "For a moment, let's forget about Jack Peters, drugs, alcohol, and whatever else. What about this graffiti stuff?"

Mom stood and began pacing with him. In unison. It was creepy. "She has to be sleepwalking. I'm not sensing any magic."

A knock sounded on the door, and we all paused, as if caught in the headlights of a car. It was the middle of the night. No one had visitors in the dead of night. Except maybe vampires . . . or nocturnal supernaturals.

"You get it," Mom whispered.

Dad didn't move.

Our front door opened.

"It's me," my sister called, the door slamming behind her. She rounded the corner, a young woman with light brown hair, black-framed glasses, and a diamond nose ring following on her heels. "Oh, and Addie Beaumont," Leda added off-handedly, amusement clear in her voice.

Mom gasped.

Adelaide "Addie" Beaumont was the granddaughter of Saundra Beaumont, a powerful witch of one of the founding families of the Luna Coven. Saundra also served on the Court of the Sun and the Moon, which meant her granddaughter, Addie, was here on business.

Dressed in a pair of ripped jeans and an old T-shirt with the logo "I'm not a witch, you're a witch" plastered across it, Addie offered us a smile. "I guess you know why I'm here?"

"So soon?" Mom asked faintly. "Now?"

Leda, who managed to look elegant even when dressed down in a tank top and skinny jeans, leaned against our sofa, arms crossed. "I'm just here for moral support. I ran into the witch on the way here."

We all ignored her.

"I hear there was a special request," Addie said, her gaze swinging to me.

I chose this moment to completely embarrass myself as an oread.

Without any thought as to how I would look, I sat down hard on the floor, lifted my leg, and pointed at my tattoo. "Check it, if you don't mind. I really do think something is wrong with me."

"Cressida!" Mom gasped.

She said it like I was doing something scandalous. It wasn't like I didn't know Addie. Anyone in Havenwood Falls with a Court-issued tattoo had to meet Addie Beaumont at some point. She was the tattoo artist who did the magic-infused designs.

Horror widened my eyes. "I mean, not that I think you messed up or anything."

Addie laughed. "I gotta say, it's refreshing when the perpetrator is this willing to work with me." She crouched before me, her gaze dropping to the elegant chain charm bracelet tattooed around my ankle. "But there's nothing wrong with your tattoo, Cressida. The tat is only part of what protects the supes in this town. We have wards and protection spells for that, too. Nothing has been set off. I checked around before coming here. Even with the empaths. Willow Fairchild said she saw you and your sister at Coffee Haven, but all she felt was anxiety."

Guilt washed over me. "You checked with them tonight? As in, in the middle of the night?"

Addie winked. "They're used to it. Problems tend to arise more at night than during the day. It's part of the job." She glanced at my parents. "We're looking into some things, but right now we're stumped. According to Tate's report, she spray-painted two buildings but claims she can't remember doing it, despite being seen by witnesses, by him, and by his dash cam."

In two days, I'd learned a lot about a life of crime. Most importantly, I'd learned there was a very exact two-step process. First, people talked *to* you. Then, they talked *about* you.

Addie stood. "According to the evidence, she's guilty, but since the victims aren't pressing charges, we're going to skip a formal review and look into this more quietly. The Court is swamped." She chuckled. "And here we thought summer would be slow and quiet." Her gaze swung back to me. "Tate mentioned sleepwalking. Is this common for oreads?"

Mom wrung her hands. "Not common, but not unheard of. There was a case I saw personally about two hundred years ago." She winced. "In Italy. In that instance, the young man stripped naked and sang in the town square, but then couldn't remember it the next day."

"What happened to him?" I asked.

Mom's grimace grew. "Back then, there wasn't any protection for supernaturals. He ended up in an insane asylum and had to be rescued by oreads. Oreads were so spread out back then, it was two years before we realized he was in there. I was part of the rescue operation."

I swallowed hard. "Oh, gods."

Addie Beaumont glanced down at me. "This isn't two hundred

years ago, and we're in Havenwood Falls. But," she turned to Mom, "she probably does need someone to watch her while she sleeps. Or maybe find a way to take some precautions. We'll look into some spells that may help."

I rose off the floor. "I'm not sure I'm sleepwalking."

Addie met my gaze. "We've done everything we can for tonight. We'll look into some oread history and helpful spells, but for now, make sure you show up to clean off the graffiti and be extra cautious during the evening hours. We haven't found anything that makes us think you're dangerous."

I started to protest.

Mom stepped between us. "Thank you. I'm sorry you had to come out so late. Can we offer you anything to drink? Eat?"

"Thanks, but no." Addie moved toward the foyer and the door. "We'll be in touch."

She left.

Leda whistled. "Well, I don't think this family has had this much excitement in years."

Dad had been oddly quiet during the entire exchange, the agitation I'd seen in him when he stormed off the couch now a palpable glint in his eyes.

Mom must have noticed the same thing, because she approached him warily. "Honey, are you okay?"

Dad shook himself. "You know, I think I'm going to go in to work early today." His voice was sugary-sweet and entirely too cheerful, even mechanical. And his words were completely unexpected. He wanted to go in to work in the middle of the night?

Leda's gaze shot to the clock on our mantle. "At two o'clock in the morning?"

Dad sprinted for the stairs. "Yes, I do believe so. There's something I want to check on."

We stared after him. Never had I ever seen my dad act like that before. Normally, he was the calm one. Mom jumped, and Dad held her back. Perfect relationship. And now he was trying to escape?

Tears clogged my throat. "Is he that upset?" I asked, my voice small and strained.

Leda and Mom shared a look.

"I'll go in to work, too," Leda said. "And keep an eye on him."

This was wrong. Everything about this was wrong, and it was all my fault.

"I think I'm going to go take a shower," I whispered.

Mom closed her eyes, worry and strain lining her lips. "It's going to be okay, sweetie."

She knew the shower was an excuse for me to cry, but she didn't stop me or try to comfort me when I left.

Inside my bathroom, I turned on the faucet, letting the water run down the drain before sliding down the closed door outside the shower stall. Completely clothed. When I was upset, I didn't actually climb into the tub. I used the shower as an excuse and the sound of running water to drown out any sobs.

Pulling my cell phone out, I clicked on Jack's name in my contact list. "Please let it go through," I whispered. "Please."

Phone service in Havenwood Falls wasn't guaranteed. I wasn't sure if that had something to do with the mountains or the Court.

"Hello?" Jack's voice came over the line, deeper over the phone than it was in person. "Cressida?" Music played in the background, along with shouts I couldn't make out. "Shit," Jack swore, "hold on, don't hang up." Static sounded over the line. Rustling, and then, "When you have to get into a dead blasted closet just to hear something," he grumbled. "Cressida?"

I hiccupped, the tears I'd been holding back flooding out in massive, unladylike sobs. Snot, sniffling, and all. Minutes passed, my crying so hard, I'm pretty sure I gave up on breathing at some point.

"Hey," Jack said quietly, finally breaking through the emotional maelstrom. "If it makes you feel better, I'm on a first-name basis with the entire Havenwood Falls police department. Pretty sure my brother isn't far behind me. Let's just say, fourteen sucks for hellhounds."

I laugh-cried, which ended up sounding like something between a squealing brake and a dying animal.

"What did they get you for?" Jack asked.

"Destruction of property," I answered on a hiccup. "They said I spray-painted two buildings in Miller's Plaza." Another hiccup. "The charges were dropped, but," sniff, "I have to clean up the mess in a few hours."

Jack went quiet, and then, "No formal review?"

From that response, I knew he'd seen his fair share of the Havenwood Falls justice system.

"They still suspect sleepwalking. There was a similar case with an oread two hundred years ago. Well, not similar. The guy didn't commit crimes or anything, but—"

"Stay on track, darlin'. What are they doing about you?"

The *darlin'* made me pause. Was he even aware he'd said it?

"They're going to look into some spells. Otherwise, be extra vigilant at night and have someone watch when or if I sleep."

"That's a good start."

I lowered my voice. "I don't think I'm sleepwalking."

Something felt off about the way I "woke" up. As if I was a puppet whose strings had just been released.

"I believe you," Jack said. He'd said something similar before, but his faith in me felt even more important now.

"Why?"

"Because you snapped out of that shit too quick in the cemetery, and your behavior while out of it was . . . off. It looked more like a case of midnight schizophrenia than sleepwalking. You were a completely different person."

"How do you mean?"

"You were cruel. Well, cruel for *you* anyway."

His words rendered me speechless, the silence long and painful.

"It wasn't you," Jack said finally. "I don't have to know you all that well to recognize that. Call it intuition. And . . . it was your eyes. One moment you were affected by my hellhound gaze, and the next you weren't."

I sighed. The sound must have carried over the line because he added, "The scariest things are the things you can't see. The worst villains are the ones you can't detect."

"That sounded smart, Peters."

"That's because I am smart."

The almost hurt way he said it made me clutch the phone. "I didn't mean—"

"Don't sweat it. I get that a lot."

"No, but I really didn't mean—"

"I know." He chuckled. "I know you didn't mean it that way. Not coming from you anyway. It's fine. Really. "

"Good."

"Now, go. Try to relax, and feel free to . . . well, call me anytime."

My heart stuttered. "Okay."

"When the service works, that is," he added with a chuckle, the sound lightening the mood.

"Same," I replied. "I mean, you can call me anytime, too."

"Goodnight, Manos."

The call ended, and I stared at the phone, the water still running in the background.

CHAPTER 14

JACK PETERS

*M*idmorning found me in the shopping center on the south side of Main Street holding a grape soda and a coffee, my hip propped against a lamppost, my gaze on the small redhead sitting cross-legged on the warm sidewalk before VIP Nails. Her hair was a crazy mass of tied-up curls, her over-large T-shirt resting over blue-jeans shorts that looked like they'd been washed so many times the seams were in danger of popping. Buckets of soapy water with large sponges submerged in the murky depths sat next to her. Earbuds dangled from her ears, her gaze focused on the crazy artwork before her.

It was the crazy artwork that got to me.

My face broke out in a grin, my gaze traveling over the giant emojis Cressida had spray-painted all over the glass VIP Nails storefront as well as Long & Associates CPA. Everything from a smile emoji to a crying emoji to the classic poop one. Cressida's sinister alter ego had a sense of humor.

Pedestrians walked past, many of them stopping to stare as Cressida vigorously attacked the graffiti, their whispers loud and harsh. Things like "isn't that Wieland Manos's daughter" and "I heard she was seen at the police station with the Peters boy" and "Irene Beckett saw her cozying up to Jack Peters next to Coffee Haven" and "what a shame." Gossip in a small town could be brutal. Anger burned low and deep inside me, the hellhound caged within wanting nothing more than to stop the rumors coming her way. She didn't deserve them the same way my family did.

Closing the distance between us, I glared at the gawkers, seriously tempted to remove the sunglasses on my face. Hell, even with the glasses on, most of them scattered, recognition lighting their eyes with fear. The beast in me loved it.

Placing the drinks I brought on the sidewalk, I crouched next to Cressida, pulled one of her earbuds free, and nodded at the graffiti. "Couldn't the Mr. Hyde part of you be a little more creative?"

She jumped, her cheeks turning bright red. "I'm mortified. Absolutely mortified."

I laughed, pushing the biodegradable cup toward her. "Maybe this will help. Caramel macchiato, extra syrup. Willow said it was your regular."

She stared at me, a complicated rainbow of emotions lighting her eyes. "Why are you here?"

The question felt timid, as if the ugly snot crying she'd done on the phone with me the night before should have scared me away. If anything, it had drawn me closer to her. People didn't open up to me like that. Because of my reputation, people didn't trust me. She had.

Grabbing the grape soda, I twisted off the lid, took a quick swig, and then set it aside to submerge my hand in one of the buckets. "I needed the exercise." The sponge splatted against the store window, soap running down the glass in colored trails. "This shit is supposed to be good for fighting, right?" Swiping the sponge to the right, I parodied, "Wax on," to the left, "wax off."

Cressida's laugh rang through the still morning like tinkling bells, her shoulder nudging me. "I don't think I'm supposed to have any help."

Following her gaze, I glanced up to find Dao Pham, the owner of VIP Nails, glaring down at us, her face surrounded by dark hair with streaks of neon red. Covered in tattoos that highlighted her muscled arms, she cocked a brow, her leather-encased legs ending in a pair of stiletto heels that tapped impatiently. Dao had the kind of personality I related to—guarded and full of secrets. The story of my life.

I winked at her, even though I knew she couldn't see it, and then dropped my gaze. "Don't worry. I'd love to be a fly on the wall if she calls this in. The Kasuns will be too impressed I'm doing community service without getting charged with something first."

The earbud that had been in her right ear dangled between us, and I scooped it up, placing it awkwardly in my left ear canal.

Cressida tried to take it back, but I covered it with my hand and leaned away, the song Fall for You by Secondhand Serenade playing in my ear. "Not my usual taste in music, but it's not bad." The only reason I knew the song was because I'd been around too many girls who did like it.

She punched my shoulder. "Whatever."

Silence fell between us, an orchestra of noises surrounding us: music, splashing water, foot traffic, and passing vehicles. Unlike the places Pops used to take us riding during the summers, it didn't get hot enough in Havenwood Falls for the streets to get that melting blacktop smell. The greasy aroma of burgers and fries wafted from the Burger Bar nearby, the grill and fryer heating for the day ahead.

Cressida swiped at the store's glass, throwing occasional surreptitious glances my way. Our shoulders met, and even though the sleeves of our shirts kept our flesh from touching, I found myself distracted by her nearness.

We took too long working on the same part of the wall, her playlist flipping from song to song, my knees bumping hers, our hands running into each other as we cleaned, soap running everywhere.

The day grew warmer, the sun moving higher in the sky, and even though I could have spent today doing other things, I was glad it was this.

Touching the earbud in my ear, I ducked my chin. "You should add—"

A squeak interrupted me, a shadow falling over the two of us, and Cressida shot to her feet, the earbuds popping out of our ears to land on the cement, her phone clattering to the ground after it.

A beautiful tall dark-skinned girl, the same one who'd been at the Apex studio the weekend I'd helped deliver art supplies, stared at us, her mouth agape. Wearing a loose green summer dress that fell to her knees, she clutched a book to her chest like a shield.

"Hey." Cressida smoothed her hands down her damp, wrinkled shirt. "I tried calling you."

The girl's gaze traveled over the storefront before us, lines forming between her eyebrows. "So, it's true? You really graffitied Miller's Plaza?"

Cressida winced. "Well, not all of Miller's Plaza, and I didn't . . ." Her words trailed off. She'd been about to defend herself, but it didn't take a strong-nosed supe or heightened abilities to sense this girl was human. There wasn't a single explanation Cressida could give in her defense that didn't reveal a supernatural connection.

"It was my fault." Standing, I shoved my hands into my jeans pockets. "She took the fall for me."

Cressida's gaze flew to my face, but I simply offered her friend a wry, unapologetic smile. I hoped the rumor got around that I'd been the perpetrator. It was something people were more likely to believe, and Cressida was the type of person who would take the fall for someone. "I certainly didn't need anything else added to my rap sheet. She's my damsel in shining armor."

If I hadn't been wearing my sunglasses, Cressida would have seen the glint in my eyes daring her to protest. Human or no, I could tell Cressida was extremely close to this girl. Which meant caring about what she thought.

"Jack Peters, right?" the girl asked, shyly.

"Last time I checked. And you?"

"Paris Callahan." She gestured at Cressida. "We're best friends," and then, as if she needed to elaborate, "since elementary school."

"Oh." Damn. Color me impressed. Shocked, I swung my gaze between them. Only the supernaturals in Havenwood Falls would understand how hard it was to remain close friends with a human for so long. It was often difficult to hide what we were capable of, especially during puberty. Really sucky things tended to happen during puberty. And then, because of a memory ward placed on the town, there was the risk of forgetting where you came from if you left Havenwood Falls for too long. Whether it be family emergency or vacation. The same risk applied to supes, but because we were aware of the wards, it was more common among the humans. Humans didn't know to return within a certain timeframe.

Paris clutched her book so tightly the cover bent, her gaze taking in the scene. "Can I help?"

"No," Cressida yelped, and then backtracked, her gaze filling with concern. "Not that I don't want you to. It's just if you get too hot or . . ." Her words trailed off again, and I got the distinct feeling that whatever she was about to say wasn't supposed to be shared. This friendship was complicated.

Paris took pity on her. "I have diabetes," she admitted. "In its severest form. They're talking about getting me a pump. So," she shrugged, "I'm not supposed to overdo it."

Cressida glared. "Why'd you tell him that?"

It was one of the perks and one of the cons of being a hellhound. For some reason, humans found it easy to share their woes with me. This was great when doing business—Pops tended to abuse the power quite a bit—but it also made for really depressing conversations.

"Don't worry about it." I tapped her book. "What do you have there?"

Paris grinned. "A crossword puzzle. Well, kind of. This one's a little different. It gives you a trivia question rather than a word clue, and then you have to fill in the blocks with the answer."

"Why don't you sit and read them aloud while we work?" Cressida suggested.

"Really?" Paris chirped, her gaze swinging to my face. For a human, she was tall, just under six foot. "You okay with that?"

"Sure."

We returned to the buckets and sponges while Paris lounged in a small bit of shade near the building. Flipping the book's front cover open, she folded it under the back.

Time stood still, a comfortable easiness linking us.

335

Scrubbing the wall, I found myself glancing at Cressida, watching as she listened to Paris, her occasional laughter transforming her face. She reminded me of the stars my mother treasured so much, bright and engaging, yet so small. As if touching her would cause an explosion.

I'd had a lot of flings in my seventeen years, having gotten my first kiss at twelve and losing my virginity at fifteen, but I'd never considered a relationship. Especially with someone other than a hellhound. It took a strong woman to commit to our kind. Dating, sex, and marriage was one thing, having children another. Hellhound births were a risky business. Our species had a very high rate of deaths in childbirth. My mother passed away a year after my younger brother was born, her body unable to completely recover from the ordeal. She'd already challenged death twice by giving birth to me and my older brother. Most hellhound families had two children at best. Anything more was pushing the envelope.

Looking at Cressida now, it was hard to imagine a future like that for her. For anyone. It was why I remained single, even in high school. The thought threw a shadow over the afternoon.

"I'd better go," I said, dropping the sponge in the bucket.

Cressida looked at me, forehead creasing.

"I've got to do some delivery runs for Cerberus," I explained. It wasn't a lie. The company could use the extra hand, especially on the loading dock, but it wasn't something I *had* to do.

If she felt the change in mood, Cressida didn't acknowledge it, a smile forming on her lips and her gaze raking over my features. Almost as if she was memorizing my face before whispering, "Thanks for everything."

"Sure thing. Later."

Paris and Cressida returned to their conversation, and I hurried to my bike. The girl rattled me like no other girl had before.

What was I thinking?

I beat my chest with my fist, damning the beast. Hellhounds were different from other shapeshifters. Even though the beast within was part of us, there were times when it felt like it was its own sentient being, separate from our human bodies. Yet, despite how complicated it felt, it was also easier to control, the change dictated by us rather than a lunar cycle or other stimulants. A hellhound never shifted on a whim. If we shifted, we did it because we intended to kill. I'd never shifted, and I hoped I never had a reason to.

CHAPTER 15

CRESSIDA MANOS

I watched Jack leave with a growing sense of trepidation, the fear his nearness had kept at bay returning stronger than ever.

"What's going on with you and Jack Peters?" Paris asked, her knowing gaze catching mine. "Looks like a lot happened in a couple of days."

There were so many things I wanted to tell her, so many feelings I didn't understand that I wanted to share. In many ways, our friendship was a one-sided affair. Everything I said was calculated, every word weighed.

"I like him," I admitted, because a simple confession was the safest confession, but it came nowhere close to touching the magnitude of emotions swirling inside of me. It wasn't just that Jack was attractive. There was something vulnerable about him beneath his dangerous veneer. He was a mythological figure created by conjecture and fueled by his solitary nature. I was the girl everyone friended but never wanted to party with. It was ironic, really. A bad boy people went to for trouble. The good girl people went to in order to avoid it.

I liked him. I liked him a lot.

What did I even know about hellhounds? Other than what my

father had told me, the stuff about their powers and their eyes being dangerous to humans and some supes. That was basic information, stuff any supe could find out. It didn't touch on the personal stuff. Were they allowed to date outside their species? Did he shift very often?

Blowing out a breath, I scrubbed the building harder, my mind occupied by physical labor and Paris's occasional trivia question. The two of us had never needed to fill silence with conversation to enjoy our time together, but for once, I wished I could spill every secret I had to her.

Just once.

By the time mid-afternoon rolled around, I'd managed to clean the remaining graffiti from VIP Nails and most of it from Long & Associates. Paris departed halfway through my progress on the CPA's office, and I took that opportunity to throw everything I had into the work, using my supernatural speed and strength when there wasn't anyone in view, my gaze flicking to the sky.

The closer it got to nightfall, the more nervous I became, my body tensing in fearful anticipation.

The CPA's office had closed by the time I completed the cleanup, shadows growing long and sinister along the asphalt. The wet sponge dropped with a splash into the bucket, and I popped my knuckles, arching my back before lifting the two pails.

I was almost to a drainage pipe when a hand closed over mine on one of the pail's handles.

A screech tore from my lungs, the sound stoppered by Jack's soothing tone in my ear. "It's getting late."

It was the only explanation he gave.

My body responded to him instantly, the anxiety I'd been feeling swallowed up by his presence. "Did you finish at the delivery company?"

"For now." He dumped the bucket he'd taken from me and started to reach for the second one.

I jerked it away. "I've got it."

He'd done enough, spending most of his day helping me clean, and I was grateful that he seemed compelled to watch out for me. Compared to that, the bucket was nothing.

"I want to." His insistence felt personal somehow, as if he was frustrated while trying not to feel frustrated.

Which made me frustrated. "I've got this."

He tried taking the bucket. "Look, Cressy, I—"

"Cressida," I corrected, yanking on the pail.

A loud crack broke through the air, the pail flying up, paint-stained water raining down, completely soaking me and splattering him. Sometimes being short sucked.

"Look what you did!" I sputtered.

"Me?"

I prepared myself for the verbal bashing I knew was coming, but it never came.

He inhaled instead, the sound so sharp, it practically cut the air. "Holy shit, you're not wearing a bra."

My gaze dropped to my shirt. My very white, very wet, and now very transparent shirt. "Holy crap!"

Bad dreams about showing up naked at school had nothing on unintentionally flashing one of the hottest guys in Havenwood Falls with my nonexistent chest.

Jack broke into a fit of coughs, his fingers running under his sunglasses to rub at his eyes.

"Why are you not wearing a bra?" he choked.

Arms crossing, I backed away from him, my cheeks flaming so hot they practically caught on fire. "It's not like I was planning to get wet in front of anyone or anything."

Oh, gods! Was I trying to ruin my life? Wrong choice of words. Very, *very* wrong choice of words. Oh, that made this worse. *So* much worse.

Jack yanked the sunglasses off of his face, his eyes searching the empty street before his stunned gaze met mine. "Why are you not wearing a bra?"

The way he said it, all disapproval and no finesse, deepened my embarrassment and my anger. Why was he still stuck on this? "You saw! I don't exactly need a bra. So, could you please drop it."

"Yes, you do!" he argued, framing my chest with his hands despite my arms guarding them. "Those are at least an A, and the last time I checked, small boobs are still boobs, Manos!"

"Oh, no, you didn't," I groaned. "No, no you didn't!"

"Sheesh!" Shaking his leather cut off his shoulders, Jack offered it to me. His undershirt was as white as mine and completely useless as a cover-up, the wet fabric revealing a massive tattoo on his chest.

I pushed my arms through the cut, turning to protect whatever dignity I had left, my fingers pinching the leather closed over my breasts.

"Dear God, Manos," Jack muttered. "I hope you know what I just did for you. Whether it has patches or no, a biker doesn't give up his cut to anyone."

I wasn't sure how to respond to that.

He tugged me toward him, wrapping a protective arm around my shoulders. "Look, the clubhouse is closer. Let's get you one of my shirts, and then I'll see you home." We moved together, making it only a few steps when he added, "Start wearing a bra!"

"Oh, get over it already!" Anger born from serious mortification rose up like a fire-breathing dragon within me. "You can't tell me—"

"Start wearing one," he roared, cutting me off. "Because now every time I see you, I'm going to wonder if you have one on, and it's going to drive me insane."

His words stunned me into silence.

Replacing his sunglasses, he grumbled, "Small boobs are still boobs."

Sudden, unexpected laughter poured out of me, so hard and so fast I found it hard to breathe, tears dripping down my cheeks. As if my body needed the humor. Considering this had to be the craziest moment ever, maybe it did. How the devil did I manage to have my boobs looked at before I'd even gotten my first kiss?

"Thank you," I wheezed.

"What the hell?" Jack shook me. "Don't thank me! Why are you thanking me?"

I nudged him, almost affectionately. "Because your reaction is making me feel like a goddess. That's a big deal, Peters. I mean, have you seen me?"

"I see you. Trust me, I'm looking right at you."

Happiness, deep and joyful, washed over me, and—for a moment —I forgot to be afraid of the dark. I was already in deep, so why not go all the way? "You're going to fall in love with me."

Jack laughed incredulously. "Are you listening to yourself right now?"

I snuggled next to him, which was a complicated feat considering our height difference and the fact that we were walking. "I'm not wrong. Just wait and see."

"Is this a one-sided, unrequited thing?" he asked. "Or are you supposed to fall in love with me, too?"

"One-sided. I like the idea of you sitting in your room all solemn and love-piney. Maybe making those tiny little paper hearts, so you can throw them like flower petals on your floor while chanting, 'she loves me, she loves me not.'"

"Love-piney? You're unstable, you know that, right? What kind of crap is that? I find out you don't wear bras, and suddenly I'm going to fall in love with you. You are one strange girl, Cressida Manos."

Leading me to the motorcycle he'd parked on the street, he climbed on, patting the seat behind him.

I didn't hesitate. One, because I'd always wanted to ride a motorcycle, and two, because I was already in this deeper than I'd ever planned to be.

It wasn't until I'd settled behind Jack that I realized what a mistake riding with him was. He seemed to come to the same conclusion, because the next words out of his mouth were, "Just hold on and don't think about it."

Wrapping my arms around his waist, I plastered myself to him, shutting my eyes as tightly as I possibly could. Yep, all dignity gone.

He sped toward the MC clubhouse, my soaked chest against his damp back, and even though we weren't technically naked and I had the added protection of his cut, it certainly felt like we were skin-to-skin. His flesh was hot, a little too warm against me, but not hot enough to burn. I hoped.

Turning my head, I pressed my ear against his back, listening as his heart thudded, strong and steady. The bike rumbled beneath us, tying the sound of the road to his heartbeat, and I suddenly understood what he loved about the ride. All of it together, his heartbeat and the sound of the bike, sounded like a poem would read, smooth and lyrical. Wind rushed against us, Jack's skin a heater against the chill.

We pulled up to the clubhouse sooner than I expected, the gravel crunching under Jack's tires, and I pressed my nose into his back, hiding, because the only thing that could make this experience more mortifying would be parading past a clubhouse full of bikers, boobs flashing in a leather cut I shouldn't have on.

Way to win the family over.

"You're in luck. No one's here," Jack said, amused. "Pops had a run tonight, and Cace's with a friend. It'll be a few hours before anyone comes back here. It isn't often the clubhouse is empty like this. There's almost always someone here. Tonight, the universe is working for you."

Parking, he slipped off the bike and offered me his hand, pulling the cut closed for me as he helped me off the seat. "I'm going to warn you—this place isn't for the faint of heart."

The front room was dark when we entered, the only lighting neon beer lights and a stained-glass orb hanging above a full-length bar. The smell of cigarettes and beer permeated the air, a testament to excess. A sagging couch and jukebox were pushed up against a wall on the side of the room, overlooking a space occupied by a pool table and extra seating.

Jack rushed me past the clubroom, tugging me into a hallway full of doorways, most of them shut. He stopped in front of the last one on the left.

"No judgment," he insisted, pushing the door open.

Chaos met my gaze, my eyes falling on books, magazines, movies, a collection of knives, and soda bottles full of change. Half-naked women adorned his walls, and I hugged myself tight, completely aware that I lacked most of what they were flaunting.

Pulling his sunglasses off, Jack's gaze followed mine, and he promptly ripped three of the posters off the wall.

"Gifts," he said quickly. "All of them. The club members gave them to me."

To lessen the awkwardness, I leaned against a desk with a broken shelf and squinted at the titles on it. "You like history?"

Pulling a closet open, Jack yanked two shirts off the wire hangers inside with a clang, offering one of them—a black one—to me. "I like the feeling I get when I study it. As if I'm standing on a battlefield or exploring places no one else has seen, and even though those things have already happened, there's so much more we can learn from the literature and artifacts people have left behind."

"So, it's human history that interests you?"

"Both. Though human history is less complicated."

"You should talk to my parents. My dad's over six hundred years old. He actually lived in France during the revolution."

"Holy shit!" Jack's eyes lit up. "Really?"

I laughed. "It's less exciting if you've heard the stories as much as I have."

"Try drunk history lessons about Blackbeard the pirate."

"Your Pops?" Turning away from him, I dropped his cut onto the bed, and then removed the wet T-shirt. At this point, I didn't care if he saw my bare back. My back was a whole lot less embarrassing than my front. I think everyone had at least one feature they'd like to change. I didn't think I was ugly. I actually liked my looks a lot, but I still hoped my chest went up at least one cup size. Then again, maybe not. I liked going braless.

"Six hundred years . . ." Jack cleared his throat. "So, you'll live a long time, too?"

"I could. It's not that oreads can't die; it's just that we're harder to kill. We don't catch human illnesses, and we won't die from a fall. We get wounded like humans do, though. We can be shot, stabbed, scratched, and so forth. We just heal from the wounds. Some wounds take longer than others to go away, but we can usually heal from them." I turned to face him. "We have the potential to live a very, very long time."

Jack's expression grew thoughtful. "Hellhounds, too. I mean, obviously, if Pops met Blackbeard. Pops is over three hundred years old. Male hellhounds tend to live longer than the females."

Jack pulled his wet shirt over his head, leaving his chest bare, and I completely lost the ability to follow along with our conversation. Tattoos covered his skin, accentuating his muscles. A chain wrapped one bicep while a skull and compass covered the other, but neither of those held a candle to the masterpiece on his chest. A three-headed beast was tattooed across his broad torso, each head with a gaping mouth holding different objects. The first head bit down on a cracked tombstone with no epitaph written on it. The second was impaled by a tree of life, the branches wrapping around its spiky head, the roots growing into its jaw. And the third held a ship with full sails, its mouth full of choppy waves.

I suddenly found it hard to breathe because something told me Jack had chosen this tattoo for extremely personal reasons.

"You should put that back on," I said, shoving his shirt back at him, and then dropping it when I realized it was the wet one.

"What?" Jack asked, amused. "Have you never seen a man's chest before?"

Not one like his. Most definitely not one like his.

"Or here, put this one on." I shoved the dry shirt he'd pulled out of the closet at him. Even going so far as to try putting it on for him. "Just, you know, back on. Like a good—"

"If you say 'good boy' like I'm some well-trained show dog, I'm going to throttle you." Taking the shirt from me, he draped it over my head and left it there, the fabric hanging in my face.

I yanked it off, letting it fall to the floor. "Aren't you, technically, a dog?"

"Not funny, Manos. Not even close to being funny."

"Yes, huh. Admit it." I pinched my fingers together and held them up. "It was a little funny. Just a little."

He glared.

I pinched my fingers even closer together. "A wee tiny bit."

He jerked me toward him, and I squealed as his large hand cupped my waist. The red hue in his eyes flared, his gaze dropping to my lips.

"Oh," I whispered. "You're not . . . I mean you're not going to, uh, kiss me, are you?"

"Cressida?"

"Yeah?"

"Shut up."

His lips fell on mine, the gentle way he kissed stealing any thoughts I had about stopping him. He tasted like the grape soda he seemed so fond of—if the change bottles on the floor were any indication—his tongue touching mine. I sighed, letting him take the lead, my body relaxing into his. Time slowed, his lips and tongue testing, nipping, and soothing mine, sending tingles of sensation zipping through my body.

His head rose, his gaze searching mine. "What the hell am I going to do with you?" he whispered. "You're too small to get under my skin the way you do."

The words startled me, and I placed a hand against his chest, my palm splayed over the tree-impaled beast head. "For a first kiss, that wasn't bad at all. I think my heart hurts."

As if he'd been burned, Jack released me, and I stumbled toward his bed. "Oh, darlin', we definitely shouldn't be doing this." Leaning down, he swiped his shirt off the floor and tugged it over his head, the fabric swallowing the beasts on him. "Come on, let me get you home before I do something I regret."

As I followed him out the door, the illogical part of me, the insane inner Cressida, couldn't help but wonder what being a regret would feel like.

CHAPTER 16

JACK PETERS

*I*knew by the way Cressida tensed behind me that something was wrong when I pulled up to her house, her reaction completely wiping clean the conflicted thoughts I'd been having on the drive over. The Manos place was the perfect example of a mountain home—stone and wood with a wraparound porch, two chimneys, and a line of inviting rocking chairs overlooking the mountain. The windows blazed with light from the second story down.

As soon as I cut the engine, I took Cressida's hand in mine, slipping it off my waist before cradling it in my palm. "What is it?"

"All the lights are on."

I glanced back at her. "That's not normal?"

"What time is it?"

Fishing my phone out of my pocket, I clicked on the backlight. "After eleven." We'd been riding for a while after we left the clubhouse. I hadn't wanted to take her directly home, and she hadn't stopped me. Her embrace during the ride had felt good. Comforting.

Cressida tugged on her ear while worrying her lip with her teeth. "I don't guess it's abnormal. But mom knew I'd be out because of the cleanup, so she wouldn't have waited up. And Dad's usually in his office after dinner, but the car's not here." She stared at the windows.

"Mom's really into conserving electricity when she can. I don't know . . . something doesn't feel right. Every single light is on."

Slipping off my bike, I forced her behind me and preceded her to the door. "I'll check it out first."

"No!" She grabbed me by the arm. "You can't! If nothing's wrong, how do I explain you crashing into my house? They don't even know I'm with you."

"Fine, then we go together," I stated firmly. I wasn't taking no for an answer.

She frowned, her hand closing over mine on the door knob. I fisted my free hand, lifting one finger, then two, then three.

We burst through the opening, the light in the foyer hitting us in the face. Beautiful Persian rugs lined polished hardwood floors that reflected fine crystal chandeliers, the front room leading to a living area on the left, a kitchen on the right, and a staircase down the center.

"Mom?" Cressida stepped forward cautiously, her heart beating so loudly, I could hear it in my ears, the smell of her fear strong in my nostrils. The hair on my arms stood up, the beast in me crouching, muscles bunched.

Footsteps pounded on the stairs, startling us. A frantic, barefoot, auburn-haired woman stepped onto the landing, running past us into the kitchen. Theia Manos.

"Mom?" Cressida followed her. "What's wrong?"

She didn't spare us a glance. "I hate that cat. Hate it! Do you hear me? Hate it! Where did you put it, you lousy little feline?"

Theia rushed through the kitchen, forcefully slamming drawers and yanking open cabinets, her body a flurry of madness, her movements violent.

"Mom!" Cressida's voice rose. "What's wrong?"

The woman's head shot up, her unfocused gaze landing on her daughter. Pure evil stared back at us. "Ah! You! You, you, you, you, you! Do you have any idea what your cat has done?"

I'd seen this look before, back when I'd caught Cressida in the cemetery. Only her mother's stare was a lot more brazen, a lot more cruel.

"Slink?" Cressida's voice shook, and I gripped her arms with my hands, steadying her.

Theia growled. "That cat's been dropping my jewelry into the toilet! The toilet! Why the hell would she drop my jewels into the toilet?"

"What? Mom, Slink doesn't mess with jewelry. Just suits and shoes."

"Then where is it!" Theia shouted. "Where the hell is it! She took it from me!"

Cressida stumbled into me, a whimper rushing past her lips, my arms becoming a vise around her. My beast roared.

Theia laughed, the sound hollow and eerie, before streaking out of the room, her movements so fast, I barely saw her brush past me, even with my hellhound abilities.

"Mom!" Cressida panicked, spinning to face me. "That's not my mother."

She didn't have to tell me that. "I know."

The sound of a cat yowling filled the house, pitiful and loud. Desperate. Like screams heard just before someone or something died.

Cressida screamed. "Oh, my gods! She's killing my cat."

Grabbing her hand, I yanked Cressida toward the stairs, following the cat's screeching, panicked adrenaline feeding the beast inside me. He snarled, pacing.

We found them in an upstairs pastel blue bathroom, her mother kneeling on a fuzzy bathroom rug, her hands shoving a tortoise-hair cat into the toilet, its head down. Over and over again. "Find my jewelry, you despicable beast!"

The cat fought for its life, clawing for purchase, its nails lacerating the skin and drawing blood on Theia's arms.

"Mom!" Cressida threw herself at them, tackling her mother against the tub.

The cat fell, water flying from its wet fur, its entire body trembling. I tried approaching it, but it hissed, blurring past me into the rooms beyond. Cats and hellhounds didn't mix. I hadn't met one yet that liked me, even when I was trying to save it.

349

Gripping her by the arms, Cressida shook her mother, repeatedly. "Mom!"

Theia fought her, her clawed-up hands going for Cressida's throat.

"Watch out!" I yelled.

The beast in me leapt, and I doubled over, taking slow, deep breaths to avoid shifting. If I shifted now, someone was dying.

Cressida flung herself to the side, ducking down just as her mother's hands closed over the spot where'd she been.

Sobbing, Cressida sat up, her expression resolved. "Oh, Mom. I'm so sorry."

The words rang through the bathroom, the apology a precursor to the slap she suddenly gave her mother across the face, the force of it sending Theia reeling into the bathtub, the apology hanging heavy in the air.

Silence fell.

Downstairs a door slammed open. "Mom! Cressida!"

Cressida scrambled to her feet. "Leda!"

Feet pounded on the stairs, and a harried, blond-haired woman in a wrinkled black business suit ducked into the room, stopping short when she caught sight of the scene before her. "Oh, my gods!"

Theia groaned. "Leda? Cressida?" She pushed herself up against the tub, leaving a faint trail of blood behind her. "What's going on?" She shook her head, blinked, and then glanced at her arms. "What is this?" Troubled eyes slid to Cressida. "Did you do this?"

"What? Mom, no!" Cressida objected.

Leda gasped, supporting herself on the doorframe, her astonished gaze finding her sister's face.

The horror of the situation suddenly dawned on me. Cressida had committed several minor crimes in the middle of the night, first by painting a tombstone, then by tagging two buildings. As far as her family was concerned, whatever strange ailment she seemed to have *only* affected her. Theia had apparently forgotten what she'd just done. It was the same thing that had been happening to her daughter.

Cressida's mouth fell open. "No," she gestured at me, her eyes full of desperation. "I've been in town cleaning graffiti. We just got here.

All the lights were on when we came in." Her gaze shot to Theia. "Mom was running around the house, yelling something about my cat and jewelry. Then she tried to drown Slink." Eyes pleading, she touched the claw marks on her mother's arm gently. "Slink did that, Mom. I didn't do this. I swear! You were trying to kill Slink."

It was way past time for me to step in. "Cressida's right, Mrs. Manos. You weren't acting right when we arrived. I've seen that same crazed look before—in the cemetery, on your daughter's face. We need to figure out what's going on here."

Leda's blue-eyed gaze shot to my face. "We? What do you have to do with any of this?"

"Stop it!" Cressida warned. "He helped me. Not once. Not twice. Not three times. More than that. I told you," her gaze glanced off the faces in the room, "something is wrong here. I told you!"

"Let's just everyone calm down," Theia mumbled weakly. "Where's your dad?"

"I don't know," Leda said. "That's why I'm here. We were at work, and then he was just gone."

Theia tried to stand, but slipped in the blood. I caught her, my muscles bunching. "We need to contact the Court," she breathed against my shirt. "If what you're saying is true, Cressida, then whatever is causing this is somehow undetectable. First you, then me and your dad . . ."

We moved out of the bathroom, Leda and Cressida in the lead while Theia leaned on me for support.

"Do you remember what you did?" I asked Theia.

She shook her head.

"What about before? Did you fall asleep earlier?"

"No, I don't think so." She frowned.

A terrible feeling bloomed in my chest. Wieland Manos was missing, and Theia Manos had gone mad while awake.

Ahead of me, Cressida turned. Her green eyes were unfocused, her pupils dilated.

Whatever this was haunting the Manos family no longer needed them to sleep.

"For the love of . . ." I shoved Theia at Leda. "Go! Take your mom! It's got Cressida!"

By some terrible twist of fate, I had to start falling for a girl who happened to be an oread.

Cressida took off, a blur in my peripheral vision as she tore past me. And there was the crux of my problem. Oreads were too damn fast.

"Shit!" I tore through the house after her, yanking open every door I came to, my thoughts flying back to the cemetery, to the first night Cressida had been possessed by whatever took hold of her now. That version of Cressida, the Mr. Hyde to her usual, fun-loving Jekyll, had been amused by me.

"That's it!" I shouted. "I'm going to spend the rest of my life feeding you the most decadent, richest foods I can find, so you become completely unable to run."

Laughter floated down the hall toward me, and I paused, listening.

"That's right," I murmured, following the sound. "Keep it up, you bastard." The beast in me jumped for joy, claws springing out. "Not tonight, hellhound," I soothed. "I really don't want to go down in history for eating my first girlfriend."

The laughter grew, high-pitched and unnatural, the sound leading me to a room at the end of the hall. I knew even before I entered that it belonged to Cressida. It smelled like paint and coconuts.

The door creaked when I pushed it, swinging open to reveal a simple room with a bed and white dresser on one side, a desk and full-length mirror on the other. Art work exploded on her walls, the space full of colorful canvases and shadowbox shelves holding sculptures and pottery.

But it wasn't the artwork I stared at now. It was Cressida.

She stood in front of her full-length mirror, a carpet of curly red hair laying at her feet, a pair of scissors clutched in her hand. The horror of it made me freeze. Whatever was inside Cressida didn't just want to make her do bad things—it wanted to hurt her, too. Every single time it inhabited her, it found a way to strike out. By alienating her, turning her into a criminal, and now this.

"Why?" I asked softly, ever so carefully edging my way forward. "Why do you do this? Every single time you take her, you find a way to hurt her. Why are you so dead set on hurting her?"

Cressida turned, her head cocking to the side, her hand fluffing the newly shorn ear-length curls. "Because of who she is."

I took another step forward. "And who would that be?"

Laughing, she twirled the scissors, fisting them in her hand before placing them against her neck.

My heart stuttered, the beast in me causing my skin to run hot.

"The backbone of her family," Cressida answered. The scissors inched forward.

I have never moved so fast in my life. In a blink, I was in front of her, my hand wrapped around hers on the scissors, the point just piercing the skin.

A drop of blood welled up on her neck, rolling like a tear down her collarbone.

"Let her go," I growled. Unfocused eyes peered into mine, and I used my shoulder to knock off my sunglasses. "Let her go." Cressida recoiled, my naked gaze holding hers. My eyes had worked before. Whatever this was, my gaze was its weakness. "Let her go."

Cressida slumped, her hand becoming limp, and I let the scissors fall to the floor, my arms catching her in my embrace.

"Jack," she whispered. This voice, this girl, was mine.

CHAPTER 17

CRESSIDA MANOS

"*I* know how to make it leave you alone."

Those were the first words I heard when I came to, my body draped in Jack's arms, his red-hued gaze on my face. "It happened again?"

"It can't handle looking into a hellhound's eyes," he replied.

We were in my bedroom, the art-covered walls a kaleidoscope of colors, all of it suddenly too bright and too much.

Letting my head fall, I started to turn my head, but Jack's hand stopped me. "Don't," he pleaded.

Somewhere in the house, my mother and sister called my name. My head felt light. *Too* light.

"What is it?" I whispered.

Jack looked away.

"Cressida!" My sister's voice rang out from the open doorway. I lifted my head, my gaze finding her weary face. My mother hung onto her for support.

One look at me, and Leda's eyes widened. "Oh, Cressida."

Mom gasped, her hand flying to her mouth.

Fear pricked my skin. "Jack," I whispered. "Is there something wrong with my face?"

Setting me down gently, Jack slid his arm around my waist, took my chin in his hand, and tilted my head toward the mirror.

A moment passed, my eyes adjusting to the image before me and the ear-length red curls that framed my face. The cut was crude, the bottom uneven. I looked like little orphan Annie. Only older.

"Oh, thank the gods!" I exclaimed when I finally found my voice. "I thought something had happened to my face!"

In the mirror beside me, Jack cracked up, his laughter deep and satisfying.

"Your hair!" Mom cried from the doorway.

I touched it tentatively. "Hair grows back. You can't grow back a face."

Jack's laughter grew. "I should have known." He hugged me from behind, his chin resting on the top of my head. "I should have known this wouldn't bother you."

Downstairs, a door slammed, completely shattering the moment.

"Dad!" Leda and I cried.

Jack rushed to the door, leaving me behind. "Stay with your mom and sister. If he's been taken by that thing, then he needs to look into my eyes."

Love is like a Band-Aid. Anything bad needs to be revealed straight from the get-go. Rip. Over. One thing the Manoses had never been good at was waiting. By pure luck—and because Mom and I were sucked dry of energy—Jack made it to the stairs first.

"Honey!" my dad shouted. "Cressida! Anyone home?"

We all looked at each other.

"He sounds okay," Leda hissed.

"Like he always does," Mom agreed.

None of that meant anything.

Jack took a step down. "I'm going in first."

My mother scowled. "And if he's not being possessed, you're going to give him a heart attack."

"I thought oreads couldn't die from human illnesses," Jack said smoothly.

355

Mom threw me a dirty look. "How long have you known this guy? And you're already spilling secrets."

I pouted. "You tried to kill my cat." Speaking of, where was Slink?

Jack rushed down the stairs, Leda on his heels. Mom and I moved much, much slower.

"Dad!" Leda called.

Wieland Thanos stepped into the foyer from the kitchen, confusion etching his brows. "Why are all the drawers and cabinets open in here?"

His gaze rose, his entire body freezing when he caught sight of Jack, a snarl curling his lips. Something moved in his eyes.

Jack tackled Dad before my father could make a move, his hands grasping Dad by the face.

"You can't have the jewel!" Dad screamed, his voice full of greed and desperation. "It's mine. Only mine!"

"Look at me!" Jack snarled, thrusting his nose against Dad's, eyes locked.

Thrashing twice, my father's body went limp.

Everything about the last week ran together like one of those melted crayon wax projects my mother used to help me do when I was a child—images and conversations bombarding me, with one important fact standing out the most.

Sagging on the stairs, my fingers gripped the rails, my warm, flushed face pressed against the wood.

"It's the delivery," I said, my gaze flashing to Jack's face. "The weekend delivery, the one you and your father brought to the store Saturday. The jewel dad bid on. This all started after we received the jewel. It has to be the jewel! That's what's causing this."

Jack released my father.

Dad slid to one of the Persian rugs on the floor, the red, black, and tan patterned carpet a part of Dad's collection of antique treasures. Considering Jack's love of history, I wondered how impressed he'd be if he knew the rug was an original, the piece dating back to the Safavid period.

Mom and Leda fell into a thoughtful silence, my words sitting heavily between us. It all made sense. Mom and Dad's strange tension-filled behavior, their odd argument, the sudden fascination with the emerald at work, Mom attempting to kill my cat over lost jewelry, and my father's jealous obsession. It all came back to the jewel.

Jack trotted up the stairs. "Would a jewel have that kind of power? Enough that even the Court couldn't detect it?"

Exhausted, he sat a step below me, his hand gripping the same rail my hand gripped, our fingers brushing. This night felt long, even if only a couple hours had passed, and now that we'd discovered the mysterious villain plaguing us couldn't hold a hellhound's gaze, Jack was being forced to play the longest game of "see who blinks first."

"We could check Dad's records at the store," I suggested.

Above me, Mom groaned, her injured arms cradled against her body.

A ball of dark fur tiptoed along the upstairs landing, slinking carefully down toward me, the cat curling into a shivering ball at my back. Slink avoided both my mother and Jack, her usual playfulness subdued.

The last week and this night had left mental and physical scars on all of us.

"We need to contact the Court," Leda said.

"Wait. I want to talk to my father first," Jack insisted. "He'll have records on the delivery, and some insight on the seller. Plus, if the jewel is the source of the problem, we'll have something to turn over to the Court. Until then, no one goes near the stone."

"I don't think staying away from it is the solution. I've never even seen it, and it's still affecting me." On a whim, I reached out, running my fingers through the top of Jack's hair. His eyes fell shut, the lines on his face smoothing.

Dad stirred below, his lanky body coiling as he pushed himself off the floor. His hair was a spiky mess, his navy-blue polo shirt was pulled haphazardly out of his slacks, and his pockets were turned inside out.

He peered up at us, his green eyes clouded with confusion. "I think I've misplaced something."

Tense and alert, Jack shot down the stairs. "Mr. Manos?"

"I'm pretty sure I've misplaced something." Pressing his fingers against his brow, Dad tapped it repeatedly. "It was right here just a moment ago."

Pulling herself up against the railing, Leda whispered, "Is he possessed?"

Jack peered into Dad's eyes. "No, I'm not getting anything."

My stomach ached, my hands clutching my abdomen. "The jewel has driven him mad."

A faint sob shook Mom's frame, a tear slipping down her cheek.

My heart broke. Oreads depended on family, on the tight bonds formed between us. It gave us strength. What was happening to us now tested that.

Jack fished his phone out of his jeans pocket before meeting my gaze. "Keep an eye on your dad. I'm going to go find my father. If something happens before I get back, slap whoever is affected. That seemed to work before with your mom in the bathroom."

"And if it doesn't?" I asked.

Jack frowned.

"We'll make it work," Leda promised. "Just go get your dad, biker boy. We need answers and help before this gets worse."

Jack's gaze found mine, concern flicking through his eyes, before he rushed out the door.

CHAPTER 18

JACK PETERS

When I returned to the clubhouse, it was no longer empty. Unconscious bodies littered the space, the forms sprawled across the floor, the threadbare sofa lining the wall, and the pool table resting in the center of the room. Half-naked women spooned with men in leather vests sporting a sword-impaled skull and patches. Empty beer bottles and specially mixed brews from Sanguine's Elixirs dripped sticky liquid onto scarred hardwood floors. Blood, alcohol, and God knew what else. I was suddenly glad Cressida and I had left when we did. More than likely, these guys had stumbled in from Silk after enjoying way too much alcohol. It wouldn't surprise me if Melaina had kicked them out. The members got rowdy when they got drunk.

The prospects were going to hate cleaning up the mess.

Anxiety over leaving Cressida and her family chased away all other thoughts, the apprehension eating at me as I picked my way around the bodies and walked toward a door at the back of the room, my stride full of purpose and determination.

I knew he was in there, and I knew he was awake. He always was.

The door made no sound when I opened it.

Inside the room, my father sat at a long mahogany table, his head bent over a stack of papers, his fingers twirling a knife. I watched it spin on the wood.

"Pops."

Liam Peters looked up, his hard gaze finding mine, the sunglasses he always wore pushed up on top of his head. The glasses held back his too-long sandy hair, his face covered in scruff. Tattoos lined his arms.

"Pops, I need your help."

Liam eased back in his chair, rolling it back, the seat creaking as he crossed his ankle over his knee, his hand resting on his leg. Waiting.

"There's an issue with one of the deliveries we made. I need some information on it," I said.

"Does this have anything to do with the Manos girl?"

I paused. "How did you know?"

"I've been watching you. And them."

I recoiled.

Amused by my reaction, Pops reached out to tap the papers on the meeting room table. "I didn't get the position I have at this club for nothing, son. It's my job to keep my ear to the wire. When I heard your girl had been arrested and that Addie Beaumont was looking into the oread problem, I did a little digging."

He pushed the papers my way.

I leaned over the table, thumbing through the top few documents. The arrest report for Cressida Manos, including a detailed monologue from Cressida claiming her innocence.

"Why?" I asked. Pops wasn't one to involve himself in Havenwood Falls drama, especially something as small as a sleepwalking incident.

"My first job is protecting you and your brothers. My beast knew something was wrong. If it involves my club or my family, it's my business," Liam said firmly. "And you wouldn't have helped the Manos girl clean graffiti in the middle of a shopping center if you weren't interested in pursuing something with her. You may not always like what I do for a living, son, but everything I do is for you, your brothers, and this brotherhood." He tapped his face. "I've got eyes everywhere."

"She's not sleepwalking."

"Keep reading," Liam prompted.

I flipped the pages over, revealing an account sheet, the file listing a wire transfer for funds to a man a few towns over. Belen Cirillo.

"That's the seller of the jewel Wieland Manos bid on," Pops informed me.

My head shot up, anger marring my features. "You know it's the jewel? Why didn't you say anything? Why didn't you *do* anything? Do you even know what that family has been through? This week and tonight?"

Pops threw me a warning look. "I wasn't a hundred percent positive until last night, and I only work with positives." He leaned forward. "That delivery gave me a bad feeling from the start. I would have investigated this even if you hadn't started taking an interest in Wieland's daughter. It didn't take a lot of deductive reasoning to realize it was after our delivery that things started going wrong for the Manos family."

We were running out of time. The jewel's power was getting stronger, the effects growing. It had gone from affecting Cressida in her sleep to driving Wieland Manos mad.

"What did you find out about the jewel?"

Pops stood, gathering the papers in his hands. "Let's discuss this with the Manos family. I can end this for them now. Tonight. Before it gets worse."

Being the son of Liam Peters wasn't easy. Pops was a known outlaw with a list of vices three hundred years long. People judged me based on his past and his present decisions, while also expecting me to take over for him in the future. At times, I hated it. But then there were times—like now—when I looked at my father, and I realized just how mighty he was, how easy it was for him to fix a problem the rest of us shed blood and tears over, with a simple stack of paperwork.

The beast in me growled, frustrated. I'd wanted a fight. I wanted to be a hero.

Pops squeezed my shoulder, sensing my anger. "The beast is always restless, son. It's just the way it is for hellhounds. But you listen to me, and you listen to me good. You don't release the beast until you're prepared to deal with the consequences. I've got a lot of blood on my hands. The longer I can keep that blood off your hands, the better. Some things are better resolved by paperwork and politics than violence. The difference between a good leader and a great one is knowing when to deal with things this way," he waved the papers at me, "or that way." His eyes flared, flames burning in their depths, and for a moment I caught a glimpse of the beast that was my father.

"Let's ride," he said.

CHAPTER 19

CRESSIDA MANOS

The healing claw marks on Mom's arms and hands had gone from angry and red to pink and bruised, the blood having crusted up as it dried. She hissed when I dabbed it with antiseptic, the skin still scratched enough to burn.

"I'm sorry," Mom said, her gaze raking over my face as I unrolled a ball of gauze. "I'm sorry I didn't listen to you."

"I'm not angry," I promised. "Truth is, I wouldn't have believed me either. No one sensed the magic, and there *are* past cases of sleepwalking oreads."

I started to wrap Mom's wounds, but she touched my face, stopping me. Honestly, the wounds wouldn't last long enough to need bandaging, but doing it made me feel better. "It doesn't matter. I should have trusted you. You've never given me any reason not to."

Tears welled up at the back of my eyes, and I blinked to keep them from falling.

Dropping her hand, Mom smiled gently. "Your father and I waited a very, very long time to have children, and it wasn't until we settled in Havenwood Falls that we were even sure we wanted any." Her gaze grew distant. "Lord, your father could be impulsive. When he bought the old Campbell's Market from Callum Campbell and told me he wanted to put a jewelry store in it, I thought he'd lost his mind. New town. New business. It was all so overwhelming, but it was opening Summit that led to having you girls, so it turned out to be the best decision we ever made."

Mom rambled, telling the same story I'd heard repeatedly over the years, the familiar tale soothing her frazzled nerves. In many ways, I was a lot like my mother. We rambled when we had nothing to say and grew quiet when we had too many words.

"I called in someone to help at the store," Leda said suddenly from the kitchen door.

I looked up from where I was sitting at the table. "How's Dad?"

"Not much better," Leda admitted, rubbing her eyes. "I should have known something was off. Things have been weird at the shop. Dad's been more spastic than usual. It's just . . . I've been distracted."

"Don't start blaming yourself," Mom told her. "You do that, and everything else around you will start falling apart. None of this is anyone's fault."

"Still." Leda tugged on her wrinkled blazer.

We all needed a change of clothes and a bath, but I was afraid to do anything until Jack returned.

Mom's gaze grew soft, a smile on her lips. "Falling in love is a complicated thing, isn't it? So small in the bigger scheme of things. But it feels so big when it's happening, as if the entire world revolves around one person and the moments you share with them."

Leda and I shared a look.

Mom snorted. "Oh, don't look at each other like I'm crazy. I've been watching the two of you, even through all this mess. I know you're both seeing someone. Or, at least," she glanced at me, "talking to someone."

Leda recoiled. "Let's focus on Cressida's relationship. She's the one seeing a biker."

"Oh, no!" I stood. "I see exactly what you're doing here. Using me to avoid your relationship woes."

"That's because we don't have a relationship."

We all froze.

"We?" I asked. "Ha!" I clapped my hands in triumph. "You just said we. There's potential there, or you wouldn't be protesting so much."

Gliding into the kitchen, Leda ruffled my short curls. "Did you kiss the biker yet? You two looked awful cozy on the stairs earlier. Very domestic."

"Oh, you!" I swatted at her.

"Does this mean we're supposed to call you his old lady now? Is that a thing?"

"I'm warning you . . ."

"Not that I'm against the whole leather look they've got going on. Have you seen the Melaina Savage woman?" My sister whistled.

"Leda!"

Mom smiled a tired, wistful smile. "I love you girls." An emotional silence, full of affection and amusement, washed over us.

A crash in the living room shattered the moment, and we rushed out of the kitchen, completely on edge.

Dad crawled on the floor toward us, dragging himself into the foyer, his body convulsing.

"It's going to kill me," he cried. Rolling over, he beat the back of his head against the floor and clawed at the Persian rugs, bunching the fabric in his hands. "It's going to kill me." His eyes rolled into the back of his head. "And then it's going to kill all of you."

A half-laugh, half-sob spewed from his lips, tears leaking from the corners of his eyes. His legs kicked violently, his head beat, beat, beating, until spots of blood appeared beneath him.

Leda rushed to his side, tears pouring down her face as she threw herself over his legs. I fell to my knees behind his head, my hands gripping his face, my arms straining desperately to hold him still.

"Stop, Dad!" Leda pleaded.

He screamed, the sound full of agony and despair, as if he was seeing the end of the world. "Dying," Dad whispered. "We're all going to die."

"Please make it stop," Mom begged, kneeling next to us. "Whatever this is, please make it stop. I can't stand it anymore."

The quickest way to defeat an oread was to defeat its family.

Dad screamed and screamed and screamed.

The door to the house flew open.

A hard-faced Liam Peters marched in, his sunglasses missing, his combat boots coming to a stop on our expensive Persian rugs, Jack on his heels. The hellhounds should have looked out of place in our formal foyer with their large statures, leather cuts, and massive builds, but Liam and Jack owned whatever space they entered.

"Get it together, Wieland," Liam commanded. He gestured for us to move away, and my sister and I backed up, letting the biker take our place.

With no finesse whatsoever, Liam grabbed Dad by the collar, lifted him up until they were eye to eye, and then growled, the sound coming from way deep down inside of him. His eyes flared, flames leaping in his pupils, his voice dangerously low when he demanded, "You asshole of a god, it takes a coward to fight the way you do. How about you do me a favor and pop out of the oread here?"

Dad's back arched.

Liam grinned, baring teeth that weren't quite human. "Release him!"

Dad slumped, his hands searching for purchase on Liam's arms. He gulped in breath, his face turning red. "You think you know how to defeat me, don't you?" Dad asked wearily.

Jack stepped forward. "You looked into his eyes, Pops. Why isn't—"

"You don't want to tangle with me, god," Liam warned.

"If it isn't them, it will be someone else. I'm never finished." Dad laughed weakly.

Liam shook him, lifting his chin so that his eyes rested on the hellhound's. "It's gods like you that give supernaturals a bad reputation."

Dad panted, visibly fighting against the hellhound's gaze. "Of course, his daughter would have to fall for one of you."

"Her lucky day, I guess," Liam retorted. His eyes flared, and Dad sagged in his embrace, as if whatever had possessed him had suddenly fallen out of him.

"Wieland!" Mom fell against them, her bandaged hands clinging to her husband, and Liam released him into her embrace. Mom hugged Dad to her. "Wieland."

His arms snaked around her waist.

"Okay," he gasped. "Okay, I'm okay." His eyes cleared, the pain that had been lining his face ebbing away. "Thank you." Together they scrambled to their feet. Dad shook, his body leaning on Mom for support. "What was that? What was in me?"

Unlike with Mom and me, Dad's memory seemed intact.

"Ancient Greek power at its best." Liam leaned against the foyer wall, arms crossed. "You really do know how to purchase jewelry, Manos."

Jack came to me, pulling me into his embrace, his arms falling around me. The move was a little showy for Jack, and I wondered if this had something to do with his dad.

Liam nodded at his son, a look passing between them.

"Goes to show that some things can be ended without violence." Pulling a rolled-up sheaf of papers out of his back pocket, Liam offered them to my father. "I need to confiscate the emerald you purchased from Belen Cirilo, whether I have to get it from here or from Summit."

Dad accepted the papers. "What's this?"

"This is about ending the tragedy in store for your family if you don't concede the jewel. Things are bad now, but they're only going to get worse if that emerald remains in your possession." Liam tapped the papers. "There's a copy of your sales receipt along with a certificate of authenticity the seller failed to give you. I'm having a tough time finding out where Belen got the jewel in the first place, but these papers date and identify the emerald. Your ancestry is Greek, right?"

My mother read the papers over my father's shoulders. "It is."

"Then I assume you've heard of the Necklace of Harmonia."

Mom gasped. "No!" She thumbed through the papers in Dad's hands. "It can't be. The necklace was lost a long time ago."

"As a whole," Liam said, "but it survived in pieces."

Mom's face lost all color.

367

"What is it?" I asked.

Liam inhaled. "Made of gold and jewels, the clasp two open-mouthed serpents, the necklace was forged by Hephaestus, a blacksmith god, as punishment. His wife, Aphrodite, had had an affair with Ares, the god of war."

Jack's arms tightened around me, his voice steady when he added, "It pissed him off, and Hephaestus offered the necklace to Harmonia as a wedding gift."

Mom sucked in a breath, and her brows creased. Because of her heritage and her age, Mom knew things about history most of us would have to research to find out.

"Harmonia was the daughter born of Aphrodite's affair with Ares," she continued. "The necklace was cursed to bring misfortune to all who owned it. It starts by causing small, overlooked mishaps, but in the end, it destroys its owners and their families."

"Why couldn't the Court detect it?" Leda asked.

"It was forged by a god to curse other gods," Mom answered, her voice awed. "Created with very ancient magic, the necklace was formed using a protection spell that made it undetectable. Otherwise, it never would have been worn by the gods, queens, and princesses Hephaestus wanted to destroy."

"A lot of supernaturals would pay big money to own it," Liam said, a mischievous glint in his eyes. "There are collectors who would do anything to break the protection spell and emulate it."

My father's hands fisted around the papers in his hands. "As dangerous as it is, you want me to hand it over to you? How many buyers do you already have lined up?"

"You really think I'd sell it?" Liam snorted. "In the wrong hands, that jewel could cause a lot of problems for all of us. I've already contacted the Court. I'm handing it over to them."

"You expect us to believe that?" my sister asked.

"Leda!" I gasped.

"It's okay," Jack whispered in my ear, his warm breath sending shivers down my spine.

"I'm not asking you to trust me," Liam told us. "As soon as you let me know where to find the jewel, a member of the Court will meet me there. I'm just the one transporting it."

"Why you?" Dad asked.

"Because the jewel doesn't affect hellhounds. Not in the typical way. You've seen what our stare can do for those under its influence. That's why Cressida getting to know my son when she did turned out to be a good thing. For them both."

"How?" Leda asked.

"Because Jack kept this from turning into a big problem for this town," Liam replied. "Not only because he was invested in protecting Cressida, but because *I* was invested in protecting him. Owning the jewel would cause just as much misfortune for hellhounds as it would you, but because hellhounds are forged from the same fires that created the jewel, the dark curse attached to it can't physically inhabit us. Besides," Liam shrugged, "I may have a hidden agenda."

"Pops!" Jack exclaimed.

His father smiled, but it didn't quite reach his eyes. "I moved my boys and my business to Havenwood Falls because it provides protection for my men and their extended families, a safe place away from my outside business ventures. The stronger this town is, the safer my club is from my enemies. If the Court can crack that protection spell and add it to their already strong wards, I'm a hundred percent behind it."

Liam inclined his head at my father. "Good job, Wieland. You may have brought something potentially disastrous to your family into this town, but you're getting the chance to turn it over to a greater cause." Sarcasm dripped from the biker's words, his smile hiding a warning I didn't miss. If my dad didn't turn over the jewel, Liam wouldn't have any problem taking it from him.

"This will stop if we hand it over?" my mother asked. "There's nothing else we have to do? No fighting?"

Liam swore, his gaze flashing to Jack. "What is it with people wanting violence today?" He snorted. "That's all you got to do. You'll be passing it and the curse on to the Court. They'll deal with it from there. There are some scary sons of bitches on that Court. I wouldn't worry too much about them or us."

Wieland swallowed hard. "It's at Summit. Take it. I just want it away from my family."

Liam pushed away from the wall and clapped my dad on the back. "See? Quick and painless. Let's ride." His gaze flicked to Jack, and then to me. "I'm guessing you're staying behind?"

"Yes, sir," Jack replied.

Liam studied us—his son and the small nymph with badly chopped off hair and no boobs—and he smiled. "You might want to think long and hard before you take on my hardheaded son, Miss Manos, but if you're up to the challenge, you'll have the club at your back."

With those words, he left.

My father followed him out the door, pausing long enough to mutter, "That may be easy for him to say, but I might have to give this some thought."

Mom shooed him away.

Leda stretched, moaning, and then popped her fingers. "Well, that was enough excitement for me. I need a shower and a change of clothes, so I'm out. I may even take the day off."

"To spend with your girl?" Mom asked hopefully.

"Mom!"

"At least give us a name. Just a name," Mom begged.

Leda paused. "Nikita . . . but, Mom, I don't really know how she feels about me. It's more like I'm into her right now, so no dinner or marriage plans, okay?"

"Fine." Mom waved her hands at the door. "Go!"

With a winsome smile, Leda disappeared. Dawn was coming, the day ahead now full of new possibilities.

Mom's attention turned to Jack and me.

"Nope," I said. "I'm grabbing a quick shower, a change of clothes, and then we're out, too."

Mom's face fell. "Okay, but," she touched the ends of her hair, wincing, "maybe stop by Shear Magic while you're out. Once they open."

"Time me!" I told Jack, pulling free from his embrace to make a run for the stairs. "If I'm not done in ten minutes, we're probably stuck here."

He grinned and started to count, "One, two, three . . ."

"Use your phone," I called down, halfway up.

"It died. Six, seven, eight . . ."

A quick shower had never felt so good.

CHAPTER 20

JACK PETERS

HOURS LATER

For the first time since meeting Cressida, it was just me, her, and no agenda. Bright light poured into Apex Art Studio from the street beyond, the smell of wet clay thick on the air as Cressida took a seat at the potter's wheel, an unformed lump before her.

Across the room, she'd set up a group of tables and a myriad of art supplies. At each seat, a ceramic piece rested, the white surface clean and ready to paint, a "Happy Birthday" sign hanging from the ceiling above.

"Have you ever done this?" Cressida asked.

"What? Art or pottery?"

She laughed, patting the stool behind her. "Try with me."

If you'd asked me a week ago if I'd ever be found dead at an art studio shoving my hands in wet clay, I would have said hell no. Now, standing here, I still found it hard to believe. And yet, something about the smell and sight of it felt like possibility. Like the beginning of a journey I never would have thought to take on my own.

"I'm going to be really bad at this," I warned, dragging a second stool over. Settling in behind her, I braced my long legs on each side of her, my arms falling over her head. Her shorn curls, the strands recently cut at the salon in town, teased my chin as I leaned forward.

She took my hands in hers, lining them up. Compared to hers, mine were huge, and I marveled at the difference.

"They're stronger than they look," Cressida whispered.

"What?"

"My hands," she replied. "They are much stronger than they look."

With one fluid movement, Cressida started the potter's wheel, placing our hands against the clay. She molded it expertly, the material cool against our fingers, my chest pressed against her back. I rested my head on her shoulder, my breath mingling with hers.

"What does the tattoo on your chest represent?" she asked me suddenly.

Watching our clay-covered hands, I whispered, "The beast in me, and the three things he feels most defines him."

She turned her head, her gaze catching mine briefly before returning to the clay. "What defines him?"

There was something hesitant and uncertain about the way she asked me, and I found my lips curling in response, the need to reassure her so strong, it nearly knocked me off the stool.

"First," I answered, "is the tomb—this need to be near the dead, to help the souls of those passing on. The tomb is where his mother is, and while for most people that's a sad place, for his mother it's safe and warm. The same way it will be for me someday."

My hands abandoned the clay, my wet fingers running over her fingers, entwining and then disentangling. Learning. Feeling. "Second, there's the tree of life, its canopy connecting the beast to the sky, its roots connecting the beast to the ground. Reminding him that you can exist in two places at once."

Turning my head, I placed a gentle kiss on her neck, my lips moving over the healing wound the scissors had left behind on her skin. "And finally, there's the ship at full sail, moving over choppy waves. There's a quote that says, 'A smooth sea never made a skilled

373

sailor.' The ship reminds the beast to learn from his mistakes, to take them for what they are: just another wave to break through."

I had completely abandoned the project before us, my clay-covered hand coming up to cup her face, my free hand sliding along her skin just under the hem of her shirt. I didn't dare go any higher.

"I'd like to try this," I said suddenly, surprising myself.

Cressida's head turned, our faces so close, our noses brushed. I liked hugging her from behind. If I leaned over far enough, I could fold her into me, keeping her safe forever.

"Try what?"

We were whispering, our breaths mingling.

I swallowed. "Being in a relationship."

Her eyes widened, and I could make out brown specks among the green in her gaze, a light line of blue tracing the center. Earth, water, and wind. My eyes were the fire.

"I—" she began, but I silenced her with a kiss, my lips tasting hers. Long, deep, and searching.

When I pulled back, she was breathing hard.

"That was in case you decided against a relationship."

"Why would I decide against it?" Cressida's newly short hair matured her features, widening her eyes and thinning her face, and I brushed a kiss on her clay-marked cheek.

"Hellhounds have bad tempers, we're incredibly hot-natured, we're possessive, and . . . our women often die in childbirth." I added the last one quick, almost as an afterthought, my lips spitting out the words.

Cressida froze. "What?"

"It's just something you should know. Not that you're considering marriage or kids. It's just that . . . I've never taken a girlfriend because I didn't want to get attached. Getting attached means possibly losing her one day. I think if we date, I may get attached."

For a long moment, Cressida stared, not saying anything. "Is that how your mom—"

I nodded.

"Oh."

My gaze dropped. "Hellhounds are tough. My brother likes to say we're badass. I don't know about that. I think we have the same vulnerabilities as everyone else. If I'm being honest, I think we have more. Or at least I do. I'm afraid of things. I'm afraid what will happen if I shift one day. I'm afraid of what being a part of my father's club may mean. *If* I decide to prospect in. I'm afraid of falling in love, because I'm scared losing the person I'm with will make me hate death." I snorted. "Which is another reason not to date me. I like cemeteries. Candlelit dinners in graveyards probably aren't very sexy. Not to mention the danger. Your family accidentally stumbled into bad luck because of your father's hobby. My family goes looking for danger just because."

Cressida touched my face, running her thumb over the bridge of my cheek. "What do you see when you look at me?" she asked.

"Cressida," I answered, and then, "you are absolutely beautiful."

She grinned. "And that's why the rest of that doesn't really matter . . . yet. We can take it one day at a time. Moment by moment. I've seen myself in a mirror, Jack. I like who I am, but I know what other people think of me, too. If you see beauty, then that means you're seeing more of me than most. I'd like to try the relationship thing, too."

"Thank God," I groaned.

Our lips fell together, a new promise sealed the way it should be.

Things could change between us. Especially if I joined SIN or if one of us went away to college, but right now, in this moment, I was proving her right. She told me I'd fall in love with her.

I wouldn't call this love yet. Mostly deep interest. We hadn't known each other long, but I had a feeling I was going to fall very, very hard.

The kiss ended, and I stared at her, no sunglasses between us, my eyes saying what my lips couldn't. Not yet. This was still too new.

If you're with me, I will protect you.

EPILOGUE

CRESSIDA MANOS

A WEEK LATER

*B*eing the sudden girlfriend of a hellhound had its advantages. Mainly that no one, and I mean no one, had the courage to mess with me. It also kept people from asking questions. No one bothered me about the weird things I'd done the week before. No one dug into the mystery about my family, even though the appearance of Court members at our jewelry shop when they confiscated the jewel must have raised eyebrows. Even the gossips left us alone.

Jack and I had been lucky. I'd heard stories about things that had happened in Havenwood Falls—things that had been covered up, but that most of the supernaturals ended up hearing about anyway. Many of them were tragic, with huge fights and lots of complications. The start of our relationship was a lot less dramatic compared to that.

For me, the solution to my problem had been a bad boy with a bad reputation, the beast he was afraid of and his very scary father the answer to my family's problem. We'd been saved before anything truly dreadful could happen.

I hated the jewel that caused it all, but it had also introduced me to my first love. At least, I was pretty sure I loved him. No way in hell I was telling him that, though. He'd probably run before he gave this relationship thing a chance. And I wanted desperately to give it a chance.

The sound of cats hissing and yowling pulled me out of my thoughts, and I grimaced, my hands quickly deserting the cage they'd been stuck in before slamming the door shut.

There were some disadvantages to being with a hellhound, too. The most glaring one was the fact that cats couldn't stand them. It made my work at the animal shelter a lot more difficult.

"You could warn me before you show up," I called out.

Jack, sans sunglasses, rounded the corner, entering the cat area of the shelter, his combat boots thudding over the linoleum floor.

"I can't help it if they can't see what a good guy I am."

I arched a brow. "Maybe they're warning me away from you."

"They'd change their minds if they saw what your mom did to that Slink cat of yours."

I glared. Slink still hadn't quite recovered from the incident. She had developed a severe phobia of my mother, which was causing all kinds of stress at home. Namely that Slink was suddenly all about destroying Mom's things, and Mom felt too guilty to scold her for it. "That was low, Peters."

He grinned. "Take a ride with me, Manos."

"I'm working."

"Take her," a female voice insisted. Isa came into view, stuffed her hands into the pockets of her white lab coat, and smiled. Widely. "I've been telling her she needs to get out more. Like normal teenagers. All she does is work and volunteer. And it's not busy today."

Jack's head hung, his hand hastily shoving on a pair of sunglasses before he looked up.

Isa pulled back the sleeve of her lab coat, revealing her tattoo. "It's okay. I know better than to look in your eyes, hellhound."

He frowned. "You smell human."

"I am human," she admitted. "But I've got some extra special abilities. Tell your dad if he keeps parking so close to the back of the building when he makes deliveries, I'll be glad to show him some of those abilities." She grinned mischievously. "The cats really don't like you guys."

Surprised, Jack laughed. "I'm not sure you really want me to tell my pops that."

"Oh, no, I really, really do," Isa said. "Now scoot."

Jack laughed, then reached out to grab my hand. "You heard the woman, Manos."

We left the shelter, the two of us hand in hand when we approached his bike. Something told me that with Jack's connection to the motorcycle club, and his possible future with them, the way we'd met was just the beginning.

I was a little scared of our future. Getting to know Jack was one thing. Being in a relationship with him was going to be a whole different kind of adventure, and I had a feeling it was going to be a lot scarier than what happened with the jewel from the Necklace of Harmonia.

WE HOPE you enjoyed this story in the Havenwood Falls High series of novellas featuring a variety of supernatural creatures. The series is a collaborative effort by multiple authors.

Stay up to date at www.HavenwoodFalls.com

ABOUT THE AUTHOR

R.K. Ryals is the author of emotional and gripping young adult and new adult paranormal romance, contemporary romance, and fantasy. With a strong passion for charity and literacy, she works as a full-time writer encouraging people to "share the love of reading one book at a time." An avid animal lover and self-proclaimed coffee-holic, R.K. Ryals was born in Jackson, Mississippi, and makes her home in the Southern U.S. with her husband, her three daughters, two playful cats named Delphi and Paris, and a coffeepot she honestly couldn't live without. Should she ever become the owner of a fire-breathing dragon (tame of course), her life would be complete. Visit her at www.authorrkryals.com.

ACKNOWLEDGMENTS

I am so thankful to be a part of the Havenwood Falls journey. Writing Jack and Cressida's story was an adventure I will never forget. Not only because I felt a kinship to these characters, but because I loved writing a love story that doesn't start off in a typical way. I have high hopes for these two characters in the future.

This story would not have been possible without our fearless leader, Kristie Cook. Thank you so much for creating a town that brings authors and characters together in a unique and amazing way. I am so grateful that you are a part of my life.

I am always blown away by the amount of people it takes to bring a story together. There are so many that I want to thank.

First, I have to thank my husband, whose patience and diligence is always such a support for me. This novella was written during a very chaotic time in our household, and he handled it all like a champ. To my daughters, who inspire me on a daily basis. I am truly blessed with amazing children. They have passion, determination, and resilience. Raising them to be the strong women I am watching them become humbles me.

A heartfelt thank you to my personal assistant, Christina Silcox. Not only does Christina assist me so much in life, she is a beacon of strength. I am amazed by everything she does.

To Melissa Wright, Jessica Johnson, and Amanda Engelkes, who are always letting me use them for a sounding board. Your input and your suggestions always mean so much to me.

A special thank you to a group of loyal women who have followed me since the beginning of my career. To my Archive girls and my

Scribes group. The dedication you have shown me is not taken for granted.

There are no words big enough to express how grateful I am to be a part of the Havenwood Falls family. Huge thanks and crushing hugs to the Havenwood Falls authors who let me borrow the wonderful characters that make this story so strong. To the rest of the Havenwood Falls authors for the characters they've created. This town is possible because of all of you.

A massive shout out to Regina Wamba for the beautiful cover art. You are seriously incredible.

To Liz Ferry and Kristie Cook for your amazing editing. You make these books so much stronger.

Finally, to my readers, you take my breath away. It means the world that you read my words. I am extremely grateful for your support on this insane journey full of crazy twists and turns. My love to you always.

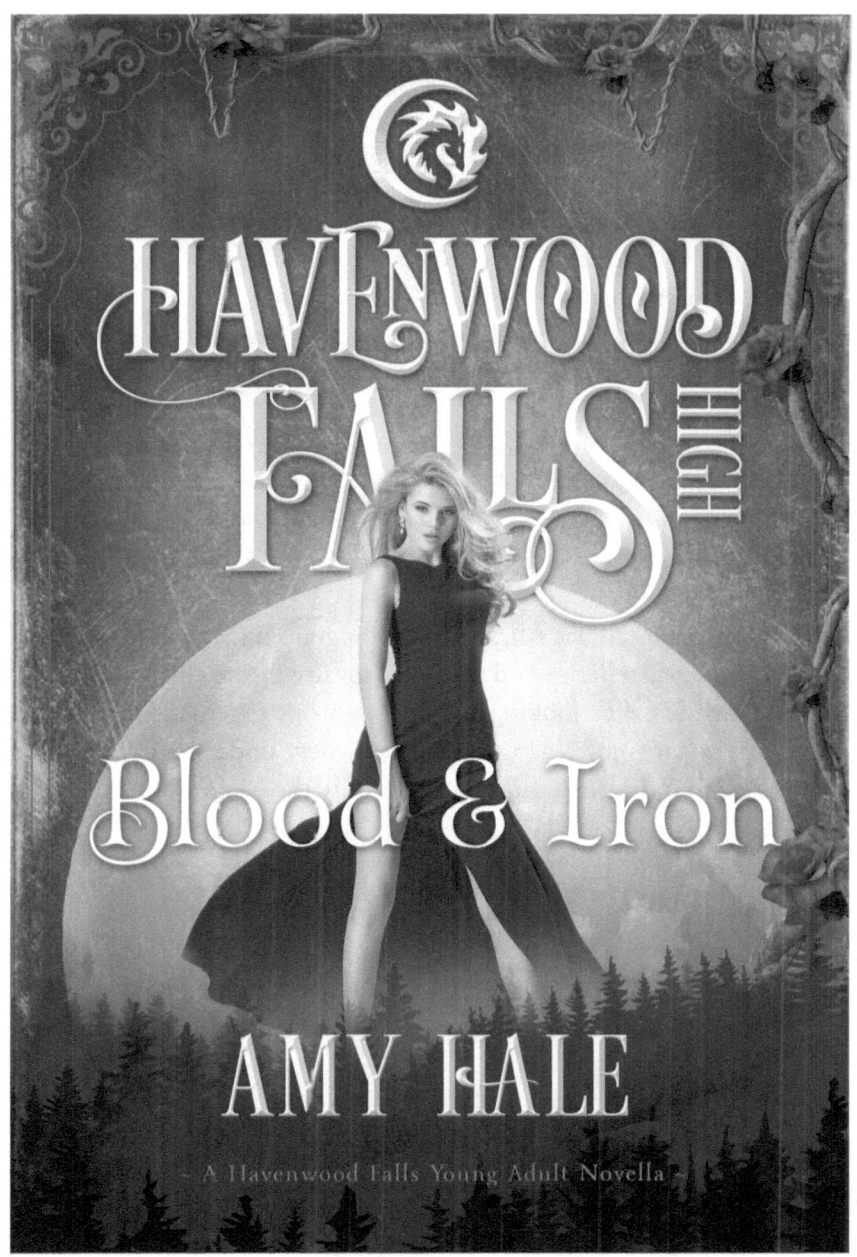

Havenwood Falls High

Blood & Iron

AMY HALE

A Havenwood Falls Young Adult Novella

Blood & Iron (A Havenwood Falls High Novella) by Amy Hale

Miranda Saunders has spent her sixteen years playing by the rules. She's known for her impeccable style, good grades, and overall positive influence in Havenwood Falls. But in the vampire community, she's an oddity. Born a vampire, from a situation deemed impossible, Miranda's origins are an enigma to everyone. When a photo surfaces that brings up questions about her long lost father, she is determined to find the answers. That search lands her directly in the path of trouble—fellow vampire Kai Reynolds.

Having recently graduated from Havenwood Falls High, Kai is tired of being told how to behave. Ready to break out of the mold he's been cast in by his parents and the town's supernatural leaders, he becomes a prospect for the SIN motorcycle club—something his parents loathe.

But when he catches Miranda snooping around the clubhouse, he has to choose: turn her in and prove his loyalty to the club, or help her find the answers she's looking for. If they work together, they're both taking risks far more dangerous than they understand. And the mystery surrounding Miranda's father is only the beginning.

BLOOD & IRON

AN EXCERPT

A bell rang. The loud clanging resonated from somewhere nearby. I was certain it was a familiar sound, yet at that moment, it seemed foreign. I couldn't register the meaning, only that it was annoying, and I wanted it to stop. I closed my eyes and rubbed my temples.

"What's wrong with you?" a grating male voice spoke near my ear.

I snapped to attention. "What?" I turned to find myself uncomfortably close to Gary Smithson, one of our notorious school bullies. His dark eyes stared back into mine. I placed a hand on his chest and pushed him away. "Nothing. I'm fine."

"You don't look fine. Are you on drugs or something?" He smirked, and I knew he'd just *love* to spread that specific piece of gossip around school.

"No, moron. I'm not on drugs. I have a headache. Now go away before I tell the entire school that you still sleep with a night light."

His eyes grew wide. "What? How . . ." He looked around and ran a hand over his brown buzz-cut hair. "You're such a freak."

Then he strolled away, his stocky build shifting side to side as he pretended I hadn't just nailed his fear of the dark, which was common knowledge in vampire circles, or more precisely due to the vampires in those circles.

I sat at my desk a moment longer as the classroom continued to empty. I'd done it again. For the past several weeks I'd been having involuntary moments where my consciousness seemed to check out, like my body was present but my mind was elsewhere. Each time I found myself mentally transported, often surrounded by mist or fog, and I was always looking for something . . . or someone. I never found whatever it was, and it always left me feeling empty. I also woke from this odd trance with a headache.

I gathered my books and made my way to my locker, willing my head to clear before I had to face the rest of the day.

My best friend Zoey reached my locker about the same time I did. "I'm so glad it's Friday and only a half day. I'm already tired of this school year," she moaned.

I chuckled. "It's barely been a week."

"I know. I'm just over it already," she grumbled.

"One day you'll look back and wonder how it all went by so fast." I repeated the words I'd heard adults say dozens of times.

She rolled her eyes. "Hey, I've gotta help my dad at the shop for a little while after I leave here, but then I'm free if you wanted to watch a movie at my house or something." Her mood brightened significantly at the subject change.

"Uh, yeah. Sure." I dug through my purse, looking for my house keys.

"Are you okay, Miranda? You've seemed kinda distracted lately. And you look tired."

"Do I?" I glanced at myself in my locker mirror. I did look a little tired, although only those closest to me would have really noticed it. My shiny long blond hair was still perfectly in place. My makeup was flawless and accented my features impeccably. Looking amazing was just one of the perks of being a vampire. My eyes, though . . . the gold flecks that were scattered within the dark irises were usually luminous. Now they seemed dull and joyless.

"Have you been sleeping okay?" She placed a hand on my arm.

"Mostly. I seem to just randomly zone out a lot. And I've been having some strange dreams. Like I'm chasing something or being chased. For some reason, I've had a lot of anxiety off and on. It hits at weird times. I can't seem to shake it." It sounds odd, vampires sleeping, but my mom and I, we're not your average Gothic vampires. Truth be told, we're not average in any way.

I hadn't told anyone about the dreams, the anxiety, or the trances, but Zoey was my confidante. I could tell her anything. She knew my darkest secrets, like the fact that I was a vampire. And I knew hers, such as her being a dragon shifter. Those were the kinds of things you took to your grave when roughly half the population in your town was human.

"Want to talk about it?" She glanced at her watch, and I knew she needed to get to her dad's shop.

"We can later. I'll meet you at the store after I've dropped some stuff off at home." I gave her a quick hug.

"Great, see you in a bit." She dashed down the hall and out the front doors of the school.

I loaded my backpack with the books I needed to take home and slung it over my shoulder. It was a relatively nice day, and I was glad I'd left my old car at home. It hadn't been running particularly well, and I enjoyed walking, when the weather was nice anyway. The exercise gave me time to think, and this was a day I needed it more than ever.

I mulled over various issues as I walked, trying to decide which one might be the cause of the unsettled feelings I'd been fighting. I'd just celebrated my seventeenth birthday, but it wasn't a major milestone like eighteen or twenty-one. It didn't have the feeling of big changes and responsibility that I assumed would come with those ages. I hadn't seen a lot of my mother lately, but I assumed that was due to a heavy workload. Being a marketing analyst could be demanding work. Most of the time, she worked remotely, but now and then she had to travel to the main headquarters in Denver. I didn't even know what her company sold. It had something to do with computers or something. Whatever it was, it paid the bills. It was just her and me, and Mom worked hard to provide for us. I had no siblings, and I didn't even know who my father was. Mom didn't talk about him.

Nothing I thought of fit. I couldn't describe the feeling other than to say it felt like I'd lost something important. And that I only had so much time to find it before it was gone from me forever. It was ominous and frightening. Despite what the movies said, Gothic vampires couldn't see into the future or read minds. At least, I'd never met any that could. And although I wasn't a normal Gothic vampire, I still didn't think visions or trances were something I should be experiencing. It felt . . . wrong. So I'd been left with this void I didn't know how to fill, and disturbing episodes I couldn't explain.

I unlocked the door to my house and put my backpack on the kitchen table. I scribbled out a note for Mom letting her know I'd be with Zoey the rest of the day, then I locked back up and walked toward the town square and Simple Treasures Pawn Shop. I hadn't quite made it to Eighth Street when I heard a noise from behind me that sounded like thunder. I felt it as well. The ground vibrated beneath my feet, and before I could even turn around, my senses were telling me to be alert and careful. I looked back just in time to see three large men on motorcycles roar past me. They were wearing leather cuts with the Swords of the Infernal Night logo on them. SIN was their acronym, and it seemed to fit them to a tee. While they appeared to be ordinary bikers, something about them gave off a vibe that they were anything but. That ominous feeling intensified, and I was anxious to get to the pawn shop.

I reached the store and walked in to find Zoey dusting a shelf loaded down with various old junk. None of it looked very valuable on the surface, and I couldn't see why anyone would want to buy it. There were belt buckles, military patches, medals, watches, small trinket boxes . . . all of it appeared beat up and dull. I assumed they held some kind of historical value, so maybe that was the attraction.

"What's all this junk?" I asked as Zoey lifted a small metal box.

She quirked one eyebrow up at me. "Junk? It's not junk. It's . . ." She waved her hand over it, as if that would somehow explain the purpose of the items before her. "It's . . . sentimental history."

"To who?" I crossed my arms. "The people that should care about it have pawned it."

Zoey opened her mouth, then shut it again. "Good point."

I laughed and nudged her side with my fist. Just being with her lifted my spirits. "How long do you work today?"

"Not much longer. I have to finish this shelf, then Dad said I had the rest of the afternoon free as long as nothing else came up. What kind of movie should we watch?" She pushed her raven black hair behind one ear, revealing some of the mother-of-pearl strands that ran through her tresses. Her hair was gorgeous, although she thought it was odd. I'd often told her it was a perfect accent to her stunning blue-gray eyes, but again she disagreed.

"Something funny." I didn't need anything scary or with major drama.

She glanced at me sideways as she continued to dust the shelf. "What? No campy slasher film? Blood and gore?" She turned to me. "Are you afraid it'll make you hungry?"

"No!" I nudged her again. "You know I'm not that kind of vampire."

"So if they were slaughtering woodland animals, you'd get hungry?"

I glared at her. "How do you like your humans? In barbecue sauce?"

Zoey laughed. "Sorry. You know I gotta tease you now and then." She dropped her rag on the counter and turned to face me. "Okay, well, what's the plan?"

"A funny movie. Or we could just hang out around town. See if there's anything new at Callie's . . . something like that."

Zoey shrugged as she picked up the rag once more and wiped down the last belt buckle on the shelf. "Sure. Any of that's better than doing nothing."

"Well," I sighed with dramatic flair, "I'm glad hanging out with me ranks just above 'doing nothing.'"

She put her hands on her hips. "Don't go all diva on me. You know what I meant."

I smiled. Someone in the hallway at school had once loudly called me a diva because I wouldn't hang out with her. While I was particular about my clothes, food, and who I spent time with, I was far from a diva. I was just very discerning where my tastes were concerned. That, and I wasn't your average vampire, so there were things about me I'd rather not divulge except to my closest friends. Spending time with me would ultimately bring those things to light. The biggest one was that I couldn't stomach human blood. I'd bring it back up every time. So instead, I fed on animal blood, which in my mind seemed cruel too, but it was better than starving to death. Human food was okay, and I'd eat it at times, but to really survive, vampires needed blood.

It was my turn to tease her. "Oh, you haven't seen a diva attitude yet. Just wait until I get my hands on Jordan. I'm gonna unleash the beast."

Zoey laughed. "Why?"

"Because I expected him to bring you one of those gorgeous flowered dresses from his vacation in Hawaii, and instead he brought you a T-shirt," I grumbled.

"Oh, you wouldn't. Besides, this is the first real vacation Jordan and his mom have taken since . . . ever. His dad wouldn't do things like that for his family. I'm glad they got to go. All I asked him to bring back for me was his gorgeous smile, tan buff bod, and photos from the island."

"I'm glad he went too, but still . . ." I crossed my arms in front of my chest. "I wanted to see you in one of those dresses like they always show people wearing on TV."

Zoey laughed. "Yeah, that wouldn't stand out on my super pale flesh at all."

"Hey, I'm the fashion maven of the two of us, and I'm telling you. It'd be perfect on you."

She waved me away as she put her cleaning supplies under a nearby cabinet. "Let me go see if Dad needs anything else. Maybe I can knock off now and we can grab lunch before we take off for the day."

I browsed around as she disappeared into the back room. The bell above the door rang, and I turned to see Zoey's grandfather, Lawrence Mills, slowly stroll into the room, his cane clicking on the hardwood floor as he moved. A young man with blond hair and an armload of boxes followed directly behind him, the pile teetering precariously every time he took a step. I recognized him as Glenn Williams when one of the boxes shifted and revealed his face. He used to go to school at Havenwood Falls High before he graduated last year.

"Miss Miranda. How are you today?" Mr. Mills smiled at me, but it never felt like he meant it. He had a tendency to creep me out.

"I'm well, thank you, Mr. Mills." I stood with my hands behind my back, hoping he didn't sense my discomfort.

"Glad to hear it." He turned to Glenn behind him. "You may put those on the counter."

Glenn did as he was told. Mr. Mills handed him some cash, and he scurried out of there as fast as he could. I didn't blame him. I didn't want to be around this cranky old dragon any longer than I had to, either.

"Please tell my son that I have some new items for inventory. He can keep what's valuable for the shop and toss the rest. I have an appointment, so I can't stay."

I nodded. "Happy to pass the message along, Mr. Mills."

"Thank you, girl." He turned and walked out of the store, not appearing to give me, or the business, a second thought.

Zoey and her dad, Tristan, came out of the back room a moment later.

"Was someone here?" Tristan glanced around. "I heard the bell, but I was on the phone."

"Yes, Mr. Mills dropped off those boxes for you. He said to keep the valuable stuff for the store and throw away the rest." I gestured to the boxes stacked on the glass countertop.

Tristan nodded. "Okay. Listen, girls, before you take off for the day, would you mind sifting through the boxes and let me know if there is anything special that catches your eye? I have a few more phone calls to make before I can take a lunch break."

"Sure, Dad," Zoey replied.

I nodded in agreement. I was happy to be helpful in any way I could.

An hour later, we'd just finished rummaging through the fourth box and still had one box to go. My stomach was growling. Tristan had ordered pizza for us. And while I was happy to help eat it, I'd soon need real vampire nourishment. I'd have to run by Sanguine Elixirs to pick up my own special blend.

We nibbled on the pizza as we sifted through the last box. I was mindlessly examining a small photo album, enjoying all the old photographs and wondering what kind of life each person led. Most of them looked to be taken sometime in the sixties or seventies. But one photo stood out from the rest. I removed it from its sleeve and studied it closer.

"This is weird," I said as I continued to stare at the photograph in my hand.

"What is?" Zoey leaned over to see what I was looking at.

"That's my mom. It's many years ago, but that's her." My mom was a vampire as well, so she didn't age, but it was obvious by the clothing style that the photo had been taken sometime in the nineties—a few years before I was born, at least. Her blond hair was a tad longer than it was in its current shoulder-length cut. Unlike me, she had bright blue eyes. Her slim five-foot-seven-inch frame wore a tight pair of stonewashed jeans and a tank top with what I assumed was a band name. She stood with a group of tough-looking motorcycle guys, her arm around one man in particular. He was a few inches taller than her, with sandy blond hair and dark eyes. His build was lean and athletic. He had more of a southern rock look going on, with his leather pants and tattered cowboy hat.

The smile on Mom's face was huge. She looked carefree and truly happy. I wondered why I'd never seen that side of her before. Sure, she smiled and laughed at times, but even then, there was a solemn sadness underneath. I could sense it, and it made me ache for her. Her most common mood was stern, serious, and worried. I'd never understood it.

Purchase *Blood & Iron* where books are sold.